GOLD CREEK KILL

The clatter of hoofs over loose rock startled the two miners seated next to Black Hawk as four men rode single file from the dense woods and pulled up before the group.

The two miners looked a little uneasy by the sudden appearance of the armed riders and they stood up slowly.

"Relax, friends. I believe I know these gentlemen," Black Hawk said, giving them a reassuring smile. The men nodded but remained on their feet.

The lead gunman stepped down from his horse and walked up to Black Hawk. "Didn't know there was any color on this stream, Hawk," he said, exchanging a knowing look with his compadre. "Seems your friends got themselves some steady ore."

The miners looked at each other and didn't answer for a long time. "You fellas looking to work some claims?" one of them finally said.

"Now, do we look like miners, son?" the hard case responded, pulling aside his frock coat and exposing the walnut butt of his Colt. He smiled at the two miners with eyes cold as the mountain stream flowing nearby. And, before his smile faded, his hand dipped down and his gun flashed fire, once, then twice. Seconds later, the two miners lay dead by the campfire, their hearts shot through.

"Well, boys," Black Hawk said, stepping over the bodies, "looks like we got us a paying claim."

GOLD RUSH REVENGE

JESS McCREEDE

PINNACLE BOOKS
WINDSOR PUBLISHING CORP.

For Sylvia, who keeps me on track.

PINNACLE BOOKS

are published by

Windsor Publishing Corp.
475 Park Avenue South
New York, NY 10016

First printing: September, 1992

Printed in the United States of America

Chapter 1

"Jack Dawson! Figgered to find you here," an old man said, sidling up to the tall man quietly drinking at the bar.

Jack Dawson turned his head and stared at the apparition before him. The old man, dressed in greasy buckskins and carrying a Plains rifle in the crook of one arm, looked as thought he had just walked away from a campfire. A sandstone pipe, clinched between his teeth, emerged from a bushy beard the color of Great Basin alkali.

"Spivey! Thought you went under last winter over on the Ruby?" Dawson clasped Coot Spivey's hand in his own.

"Got to admit, Jack, it was touch and go fer awhile. Been Comanche or Sioux, don't expect I'd be standing here now. But they was Bloods and you know well as I do, they ain't the kind to stand up to a stiff fight fer long." Dawson nodded in agreement.

"Let me buy you a drink?"

Coot Spivey shook his head. "Ain't got the time, Jack. I've signed on to lead an emigrant train to Oregon country and we're pulling out within the hour."

"All the more reason to have a final drink with a friend," Dawson said, motioning for the bartender to bring another glass. He poured Spivey three fingers from the bottle before him. Spivey's blinking blue eyes shifted from the drink to the door. He was torn between the need to leave and a desire to stay and drink with his friend.

Coot Spivey accepted the proffered glass from Dawson.

He removed the pipe and licked dry lips while the tall man by his side grinned.

"Guess it won't hurt none to have one drink."

"Now that's the old Coot Spivey I know," Dawson shot back with a friendly slap on the old man's shoulders. They both downed their drinks and Dawson instantly refilled their glasses.

Coot caught his breath and looked over at Dawson. "That's damn fine sipping whiskey, Jack." Without further prompting, Spivey drank the second glass down slowly, savoring the taste of the smooth Irish whiskey.

"Most times, can't afford more than rotgut cut with plug tobacco and bad water. Don't hurt to splurge once in awhile," Dawson remarked.

"It shorely don't," Coot Spivey whispered as he lifted another glass to his lips. This time when he emptied the glass, he turned it upside down on the bar. "I'd love to stay here and buck the tiger with you, Jack, but I got to git across the river to them wagons. Won't do me show up with a snootful first day out."

"Why leave so late in the afternoon?" Dawson said, pouring himself another glass. "Ain't likely to gain much ground with only three hours daylight left."

"Know that. Fact is, it weren't their idea. It was mine." Spivey looked a little sheepish as he toyed with his pipe. Finally he knocked the dottle from it and repacked the pipe with fresh tobacco and put a lighted match to the blackened bowl.

"What is it then?"

"A mite of trouble, that's all," Coot said through a haze of blue smoke.

"That why you looking for me?" Jack said, eyeing his friend sharply.

"Got nothing to do with it," Spivey said, realizing how he had been easily deflected from his original purpose of locating Dawson by the premium whiskey.

"Coot, you ain't changed a bit." Dawson sounded exasperated. "Trapping beaver in a dry wash is easier than pulling information from you."

Spivey gave Dawson a sly grin. "Know someone else ain't too free and easy with their lip."

"Dang it, Coot—"

"Okay, okay," Spivey said, holding up his hand. "Didn't come in here to unload my troubles on you. Only wanted to let you know there's a group of men looking for someone to guide them west. I thought of you after Red down at the Chicago said you jest blew into town." The Chicago was one of the oldest saloons in St. Joe and was a favorite for most rivermen and trappers when they hit town. Dawson had stopped there first after dropping his bedding gear and rifle at the hotel that afternoon.

"Not interested in guiding emigrants nay more," Dawson said, tipping the half-empty bottle over his glass and filling it to the brim. "Me and Tom Fitzpatrick done more than our share of late and I for one have had enough of green farmers and their snot-nosed young'uns."

"They ain't farmers, Jack. They're prospectors, looking to tie into the Pikes Peak rush." Dawson laughed uproariously and downed the drink in one quick swallow. He was slowly getting drunk and he didn't care who knew it.

"Hell, they don't need me to guide'm then. All they got to do is follow the trail of garbage scattered from here to purgatory left by those farmers."

"That's just it," Spivey persisted, "they ain't looking to go by the Oregon route. Want somebody who knows the country and can lead them straight to the diggings by the short trail. I'd do it myself if I hadn't signed on with this wagon train." Dawson still didn't look interested. "They willin' to pay well," Spivey added.

"How well?"

"Two-fifty."

"Ain't interested," Dawson said flatly, turning back to the bottle.

"That you talking or the whiskey?"

"Damn it, Coot, don't rile me," Dawson warned his friend.

"Just tell me this," Spivey said, acting as though he hadn't heard Dawson's outburst, "what is it you going to do now that spring is coming on? Ain't no money to be had in St. Joe less you willin' to steal or kill fer it."

"Plan on taking trade goods down Santa Fe way if you got to know. That way, won't be nobody giving me lip about how tough life is on the trail and how they hadn't planned walking for fifteen hours a day under a broiling sun with bawling kids underfoot. Be just me and a string of pack mules . . . no complaints and no fool questions to contend with."

"That's gonna take a sight of money."

"Got more than enough to handle the charges," Dawson said, patting his coat pocket. "Me and old Fitz done all right last year. Figure I can triple my money."

"Can't deny the Santa Fe trade ain't been a good idea of late, but should you change your mind, them prospectors are staying over to the Barton House." Thirty years ago the Barton House was an impressive structure where St. Joe's elite attended gala balls and prosperous businessmen met to discuss the burgeoning trade along the Missouri Riverfront. Now it was nothing more than a ramshackle place where rivermen, trappers and the lower rungs of society hung out.

"I won't," Dawson said with finality. "Now what's got you leaving town in such a hurry?"

Coot Spivey prefaced his answer by starting out, "Jack you known me more'n twenty years now and you know I ain't one to duck trouble when it comes my way." He looked at Dawson for confirmation. The tall man nodded his head and waited for Spivey to continue.

"I been seeing this lady friend on what you might say a regular basis over the last few weeks." Dawson gave him a knowing smile which Coot Spivey pounced on immediately. "Don't look at me that way, Dawson. I admit there's more smoke than fire in this old chimney but the furnace still works when I need it!"

8

"Never meant to imply otherwise," Jack said pouring them another drink over Spivey's objections. "Please continue." His speech was slightly slurred now.

Somewhat mollified, Coot Spivey picked up the glass of whiskey against his better judgement and drank half of it. "Whiskey like that has a way of slipping up on a man," he said, placing the half-empty glass on the bar. He felt the warm explosion in the hollow pit of his stomach for the third time.

"You were saying?"

"I'm a-gittin' to it!" Coot Spivey caught his breath and lowered his voice after looking around at the sprinkling of afternoon customers. "This lady friend has, ah, a husband, a riverboat captain, who it turns out is insanely jealous. I found out just how bad a case he has for her yesterday when his boat docked ahead of schedule."

"So now he's gunning for you, I take it?" Dawson said, getting the picture. He was having trouble focusing his eyes now.

"That I could handle. It's the lady friend. She made me promise I wouldn't get in a fight with him. The only way I know how to avoid him is hit the trail in a hurry. I understand he's making all the saloons in town, trying to drink them dry and saying how he's going to shoot me on sight." Coot Spivey looked worried.

"Never knew you to get your tail in a crack over a woman, Spivey. She must be some kind of looker."

"She's that and more, Jack. A lot more."

"Well, in that case you best git before her husband corners you into a gunfight." Jack Dawson smiled, lifting the glass to his lips. "And we both know you can't hit a moose with a short gun."

Coot Spivey glanced toward the door before turning back to Dawson. "Just stopped by to tell you about them prospectors is all. Good luck down Santa Fe. Don't lose my topknot, see you this fall." With that, the two trappers shook hands. As Spivey moved away from the bar, Jack

Dawson called for him to wait. He had the bartender fetch him another bottle of Irish whiskey.

Jack Dawson shoved the bottle into Spivey's hand, "Here, might help ease the pain some on a lonely night. Take care old man."

After Coot Spivey had gone, Jack ordered another bottle, deciding what he needed most besides whiskey was good company for the rest of the night. And with him carrying over twelve hundred dollars, it wouldn't do to burn the wick too close to the fuel, if he hadn't already. Tomorrow he intended to throw together a pack outfit, buy as much trade goods he had money for and strike the trail for New Mexico. Jack moved toward the door not knowing if his feet were touching the rough planking or not. *He had drunk too much!* Just as he was about to push open the door, the figure of a large red-bearded man filled the entrance. He shoved Dawson aside roughly and stepped into the saloon with eyes blazing. Already unsteady on his feet, Dawson nearly fell. Catching himself, the bottle of expensive Irish whiskey crashed to the floor, the precious liquid draining quickly through the cracks. The man never looked around at the sound of the breaking bottle or to offer an apology.

"Anybody seen a runt of an old man wearing a full set of buckskins? Got a thick gray beard," the man questioned no one directly, yet made it clear he was asking everyone present.

Jack Dawson regained his balance as anger raced through a lean frame already fueled by the whiskey. He reached out and spun the big man around, nearly tripping him in the process.

"Expect you to replace the bottle you just broke," Dawson said.

The fiery-eyed man centered his anger on Dawson and broke loose from his grip. "Ain't buying drunks booze. You shouda watched where you was going."

Without formulating a reply, Jack Dawson found himself reaching out with a knotted fist. The blow reeled the big man backward, but he stayed on his feet. For a moment,

10

pain washed over his face, but this was quickly overshadowed by the deep anger that filled his dark eyes.

"Damn you! I'll break more than your bottle," the man bellowed as he stepped in close. He landed a stinging blow that Dawson tried to duck, the punch glancing off his shoulder. Even still, numbing pain shot down the length of his arms to his fingertips like a hot branding iron. The man had power, and Dawson saw the vicious gleam that lit his eyes.

He had been in countless fights in his lifetime, most he had won. But this time, Dawson had the uneasy feeling he was going to lose. He feigned a right with his damaged shoulder, stepped in and threw everything he had behind his left, aiming at the man's square jaw. The sudden explosion in his head caused everything around him to go black abruptly.

Ham Anderson stood over the prostrate figure with his fists still clenched. "Damn trappers. They're all alike. Ain't worth wood shavings." He gave Jack Dawson a swift kick in the side and strode out the door.

Excruciating pain forced Dawson upward through the darkness. The pain in his side felt like someone was twisting a knife blade between his ribs. A moan escaped his lips.

"Take it easy, friend," the bartender said, wiping his face with a wet towel. "Expect you got a broken rib or two when he kicked you."

Jack Dawson struggled to sit up, the effort causing more pain, and he had to fight back the cry that rose in his throat. He found he could not breathe deep without it hurting.

"That . . . big . . . man . . . do this?"

"Afraid so, mister. Good thing you was out when he kicked you. Don't take much of a man to do that, especially after he knocked you flat with that big fist of his," the bartender said.

"Help me to a chair," Dawson whispered, using the man's arms as a way to pull himself off the floor. Someone stuck a chair beneath him and he settled down gratefully.

"Man was on the prod for some reason," the bartender vouched. "Just you sit still and I'll fetch you a drink." The man hurried behind the bar for a glass and a fresh bottle of Irish whiskey.

Dawson looked around him at the few patrons who were staring openly. He explored his ribs gingerly. White-hot pain shot through him every time he located a broken rib. So far, he counted three.

"Anybody know the gent that did this?" Dawson questioned those nearby. Most of them turned away, not wanting to be a party to the fight.

"I know him," a slender youth to his right said. "That was Captain Hamilton Anderson. Shipped out with him once. Man is a terror when sober and deadly when drunk. Had he been drinking much, doubt he would have stopped 'til he killed you."

Dawson tried a weak smile, but failed. "Guess I should consider myself lucky then." Dawson thought of Coot Spivey.

"Best leave the captain alone," the youth warned. "He'll kill you for sure next time." The bartender came up with the bottle and poured Dawson a drink.

"Next time, I won't be carrying good Irish whiskey in me." Dawson swallowed the drink, feeling for the first time the soreness in his jaw as he touched the tender area.

"That's the blow that laid you out."

"Yeah, it's coming back now," Dawson said ruefully. He felt for the thick packet in his coat pocket and felt the bulge. At least he still had his money.

Dawson rested for a few minutes more and finally managed to stand on his feet, despite the pain it caused. He laid some bills on the table, paying for a another bottle of whiskey.

"Much obliged for your help," he told the bartender. The bartender waved back at him and watched as Jack Dawson walked unsteadily from the bar.

Outside on the streets, Dawson was surprised to see it was nearly dark. Foot traffic, as well as mule-drawn wagons and men on horseback, rushed up and down the busy corridor like it was broad daylight. Dawson stood in front of the

12

saloon, holding on to a post for balance. He hadn't intended to let things get this far out of hand. Coot Spivey was right; good whiskey had a way of slipping up on a man.

A wave of nausea swept over Dawson. He was going to throw up no matter he was carrying a belly full of good whiskey and an aching in his side. He looked around at the busy street and staggered down an alleyway for a few feet. Dawson cried out from the pain as his muscles tightened over his ribs as his stomach rolled over, emptying its contents on the litter that covered the ground. The pain was terrible, doubling him over, and leaving him gasping for breath. He didn't notice the shadow that fell over him until it was too late. But he did feel the sudden eruption of pain at the base of his skull. As he tried to catch himself from falling, Dawson did a half-turn to see the figure of a man standing over him with a short piece of pipe in his hands. He tried to speak through the black void that was descending quickly over his eyes, but the words never came.

The man bent over the unconscious Dawson and rifled through his pockets, taking the packet of money from his coat. Next, the attacker picked up the unbroken bottle of whiskey, hesitated, and put it back down beside Dawson. The man dropped the short piece of pipe and hurried out of the alley where he rejoined the heavy foot traffic.

Chapter 2

"My God, Jack, just look at you! How long have you been in town, anyway?"

Jack Dawson managed a weak smile while the woman worked on the back of his head with a wet cloth.

"Since early afternoon," he said through hurting teeth. The back of his skull felt like he had been run down by a stagecoach.

"You smell like you've been in town a month," the woman said, wrinkling a dainty nose. She rinsed the cloth in a pan and the water turned crimson. "You best get over to Doc Mabry and have this stitched up. He can take a look at your ribs too while you're there."

"Quit fussing so woman and give me that bottle. I feel like crushed ore in a stamp mill." Dawson twisted around holding out his hand.

"Hold still! And you can forget the alcohol while you're here."

"I'm hurting, I tell you!"

"Serves you right. Why didn't you come see me first, Jack Dawson?"

"Dang it, Jenny, can't a man wet his whistle? I been up the trail eight months for chrissakes."

"Oh, I don't object to a man sipping a little whiskey, but you didn't have to go and drown in it." Dawson squirmed around on the bed. "Hold still, will you!" The woman rubbed a salve into Dawson's scalp.

"That stings."

"I only hope it wards off infection since I know you aren't going to see old Doc."

"Done told you. Whoever hit me took all my money. I can't afford a beer much less a doctor bill."

"And how you going to pay for my services?"

Dawson reached behind him and squeezed her thigh. She pushed his hand away.

"It sure won't be *that* way, Jack, as busted up as you are."

"I'm not that busted up, darling," Jack said, his voice betraying his thoughts.

"Huh! First thing you're going to do is strip off and give me those clothes so I can have them washed. After you soak for an hour or two then we can discuss payment."

While Jenny Logan arranged for hot water and a tub, Jack Dawson eased out of his shirt and stripped away the sour-smelling pants covered in his own vomit. He handed Jenny the soiled clothes which she piled by the door. She stood there with hands on hips, smiling at Dawson who looked back at the woman self-consciously, a little worse for wear.

"Well, Jack, you getting shy in your old age. Shuck them long underwear. I know they haven't been washed since last spring." Dawson smiled sheepishly and began undoing the buttons.

"You're sure being hard on a man that's suffered grievous injuries."

She eyed him benignantly. "Grievous, Jack. Never knew you to be a man of such words."

"Never had the call to use them 'til now." Dawson gave her a crooked smile and tossed her his underwear. He saw the light in her eyes as she appraised his muscular frame.

"Even stove up you don't look half bad," Jenny admitted.

"Just lemme get cleaned up, darling, and you can appreciate me a lot better up close."

"That's what I figured you'd say." Jenny turned to answer a knock at the door, and supervised the placement of the tub. Jack Dawson raced over expectantly to the hot tub of water which had been placed in the adjoining room. Jenny Logan ran the best brothel in St. Joe. Not only did she serve the finest liquor, but her girls were the prettiest around and had to toe the mark or be kicked out. There was always clean sheets on the beds and the sweet smell of windflowers to entice any man. Although Jenny was well over thirty, she had lost none of her beauty. Many a man had tried enticing the raven-haired beauty with the sparkling green eyes into their beds, but Jenny favored few requests now, preferring the quiet and solitude of being a madam. The one person she could never say no to was Jack Dawson and it irked her that she allowed him to come and go at his own choosing.

Jenny came in and knelt down by the tub. She took the facecloth from Dawson.

"Here sit up straight and I'll wash your back. And whatever you do, don't get water into that cut on the back of your head."

"Anybody around here noticed how bossy you've become since I've been gone?"

Jenny ignored him as she soaped the facecloth and began washing his broad back. He was rock hard and slabs of muscle covered his shoulder blades. She ran a hand over a puckered scar.

"How did you get this scar, Jack? I've never noticed it before," Jenny whispered softly in his ear. Dawson had his eyes closed, enjoying the back rub.

"It was the same day ol' Prince Albert Smith went under. Remember him? Always wore that dang claw-hammer coat, even in the wilderness. Claimed it warded off Indian troubles." Dawson shook his head. "P.A. was a strange one all right, but as true a friend as a man could ever ask for. Never did know his real name." She increased her strokes in a broader circular motion.

"Ah, Jenny darling, that feels good."

"The scar, Jack?" Jenny persisted.

16

Dawson cocked his head and smiled up at the woman. "I warn you, it's a kinda bloody story.

"Jaaack."

"Okay, darling, just you keep rubbing my back thataway and I'll tell you stories till the water gets cold." Jack Dawson took a deep breath. "Let's see. I believe that was in 'fiftythree. No! It was 'fifty-one. Broken Hand . . . that's Tom Fitzpatrick . . . me and P.A. had just come across Skalkaho Pass through the Sapphires when a bunch of Blackfeet, led by a mad dog Indian we all called Big Yaak, hit us at Rock Creek crossing. We were making our way back from Astoria after delivering a bunch of fool emigrants and decided to cut through the Bitterroots and scout out a new trail. Ol' Fitzpatrick was always doing that, wanting to see over one more rise or mountain chain. Got to admit, for better than twenty years, that lust to explore new country was strong in me as well. Anyway, P.A. says to us that it looked to be prime Blackfeet country when they whooped up out of the brush along the creek.

"Oww! Be careful where you rubbing. Those ribs are sore as hell."

"Sorry, Jack," Jenny said, moving away from his ribs.

"Anyway, Big Yaak, who was the size of two normal men put together, cut loose with a bone-chilling scream that put the fear of God in all three of us. All I could see was a creek bottom swarming with Indians and it was every man for himself. P.A. went down first, his horse killed by a stray arrow. This made Big Yaak plenty mad and he jabbered something to his braves for killing such a fine horse, and P.A. had a fine'un. I circled back to get P.A. while Tom covered us. When I reached down to help P.A. up behind me, I caught an arrow . . . that scar you see now on my back . . . and he took one in the brisket by stepping in front of it for me. Never will forget that as long as I live." Dawson shook his head and scooted further down in the cooling waters.

"Before you could blink, P.A. caught two more feathers and he slaps my horse on the rump, yelling for me to get out

17

of there. P.A. knew I wouldn't leave him even if he was done for, so he just turns around and charges Big Yaak. This got the Blackfeet all in a fighting frenzy and they immediately surrounded P.A. who kept slashing at them with his big knife until he went down. Me and Tom had to cut our way through a mob of Blackfeet. To this day, I still don't know how we managed to survive."

"Did you ever even the score for your friend, I mean, kill this Yaak?"

Dawson shook his head. "Tried several times, but he was a slippery rascal. Heard he was killed three years ago by, of all things, a lightning bolt while crossing the Beaverhead."

"Guess the Lord saved him for himself," Jenny said, standing up.

"Don't know why the Lord would want someone like Big Yaak, but it ain't my place to say. Hand me a towel, Jen, this water is getting cold."

Later, they lay coupled in Jenny's soft bed as twilight came to St. Joe, relaxed after a session of furious lovemaking. Dawson was half-asleep and enjoying the warmth of Jenny's soft body beneath his own. It had been too long.

"You never told me how much was stolen," Jenny whispered sleepily in his ear.

"Twelve hundred dollars," he said, his current problems settling over him again like a thundercloud.

"Jack, how could you drink so heavily carrying that kind of money on you? You know how St. Joe is."

"Don't remind me. I get sick every time I think of it, along with this damn headache which ain't never going to stop."

"What did the sheriff say?"

"Didn't bother reporting it," Dawson said simply.

"Why not? That kind of money will draw a lot of attention. He could keep his eyes open for a sudden big spender."

"Got a feeling the sheriff and me will never see that money again."

"Oh, do you, now? Well, how'd you feel about letting me up. I got a place to run in case you haven't noticed."

Dawson raised himself up on his elbows, gritting his teeth against the pain created in his side. He looked down at Jenny Logan with a sly smile, her large breasts nestled in his chest hairs.

"I got a feeling all right and it ain't about money," he said thickly as he lowered his mouth to hers.

Chapter 3

The next morning, Dawson found his cleaned clothes folded neatly over the back of a chair. As he slipped into them, he found himself looking down at the sleeping form of Jenny Logan, who was oblivious to her naked thigh exposed from beneath the covers. He felt the stirrings of desire, but checked his first impulse of going back to bed. Dawson smiled. There would be time for that later, besides, Jenny had spent most of the night seeing to her customers while all he did was sleep. He doubted if she would appreciate being woken from a sound sleep just so he could play hide the opossum.

He slipped on his boots and strapped the big, .44 caliber cap and ball Colt First Model Dragoon around his slender waist. The grips of the large Colt were oiled and well-worn and the gripstraps of brass shone like newly minted gold. Dawson took good care of the weapon which had saved his life on more than one occasion. This morning, he intended to retrieve his bedding and his .58 caliber Joslyn, a percussion, breech-loading rifle made for the U.S. Navy that he had left in the room he had rented yesterday. Other than a nagging headache, Dawson figured he was in fairly good shape.

He went over to the bed and bent down to kiss the sleeping woman who shifted slightly on the pillow. It was times like these, Dawson felt the pangs of never having taken the time for a wife or a family of his own. Raised by a drunken mother on the waterfront of St. Louis who abandoned him when he was ten years old, Dawson had grown up in a hurry. His father, he suspected, was nothing more than a passing fancy of his mother's who moved on before he was ever born.

He was out on the busy street before he found the greenbacks in his coat pocket. He smiled. Jenny had put the money there, knowing he would never ask her for a loan. Over coffee and a huge breakfast of steak and eggs, Dawson took stock of his condition and net worth and didn't like what he saw.

First, he didn't have the means of supporting himself, and he wasn't about to lay up on Jenny. And second, in the cool light of a new day with the whiskey fever lifted from him, hard reality set in where his money was concerned. There was little chance of his ever seeing it again and that forced him back to where he started. With no money and no job, he was a poor prospect for someone like Jenny. The more he thought about it, the gloomier he became. Instead of buying supplies and mules and such for the trip to Santa Fe, here he sat with just enough money to last him for a day or two . . . if he was careful and stayed away from the saloons.

He was halfway to the hotel where he had left his gear when a thought struck him. He veered toward the river and the imposing structure of the old Barton House. Just maybe, those prospectors were still around and needed a guide and scout. He could smell the river and wharfs in the morning sun as he opened the door of the aging building and stepped inside. The interior of the Barton was a mere reflection of its once elegant self. French brocaded, velvet curtains, the color of port wine, streaked with grime and discolored by age and sun, hung carelessly over the large windows in the front. The threadbare carpet of floral design was heavily stained with tobacco juice. The place smelled of old wood, stale cigars, and sweaty bodies.

As he approached the sagging desk, he realized he didn't know who to ask for. A thickset man with watery eyes and thinning hair watched his approach with a bored look.

"Don't know how to really say this, but I'm looking for several men who are staying in this establishment and are looking to head for the goldfields. Would you know these gentlemen?"

The man looked Dawson up and down, noting the discolored jaw where Ham Anderson had slugged him. For a long moment, Dawson waited patiently and was about ready to conclude the desk clerk wasn't going to tell him anything when the man roused himself enough to speak.

"Must be looking for Frank Trego. He's got a group with him just aching to start West."

"That must be them," Dawson agreed. "Do you know where I might find them?"

The desk clerk jerked a thick thumb in the direction of the wide curving stairs. "Packing most likely. Overheard one of them say they were heading off this morning and catch up with a train of emigrants that left yesterday afternoon."

Coot Spivey's train no doubt, Dawson thought.

"Much obliged," Dawson said and turned toward the stairs just as a group of men came down carrying packs and weapons.

"Trego?" Dawson asked as he came up.

A tall, slim-built man with nervous eyes and the longest fingers Dawson had ever seen stopped and looked at Dawson.

"I'm Frank Trego, who's asking?"

"Name's Jack Dawson. Coot Spivey said you was looking for a guide and scout to the Rocky Mountain region."

Trego dropped his pack and a relieved look spread across his shallow face. The others put their packs down as well.

"Right you are, Mr. Dawson. We had just about given up finding anyone. Fact is, we heard an emigrant train pulled out of St. Joe yesterday afternoon and we figured to catch up with it and tag along. But if you're willing to guide us, we're willing to pay you two hundred and fifty dollars."

A bearded fellow stepped up to Trego and whispered something in his ear. Trego looked pained by what the man

22

apparently said. Dawson waited to see what the problem was.

Trego finally cleared his throat and seemed uncomfortable at what he was about to say. He looked into Dawson's steady eyes and glanced down at his feet.

"What's the problem? You still need a guide, don't you?"

"Oh, yes. What Mr. Barnhart wants to know, and I guess the rest of us as well, is how do we know you won't just take our money and leave us stranded in some godforsaken place on our own. No offense intended," Trego offered quickly.

"None taken, Mr. Trego. A body can't be too careful around men who speak in an easy manner. I suggest you stop in at the Harvey Brother's Mercantile over on Fourth Street. Been doing business with Bill Harvey for nigh to twenty years. Expect he'll vouch for me."

Luther Barnhart pushed around Trego. "Have you been to the Pikes Peak diggings?"

"No . . . I haven't," Dawson said slowly. "Leastwise not the way I think you're asking me. I've been though that country a number of times over the years, trapping beaver and such, but that was long before gold was discovered. And on that score, I don't know much about gold."

"I think what Luther is wanting to know, Mr. Dawson, is do you know a trail that will get us to the fields in record time? We've heard rumors that over five thousand miners are due to pull out of St. Louis this spring. We only want to get there as quickly as possible."

Dawson nodded his head. "Expect that's not going to be a problem if you men are willing to put up with long hours in the saddle over some pretty rough country and discard any ideas of traveling by wagon."

Trego looked around at the other five men, receiving their nods of approval. He turned back to Dawson.

"We're more than ready to do whatever it takes to be the first in there this spring, Mr. Dawson."

"Okay, but I'm telling you now before we get out on the trail, it's going to be a tough trip across the Plains. There's no room for the fainthearted."

23

"We understand what you're saying, Mr. Dawson, and we're ready for whatever comes."

Dawson grinned faintly. "Mr. Trego, as many times as I've been across the Plains, which is considerable, I'm never quite prepared for the things that country can throw at you. Just wanted you to be prepared for the worse, is all."

"When can we get underway then, Mr. Dawson?" Trego asked. Luther Barnhart leaned into Frank Trego once more. Trego seemed irritated by the man.

"Damn it, Luther, I know what I'm doing. We can stop by and see Bill Harvey as we head out of town," Trego grumbled. In spite of himself, Dawson felt a growing dislike for Luther Barnhart.

"One more thing, Mr. Trego, I expect my money in full, in advance," Dawson said tightly. He hadn't intended on asking for it all now, but Luther Barnhart's attitude toward him changed Dawson's mind.

"Why that's preposterous!" Barnhart blurted out.

Dawson looked at the man through narrowed eyes. "It's all or none," he said flatly. "You decide to turn back once we're on the trail, where does that leave me?"

"That won't be a problem, Mr. Dawson," Frank Trego cut in. "If you would meet us, say in two hours, at the mercantile, I'll see you get your money then."

"Fair enough," Dawson said, turning to leave.

Jack Dawson let himself back into the darkened room where Jenny Logan still slept. He had stopped by the hotel on the way over and picked up his things . . . . It was a damn good thing he had paid for the room in advance, Dawson thought, now that he was flat broke. He looked over at the sleeping form. Jenny wasn't going to like his having to leave so soon, but a man without money in St. Joe was a man in trouble.

As he approached the bed, Jenny stirred and opened her eyes. She smiled up at him and held out her arms. The covers slid back exposing her nakedness.

"Where have you been, Jack?" Dawson dumped his gear on the floor and came to her. She was warm and inviting, and her musky smell aroused him immediately. They kissed briefly.

"Had to go get my gear over at the hotel," Dawson said softly in her ear. She pulled him closer to her and then just as suddenly pushed him back to look in his eyes.

"Why do you have these on?" Jenny asked, referring to his rough set of buckskins. "I had your suit cleaned and . . ." She saw the look in his eyes and knew immediately what it meant.

Dawson glanced away under her stare, "Listen, Jenny, with no money to carry through with my plans, I got no choice but to start guiding again." His voice was apologetic.

"But you just got here, Jack," Jenny protested, sitting up in bed with the covers close around her.

"Lord I know that, but it ain't my doing. Some men want me to guide them to the gold diggings in Colorado. It's easy money and I can be back by late May."

"If it's money you need, I'll loan you whatever it takes to start your Santa Fe business. I've done well, saved some, and invested the rest back East."

Dawson shook his head, "Won't do, Jenny. I'm not about to take your money or risk it either. I was the damn fool who lost his poke. Now I got to suffer the consequences."

Jenny flung her hair about her head exasperatedly and then her countenance softened. "I don't want you to leave, Jack . . . so soon."

Dawson cradled her head in the hollow of his neck. "I know, I get a little sick myself over the prospect of trading this warm soft bed here with you for hard ground."

Jenny pulled back and Dawson saw the tears spilling down her cheeks. He wiped them away tenderly.

"Hey now, none of that. We both know what I got to do."

"What about a job, Jack? Russell and Majors are looking for men to run relay stations along their pony express they

25

started just last week. I would go there with you, do whatever you asked."

"Jenny, any man would be pleased to have you by his side, but I been crawling around those mountains for most of my life. Ain't one to take orders or sit still for very long in some desolate station, tending to stage stock. I come from a different time, a different breed that's about played out."

"You're selling yourself short, Jack. You could change, settle down under the right circumstances." Her voice was soft and yielding to his touch as he stroked her naked shoulders.

"I know what you're trying to say, Jen. I want you to know I've never cared about another woman like I care for you."

She hugged him tightly. "When are you leaving then?"

"Got to meet those miners over at Harvey's in about an hour."

Jenny Logan sat up and dried away her tears with the corner of the blanket, allowing it to fall away from her body afterward. She looked up at Dawson with sad eyes. "Then we don't have much time."

Dawson looked down at her, nodded, stood up and took off his clothes.

Frank Trego and the others were waiting for him when Dawson rode up on his buckskin. Trego ran his eyes over the well-muscled stocky horse.

"Fine animal you got there," Trego said as Dawson reined in and stepped down.

"Looks to be too small to pull the load if we get in a tight and have to make a run for it," Luther Barnhart spoke up.

Dawson's face reflected his displeasure in the man.

"Barnhart, isn't it?" Luther nodded. "Well, Barnhart, since you seem to know more about proper animals, trails and such, why don't you just move to the head of the column and do the leading? I'll go on back to the woman I left crying in bed." Luther Barnhart was speechless and slowly his face shaded over with red.

"Luther, how many times do we have to tell you to watch that tongue of yours?" Frank Trego said angrily. Barnhart opened his mouth to reply but Trego cut him off, by turning back to Dawson.

"I'm sorry for the outburst, Mr. Dawson. We are prepared to hire you, if you'll overlook Luther. You come highly recommended by Mr. Harvey and I apologize for doubting you in the first place."

"Call me Jack. That's okay, expect any man with a lick of sense ought to check out who he's doing business with. Lot of grief later on could be saved thataway." Dawson looped the reins over the railing in front of the store and stepped up on the rough planking. He looked around at the group of men and at their gear. A few minutes were devoted to their horses. Dawson didn't like what he saw.

"First thing we got to do is trade those leggy horses for something with bottom." Barnhart started to offer an immediate protest but the look form Frank Trego cut him off. "Got to have mules to pack your gear, so expect on buying at least three."

Trego looked worried. "How much is all this going to cost?"

"Let's see," Dawson said, staring out into the busy street. "Most likely, I can find us decent mules for about sixty, seventy dollars apiece."

"Seventy dollars!" Barnhart blurted out. "Why we could get mules back home for twenty-five, easy."

Dawson's face turned bleak. "This ain't Indiana or Ohio or wherever the hell it is you came from," Dawson snapped back. "Most those traveling through are having to pay upwards of a hundred dollars, not that I owe you an explanation, Barnhart."

"Damn it, Luther, this is your last warning," Trego said with blood in his eyes. "Another outburst and you can hook it best way you can to Colorado. You been an ache in my side ever since we left Cincinnati." Luther Barnhart stared for a minute at Trego and finally turned around and stalked off.

"Come on, Jack, I want to introduce you to the others." Dawson shook hands with the rest of the men, appraising each for obvious strengths and weaknesses. Two were brothers, youthful and eager for adventure. They were Tom and Mike Rogers. Charles Pittman was an ex-minister who appeared to be running away from something. Pittman was the only clean-shaven of the bunch. Dawson shook hands with a big raw-boned man in his late twenties from the Pennsylvania coal mines by the name of Danny Malone. Malone was carrying around a lot of hurt in his sad eyes for some reason, Dawson concluded.

"There were two more of us, but they decided to join up early with that wagon train before we ran into you to do our scouting," Frank Trego said. "Since we are going to need both horses and mules, I wonder if we might prevail upon you to accept half of the two hundred and fifty we owe and the rest once we reach the goldfields?"

"That'll be fine, Frank. It's because of Barnhart I even asked for the full amount up front in the first place."

"Well, don't worry about Luther," Trego said, counting out the money to Dawson. "He's my responsibility and I'll see to it he stays out of your hair."

"Well, that I will leave to you. We best get to it if we expect to make it much past the river by tonight," Dawson said, stepping into the mercantile for the few supplies he would need between here and Cherry Creek. He thought again of Jenny Logan and wondered if he was doing the right thing by leaving.

William Harvey met Dawson at the counter and the pair shook hands. Harvey, round faced and smiling, cleared a space on the cluttered counter to rest his thick elbows. Like his brother, Sandy, Bill Harvey tipped the scales at three hundred pounds and seemed to be getting bigger every time Dawson saw him.

"Heard you were the brave soul going to guide those

28

eager miners West, Jack. You musta fell on hard times?" Dawson allowed himself a tight grin.

"Something like that." And then he told Harvey about being robbed of his money.

"Tough break, Jack. Anything I can do?"

"Just keep an eye out for anyone that suddenly starts spending money like it was water. Make a note of it. Should be back late May. I'll settle accounts then."

"I'll sure keep my eyes peeled, Jack, but it may have been someone who's passing through."

"It's a long shot, I know. Fact is, I really don't hold out any hopes of ever seeing my money again."

"You been over to see Jenny?" Dawson nodded as he began to pick through items he wanted. "She sure is a looker, Jack. If I was you, I'd marry that woman and cut out all this rambling. You know what they say about a rolling stone."

"Yeah, I know and if you don't start helping me put things together, I'm going to throw that stone through your window as I ride out of town." Harvey roared with laughter, his apron over his fat belly shaking like leaves in a stiff breeze. "What can I get for you?"

It was past noon before the small group pulled out of St. Joe, riding new horses and packing three mules that acted as though this was the first time anything had ever been strapped to their backs. It had taken Dawson's expert hands to get the gear tied down and the group started out of town.

"Those mules appear to be a mite green," Trego allowed.

"They'll settle down once we're down the trail a few days," Dawson said.

"Guess the price should have been a clue to their disposition."

"We were lucky to find mules for forty dollars."

"Expect you knowing that muleteer had a lot more to do with it than luck, Jack," Trego said.

Chapter 4

"What do you think, Colin?" a dark-skinned individual dressed in a heavy checked coat asked. A black beard tinged with gray covered his face and his wet eyes were never still in his head.

"Of what?" Colin Jackson asked slowly. A known gunman and outlaw, Jackson had spread his fame from the border towns of Kansas-Missouri into the Rocky Mountain region at first hints of gold. Towns along the Missouri and Mississippi breathed a collective sigh of relief upon his departure. Along with his deadly accurate guns, Colin Jackson was endowed with a violent temper when aroused. Nattily dressed on most occasions, Jackson wore roughrider's garb and carried a brace of Colt's pistols at his belt along with a large knife.

A quarter slice of moon threw an eerie light across the broken landscape where Jackson and the other gunman known only as Black Hawk sat their horses. In the distance stood a small ranch house of sod and logs. Next to the soddy was a pole corral where a cluster of horses stood quietly in the pale light.

"Looks like about a baker's dozen," Colin Jackson said, counting.

"Should we wait for the others? Handling that many horses could pose a problem if we wake up Jonas Bradley."

Colin Jackson turned his hazel eyes to Black Hawk and smiled, the pale light of the moon outlining his white teeth.

"Bradley is only one man. We can handle him."

"Okay by me, but I remember the last time someone tried to steal horses from him."

"Mandina and Lyles? Ha, born losers and you know it. Surprised they lived long enough to reach Denver City," Jackson said.

"Just the same, Bradley laid them out with that Sharps of his after they thought they were safely out of rifle range."

"I swear, Black Hawk, you sound like a man who lost his nerve."

"You know better than that, Colin," Black Hawk said coldly.

"Let's get to it, then. I got a poker game waiting for me back at the Cibola gambling hall."

Against his better judgement, Black Hawk spurred his horse toward the distant corral with Colin Jackson riding on his left. Swiftly, Black Hawk dismounted and threw aside the poles that acted as a gate unconcerned with the amount of noise they were making. Their game plan was simple; hit fast and run the horses off before those inside the ranch house knew what was happening.

As soon as Black Hawk had the gate clear, Jackson drove his horse into the corral flaying a rope over his head to get the animals stirred up and moving. Black Hawk joined in, using his quirt on the nearest animal. The squealing, snorting horses left the corral on a dead run, thundering across the rocky ground toward the rough foothills to the west. Both Black Hawk and Colin Jackson knew that rugged part of the country like the back of a playing card. The maze of rocks and gullies had served them well on more than one occasion. If they made it to the foothills, there was little danger of pursuers ever tracking them down.

A yellowed light flared in the window of the dark ranch house as they swept past the structure, driving the horses at full speed. Even in the knife blade of light, Black Hawk felt like everything around him was as illuminated as if the sun had been shining. He heard a distant shout behind him and he laid over the neck of his horse to urge more speed from

31

the animal, but more so, to present as small a target as he could to Jonas Bradley's Sharps.

Suddenly a riderless horse squealed and went down, kicking hard. A second later the booming report of a large caliber rifle filled the night air and Black Hawk tensed his back muscles even though it was too late. An instant later, they swept around the first formation of rocks that led through a narrow canyon where Boulder Creek plunged, cutting off any further shots from Bradley.

They drove the horses hard through the weird rock formations of red and brown that marked the beginning of the hogback that ran horizontal to the Plains and extended upward for two thousand feet. It was in this maze of rock, three men rode out of a slash of land covered by stunted pine and cedar. Even in the subdued moonlight, Jackson and Black Hawk had no trouble identifying them as part of their gang. The three men dropped in behind the charging horses and helped drive them through a narrow gap that led to a small valley suitable for holding a hundred head of animals at a time. Near the upper end, lay a pool of dark water that owed its existence to an underground stream that flowed down out of the high mountains to the west.

They drove the horses into the little valley, unsaddled their mounts, and a couple of the men brought in firewood. Black Hawk took the coffee pot down to the pool and filled it with icy water. When he got back to the line shack, a roaring fire was going in the little stove. Colin Jackson sat at a rickety table with a deck of cards, but his eyes stayed on the men with their backs to the heat. It was then, Black Hawk figured Colin Jackson hadn't stayed behind just to play a hand of cards. He had seen that look in Colin's eyes before . . . just like the time he gunned down Lidge Porter for cutting the cards wrong. And now it was back again.

Black Hawk added coffee to the pot and sat it on the stove lid which was glowing a deep red in the soft light of the lamp. He moved away from the others and took up a position near the door. Damned if he was going to get in the way.

32

Bennie Carter looked at Black Hawk curiously. "You expectin' Bradley to bust through that door?" He gave Black Hawk a yellow-toothed grin.

"Ain't worried about who may bust in, more like who might try to bust out," Black Hawk replied.

Carter's face sobered and his eyes narrowed a bit. "Just what the damn hell you talking 'bout, Black Hawk." Black Hawk and the gunmen at the table traded glances, and Colin Jackson shoved the cards to the center of the table and stood up. As he gained his feet, he pushed aside his coat, exposing the walnut handle of his pistol. Bennie Carter suddenly looked like a rat with no place to go. His eyes betrayed his thinking but before he could put it into words, Jackson spoke quietly, as if he were talking about horses or the weather.

"This is the third time you been late, Bennie. What if me and Black Hawk had run into trouble, where would we be now? Man ain't dependable, he ain't worth having around."

"I can explain, Colin," Bennie said hastily.

"Like the other times," Jackson cut in. "It ain't your gambling or the whores you been chasing that bothers me. It's the drinking and that loose tongue of yours . . . could get us all hanged if anybody ever found out about who we are. And I know a few prominent people in Denver wouldn't like that one bit, Bennie, not one bit." Bennie stiffened and looked like a man about to face death.

"I ain't said nothing to nobody, Colin. That's the honest to God truth."

Colin Jackson gave him a lazy smile, "I know," and then he shot Bennie Carter twice through the heart. Carter barely had time to register surprise on his face before he pitched backward to the floor.

Colin Jackson gestured to the other two men, using the barrel of his smoking gun to emphasize the point. "Drag him out of here before there's blood all over the place." Without a word, the two men who had ridden in with Bennie carried him out behind the shack and placed him on the cold rocks.

Black Hawk was numb from the experience yet he maintained facial calm as he poured them both coffee. Colin had taken his seat again and was shuffling the cards with hands as steady as if there had been no shooting.

"We're going to need a few more good men," Jackson said, taking a sip of the hot liquid.

"What for? We been getting by. Too many men can lead to trouble," Black Hawk said, taking a seat across from the cold gunman.

"Because stealing horses ain't as profitable as what I got in mind."

"What about Ford and the others?" Black Hawk said. "They won't like having to cut in two more men."

"Got a feeling once they find out what their share is from this new venture, they won't care either way. Course, I expect you and I to take the largest cut since it's our necks they'll help stretch if we ever caught."

"What you planning?" Black Hawk asked, his eyes betraying his sudden interest.

"First we got to get rid of the stock on our hands now. I figure Jim Latty and his boys can move them for us. He's been wanting to get in the horse stealing business ever since hitting Denver. Fact is, what I got on my mind, we can let Latty take over for us if he's determined to rustle horses. Need to do a little more thinking on it, then I'll lay it out for you."

Black Hawk shrugged and turned back to his coffee as the other two men came back inside and over to the stove.

"Dang, it's getting a sight colder out there," the one called Cove Stillman said, rubbing his hands over the stove to get the life back into them. The other man, Whit Coleman, true to his nature, never said a word.

"Tomorrow, I want Bennie hauled away from here, don't care where long's it's far enough so they ain't no way anybody can trace you back here," Jackson said to the two men. Colin figured it didn't really matter since Latty would be the one occupying the shack from here on out. It was just his nature to be cautious, and so for it had blessed him with a long life.

"Don't worry none about that, me and Whit'll take care of it," Cove said for the both of them. Fact is, Cove did most of the talking for them. It had been that way since they left Tennessee three jumps ahead of a posse determined to string them up for horse rustling. Nervous and quick to speak, Cove Stillman never wasted a lot of time on thinking before plunging ahead. Whit was just the opposite, slow and methodical; he liked things thought through before taking any action. Most times, Cove would get exasperated at his friend and simply barge ahead, devil take its course.

Colin Jackson stood up, giving the men a cold smile. "Guess by now, ain't nobody left in Cibola Hall but the high rollers. Think I'll ride in play a hand or two, see if I can change their luck." A consummate gambler, Colin Jackson was good enough to turn professional. Fact is, Ed Chase over at the Palace Saloon offered Jackson a job there with a sixty-forty split but Jackson only smiled and shook his head. Gambling to him was a sport, something he did for pleasure. He wanted nothing to change that for him. His real business was tied low on his left leg . . . hired to the highest bidder.

After they heard him ride away, Cove Stillman asked Black Hawk what was eating the icy gunman.

"Nothing," Black Hawk replied, "leastwise, nothing that lead won't cure." The outlaw guffawed loudly at his own attempt at black humor, but Stillman and Coleman never cracked a smile. They had seen what the unprovoked Jackson was capable of, and neither man wanted to find himself on the wrong side of the man. He had shot Bennie faster than Cove Stillman could blink. That was all the impressing Cove needed to ride a wide circle around Jackson. And if it came to a fight, Cove would make sure it was from a distance with rifles. Cove believed he could hold his own with the best of them at three hundred yards, including Colin Jackson.

Black Hawk stretched and rubbed his eyes. "Think I'll

grab some sleep. Just make sure you haul Bennie outta here at daylight. Don't want him stinking the place up." With that, the outlaw fell across a rumpled bunk in the corner and started snoring immediately. The men at the table sat there for a long time without speaking. Uncharacteristically, it was Whit Coleman who broke the silence.

"Don't like what Colin done," Coleman said slowly. "Bennie never had a chance to defend himself."

"Ha! Defend himself! Why Colin coulda ate dinner and still had time to plug Bennie. The man is faster than anything I've ever seen, either side of the Mississippi, and further more you know it."

"Just the same, it ain't fair."

"Whit, we both know dang good and well life ain't fair, otherwise we'd still be back there in them Tennessee hills. Now gimme them cards and let's see if you can lose a hand or two to me."

Chapter 5

Frank Trego caught up with Dawson as he topped a slight rise that overlooked the well-beaten Oregon Trail. Dawson waited as Trego drew rein, sending up a small cloud of pulverized yellow dust into the calm air. The others were a mile to the rear and wide-eyed at the sight of human litter that greeted them the further west they moved.

Even though they were only sixty miles out of St. Joe, there was plenty of evidence along the trail to indicate how some of the emigrants had suffered in their quest to find new homes in California and Oregon. In the dry Kansas air, discarded bureaus, clothing, rusting pieces of machinery, and even sewing machines sat beside the trail, dusty and forgotten by owners who were forced to lighten loads to save their poor animals in the sandy bottoms. Among the scattered belongings every fifty feet or so, lay the hastily dug shallow graves of those souls who had died from some disease, an accident, or who were murdered by roving bands of Indians. It was a sobering sight to the green miners who followed in the emigrant's hopeful, but dusty, footsteps.

Frank Trego drew rein beside the waiting Dawson and mopped a fine bead of mist from his brow. "Heating up some," he said, looking out across the undulating horizon creased by dried out riverbeds that were easily marked by the smattering of trees, managing to hold onto life by taking advantage of the infrequent rainfall.

"Try crossing the Plains in July if you really want to know what hot is," Dawson said.

"We making good time?" Trego volunteered.

"Should reach the Blue this time tomorrow."

"Then what?" Frank Trego wanted to know.

Dawson took a small drink from his canteen before answering. He was beginning to like the solid Trego while his dislike of Luther Barnhart continued to escalate with each passing day. The man had turned into a chronic complainer; if it wasn't the weather, it was the stifling dust or the drab meals that didn't suit him.

"We turn south, unless you want to tag along with that bunch from the wagon train," Dawson said, indicating the smear of dust that marked the trail several miles west of where they sat their horses.

Trego shook his head. "That way is too long. If we don't get to Cherry Creek by the end of this month, won't be enough space left to stand much less work a claim."

"You know anything about mining, Frank?" For a moment, Trego seemed a little flustered as he pulled a wrinkled pamphlet from his shirt pocket.

"Bought this back in St. Joe." He handed it to Dawson who glanced down at the author. It was by D. C. Oakes, the flagrantly optimistic guidebook author who had arrived at the diggings in the early fall of '58. Excited by what he saw there, Oakes kept up a steady stream of writing, extolling the mineral wealth of the region and sending it back for publication in Kansas newspapers. His twenty-five cent pamphlets sold like hotcakes to gold-hungry miners heading West. Actually they were quite helpful in warning the green miners to bring plenty of provisions and to organize into four man companies for mutual protection as well as reducing the amount of supplies needed. Dawson handed the pamphlet back to Trego.

"You know Mr. Oakes by any chance?" Trego asked.

"Know of him," Dawson said, smiling. "We'll come by a marker before we get to the Blue where some disgruntled miners, called 'go-backs,' nearly strung Oakes up, claiming he had started the gold rush rumor in the first place."

"Then what he says in this pamphlet, isn't true?" Trego asked, slightly alarmed that he had put all his trust as well as his life in the hands of a man he had never met.

"Oh, most of it is true, that part about partnering up and sharing mining equipment and such. Trouble with any guide, Frank, is that it can't tell you where to dig for gold, only how."

"Comforting thought." Trego looked at the specks of wagons lumbering slowly along in the distance and back to the trash and junk that littered the trail. "Is it going to be like this to the Blue River?"

Jack Dawson laughed in spite of himself. "It's like this right up to the very end of the trail in Oregon country. Trail really gets thick with truck and all the closer you get to the divide at South Pass. What pilgrims won't try to haul across rough country." Dawson shook his head.

Frank Trego sat there on his horse trying to visualize the accumulated waste along the entire length of the Oregon Trail. There had to be literally tons of stuff going to ruin. What sobered him more, were the marked graves that stood as a silent and grim reminder of the harshness of life out here on the lonely trail.

"Wagon coming our way," Dawson remarked. Trego set aside his morbid thoughts of the dead men lining the trail and looked out across the distant space at the approaching wagon.

"Best get moving or we'll never make the Blue by tomorrow," Dawson said, giving his big buckskin a gentle nudge. Lost in thought, Frank Trego rode along with him as they closed the distance between themselves and the lone wagon.

When they were fifty yards out, Dawson drew rein and waited for the white-canvassed wagon to come to him while he studied the driver and the passenger seated next to him. They were hollow-eyed and gaunt; their faces held none of the hopes that crowded the miners leaving places like St. Joe, West Port or Independence. The driver, who appeared to be in his middle years with a shaggy gray beard, brought the skinny mules to a halt beside the waiting riders. A thin layer of dust settled over them all.

"Howdy," Dawson said through the clearing haze. The driver scanned the riders' faces and spit a chew across the back of one of his mules.

"You'd be advised to turn back," the driver said, not wasting words on greetings.

"How's that?" Frank Trego asked.

"Ain't 'nough gold in them mountains to fill a tea cup much less go around all them pikers that's bunched along them creek beds. Me and my boy Samuel's headed back to the farm in Iowa and damn glad of it." Samuel nodded his head as if to lend credence to what his pa was saying.

"Go-backs," Dawson exclaimed.

The driver looked grim-faced. "Guess you could call us that. Fact is, it don't matter one way or the other to us. Staying around Pikes Peak a man can die. Food is scarce, but the prices ain't. Robbery and murder is an everyday occurrence."

"You paint a pretty bleak picture, my friend," Trego said.

"By golly, you continue on, you'll see just how bleak things can get. Without color to pay for the necessities of life, you'll wished you had heeded my warning." Without further conversation, the driver cracked his long whip across the back of his sorry mules. "Hee-i, getup there!"

The wasted mules lunged into their harness and slowly got the wagon going again. As it creaked by, Dawson and Trego saw the crossed out black letters against the dingy white canvass and the words "Busted, by God" substituted above the words, "Pikes Peak or Bust!"

Dawson looked over at the worried Trego. "Still got a mind to continue?"

Frank Trego jutted out a determined jaw, "I'm not turning back, no matter what. May not pan the first flake, but I'll be able to say I been to gold country."

"Just thought I'd ask," Dawson said, pointing his horse west again.

"Luther'll most likely want to cave soon's he sees the wagon. He's never really had his heart in this like the rest of us."

"I could have guessed as much," Dawson said simply.

That night they dry camped within a mile of the wagon train and Dawson watched as the sun painted the western sky red and then purple. Flickering campfires glowed back at him like angry red eyes across the gentle swale as twilight settled across the wide expanse. He thought of Jenny Logan. There was something good developing between them, genuine feelings he couldn't yet sort out. Dawson wondered if he had been wise to leave St. Joe. Maybe he should have at least taken the time to look for the thief who had stolen his money. It would have given Jenny and him a little more time together. He heard footsteps and Dawson turned around and found himself facing Luther Barnhart.

"What is it?" Dawson asked rather hard. He hated having to shift his thoughts from that of Jenny Logan to the green miner.

"Just wanted you to know that I, for one, think going on is a waste of time, money, and sweat."

Dawson allowed a thin smile to cross his rock-hard features. "And you don't intend to chip in the rest of my money if you do go on, is that it?"

Luther Barnhart looked surprised, yet recovered quickly. "That is correct," Barnhart snapped. "In fact, I would like very much for you to return a portion of the advance that constitutes my share."

It was Jack Dawson's turn to be surprised. "You got the brass, Barnhart, I'll give you that. What did you do before you took up gold mining, foreclosing on old ladies and orphans?"

Barnhart's face grew crimson, but he kept a check on his tongue out of fear for the man he now confronted. He had overheard Bill Harvey telling Frank Trego how Jack Dawson was one of the best Plainsman around and sure death in a fight with pistols or rifle.

Dawson continued, "Far as I'm concerned, you've used up your share already. Only thing you got coming back is trouble if you press it." Luther Barnhart stared at Dawson and finally stalked off in the gathering darkness without another word.

By mid-morning of the next day, the weary animals, lugging at their heavy wagons, broke into a brisk trot at the smell of water. Dawson watched as the cloud of dust mushroomed up around the wagon train. He only shook his head. Whoever was leading them didn't know much about traveling across the Plains. They were still a good twenty miles from water and if the animals continued at that pace, many would drop in their traces long before they ever reached the Blue. Frank Trego rode up and sat his horse, staring at the distant sight.

"Looks like they decided to pick up their pace," he commented to Dawson who seemed preoccupied with his thoughts. It was a full minute before Dawson responded.

"Kill their horses is what mostly likely will happen." Trego looked curiously at Dawson, but said nothing. The dry air was filled with the smell of dust.

"Barnhart's decided he wants to turn back," Dawson said, changing the subject.

Trego took his eyes from the giant yellow dust cloud and focused them on Dawson's face. "He tell you that, huh?"

"Wanted part of his advance back as well. Didn't like it much when I told him his share was already used up." Dawson smiled.

"Oh, I wouldn't worry none about Luther. He's a pain most times, I agree, but he'll stick as long as the others hold out."

"I warned you this could happen once we got good and started and we ain't seen any trouble yet. A few Indians will convince Barnhart he's needed badly back home."

"Think we'll see Indians soon?"

"Not until we get a day or so out of Ft. Riley. Most of

those hanging around the post are there to beg for table scraps and whiskey. No need to worry about them. It's the others, the ones that hang farther west in broken country so barren and dry it taxes even a coyote to live there."

"Should we join up with others to prevent an Indian attack?" Frank Trego looked worried.

"Ain't sheer numbers that sees you through, but how you go about moving across their country. The Comanche and Kiowa are getting a little tired of the white man moving in on them from every angle. Don't much blame them." Dawson pointed ahead amid the trailside clutter. Trego strained his eyes but could distinguish nothing of importance.

"What is it?"

"Up ahead, twenty yards off the trail. It's the sign I told you about." Dawson spurred his horse forward and Trego followed close behind. They drew up before a weathered headboard and Trego studied the faded words written there:

Here lies D.C. Oakes
killed for starting the Pikes Peak Hoax

A sober Trego turned in the saddle to look at Dawson. "Do you believe there's gold in those mountains?"

"More importantly, do you believe it?" Dawson countered. "I'm not the one prospecting." Dawson saw the stumped look on Trego's face and added, "Like they say, gold is where you find it." Trego didn't know how to respond to this either, instead the pair rode on down the trail through the thinning haze kicked up by the passing wagon train.

Five miles down the trail, they came upon the first of several dead mules, freshly cut from their harnesses.

"Damn fool, pilgrims," Dawson said tightly. Beside the dead mules were newly discarded baggage from wagons now too heavy to carry a full load. Frank Trego kept his thoughts to himself. He was learning: Men who made mistakes this far from civilization paid the price.

By noon they could make out the distant slit of green that

undulated across the flat country and marked the Blue River. Along the way, they passed an abandoned wagon with dead mules still hooked to its traces. There were wagon tracks where others had simply passed around the hapless vehicle and continued on their way.

"Bad piece of luck for somebody," Trego commented.

"If I were part of that train, I'd cut loose on my own rather than have somebody drive my animals 'til they died."

In two hours, Dawson led his small group deliberately to a point on the Blue River that was up stream from the emigrants by several hundred yards. They drew a lot of curious stares from silent men and sunbonneted women with babies in their arms. A dog charged out from beneath a wagon, barking loudly. A sharp command from its owner sent the dog back to the shade with tucked tail.

"That's a pretty sight," Frank Trego breathed as he looked down at the quiet waters of the Blue as it curved away from them through thickets of willow and cotton-woods. At this point, the Big Blue was some three hundred yards wide and lined with shelf rock that crumbled easily under the weight of a horse. Ten miles further down stream, the Little Blue joined with the Big Blue and grew to a width of a quarter mile in places.

"Around that yonder bend, you'll find a waterfall that drops ten feet from shelf rock into a blue hole. Water is cold and clear as ice. They call it Alcove Spring and somebody chiseled the name on a rock nearby," Dawson said.

"Sounds nice," Trego replied, "soon as we set up camp, I'll take a walk down that way."

"Be careful watering those mules," Dawson cautioned. "Let them drink a little then stake them out on that patch of spring grass so they can graze for awhile." Dawson led his own horse down to the river and both drank deeply of the cold waters. Frank Trego did the same. They moved back up to its bank and built a small fire to cook their first meal since early morning.

Luther Barnhart rode his horse down the crumbly bank to the water's edge, the animal slipping and sliding all the

44

way. Dawson and Trego stood watching the scene. When Barnhart tried to ride the animal back up the dangerous bank, the horse faltered and fell to his knees with Barnhart sawing back on the reins with all his might.

"Get down off that horse," Dawson shouted, his face an angry cloud. "You kill that horse, you'll walk the rest of the way. Won't have a man that's dumber than a mule riding him." Luther Barnhart's face filled with rage; yet he dismounted and led the poor animal the rest of the way up the tricky slope, glowering at Dawson all the while, but saying nothing as he passed by.

"How did you manage to hook up with him anyway?" Dawson asked Trego.

"Didn't. He fell in with Tom and Mike Rogers, and those boys will put up with most anybody."

Dawson shook his head, "The man is heading for trouble out here if he continues along the way he's going." Charles Pittman came over to the fire after the mules were taken care of and began slicing meat into a skillet. Of those on the trip, Pittman was the strangest to Dawson. The man was carrying around a lot of grief over something. But then, wasn't everybody, one way or another? Look at him, here he was, doing exactly what he swore he would never do again. And he had left behind his own grief in the form of Jenny Logan. He asked Trego about Pittman.

"Quiet man, hardly ever says much. But what I could piece together, Pittman left the ministry after being caught with one of the deacon's wives during a fellowship meeting. Word is, this deacon beat the wife so bad, she died. Wasn't long after the funeral, the deacon was shot to death and the preacher missing."

"And Malone?" Dawson asked. "He's got the saddest eyes of anybody."

"Danny lost his brother and father to a cave-in back in a Pennsylvania coal mine. The boy swore he would never go near another mine and drifted west to Missouri where he joined up with us."

Later, as they crowded around the fire, eating cold biscuits left from breakfast and the meat Charlie Pittman had fried, a lone horseman came riding over from the wagon train. He wore Plainsman garb and carried a long rifle across his saddle. There was so much hair about his face that only his eyes were visible beneath his floppy hat.

"Light and have some coffee, friend. 'Bout all we got left to offer," Frank Trego said. Jack Dawson studied the short man as he dismounted. Their eyes met.

"Shorty Stokes, might have known it was you," Dawson said. Stokes gave them a big smile, yet all they saw were the whiskers moving on his face.

"Jack Dawson. Thought you was lost up on the Green last year?"

"Who told you that?" Dawson asked. Shorty merely laughed and came over to the group and shook their hands.

"Figgered I might entice you fellars to join up with us, 'stead hanging back on your own. But if ol' Jack is doing the leadin' then I've wasted my time." He took the proffered cup Frank Trego was holding out to him.

"Never knew you to waste anything, Shorty," Dawson said, sipping his coffee. "Expect you was hoping to buy our mules, seeing how you're short a few."

Shorty Stokes's eyes twinkled under the shade of his hat. "Well, fact is, a few of them pilgrims did ask me to ride over and see what it would take to by one or two. Course on the other hand, if'n you was to join up with us, we could spread your goods among the wagons and make a sweet deal on them mules in the bargain."

"We ain't headin' to Oregon, Shorty," Dawson said.

"Well, shucks, you boys could tag along with us far as the South Platte and foller it on into Cherry Creek easy like."

"You sure hurting for mules, ain't you?" Dawson said.

"It's a fact we could shore use some extras. Gonna slow us down a mite if we don't come across some soon," Shorty acknowledged.

"How come you let those emigrants drive those poor animals into the ground like that this morning?"

Shorty Stokes shook his head sadly. "What I get fer

lettin' a dandy from Boston hold the reins while I scouted the Blue. By the time I got back and put a halt to their runnin' we had five mules too far gone to save." Shorty looked sad as he drank the coffee. "Guess you past'm back there on the trail."

"What you offering for the mules?" Luther Barnhart cut in. Shorty Stokes studied the man for a moment, his shrewd eyes taking in the Easterner. He glanced over at Dawson for guidance and got none.

"Well," Shorty said, clearing his throat, "depends on them mules. They broke fer pulling wagons?"

"No matter," Frank Trego snapped, "they aren't for sale . . . at any price." He gave Barnhart a cold stare.

"Hell, Frank, me and the others have had enough. We could waste a month getting to the gold fields only to have to turn around again and come home. Way I see it, cut your losses and head back to civilization with as much as we can save out of this deal."

"That's how the rest of you feel?" Trego asked the others by the fire. "You willing to throw in the towel, now that we're underway, Pittman? And you Malone?"

"Now Luther makes good sense, I'll warrant," Charles Pittman said slowly. "None of us ever figured on running into men headed the other way. Don't make a lot of sense to continue on if there's no gold to be had." Pittman dropped his eyes under Trego's burning stare.

Shorty Stokes watched the proceedings curiously. "Didn't mean to ride over here and stir things up for you," he said, not sure if the men heard him or not.

"You didn't start a thing that hadn't been brewing for two days," Dawson said, throwing the remainder of his coffee into the fire and stalking off toward the river.

"I was elected leader and I say we keep going," Trego said firmly. "We all know there'll be people ain't satisfied less they got it all and that's how I got these go-backs figured. They just weren't willing to work hard at making a claim pay." He looked at the others. "What about the rest of you?"

Tom Rogers spoke up, "I say we got to give it a go, since we come this far. Ain't that right, Danny?"

Danny Malone, the big raw-boned coal miner, worked his hands back and forth as if trying to grip some unseen object. "I vote to go on as long as things don't change and we don't run into more than we can handle."

"What do you mean by that?" Trego asked.

"You know, Indians and such."

Shorty Stokes laughed, "Maybe you should have stayed on the farm or wherever you came from 'cuz things is gonna get a lot worse the further you head west. Jack Dawson can testify to that."

Trego glared at the short man who dipped his head and fell silent. Mike and Tom Rogers nodded their heads in agreement with Malone.

Luther Barnhart glared at the men around the fire. "We're making a mistake, but I can see it's no use talking further." With that Barnhart stalked off down river.

"That's that then," Shorty Stokes said, turning to his horse and pulling himself into the saddle. "Good luck to you men . . . see you on the high lonesome," he called to Dawson who waved back at him.

Dawson came back to the fire and stood there watching Stokes ride away. He looked over the fire at Trego.

"What's it going to be?"

"We push on," Trego said firmly.

"Then let's get started. We still got four hours of daylight left."

"How we going from here?" Charles Pittman asked, wiping the grease from the skillet.

"Straight across the Big Blue. Two days out, we'll come to the Republican. We take that until it peters out in eastern Colorado. After that, it's straight across the Plains to Cherry Creek."

"That the shortest?" Trego asked.

"We can take the Oregon-California Trail. It's safe, but longer. Cuts two hundred miles across the Plains to Fort Kearney and another two hundred to O'Fallon's Bluffs as it

48

follows the Platte. From there it's roughly another two hundred miles to Cherry Creek. Then, there's the Smoky Hill, but that's to the south. It ain't much different than the Republican though. Our best bet is to stick with the Republican, but let me warn all of you, the trail from there to Cherry Creek is going to be like nothing you've ever experienced."

The men around the fire looked at one another as if having second thoughts about the decision to go on. Barnhart had eased back close to the group and was listening to what Dawson was saying.

"Just what do we have in store for us, Dawson?" Danny Malone asked worriedly.

"There's broken country, barren ridges cluttered with rocks that's a horse killer if you ain't careful. And if that ain't enough, we'll hit stretches of deep sand that can suck the strength of man or animal in a hundred yards. We'll be lucky if we make five miles a day through it. And you've never experienced dry country like this. Grass is thin and reedy, that's why I had you buy these mustang horses. American saddle horses won't last a week on such forage."

"You don't paint a pretty picture," Malone said, his face plainly worried as were the others.

"Just trying to prepare you for reality. This ain't going to be no picnic. Soon's the trees thin out, we pick up prickly pear, dwarf cactus and Spanish nettle to irritate and add to the general discomfort of man and beast."

"Others have done it, and so can we," Frank Trego spoke up.

"That's true. But both the Smoky Hill and the Republican are littered with the bones of those who didn't prepare themselves for the worst." Dawson retightened the cinch on his horse and climbed into the saddle and the others turned to their own animals, sobered by the prospects of what awaited them farther down the trail.

"I can't believe we're riding on after what he said!" Barnhart spat out.

Frank Trego looked pained. "Damn it, why don't you

just fall in with that wagon train pulling out if you've gone that soft on us. We all agreed on taking the shortest trail, but if you want to show up at the diggings weeks after us, just go ahead."

Barnhart looked ready to explode as he snatched the reins of his horse from a low limb and climbed aboard.

"Mark my words. Got a bad feeling grief is just waiting for us down the trail." With that, he jammed his heels into his horse and headed down the crumbly bank into the Big Blue. Trego and Dawson watched as the others followed.

"Fool's going to kill his horse or himself," Trego said.

"Hope it's him. Ain't the horse's fault," Dawson replied, moving forward. Trego fell in last with one of the pack mules and had no trouble coaxing the animal into the milk-blue waters.

As it turned out, grief was a lot closer than even Luther Barnhart had figured it to be. Frank Trego was the last out of the river and as his horse scrambled up the slippery bank, the pack mule lost his footing and yanked the horse backward. Rather than dallying the rope, Trego had tied it off to the saddle horn to free his hands during the crossing. Trego tried to kick free of the stirrups but the taut lead rope held him fast. Kicking wildly and squealing, his horse reared up and over with Frank Trego taking the full impact of the horse's weight as it rolled over backward. The air was crushed from his lungs before he could cry out; yet Jack Dawson was beside the flaying animals with his knife in a matter of seconds. He quickly cut the lead rope, freeing both horse and mule who regained their footing and scrambled up the bank where the others were sitting watching the scene below.

A low moan escaped from Trego's mouth as blood forced its way up into his throat. Dawson eased him over on his side so he could breathe better. The sharp rocks pressed into his caved-in ribs.

"Frank, can you hear me?" Dawson shouted in the man's ear. "How bad you hurt?" Trego opened his eyes to a world of excruciating pain.

"God, Jack. I feel awful," he said weakly. He tried to spit the bright blood that flooded his mouth, but all it did was dribble out, staining the rocks. Malone and Pittman scrambled down the loose rock beside Dawson.

"Help me get Frank up to level ground. Be careful, think his ribs are smashed. Might have punctured a lung." Between the three of them, they managed to carry Frank Trego up the steep slope, with the injured man crying out at every step.

"Sorry, Frank, but we gotta get you away from this river and onto solid ground so's we can have a better look at you," Dawson said. They eased Trego to the ground among the mixed prairie grass and yellow cone flowers.

"Told you this could happen. Now what we gonna do?" Luther Barnhart said.

Jack Dawson whirled around to face the unhappy man. "I hear one more word outa you, I'm gonna cut that damn tongue from your head," Dawson snarled, a savage looked etched across his face. Barnhart blanched under the raw fury that confronted him and he dropped his head and turned away.

Dawson knelt down by Trego. "Somebody fetch my canteen," Dawson urged. He studied the pale face on the ground. The man was barely breathing. A canteen was shoved into his hands and Dawson lifted Trego's head and trickled a little water into his mouth. Trego worked his jaws, but the water, now mixed with blood, ran back out of his mouth. He opened his eyes and looked up at Dawson.

"I'm done for, Jack," he whispered. "Feel like everything inside of me has busted loose."

"That was a mighty bad fall, Frank. You hold on. We going to get you to a doctor."

In spite of the pain, Trego found room for a small smile. "Hell, Jack, this ain't St. Joe. And I'll never last long enough to make it back."

"We ain't going back," Dawson said grimly. He stood up and looked around at the stone-faced men. "Couple of you men take an axe and get to chopping me a few cottonwood

51

poles. We got to make a travois for Frank. There's no way he can sit a horse now." Tom and Mike Rogers hurried off with the axe. "Charlie, you and Danny get some rope and several blankets and bring them over here. Barnhart, take the mules and stake them out on that grassy area over there." When Dawson turned back to Trego, the man managed a little humor although his eyes were dull with pain.

"Looks like Luther's got his wish, grief arrived early."

Chapter 6

Except to those weary emigrants just coming off the trail, Denver City wasn't much to look at. The bustling little mining settlement of three thousand was a mixture of old and new. A huddle of thrown together mud huts, log cabins and a few clapboard buildings which stood amid tent saloons and bawdy houses where liquor and gambling ran twenty-four hours a day. Stray dogs and pigs littered the rutted streets. Of the more imposing buildings in the newly incorporated city, Uncle Dick Wootton possessed the oldest. The Broadwell, the Vasquez and Clark and Gruber's mint were constructed a year later and represented the best Denver City had to offer. Yet the long, sloping two-storied log structure Wootton called the Western Saloon and Hotel on Ferry Street served as a meeting place for Denver's first elected officials and newspaper. It was in Wootton's loft that William Byers first set up his newspaper business, *Rocky Mountain News,* for a short period.

It was William Byers, as much as anybody, who helped turn the tide against the "go-backs" by writing scathing editorials. When it looked as though the gold rush would peter out, Byers hitched a fast team to a light wagon and drove a few well-fixed miners back East where they displayed gold dust for the world to see and know the truth: There was gold in the Rockies after all!

A few doors down from Wootton's place on the opposite

side of the street was the Cibola, one of the more lavish gambling halls in the territory.

The Cibola was lively as Colin Jackson rode up to the hitch rack and stepped down. Raucous laughter and a loud piano drifted out of the gambling hall and mixed with the crowded street traffic.

Jackson stepped into the Cibola and spotted James Reid at the bar who waved him over.

"Howdy, Colin," Reid said, shaking the gunman's hand. "You'll find A.C. at that back table along with a few of his lawyer friends." Then he smiled and winked at Jackson. "A.C. is skinning them at poker."

"Guess I'll join in and get my fair share as well. Give me a bottle and a glass." Reid reached under the bar and brought out his best whiskey and a clean glass. Without a backward glance, Colin Jackson moved off to join in the high-stakes game.

James Reid watched as the gunman drew up at the table and, after speaking, pulled up a chair and sat down. Reid shook his head. Never would he play with a man like Jackson. Not only was he highly skilled at cards, the man was like ice. You could never tell if Jackson was losing badly or on a wining streak by watching his face.

Reid was an old hand at reading men. And Colin Jackson was as dangerous as they came. An old Missouri riverboat pilot, Reid first built the one-story log and frame building in 1859, calling it Reid Hall. Later, with James Gordon, a young engineer, as a partner they changed the name to Cibola Hall. It now boasted a large stage where amateur plays were conducted at hugh profits to both Reid and Gordon. Cibola was also the place where the burlesque of a trial was staged by self-appointed Samuel Rooker, father of renegade John Rooker, the shotgunned slayer of one of Denver City's most colorful gentleman gamblers, Jack O'-Neil. Even though such powerful members of the community as William Byers and Mayor John C. Moore denounced the travesty, John Rooker stood acquitted of the murder just the same.

At the table with A.C. Ford was Mayor Moore, Alexander Hunt, Judge John Sherman and Judge Hiram P. Bennett when Colin settled himself into a chair. Ford and Jackson exchanged knowing glances.

"How's the night going for you, Colin?" Ford asked, offering the gunman a cigar. Jackson bit off the end and ran a wet tongue over its black length before inserting it into his mouth. Judge Sherman, sitting to Jackson's right, produced a match and lit the cigar.

"Much obliged, gentlemen," Jackson said. "I figure in such illustrious company, the night will be a lot more profitable than it has been already." Ford smiled and expertly shuffled the cards.

"Well, Colin, you'll find the law here more than willing to take your money, won't we, boys?" There was general laughter all around the table as Judge Bennett cut the cards and Ford dealt them. The majority of Denver City's judicial system sat at the table playing poker, except for Judge William Slaughter. Everyone looked at his cards. Alexander Hunt was the first to fold after second cards were dealt. Hunt, a tall, elderly yet energetic lawyer from Illinois, had the respect of his peers as well as the miners, having been called on to preside over the People's Court on more than one occasion. Slaughter now held that position. Hunt had made a fortune in the goldfields of California before losing it all in the national panic of 1857. And now, two years later, he had established himself as a respectable lawyer as well as a lumbering and real estate magnate.

Colin Jackson stayed in for the ride even though he held only a pair of sevens. The bluff didn't work and Judge Sherman raked in a sizeable pot.

"Just keep on playing hands like that Colin and we'll stay here all night," Sherman said, smiling broadly. Jackson's hooded eyes never reflected the humor his thin smile indicated.

Jackson caught the necessary cards to build a royal flush and suckered the two judges into raising twice more before they called.

"Dang and I thought we had him on the run," Mayor Moore said, tossing his cards into the discard pile. Jackson raked in the money which he estimated was several hundred dollars. The greenbacks Jackson left on the table while he slipped the gold coins into his coat pocket.

"Gentlemen, ante up," Jackson said as it fell his turn to deal the cards. Three hours later, the game broke up with Jackson still holding most of the winnings. Jackson followed Ford to the bar for a nightcap. It was nearing midnight, and the Cibola, like every other establishment of its kind in Denver City, was jammed pack with boisterous miners, green emigrants wanting to belong even though they had yet to pan the first Rocky Mountain gravel for gold, and an assortment of confidence men, gamblers and footpads. Ford and Jackson downed their drinks and the lawyer motioned for the gunman to follow as he led the way out of the saloon. On the street, the din was not quite so bad and Ford turned to Jackson.

"Let's go over to my office so we can talk in private." The gunman nodded and Ford led the way to his office three streets over on Fifth. Once inside, Ford poured them both a brandy from a bottle he kept in his desk. A.C. Ford looked keenly at the gunman as he settled in behind his desk.

"You probably made more tonight gambling than you did off the horses you and Black Hawk stole."

"I have no doubt," Colin Jackson replied, unsmiling. "Bradley's horses ain't the best I've ever seen."

"True, but they'll still bring good wages. You know how hard horses are to come by out here."

"Still, after everything's divided, my share ain't enough to keep up my gambling habit."

"Meaning?" Ford wanted to know.

Colin had taken a few of the gold coins from his pocket and was playing with them. He looked at Ford with wet black eyes.

"Meaning I'm through messing with horse rustling. Not enough money in it to make it worth my time anymore.

Besides, a man can be hung for horse stealing same as murder."

"I see," Ford said, leaning back in his chair, yet not really seeing at all what Jackson was driving at. They had a neat rustling ring going here with nobody to interfere with the operation. True, by the time some of the ring members received their share, it didn't seem like a lot in the beginning, but it added up fast after a while if a man was careful.

"Don't think you do, A.C."

"Spell it out then, Colin. Hell it's getting late and I promised to stop by Sarah Jane's tonight." Here he leered at Jackson who ignored the obvious. Sarah Jane Vailes was Ford's mistress which he kept, yet refused to live with. Colin Jackson found it an odd arrangement since Ford wasn't married, unless the attorney didn't want the respectable citizens of Denver to know he engaged in such shenanigans. Even that idea was crazy. Most everyone in town knew Ford's arrangement.

"Just this. I been thinking it would be a lot more profitable if we, that is me and you, decided to do a little claim-jumping now and then. The others don't have to know, except Black Hawk, I mean."

Ford's face clouded over. "I don't know about that, Colin. Jumping claims can bring down a lot of heat among the miners, much less the authorities."

Jackson found himself laughing at the last part of Ford's statement. "Hell, A.C., you and the others *are* the law."

"That's just it. Stealing horses is one thing. Not everybody's affected, but you go and have a rash of claim-jumping by professional gunmen and the miners will cry for somebody's blood."

"I know what you're saying, but hear me out. First we don't just jump any old claim. We take our time and pick one that's producing well and is sorta isolated from the others. We move in, kill the owners and start operating it ourselves. In a few days, we file on it legal-like and that's that." Jackson could see the wheels beginning to turn in

Ford's head and knew he liked the idea despite the obvious risks.

"We would want to make damn sure it was paying well before we made our move. Last thing we need is to have the heat directed at us over some two-bit claim."

"Absolutely, and with the others in the ring cut out, the profits should be substantial for you, me, and Black Hawk."

Ford nodded, yet his eyes showed a trace of concern. "The others find out what we're doing, there'll be hell to pay."

It was Colin Jackson's turn to smile as he patted the butt of his pistol. "That's why I'm here. Anybody goes snooping, we'll just take them out. And that means anybody, judge or no." He raised his glass of brandy in a salute and slowly Ford did the same. After they drank, Ford asked one more question.

"You think Black Hawk will go along with it?"

"He's like I am, tired of getting shot at by ranchers over a few raw-boned nags. He'll jump at the chance to make some real money."

"I'm telling you, Whit, we got to move these horses at first light. You shoulda slept 'stead of plowing furrows all night with your pod."

"It was Bennie that kept me up. You sent me looking for him don't forget," Whit Coleman said to Black Hawk.

"Yeah, and see what it got for Bennie, don't you? . . . an early grave. Swear women ain't nothing but trouble don't care how you slice it."

"Still don't see why we got to move these horses just yet. Ain't no way Bradley's gonna track us in here."

"Maybe not," Black Hawk responded firmly, "but we ain't about to take the chance and that's that, so git saddled up."

They started the horses, all forty head, back down the narrow valley by the time the sun touched the red rimrock. Whit Coleman was still grumbling to his partner, Cove

Stillman, who merely shrugged. As far as he was concerned, the whole deal kinda soured, starting with the unprovoked shooting of Bennie Carter.

"Way I see it, Whit, the sooner we get these horses outta here, the sooner we get our money."

"Another thing that's eating at me. How come we don't get an equal share?"

"How do you know we don't?" Cove asked. "Remember, it's more than just us, Colin, and Black Hawk in this deal."

"Yeah, but how many more?" Whit persisted.

"Don't nobody knows that, but Black Hawk and Colin."

"Right you are. So how easy would it be to just add a few more members to this secret vigilante committee and skim off a little more of our share? I can tell you, it would be easy as pie."

"Maybe so, but I ain't about to buck Colin Jackson just to ask him the number. Dead men don't need answers to questions."

Black Hawk came riding up, driving two stray horses. "What's got into you two. Keep your mind on business," Black Hawk snapped, riding on by to nose the first horse though the narrow opening. Cove Stillman spurred his horse to the other side of the herd just as a loud boom echoed across the narrow valley. He looked back to see Whit Coleman reel in his saddle and then slump over the neck of his horse. A black smudge against the deep blue sky marked the shooter in the high rocks. Cove immediately pulled his rifle as he heard Black Hawk cut loose somewhere up ahead with his rifle. Cove put the spurs to the big gray he was riding as another booming shot whipped a bullet past his head, sounding like a large bumblebee in flight. He didn't look up from the neck of his horse until he was safe in a nest of rocks. Cove dropped off his horse and flattened himself against the sharp rocks, his eyes scanning the rim-rock. A large puff of dark smoke lifted away from the rocks followed by the roar of the big gun a second later. A horse squealed in pain and Cove turned to see Whit Coleman being pitched head over heels as the wounded animal's front feet collapsed under him. Coleman landed in a heap, unmoving.

Cove sighted over the rocks and pumped four shots out as fast as he could. Across the valley, Black Hawk cut loose and he heard a man scream from the rocks above. Cove watched as a man stood up suddenly, swayed gently in the morning breeze and then plunged down the face of the rocks. A long silence fell over the valley, but Cove Stillman stayed put just in case there were others in the rocks. He saw Black Hawk leave the shelter of a small tree line and ride over to where the fallen man lay in a heap.

Cove stood up slowly and looked around. *Who the hell had been doing all that shooting?* He trotted over to Whit Coleman who lay on his back staring up at the cloudless sky with unseeing eyes. A gaping hole in the side of his neck told the tale. He heard Black Hawk riding up and he turned to meet the outlaw leader with excited eyes.

"First Bennie and now Whit," he said, his voice breaking.

"It was that damn Bradley fellow. Can't believe he'd track us in this far." Black Hawk looked down at the shaken outlaw and over at the still form of Whit Coleman. "Damn fine shooting, I'll give him that, not that he'll ever lift another rifle now."

"What we gonna do now, Black Hawk? The two of us can't keep this many horses together once we clear this valley."

Black Hawk nodded. "For once you're right, Cove. Best let them go back to grazing 'til I check with Colin. We got to find a couple more hands and that's a fact."

"Guess I'll bury Whit," Cove Stillman said, making his way back to where he had left his horse. It seemed death had come to this peaceful valley for supper and stayed over for breakfast.

Chapter 7

It was a long and jolting two day ride south for Frank Trego on the travois to Kaw River and Fort Riley. Most of the time he was blessedly unconscious even though Jack Dawson tried to be as careful of the rough trail as he could. Trego's body, now swollen and dark from accumulated blood, shook like a sack of jelly every time the travois struck a stone or dipped into a shallow swale. It was near sundown of the second day following the accident when Dawson pulled into the fort with the others tagging along behind like lost sheep.

"Where'll I find the doctor?" Dawson asked the sentry on duty.

"What you got there mister, sick Injun?" the young soldier asked.

Irritation flooded Dawson's tired mind and he snapped at the trooper in a cold voice meant to be obeyed, "Need the doctor, *now!*"

The sentry snapped to attention. "Straight across the parade grounds, third building on the left, sir."

Dawson moved on with the sentry calling after him, "You best go around. The colonel'll have your hide if you cross the grounds with that thing." Dawson rode on, ignoring the soldier.

The trooper looked exasperatedly at Barnhart and the others. "Wouldn't want to be in his boots when the colonel sees this," indicating the marks left by the travois.

Dawson crossed the skillet-flat parade grounds, leaving behind him two deep furrows where the travois dug into the smooth earth. He pulled up at the post hospital, stepped down, and walked back to where Trego lay like a large bull buffalo. His face was barely recognizable from the bloat.

"We're here, Frank," Dawson whispered in the injured man's ear. "I'll get the doctor." Frank Trego's eyes fluttered open and he turned his head and watched as Dawson climbed the two steps and pushed open the post hospital door. Trego closed his eyes again and continued his shallow breathing pattern. With a crushed chest, it was just too painful to breathe deep.

Dawson sat on the front stoop of the hospital and watched as night descended over Fort Riley. Troopers moved back and forth tending to their last minute duties, casting sideways glances at the man slumped on the porch steps. The others had taken the horses and mules over to the livery for a ration of oats and hay afterwards, stopping by the sutler's for post whiskey and tobacco.

It was pitch black before the door opened and a young trooper in a white smock spoke softly to Dawson. Dawson stood up and followed the soldier inside and was assaulted with the smells that went along with the attending of the sick. A balding man in his late fifties met Dawson and held out his hand. Dawson shook the soft hand and noticed the sadness in the man's eyes.

"I'm Dr. Murray Gart."

Dawson gave his name, then inquired, "How is Frank?"

"Are you a relative?" Gart asked.

"No, I'm guiding Frank and a few other men to the gold fields at Cherry Creek."

"I'm afraid I've got bad news, Mr. Dawson. Your friend is too far gone for me to offer much beyond painkillers and prayers. Jimmy said a horse rolled over him," Gart said, indicating the young orderly.

Dawson nodded, "You tell Frank?"

"Didn't need to. He already knew. I commend your

62

bringing this man all the way to Fort Riley like you did, but you could have saved him the trip. I'm sorry."

"Can I see him?"

"Oh, yes. As a matter of fact, he asked for you." Dawson followed the doctor down the hall and into a room pungent with a smell he couldn't place. Frank Trego lay on a bed, his bloated body covered to the neck with a white sheet. The only things that seemed alive about him were his eyes.

"How you feeling, Frank?" Dawson whispered after the doctor departed the room, knowing how stupid that must sound to a dying man. It was all he could think of at the moment.

"Pain's gone, Jack. That army doctor knows how to dose a man up. I feel almost good enough to get up off this bed, till I look down at myself." Dawson didn't know what to say. He had seen death many times, in various ways from shootings to drownings, but the worse death was the lingering kind. A man snuffed out in an instant didn't have time for last minute pain, instructions, or goodbyes. But a man with a mortal wound got to know pain as intimately as a woman. On the plus side of the ledger, a slow death gave a man time to think and plan for it, yet there was always the awkwardness that existed between those dying and those that went on living. Words never came easy to a man at such times, and Dawson was as ill at ease as any man could be.

Trego gave Dawson a smile, "Relax, Jack, ain't nothing you can do, I know that. Fact is, I knew it back there on the river and so did you, my friend."

"Had to try, Frank."

"Know you did. Luther would've waited for a day and when I didn't oblige him by dying, he would have left me to the wolves." Trego looked deep into Dawson's ice blue eyes. "Never known a man like you before, Jack Dawson. I'm mighty proud to have ridden with you." Trego stuck his hand out from beneath the sheet and Dawson gripped the swollen hand tenderly.

"If it's any consolation, you got the stuff it takes for a

man to make it out here in this country. You woulda done fine, Frank, of that I have no doubt."

"Thanks," Trego whispered, closing his eyes. "That means a lot to me coming from you."

"Frank, is there anything I can do? Anyone I can contact back East? They got a telegraph here or if you want you can write a letter. The stage'll take it back to Leavenworth when it comes through."

Trego shook his head. "Got nobody anymore. Been on my own since I was a shaver. Pa died with the fever when I was five and my ma died having me. Got nobody," Trego repeated. Trego roused himself long enough to say, "You take my share of the gear and anything else that's mine, Jack. Just don't give them others nothing belongs to me." Dawson promised the dying man that he would.

Dawson never left Trego's side for the rest of the night. Several times Doc Gart came by and checked his condition and quietly left. Dawson watched as a fever took hold and Trego's bloated face turned blood red. He piled blankets on the shivering man and watched him take his last breath as the sun broke over the flat horizon. Dawson covered the man's face and went out into the early morning chill just as a solider emerged from a building and began playing reveille. Not one of Trego's companions had bothered to come by and check on him, and Dawson felt a cold fury in the bottom of his stomach where they were concerned.

He thought again of the promise he had made to Trego and he hitched his gunbelt around so the butt of the big Colt was in easy reach and started for the livery. He may be forced to gut shoot the lot of them, but damned if they would ride away from here with anything of Frank's. And if they still had a mind to continue to the Rockies, they'd have to get there best way they could. Be damned if he was leading a bunch of sonsabitches like them one step further. He had quit the minute Frank Trego died.

As it turned out, Dawson found Barnhart and the others with the spirit gone out of them to continue West. They had spent their time talking with several wagons who lumbered in during the night off the Smoky Hill Trail and listened to the harrowing stories of starvation, thirst and, worst of all, the lack of gold.

"We're cutting our losses and catching the East bound stage this morning," Luther Barnhart said defiantly when Dawson found them going through their gear. "Done got our tickets." The Leavenworth and Pikes Peak Express coach, started by Majors and Russell in May of '59, ran from Cherry Creek to Leavenworth, Kansas and charged one hundred and twenty-five dollars one way.

"The army bought our mules and we sold most of our supplies to a wagon train headed east," Charles Pittman spoke up.

Dawson looked at the men with cold eyes; none had bothered to ask about Frank Trego. He went over to his horse and doled out a generous portion of oats from a burlap sack, the silent men watching his every move. When he was done, Dawson turned back to the mute men.

"Don't figure any of you care a whit, but Frank died a little while ago." His voice was as cold as stone. Danny Malone shifted his feet and looked down at the ground while the others merely stared at him.

"Couda told you Frank wasn't going to make it," Barnhart finally said. Dawson looked at the man with open contempt.

"You best leave Frank's gear and horse be," Dawson warned. "And the mules," he added as an afterthought.

"We all got good money tied up in them mules," Barnhart shouted, "ain't that right boys. Frank didn't buy'em with all his money." Luther Barnhart looked at the others. It was Pittman who saw the bleak look on Dawson's face. A look he had seen once before on a man about ready to kill after finding his wife with another man.

"Let the mules be, Luther. We got rid of most of our stuff and enough left over for stage fare," Pittman added quickly.

"Hell, Charlie, we gonna forget the mules *and* the money we advanced Dawson?" Barnhart's face was livid.

"That's just what we are going to do, Luther."

"I'm going to sell the mules and Frank's gear to pay for a coffin and burial. The rest I'm giving to the post commander to distribute to needy people passing through," Dawson said softly, although he didn't feel he had to tell them this. He didn't want Barnhart to get down the road and bad-mouth him to every piker he saw.

"As for the money paid me so far, I keep," Dawson said flatly. "Anybody got a problem with that can jerk iron, because I'm tired of dealing with your kind. You all make me sick to my stomach." The blood drained from Barnhart's face under the cold steady stare of Dawson's eyes. Dawson waited for a full minute and seeing no resistance, turned his back to the men. As he stalked off, he warned them for the last time.

"I find anything of Frank's missing, I'll hunt every man jack of you down and put a bullet in you."

"The nerve of that man!" Barnhart said after Dawson had disappeared from sight. "What gives him the right to Frank's stuff?"

"That big Colt he's wearing on his hip, Luther, case you ain't never noticed it before," Charlie Pittman said wearily. All he wanted to do now was clear out of this part of the country and away from Barnhart. He figured his best bet was to catch the first steamer headed south down the Mississippi, maybe to New Orleans. It was either there or a grave if he showed his face back home.

"He would never have dared to shoot us," Barnhart said with confidence, "especially here in front of the army."

"You don't know men like Jack Dawson, Barnhart," Charlie said, turning to pick up his belongings. "Another mouthy word from you and I'd expect we'd be burying you alongside Frank this morning." Luther Barnhart glanced sharply at Pittman and then at the others standing nearby. His jaw hung open and he looked once more in the direction Dawson had gone, his mouth suddenly dry.

* * *

It was noon before Dawson finalized the details concerning the use of Trego's money and gear. Colonel James Witte had been angry over the ruts in his parade ground, but this quickly passed as he listened to the details from one of his men and after talking further with Dawson about the use of the money.

Dawson led his horse and pack mule over to the post hospital and found Gart hard at work setting a soldier's broken leg from an early morning wagon accident.

Dawson extended his hand to the doctor, "Just wanted to thank you for what you done for Frank. His dying was made a lot easier because of you."

"Sorry I couldn't do more." Then Gart looked keenly at Dawson. "You must have been good friends."

Dawson shook his head. "Only known Frank a week but he was a good friend."

"Yes, Mr. Dawson, I can see you were." They shook hands and Gart followed Dawson back to the porch and watched him mount his horse.

"You know you could stay a few days. I got a spare room in the back you can use. You've not slept all night."

Dawson gave the doctor a sly grin, "Thanks, but it's all the same to you, I'll catch a few winks down the trail."

"Yeah, well, I know the place smells to high heaven. Good luck to you then . . . wherever you're headed."

Dawson backed the big buckskin away from the railing. "Well, I always like to finish what I set out to do. Think I'll go have a look-see at the goldfields for myself. A man never knows. . . ." With that he led the pack mule clear of the fort making sure he stayed off the parade grounds.

From the hospital porch, the post surgeon watched until Dawson disappeared from sight, whispering under his breath to himself, "A man can't have too many friends like that." With a sigh, Gart stepped back inside to check the condition of the solider with the broken femur.

Chapter 8

Henry Stiles was a man of immense confidence and daring despite his inexperience at crossing the broken country, pushing his single wagon deeper into the vast sea of waving grasslands. For ten days now they had proceeded along the Smoky Hill River, past the chalk hills that either reminded Mary Stiles of tall chimneys or distant castles. Their son Jonathan had picked up a few rock specimens showing the fossilized remains of small insects and tiny fish. Studying these rocks close he asked his mother a thousand questions about the tiny embedded fish and how they came to be where there was no ocean. The boy showed the natural curiosity and wonder of an eleven year old one minute and the wisdom and maturity of a man the next. He seemed quite grown-up when he rode out in front of the straining oxen to scout the trail next to his big shouldered father, his wavy hair flashing in the sun.

Mary Stiles smiled with the knowing pride of a parent that her son would one day amount to more than what her shortsighted husband intended. Her reverie was interrupted by a voice from the rear of the lurching wagon.

"Mother, I can't find it," Melissa Stiles wailed.

Mary Stiles turned her attentions from the plodding oxen and stuck her head into the wagon. "Take those blankets from that chest," she indicated to her daughter. "It's in there. But be careful with it. If it's broken, we'll have to settle for looking in a basin of water to comb our hair. Your

68

father would be upset as well if he couldn't use it for shaving."

"I *will* Mother," Melissa said, tossing aside the blankets and popping open the leather trunk. The mirror lay on top wrapped in a thin piece of cloth. Next to it was her father's straight razor and shaving brush. She unwrapped the mirror and let the trunk lid fall back into place. She cocked her head from side to side as she brushed out her long saffron-colored hair. At eighteen, Melissa's sunburned cheeks enhanced her natural beauty, her flawless skin, and wide-set dark green eyes. Already matured into a full woman's figure, Melissa had the body most men would kill to possess. Satisfied with her looks, she repacked the mirror and joined her mother on the hard spring seat.

"Did you wrap it up again carefully?" her mother asked.

"*Yesss,* Mother," Melissa said, rolling her eyes.

"It's just I doubt there's another one to be had at any price in Denver City . . . if we had the extra money."

"I still can't believe we left the wagon train," Melissa said, looking out across the distance to where the sky and land joined as one. "I *hate* this."

"Young lady, your father is doing the best he can. It wasn't his fault we lost the farm. Everyone had to give up something during the panic three years ago. We held on as long as we could."

"I don't see why we had to leave Ohio for this."

"It's a chance to start over, to build a new life in a land where we can grow with the times."

"You sound like pa."

"Melissa Stiles!" her mother said sharply and Melissa backed off just a bit.

"What if father doesn't find any gold? What are we going to do then? Take in washing and ironing until our fingers bleed from scrubbing other people's filthy clothes?"

"If we have to. And you, young lady, had best watch that sassy tongue around your father. He's only doing this for us."

Melissa Stiles laughed out loud to the spring wind that

69

moved the long grass around like a giant unseen hand. On the distant horizon, a few clouds billowed up from the ground like giant forest fires of white smoke, except there were no trees to burn.

"Father is doing this because *he* wants to and you know it. Mr. Scatherson offered him a good job in his foundry."

"What did I tell you about that tongue of yours," Mary Stiles warned.

Melissa fell silent. It was always the same. Her mother would never tolerate a single harsh word against her husband, even when the truth was being spoken. Even though she had asked, Melissa knew perfectly well why they had left the wagon train. She had only wanted her mother to confirm it in her own mind. Her father's incessant questioning of the train captain's ability to guide and the final eruption of hot words, drove him to seek his own way across the wilderness. Never mind the fact that the train captain had crossed the Plains many times in the past. Never would she blindly follow a husband like some thistle in the wind. She would be the one to set the rules, Melissa promised herself.

Henry Stiles rode back to the swaying wagon on a big dapple gray and swung in along side. He immediately caught the strained looks between mother and daughter and he squelched the idea of asking them how they were enjoying this beautiful spring day.

"See that line of trees up ahead, oh, maybe three miles out?"

Mary Stiles pulled her sunbonnet lower over her eyes and looked in the direction her husband was pointing. She nodded her head.

"That's where the river forks. One branches to the northwest and the other fork runs almost straight south. We'll spend the night there and decide in the morning which fork we should take, although the north fork looks to have the most water."

"Whatever you say, Henry," Mary Stiles said. Henry Stiles moved away from the plodding wagon to rejoin his young son and Melissa mimicked her mother with a sarcastic tone in her voice.

"Whatever you say, Hennnry," she drawled out.

"Child, whatever is the matter with you?" her mother snapped. "Don't let me catch you doing that again!" Melissa pouted. "Why can't you be more like Jonathan, so grown-up and willing to do whatever is necessary to make our lives better."

"I didn't want to leave all my friends I'll never see again," Melissa blurted out. Mary put a comforting arm around her daughter's shoulder.

"I know, I know, Melissa. We all left dear friends back there," Mary said wistfully.

Melissa turned to her mother with tear-stained eyes. "Will things ever be the same again, Mother?"

Mary put on her best smile even though she felt like crying along with her daughter. "Things will be even better than you ever dreamed, Melissa. With the gold your father will mine, we will be able to afford things your father would never have been able to buy working in the foundry." They watched as Henry stopped to confer with his son and then ride on toward the river, still a mile ahead.

"When will we reach Denver city, mother?"

"Hard to say, child. Another two weeks I suppose." The wagon lurched over a protruding stone, jarring them hard.

"Guess we should walk awhile and give these poor animals some relief," Mary Stiles said, shifting her bottom on the hard plank.

"Look, Mother!" Melissa pointed toward the river. Mary looked up to see her son riding like the wind, his long hair flashing in the sun.

"Your father will take a hickory switch to him for riding—" Mary's voice faltered and she rose up out of her seat as her son drew nearer. There was pure terror in his eyes as he continued to flog the old draft animal he was riding.

"What is it, Jonathan?" Mary screamed at her son.

"Oh God, Mother, look!" Melissa pointed beyond Jonathan. Together they watched in horror as Henry Stiles, with

71

blood streaming down his face, slapped at his horse with knotted reins. What made their blood run cold was the two dozen brightly painted Indians pursuring Henry Stiles, their lances glittering like molten steel in the bright sunlight.

"Get the rifle, child! Hurry!" Mary said, pulling back on the reins to stop the wagon. They could hear the charging thunder of hoofs across the dry prairie. Melissa scrambled into the back of the wagon just as Jonathan drew up in a cloud of dust and jumped off the blowing horse.

"Get inside, Mother. Father and I will hold them off." Mary hesitated. "Do like Father says and pass me the rifle. Hurry, Mother, they're gaining on Father," the boy said, looking back at Henry Stiles who was riding for dear life now. The yelling Indians' cries floated to them on the suddenly still air.

"Be so careful, Jonathan," his mother said, taking the rifle from Melissa and passing it to her son. "Remember, I love you so much."

"I know, Mother. Now get inside and close the drawstring as tight as you can get it." Jonathan squatted down in the hip-high grass and took careful aim at the nearest Indian. When he had the big rifle centered on the Indian's chest, Jonathan squeezed the trigger like his father had taught him back when they hunted rabbits on the farm. Jonathan could not see the big Indian lift up from the neck of his horse and tumble to the ground through the haze of yellow smoke from his rifle. Seeing one of their number shot from his horse only sent the remaining Indians into a frenzy. Their cries for blood rose loud enough to cover the sound of Henry Stiles's approach.

"Father, are you all right?" Jonathan asked as Henry Stiles skidded to a halt beside the wagon.

"I'm okay, boy, now scoot 'neath the wagon and cover the tail gate with your rifle. We're surely in for it now," Henry said desperately. He dropped the reins of his horse and dove under the wagon just as the Indians descended on them with a thunder. With reins flapping loose, Henry's horse shied away from the milling Indians, his nostrils flaring wide. An Indian with a face painted red grabbed for the reins and missed. Henry sent a bullet through the man's stomach. The Indian howled and retreated from the scene, holding onto his horse for support.

Suddenly the air was filled with flying arrows and both oxen were killed immediately. Henry wiped the blood spilling into his eyes and sighted down the barrel of his rifle as the Indians circled the wagon, yet growing closer with each passing turn. He fired at the circling mass and saw an Indian tumbled beneath the horses.

"Henry!" Mary Stiles screamed.

"For God's sakes, Mary, keep quiet," Henry said, jacking another shell into the Henry. God was he glad he had taken the forty dollars to buy the new fifteen shot .44. He heard his son fire again with the old single shot and an Indian screamed out. He fired off six more rounds, three of them finding their mark before an arrow slammed him in the thigh. He stifled a cry, knowing it would only cause his wife to worry further and hadn't the time to deal with that.

A large Indian with trailing feathers down his back rode back and forth in front of the wagon urging his warriors on. Henry sighted his rifle on this Indian, but in the hazy dust kicked up by the pounding hoofs of circling horses, he was unable to draw a clear bead. Finally, Henry turned to another target as an arrow glanced off the side of a spoke and buried itself in his neck. This time Henry Stiles could not stop the strangling cry that tore from his lips. He dropped the rifle and grasped the embedded arrow. Blood gushed over his hands. Henry turned toward his son and found him staring at him, white faced. He tried to speak, but the words froze on his lips. Suddenly the bright sun was no longer quite as brilliant and the taunting shouts from the Indians seemed muted and far away.

Jonathan cried out his name, but Henry Stiles was beyond caring. His father flopped over in the spring prairie grass and lay still.

Jonathan grabbed up the warm Henry rifle just as something slammed him hard at the base of his skull. He toppled over next to his father without a whimper. Suddenly the Indians fell silent and as the dust settled around the little wagon, a sobbing wail rose up from behind the white canvass.

Tall Feather motioned his men forward and two braves jumped to the seat of the wagon and ripped open the cloth with their knives. Another brave dismounted and picked up the rifle that shone like the sun and handed it to Tall Feather who examined the weapon. He had never seen such a gun and he turned it over and over in his hands. No gun he had ever known could shoot so many times. A smile played across his grotesque features and he held the shining rifle aloft so all his men could see it.

"Hii-eee!" Tall Feather shouted. The others joined in, lifting their bows and flashing lances upward into the blue sky, their prancing horses stirring up clouds of yellow dust amid the laughter and shouting.

A pistol shot halted their cries and Tall Feather looked toward the wagon where Lame Deer was clutching his side. Blood dribbled between his fingers as the stillness deepened around the wagon.

Instantly, the squat warrior beside Lame Deer leaped into the bed of the wagon and wrestled the smoking revolver away from the wide-eyed woman and pulled her to the front of the wagon.

"Please, please. We mean you no harm. Why are you doing—"Mary Stiles screamed pitifully when she saw the bodies of her husband and son. Without further regard for her safety, she tore free from the short Indian and leaped to the ground beside the bodies. Lame Deer and two others began looting the wagon.

She stroked her son's beautiful hair that now lay carelessly about his face.

"Oh, Jonathan," she sobbed. "Oh God, what have we done!" She crumpled to the ground wailing loudly. She looked over at Henry Stiles in death, the blood from the neck wound covered his chest and pooled beside him on the dusty ground. Mary couldn't bring herself to touch him.

Meanwhile the looting of the wagon continued with the stoic Tall Feather watching the grieving woman with feigned interest. Several men near him made a few obscene gestures, laughing, but Tall Feather remained aloof and silent.

Suddenly a new scream rent the air, higher pitched and desperate. Lame Deer, now forgetting about the bullet burn on his side, had moved the large trunk and pulled the crouching Melissa Stiles from behind it.

"Melissa!" Mary Stiles screamed and jumped up, rushing to her daughter's defense. Lame Deer flung the young woman to the ground, laughing as Melissa tumbled hard on her shoulder, her petticoats flying up to reveal shapely legs.

Mary Stiles hovered over her daughter, pulling down her dress, while helping her to her feet.

"Oh, Mother, what will they do to us?" Melissa's eyes were like a frightened deer cornered by a cougar.

"Hush, hush, child," Mary said, as they held one another in their arms. "We must be brave . . . show them no fear." When Melissa saw the bodies of her father and young brother, her legs buckled and would have fallen except for her mother.

"I know, child. It's awful, but we must bear the pain. Father would want that," Mary whispered. Lame Deer had been going through the trunk and he now held up the mirror and blinked as it caught the sun and flashed in his eyes. He said something to the tall Indian on horseback and held the mirror out for Tall Feather to see. Lame Deer could not understand why the sun did not flash as before and he looked back into the mirror at his reflection. This time the angle was different and there was no bright flashing of light. Tall Feather rode over and took the mirror from Lame Deer. The two women hugged one another and watched as the big Indian looked into the mirror. He glanced down at the women and nudged his horse over and held it out to the one with the hair like ripe corn.

"Go on, child, take it. We don't want to make him mad," Mary said.

Melissa glanced up at the big Indian and their eyes met; his were like the dark liquid pools of a wild animal and Melissa looked quickly away. Tall Feather shoved the mirror toward her. With a tentative hand, Melissa reached out and took it from the Indian. Several other Indians broke into grins and talked among themselves while gesturing at the women. The exchange only heightened their anxiety even more.

The women watched as more Indians jumped into the wagon and began throwing their possessions over the side as if they were searching for something specific. All the things that, just minutes before, Mary Stiles had cherished and considered too important to leave behind were ripped opened and thrown into the dust at her feet. Howls rose up from the wagon when it seemed it had been emptied without finding whatever they had been looking for.

"Give me the shells for the rifle," Tall Feather said to Lame Deer who held a box of metallic .44 cartridges for the Henry in his hand and bottle containing a blue liquid in the other. Lame Deer pitched the box to Tall Feather, uncorked the bottle and took a long drink.

"That Indian is drinking father's shaving lotion," Melissa said, amazed.

Lame Deer took the bottle from his lips and spit over the side of the wagon, gagging. Several others laughed and the squat Indian, who had dragged Mary Stiles from the wagon, snatched the bottle from Lame Deer and sniffed the opening. His face showed his displeasure and he smashed the bottle against the side of the wagon. Lame Deer looked sick as he jumped down from the wagon and bent over Henry Stiles who stared upward with unseeing eyes.

Mary and Melissa Stiles watched in horror as Lame Deer swiftly scalped the dead man. Mary stifled the impulse to cry out over such mutilation, instead she forced her daughter to look away from the gruesome sight, knowing that her son was next. She tried to steel herself against the thought of Jonathan being subjected to such treatment, taking comfort

76

in the fact he was beyond any pain the Indians could inflict on him now.

The big Indian said something to them and Mary looked up through her tears as he held out his hand to her daughter, making the motion for her to mount behind him.

When Melissa realized what was being asked of her, she clung even tighter to her mother. Mary Stiles forced her daughter to look at her.

"Listen, child," she whispered, "if we are to survive until somebody rescues us, we must do as they ask. He only wants you to ride with him. Please do as he says," Mary whispered gently to her daughter. Melissa looked one last desperate time at her mother and took the big Indian's hand.

Tall Feather lifted the girl effortlessly to the back of his horse. He gestured for her to hold him. Melissa still clutched the mirror in one hand.

Henry Stiles's horse was brought around and Mary mounted the animal while Lame Deer held the reins. He looked at her with eyes that seemed without emotion. Mary looked at the three-inch burn on his side now clotted over.

"I'm sorry about—" she faltered and looked away when she realized that her husband's bloody hair hung from his belt. Somebody fired the wagon and it was burning furiously, dense gray-black smoke curled upward into the prairie sky.

Tall Feather gave the signal and the others gave a series of shouts. With their dead across their horses, the Indians thundered away from the wagon following the south fork of the Smoky Hill River. Mary managed to take one last look back at the burning wagon and the prone figures of her loved ones. Turning to face front again with tears streaming down her face, there was a hardness about her now, a resoluteness in her eyes that revealed a determination to survive no matter the odds.

Chapter 9

Now that he was free of Barnhart and the others, Jack Dawson had chosen an even more direct route to Denver City than the Republican River Trail. Cutting directly across the undulating prairie until he picked up the Smoky Hill River three days out of Fort Riley, Dawson had saved himself another three days by not sticking to the longer route the emigrants had to follow because of their lack of trail knowledge and their need for less rugged travel.

Now six days on the trail, Dawson had made camp at Russell Springs, fifteen miles west of the chalk bluffs that so fascinated Jonathan Stiles.

By early next morning, Dawson was up and moving. It was one of those spring mornings that made a person glad to be alive. Bright pink flowers lay in swaths across the Plains, soaking up the remnants of moisture from the crisp morning air. Dawson knew a rancher near Wichita who called these little ground-hugging flowers, cowboy's delight. After a bleak snowy winter here on the Plains, Dawson saw how the little flowers could have gotten their name.

It took Dawson a few minutes to separate the dark smudge on the western sky from the other low clouds forming in the distance. Something was definitely on fire. Dawson pointed the big buckskin in that direction while checking the loads in his Colt and rifle. Dawson approached the thin trail of smoke by keeping a small drainage between himself and the open country. When it looked like he was directly opposite the smoke, Dawson tied his horse and pack mule to a low scrub pine that had somehow found its way from the higher reaches to the west as a seed and lodged in the folded hillside where it had grown into a stunted tree.

Taking his rifle, Dawson climbed the small rise and peered down at the smoldering ruins of a wagon, some two hundred yards out. His practiced eyes caught the tawny movement of an animal and Dawson separated the coyote from the surrounding countryside. There was no other signs of life, yet Dawson waited another half hour to be sure. Another coyote soon appeared over a low rise to the west, slinking along with his nose pointed toward the wagon. Whatever was down there was dead, Dawson concluded and he stood up.

The approaching coyote froze instantly in his tracks, sniffing the gentle breeze. With keen eyesight, the wary animal stared at Dawson, but the gnawing hunger was greater than his fear of the man and he loped toward the charred wagon, keeping his ears alert for sudden danger from Dawson's direction.

Dawson dropped back down the rough slope and stepped into the saddle. He left the crease of land at a lope. At the sound of approaching hoofs, the two coyotes pulled back for a hundred yards and circled with their noses into the wind, licking their mouths.

Jack reined up and sat there for a few minutes surveying the grim scene, heavily laced with the stench of death. There was nothing left of the wagon but a few pieces of charred floorboards and half-burned wheels. The two dead oxen lay with their entrails trailing out across the ground where the coyotes had been feeding. It was only when he walked his horse around to the other side of the smoldering remains that he saw the blackened and bloated bodies.

Dawson had already taken notice of the numerous unshod tracks and knew instantly what had happened. What he couldn't figure is why anybody, even a green emigrant, would strike out across the prairie all alone. He stepped down from his horse and came over to where the bodies were half-covered by the burned wagon bottom.

"Damn!" Dawson muttered as he realized one of the bodies was that of a young boy. Both had been scalped. Dawson looked around at the scattered items, some had been partially burned as the fire spread outward from the wagon. There were the usual things most pilgrims felt were necessary: a washstand, heavy silverware, chest of drawers, and a sewing machine. The heavy trunk had escaped the fire and Dawson poked through the contents that lay scattered around it. Suddenly, he realized he was looking at women's clothing, blouses and undergarments. What bothered him more was the fact that it looked like the clothing was of two sizes, indicating a younger woman, possibly a daughter.

Dawson stood up and looked out across the broad expanse, knowing what the women faced as captives. He walked back over to the dead man and freed the arrow in his neck. Dawson studied the blue and red stripes painted the length of the turkey-feathered shaft. There could be no doubt, the Indians that attacked the lone wagon had been Cheyenne. Their trail headed toward the South Fork of the Smoky Hill River. They would not go far to rid themselves of their dead, if the man by the wagon had given account of himself. From the looks of things, the attack had occurred yesterday. He estimated mid-morning by the sand that had fallen back into the tracks of the horses and the small trails of insects that stood out plain in the deep grooves.

Dawson spent two hours digging two graves in the thickly matted sod using a half-burned spade he had uncovered in the rubble. By the time he had finished, Dawson was sweating heavily under the noon sun. He smelled of putrefying flesh, and the odor burned his nostrils and stung his eyes.

Dawson mounted his horse and followed the Indian's trail down to the river. He saw where they had spent several nights among the thick brush by the river, waiting for that right moment when some dumb emigrant would come along. Dawson shook his head at the folly of some men as he stripped off his shirt and washed himself in the cold river to rid himself of the stink of death. Across the river an eagle screamed at Dawson from the thick tree line, rose loftily on the heated currents of air and disappeared to the north.

Once he was relatively free of the odor, Dawson built a small fire and made coffee while he sliced a few pieces of bacon into a skillet. The labor of burying the two bodies had left him weak and hungry, despite the grisly situation forced on him.

As he ate the bacon, Dawson studied the tracks left by the departing Indians. It was clear to him they expected no pursuit. Another green emigrant coming down the trail wasn't about to go running off to chase wild Indians. They would merely acknowledge what had happened to some poor unfortunate souls and hurry on, thankful that it hadn't happened to them.

So what was he thinking? Dawson poured himself more coffee and thought about it some more. It was none of his affair. Fool man should never have wandered off alone. Now he had gotten himself killed along with his son and his womenfolk taken captive to face a fate worse than death. Dawson poured the remainder of his coffee on the fire, shoved his skillet and pot back into place aboard the mule and stepped into the saddle. He was heading to Denver City, he decided, and nothing was going to deter him from his goal.

He left the screen of bushes and took the South Fork, which a hundred yards below, where the North and South Fork split, looked more like a gully where only a narrow trickle of water flowed, no more than a yard wide. Dawson had heard of those emigrants who had insisted on taking the North Fork of Smoky Hill thinking it was the main river. Yet he knew the river only snaked upward and finally petered out, leaving the emigrant to face a wide stretch of broken dry country where water was scarce and mostly alkaline when found. He also couldn't help but notice that the Cheyenne had stayed with the South Fork and Dawson began to wonder just where they may be headed.

Fifteen miles out, the Cheyenne's trail crossed the deep

slash of gullied ground that was the South Fork of the Smoky Hill River and headed out across broken country covered with thin grass, sage, and prickly pear. Where the land folded over, trapping what little moisture was in this country, dark green Rocky Mountain juniper took root, displaying their white berry-like cones of fruit, a favorite of birds and ground squirrels.

Dawson sat his horse and studied the hoofprints left by the Cheyenne. There were at least a dozen, possibly more, too many for one man to consider. The heated breeze brought the smell of the pungent juniper to him. It was a pleasant odor and welcome after the gruesome task he had been through with the dead emigrants.

A tiny speck jumped into his line of vision and Dawson studied the slow moving object for a time. At first he thought it was some wild animal on an afternoon prowl for food in a land scarce of shelter or sustenance. Then, he saw it stumble and fall as if hurt. Only one thing he knew fell like that. A man.

Without thinking, Dawson kicked the buckskin in the ribs and down the rutted embankment of the South Fork. He splashed across the thin layer of muddy water and topped out on the other bank. He searched the area ahead where the man should be, but nothing moved in the distance. Had he fallen and couldn't get up?

Dawson knew he had to be careful as he rode north over the tracks left by the Cheyennes. A man could be ambushed out here and no one would ever be the wiser to his disappearance. Just in case it was a trap laid to snare him, Dawson unlimbered the rifle and cut a wide circle where he had last seen the man . . . at least what he thought to be a man.

Doubling back down a narrow rocky draw choked with prickly pear and a few scattered juniper brought him adjacent to the area he was sure the man was at. When he cleared the draw and studied the horizon, he was surprised to find a man sitting on a rock some thirty yards out. Bareheaded with a crown the color of autumn alders, the man appeared to be in his sixties with a huge gray mustache.

His clothes were weathered to the color of surrounding rock and over his linsey-woolsey shirt he wore a pair of faded red suspenders. The man appeared to be in a daze and apparently had not seen Dawson.

Jack Dawson started forward and the mule cut loose braying at the sight of the object on the ground and pulled back on the lead rope. Dawson cursed under his breath for having to take his eyes from the man to deal with the frightened mule. When he had the mule under control and calmed down, Dawson turned back to find the man standing there with a big rifle aimed at him.

"Take it easy with that cannon, old man," Dawson warned. "I mean you no harm." The man continued to stand there for a few minutes in silence, the rifle never wavering. Suddenly he lowered the weapon and waved Dawson over.

"Reckon if you had been up to no good, you would'na been messing with that mule thataway," he said, as Dawson rode up.

"What happened to you?" Dawson asked. The man smiled ruefully and shook his head.

"Near got my hair lifted by a bunch of proddy Cheyenne this morning, leastwise what I got left 'round my ears. Been walking for the last four hours to the only source of water hereabouts and that's the South Fork." Dawson relaxed in his saddle, thankful at least that the man was no tenderfoot to this country. He had had enough dealings with emigrants, farmers and the like to last him a lifetime. Dawson tossed him a canteen and the man uncorked it and took a long swallow and handed it back to Dawson. At least he had the common sense not to drink too much the first few minutes. Dawson stepped down and extended his hand.

"Jack Dawson."

"Josiah Catt," the man said, "that's two tees," he said, his gray eyes twinkling in spite of his predicament.

"What happened?"

"Not much to tell," Catt said rather ashamedly. "Dang Redskins caught me early this morning fresh out of my blankets. Barely had time to grab my Sharps and headed to some rocks. Figger I'd been done for 'cept I kinda kept them at long range after I killed two of them. Kept me pinned down there for better'n three hours while they helped themselves to my camp, eating my grub and drinking my coffee while I was wedged in them rocks like a pocket gopher."

"You're a mighty lucky man," Dawson said, wanting to ask the question that was burning a hole in his mind, but waiting for Catt to mention it. As if reading his thoughts, Catt's face sobered.

"They got two white women with them." His voice was soft, yet seemed as hard as steel when he said it. Dawson shook his head.

"Damn! I was hoping I was wrong about that. Came across this pilgrim's wagon near the forks of Smoky Hill. Buried a man and a boy."

"Must be part of'em," Catt said. "The younger woman had hair as yeller as placer gold and purty too."

"How were they holding up?"

"Hard to say, but the mama, if that's who she is, seemed to be in control. There is one bit of bad news though. Tall Feather is leading that bunch and he's claimed the young'un fer himself."

"Tall Feather!" Dawson exclaimed.

"Know him, do you?"

"Been to his main village one summer when he was camped five miles from the Platte up Lodgepole Creek. We didn't part the best of friends after Tall Feather decided he wanted not only my horse but my pelts as well."

Josiah Catt's eyes narrowed. "Dawson," he said slowly, "I heered tell of you. Didn't you usta run with Fitzpatrick and them other trappers twenty years er more ago?"

"I know a few trappers, Tom Fitzpatrick being one of them. Fact is, Tom and I guided wagon trains to Oregon country for near ten years."

"How come you ain't doing the same fer all them green miners chomping at the bit to head out to the diggings?"

It was Dawson's turn to be a little shamefaced. "Fact is,

I was doing that very thing when we had an accident and one of their men died. Sullied them on taking another step West. I left them to catch the Eastern stage back to Missouri at Fort Riley."

"That's fine. More of 'em was do to that, this country may not be too bad a place to stay."

"Hungry?"

"I'd be obliged fer a bit of grub if you can spare it," the old man said.

"Stocked up with plenty before I left the fort. Got some cold bread and meat left over from the noon meal if that'll suit you?"

"Be jest fine." Dawson watched the old man eat, his thoughts straying to the women and wondering if he was really going to do what he was thinking.

"Know what you thinking," Josiah Catt said, between mouthfuls. "But without a few extree men, we ain't likely to do much fer them women."

"How did you know I was thinking that?"

"Because it's something been eating at me ever since I caught sight of 'em."

Jack Dawson rubbed his jaw thoughtfully, "Only settlement of any kind I know of is Potter's on the South Fork of the Republican, but that's near forty, fifty mile from here."

"That's right and guess who's a-headed thataway?" Catt said, wiping a few crumbs from his bushy mustache.

"Tall Feather!"

Chapter 10

The rawhide bonds cut into Melissa Stiles's wrists but she hardly noticed the pain, her senses dulled by the nightmare of the last twenty-four hours. Once the Indians had disposed of their dead, the big Indian had given Melissa her own horse to ride, although he still held to the reins.

Melissa wet her cracked lips, tasting the salt that was her blood. Only at the river were she and her mother allowed their first drink. The water, thick and laced heavily with silt, gagged Melissa. She drank only a small amount, hoping there would be better water later on. That had been an error in judgement she would not repeat again. When they stopped at a small pool of stagnant water, she steeled herself against the need to retch. Melissa looked back now at her mother who seemed to be holding up under the circumstances. Mary Stiles returned her discreet smile and Melissa knew as long as they were together, they could survive whatever the Indians had planned for them.

The big Indian, who was obviously the leader, had kept them apart during the night as well as during the long, dusty ride. Several Indians had come by during the night, making obscene gestures at Melissa and rubbing their hands over her breasts and body. Once, the big Indian caught them doing this and he gave them hell in his own tongue. After that, Melissa was left alone. Later, when the big Indian came to her and spread his blanket for Melissa to lay on, she was afraid of what he might do and refused his offer. He simply stretched out and fell asleep while she sat on her haunches, dozing through the cold night. Melissa had been stiff and tired when they broke camp the next morning. She prayed her mother had not suffered at the hands of the other Indians during the night.

Suddenly, Melissa realized they had stopped and she looked at the big Indian who motioned for her to dismount. With aching limbs and eyes that felt like they were full of sand, Melissa slid off the spotted pony and leaned against the animal, too tired to even think anymore. Unexpectedly, she realized her bladder was painfully full and demanded immediate attention. How could she make them realize she needed privacy to void herself? She looked at the big Indian who had lifted a rawhide bundle from the back of his horse and brought out something that resembled thin flat cakes of berries and bits of meat. He offered her one and Melissa accepted, motioning for him to free her while she pointed at her belly, trying to make him understand her need. He only shook his head and began eating.

Melissa took a small bit of the dried cake in her mouth. It was a few minutes before she could mix enough saliva with it to discern the taste. When she had, Melissa found the cake delicious. She marveled at how something that looked so awful could taste so good. She quickly consumed the small cake and held out her bound hands for more. The tall Indian looked at her and gave her two more, saying something she couldn't understand. When she thought he wasn't looking, Melissa slipped one of the cakes down the front of her dress where it lodged in her corset stays.

The other Indians were eating as well, yet nothing had been offered to Mary Stiles. She simply stood by while they ate, trying to ignore them.

Melissa pointed to her mother and back to the sack that her Indian benefactor was holding. He hesitated and looked from the girl to the woman who was being held several yards away. Again he said something to her and shook his head, retying the bundle behind his horse again. The message was plain enough, Mary Stiles would get nothing to eat from the tall Indian. Was he letting Melissa know the other woman was not his responsibility, only her? And then the impact of what she was thinking hit Melissa full force, causing her heart to squeeze tight in her chest. She was to be his woman . . . his squaw. Her mother was not his concern.

Melissa looked quickly at her mother who tried to reassure her things would be okay. What were they to do? Melissa could not bring herself to think of lying down with this smelly Indian. That was something she had been saving for her husband. She felt desperate, yet the insistent pain in her bladder forced her mind back on her immediate problem. Melissa looked around for a place that would offer a little privacy. When she realized the Indians were mounting up again, Melissa simply lowered herself to the ground and emptied her bladder in the sand, her face reddened by the bold act. The Indians paid her no mind and she quickly remounted the pony keeping her eyes averted from the wet spot. She wondered when the Indians ever relieved themselves. None seemed to pause long enough for such things.

They rode across the broken, arid country for the rest of the day without pausing. It was as if the Indians were suddenly in a hurry, yet Melissa could see nothing that indicated a change in the sameness of the terrain. It was as if this world of waving grass and broken ridges had swallowed them up. The vastness created an isolation within Melissa she had never known before.

Near sundown, the leader called a halt at a small trickle of water that was clear and cold. Melissa had never tasted anything so good in her life and she drank deeply, splashing water on her sunburned skin.

"Not too much at one time, child," Mary Stiles said gently. Startled, Melissa found her mother kneeling beside her in the fading light.

"Oh, Mother!" Melissa cried, and the two women hugged one another awkwardly with their bound hands.

"Don't cry, Melissa. You mustn't show them weakness.

They will not understand." Melissa reduced her crying to a sniffle.

"Here, Mother," Melissa said, retrieving the dried cake from her bosom and shoving it into her mother's hands.

"I can't take your food, child."

"The big Indian gave me plenty, I saved this one for you. Eat it please."

Mary Stiles quickly ate the small cake and washed it down with more cold water as she looked around at the Indians who seemed excited over something.

"Something's got them stirred up. Wonder what it is?" Mary Stiles said.

"Do you think they will let us stay together tonight, Mother?" Melissa's frightened voice betrayed her true fears.

Her mother turned to her, "Listen, if we become separated somehow, I want you to remember that surviving this is more important than anything they can do to you. *You* must survive at all costs, do you understand?"

"You frighten me, Mother. What are you saying? I don't want to live if you're not there with me."

"Hush that kind of talk, Melissa. You have your whole life to look forward to. I'm simply saying, if there's ever a chance for you to escape, I want you to take it."

"But, Mother—"

"No more. We are fighting for our lives here, Melissa and it's time for you to grow up. They . . . they may try to do things . . . what I mean, these savages think nothing of violating—"

Melissa placed a bound finger on her mother's lips. "I understand, Mother, and I've prepared myself for that when it comes. But I still won't desert you." Melissa's voice was firm and resolute and Mary's shoulders sagged.

"We shall see, darling one. God, how I wished Henry had taken the time to tell me more about this big country. Even if we were to escape, what direction would we head toward?" Her voice was filled with despair.

"I would rather die under an open sky with you there

than stay here like this," Melissa said, holding her mother's hands in her own.

The leader came up to them in the darkness and motioned them over to the small fire. The women, still clinging to one another, went over and sat down on blankets that had been spread out for them near the fire.

This time, when the leader offered Melissa more of the dried cakes from his sack, she managed to grab a half dozen of them in the darkness before he took it away without offering her mother any. After he walked away, Melissa slipped her mother four of the thin cakes. They ate in silence while watchful eyes glittered at them from the other side of the campfire.

The leader squatted by the fire and studied the Henry carefully. He pulled down on the lever of the rifle and a big brass cartridge leaped into the air. The Indian's hand snaked out and caught it in flight. The women watched while he rolled the bullet around between his forefinger and thumb. He turned the rifle on its side and pushed the nose of the bullet into the side chamber until it disappeared. The other Indians were watching Tall Feather closely. None of them had ever seen a lever action rifle before.

Tall Feather extracted another shell from the box and tried to shove it into the slot as well. The bullet jammed halfway in and the big Indian frowned. He was forced to use the tip of his knife blade to remove the bullet. Henry Stiles had just finished loading the weapon when the arrow caught him in the neck.

"It's full," Mary Stiles blurted out. Dark eyes turned to stare at the woman. The dull gleam of brass reflected by the light of the fire sent a pang through her. She recalled how proud her husband had been of the repeater and talked how it would make a difference if trouble should happen upon them.

Tall Feather stared at the woman for a minute, trying to understand what she was saying. He hefted the rifle and Mary Stiles nodded her head. The Indian came over and knelt down before the women. His eyes were like two black holes, devoid of any emotion.

Slowly, Mary Stiles reached out with her bound hands and took the rifle from him. She tried to work the lever but it was too awkward with her hands tied.

"Untie my hands," she told the Indian, holding them out to him. He looked at the woman and down at her bound wrists. Instantly, the knife came out and sliced through the rawhide string. Mary nearly dropped the rifle as blood pulsed through her numb fingers, sending shooting pains up both arms.

"Oh, that hurts," she cried out, never letting go of the rifle.

"Mother, what are you doing?" Melissa said, frightened.

"Don't worry, child. I'm trying to gain a little of their trust." With that she jacked a shell into the rifle and ejected it the next instant. She repeated the procedure until fifteen brass shells lay around her on the blanket. The big Indian looked amazed, and he touched the shells to make sure they were real. The other Indians craned their necks around the fire, trying to get a better look at the demonstration.

Next, Mary Stiles showed the big Indian how to load the Henry by replacing all the shells through the slot in the brass frame after jacking one into the chamber. When she was done, Mary handed the weapon back to the Indian who held the rifle like it was suddenly alive, his eyes roaming up and down its length. He walked back over to the fire, smiling and holding the rifle up so the rest could see the powerful weapon.

"I think you've just showed him how to kill quicker than he ever thought possible," Melissa said solemnly.

"If it gains us a little trust and buys some time, it will be worth the risk." It had not escaped Mary that she had not been bound again.

They watched from the blanket as the Indian repeated what Mary had shown him. When he had the cartridges laid out in a row at his feet, he said something to his men and they burst into laughter. Tall Feather scooped up the brass shells and loaded them into the rifle magazine, one at a time. He didn't fail to remember to jack a shell into the chamber before loading them all. Once this was done, he spoke again and this time the others turned to their blankets while their leader stayed by the small fire, holding the Henry close to his chest.

"Let's roll up in these blankets and I'll untie your hands," Mary said to her daughter.

"Are you sure?" Melissa said. "What if they get mad . . ."

"I think it's time for them to give us a little something in return," Mary whispered as she worked at Melissa's bonds after they had the blanket over them. "That big Indian knows full well he didn't retie me. It will be all right, you'll see."

They lay there a long time looking up at the glittering stars.

"Have you ever seen country so big and open?" Melissa asked, sleepily.

"I know. The vastness makes you feel insignificant, almost unimportant." It caused Mary to wonder, if in all this empty space, was there another living soul to mark their passing?

"I wonder if that poor old man the Indians chased into those rocks escaped," Melissa said. "And if so, where could he go, how could he survive in such desolation?"

Caught up in their own predicament, Mary had nearly forgotten about the white man the Indians had surprised that morning. There was another living soul out there after all, and Mary held that thought close to her for some time before answering her daughter.

"We can only pray that he does, Melissa, and reports of seeing us. There's little hope for rescue if he dies."

As Melissa drifted into a troubled sleep, she prayed for the souls of her father and brother. She prayed, too, for the old man's safety so he might tell others about them.

They were awakened by low voices in the gray dawn of a new day. Both women were startled to see the Indians with their faces painted. Some had even stripped down to breech-cloths in spite of the predawn chill and were busy painting red and blue stripes down the length of their legs and across their chests.

"What's happening, Mother?" Melissa asked, frightened. She hugged the blanket to her, her big eyes taking in the scene.

"Looks like they may be getting ready for battle with someone," Mary Stiles said.

"Oh God, no!" Melissa whispered. Then as quickly, "If it's white people, there may be a chance for us to escape." She looked at her mother with questioning eyes.

"Maybe. For now we must wait and see. Remember to keep your hands beneath the blanket," her mother cautioned. But the leader had not forgotten and he came over and bent down by them, his face looked fierce and somehow different with the paint.

The Indian drew aside the cover and looked down at Melissa. There was no mistaking the meaning of his open stare and Mary Stiles knew then they would never pass another night in safety. He removed two leather strings from his belt and retied both women, yet not as tight as before. He said something and stroked Melissa's yellow hair before turning away.

The Indians quietly gathered their lances, bows, and what few single-shot rifles they had and departed the still dark camp, leaving a young brave to guard the women. As soon as Tall Feather and the others had gone, the brave got up from the fire and came over to the two women with two tins of coffee. Mary Stiles accepted the coffee gratefully and tried to reassure the young Indian with a smile. Melissa only gave the young Indian a hard stare for she recognized him as one of those who had fondled her earlier. But now, without the others around, the Indian seemed shy in their presence. The young brave retreated to the fire and sat back down. His only visible weapon was the hunting knife at his belt.

"Where do you suppose the others have gone?" Melissa whispered, sipping the weak liquid.

"You saw their faces. I'm afraid it can only spell more trouble, but for who I haven't a clue."

Chapter 11

Potter's Settlement grew up on the banks of the South Fork of the Republican River haphazardly by a stroke of bad luck, or at least that was what Elijah Potter called it at the time. Only later, did he come to change his mind.

While on his way to the Cherry Creek diggings, along with the other hopefuls traveling the Republican River Trail, Potter found himself with a busted axle wagon when he tried crossing the gullied river at South Fork. A merchant by trade, Elijah Potter was hurrying to the goldfields, not to mine for gold, but to establish a store and his heavily loaded wagon was stuffed with a variety of dry goods, food stuffs, and light mining equipment.

In order to affect repairs to his wagon, Potter had been obliged to unload most of his things. When other emigrants paused by the river to catch a final breath before the dry cross-country run to Denver City, Potter found himself doing more business with his trade goods than he was at fixing the wagon.

And now a year later, Potter was still there by the river but so were two mud-hut saloons, and a small corral where a man swapped prairie-worn animals he had fed out on the grassland north of the settlement for a modest rate of exchange. Not long after, a family from Arkansas established a vegetable farm down river by ditching and irrigating their fields from the Republican.

Rounding out the inhabitants of Potter's Settlement,

were the Kelsey sisters who kept a fourteen-year-old boy around to do their chores. Although the older of the two sisters looked as though life had ridden her hard, with such scarce commodities about, Kathleen Kelsey found her services were still in great demand here on the bleak Plains. Iris Kelsey looked to be a good ten years younger than her sister; slim, big busted, yet with a soft kind of beauty about her that failed most working ladies rather quickly. Both women had startling red hair and blue-green eyes and became an immediate success in Potter's Settlement, drawing all manner of lonely men from every corner of the open Plains for miles around.

The Kelsey sisters proved to be good for saloon business and for Potter's store as well, bringing in trade from other remote settlements, hide hunters and a score of hard-eyed gunmen who passed through now and again. And even though Potter was well into his sixties, he had succumbed to both women on several occasions, yet retaining enough of his New England trait by working out a trade for their favors from his supply of goods. Hard currency was hard to come by here on the open Plains.

Potter put the boy to work in his store which was really nothing more than an adobe cabin cluttered with sacks of trade goods, boxes of staples, and a variety of tinned products from tomatoes to oysters. With no counters or shelves to hold these goods, there was barely walking room amid the piles of clutter.

All in all, Elijah Potter was rather proud of what had happened here on the banks of the South Fork. And he had yet to lay eyes on the Rocky Mountains.

As was his usual custom, Elijah Potter rose before dawn from his bed he kept in one corner of his store, fired up the little stove to ward off the chill, shoved what was left of last night's coffee on the fire, and stepped out back to relieve himself.

In the dawn of a cloudless day, Potter lined himself up with the ten foot deep slash of earth, put there by some ancient riverbed that once may have been part of the Re-

96

publican and unbuttoned his pants. He leaned back and was all set to go when Potter lifted his eyes to the surrounding sagebrush and froze. Coming at him through the low shrubs were a dozen painted Indians, their freshly painted faces seemed to shine even in the dull light.

Without bothering to rebutton his pants, Potter scrambled backwards toward his store, screaming at the top of his lungs, "Indians!" Behind him, the Indians broke into a war hoop, and suddenly the little settlement was crawling with yelling savages.

A few horses were still tied to the hitch posts in front of the two saloons and Potter's screaming brought several patrons boiling outside with revolvers cocked. A bitter, but short, fight erupted there in the middle of the narrow street. The Indians swarmed around the badly outnumbered white men. When it was over, four white men lay dead alongside the body of one painted warrior.

Elijah Potter barred the back door of his store and started for the front with rifle in hand. Before he could cover the distance, the front door burst open and two Indians rushed him. With no time to aim, Potter snapped a quick shot from his hip, shattering the only glass window in his place. Cursing loudly, Potter dropped the rifle and grabbed for his pistol but it was too late. The first Indian to reach Potter plunged a knife into the man's ample stomach, cutting upward into the breastbone and heart.

Air rushed from Potter's lungs with an audible gasp as he raised up on the tips of his toes, trying to rid himself of the deep cutting knife. Dark blood spurted out across the sacks of flour and canned goods. Potter sagged against the Indian as his life pumped out of him. Contemptuously, the Indian pulled his knife free and shoved Potter backward. The storekeeper collapsed among the crates and boxes.

From the floor, Potter watched, with fading vision, as the two Indians plundered through his stock, his mouth working silently in protest.

The howling Indians rushed into both saloons and pulled their fighting and kicking owners, back into the streets where both were immediately shot full of arrows and scalped.

Tall Feather motioned his men toward the lone plank building standing fifty yards from the rest, and several warriors leaped atop the horses standing hitched at the rail. Kicking and yelling loudly, they thundered up to the darkened building. The nearest rider leaped from his horse, holding his lance high over his head as his feet touched the rough planking that served as steps.

A puff of white smoke appeared at one of the two windows and the Indian flew backward, landing in the rutted street. Blood pumped from a chest wound. Feebly, he tried to rise and was shot again. This time he flattened out and lay still. The other three Indians circled the small building, hanging over the neck of their horses to keep from being hit.

Tall Feather was drawn to the scene by the gunfire and the body of Lame Deer now stretched out face up on the ground. A bullet whizzed by his head as he rode up. Immediately, he slid to the opposite side of his horse and angled his pony toward the back of the building. Kicking free of his horse, Tall Feather leaped to the ground and ran up to the back door which he found unlocked. Meanwhile, his men kept up a constant barrage of arrows and rifle shots into the building from the front.

Tall Feather slipped inside. Holding the Henry, Tall Feather was drawn to the front of the structure where he could hear voices and an occasional rifle shot.

He stepped quietly into the dimly lit room and was surprised to find that it was two women who were doing all the shooting. One of them turned as he entered the room and pointed a gun at him, warning the other woman as she did so.

Tall Feather reacted instinctively, shooting the woman through the head with the Henry. The other woman screamed as Kathleen Kelsey fell into her sister's arms. The rifle she was holding clattered to the floor. Tall Feather strode over and retrieved the weapon. He flung open the door and called to his men who rushed around Tall Feather and grabbed the grieving Iris Kelsey who still clung to her dead sister. The Indians dragged her, kicking and screaming, from the building. Tall Feather watched impassively and bent over and loosened the dead woman's scalp with his knife. He held the thick scalp of red hair high in the air and, throwing back his head, gave a loud war cry.

They had hit the farmer and his family from Arkansas before first light, killing both the man and his wife and two young boys as they slept. They had been the first to die this morning. And now the bloody carnage of Potter's Settlement was over and the Indians turned to raiding whiskey from the saloons and hauling out sacks of tobacco, sugar, and blankets from Potter's store.

Tall Feather strode over to the distraught woman who had been tied to one of the railings. He showed her the bloodied scalp, grinning at her. The woman turned pale and struggled hard to free herself from the leather bonds, screaming all the while. The big Indian laughed, stepped close to the woman and slapped her hard across the mouth. Iris Kelsey sank to her knees in the dirt, sobbing loudly, her hands pulled tightly over her head by the rawhide bonds.

Several of the Cheyenne warriors rode back and forth in the street, shouting their victory and drinking freely from bottles of whiskey. As one of them flashed by Tall Feather, he pitched him a half-empty bottle. Tall Feather took a long swallow, feeling the whiskey burn as it went down. At that precise moment, Tall Feather felt invincible as he gripped the rifle that shone like the sun in one hand and the bottle in the other. With the rifle, he had killed the white man who had tried to hide in the corral from him. In less time than it takes for a man to blink, he had shot the white man twice with this new and deadly rifle. No one in the Bow String Society had such a fierce weapon as his. Along with the whiskey that raced like fire through his veins was the desire to be a great leader like Hump Back Wolf or Dull Knife. Today, Tall Feather knew he had started down the path to greatness.

* * *

As the first sounds of distant shooting reached the camp, the young Indian jumped up and walked swiftly away from the fire, pausing some distance away.

"There is fighting nearby," Mary Stiles said to her daughter as she gained her feet.

"What are you doing, Mother?" Melissa asked.

"I need to know if they are attacking a white settlement. If so, there may be a chance for us." She reached down and helped Melissa to her feet. "Regardless, we must be ready to take advantage of the situation."

The two women hurried after the young Indian who heard their approach and turned quickly around, his black eyes filled with alarm. Mary Stiles gave him a smile and indicated they wanted to watch as well. The distant popping of rifles forced the Indian's eyes back to the battle scene below.

Mary and Melissa Stiles looked out across sloping land that gave way to a thin line of green that marked the passage of a river. Black smoke was boiling up into the early morning air from several different points and they could see tiny figures running wildly about. Their faint cries came to them over the broken terrain on a gentle breeze.

"My God!" Melissa said, her eyes mirroring disbelief. "Those poor people."

Mary Stiles only stared at what she knew may well be their last hope of gaining freedom as Potter's Settlement was put to the torch. There was no time to waste thinking about the fates of the people in those houses. What worried her more was the whiskey she knew the Indians would find down there. With alcohol in their captors' blood, Melissa and she would never be safe again. Just thinking of what the big Indian intended for her daughter was almost too much to bear. Mary Stiles made up her mind. The time had come to act. She would rather see her daughter die fighting than being savagely attacked by that Indian tonight.

Mary Stiles nudged her daughter who could barely turn away from the carnage spread out before her.

"Follow me back to the fire," Mary whispered.

"But, I thought you wanted . . .?" Melissa saw the distressed look her mother gave her and she obediently turned back toward camp.

Mary glanced back at the young Indian who seemed to not have noticed their departure. Back at the fire, Mary worked feverishly to untie Melissa.

"What are we going to do?" Melissa whispered.

"We must get away . . . now, before the others come back. It's our only chance." Once the rawhide thongs had been removed from Melissa, she untied her mother easily. Mary had kept constant watch on the young Indian who had yet to look back at them.

The only animal in camp was the old draft horse that once belonged to Jonathan and was now the property of the Indian that was suppose to be guarding them. The horse was old and slow, and Mary realized their chances of escaping meant leaving immediately. They had to put as much distance between them and the Indians before they returned. The horse was tethered to the limb of a scrub juniper a few yards beyond camp.

"Listen, child," Mary Stiles said, her eyes glued to the back of the Indian. "Go over to old Jake and ease the reins over his head and be ready to ride as soon as I get there."

"But, Mother—"

"Do as I say, Melissa. Now go!" Mary Stiles gave her daughter a gentle shove. As she walked slowly toward the horse, Mary bent quickly over the campfire to pick up a few scraps of food and a water bag made of skin. It was at that time the Indian decided to turn back to camp and Mary realized the time to act was now. The others could very well be on their way back.

With restrained effort, Mary Stiles stood up and walked casually away from the fire, going directly to Melissa who had thrown the reins around the animal's thick neck. With every step, she expected the Indian to call for her to stop, but no such order came. When she came up to Melissa, she saw the fear deeply etched on her daughter's face. Moving quickly, Mary Stiles slung the water bag over her head and grabbed the reins.

"Get on quickly," she ordered Melissa who sprang to the broad back of the horse, her dress riding up past her knees.

The young Indian shouted at them. As Mary Stiles pulled herself up behind her daughter, she held to the reins and kicked the fat animal in the ribs as hard as she could. The Indian was running now, yelling at them to stop. Mary Stiles turned the draft horse's head and started back down the trail at what seemed like an agonizingly slow gait.

"Make him go faster, Mother," Melissa said, looking behind them at the running Indian who appeared to be gaining ground.

"I'm trying," Mary said, kicking the animal over and over. The big draft horse broke into a lope and gradually pulled away from the running Indian.

"We've done it, Mother!" Melissa shouted, holding to the horse's mane and looking back at the Indian who had stopped running and was standing there staring after them.

"We're not out of this yet, child. First we must get as far away from camp as possible before the others get back. Then we must turn old Jake loose and take to the rocks."

"Mother, without a horse we won't make it," Melissa said, concerned.

"Melissa, honey. You see how slow Jake is. We cannot hope to outrun them. We'll hide somewhere and wait until dark before we do any traveling. Once they find the horse, and not us, they may decide to go on and leave us be."

Mary Stiles meant for her voice to convey a strong sense of conviction, yet it came out threaded with inner doubt. How could two women, new to the raw frontier, possibly hope to escape from men born to wild country? What were they going to do if they managed to escape? Mary wondered. She had no idea where they were in relation to known trails or other settlements like the one the Indians had just attacked. They had water for now, but where would they find more? To her, this land was dry and forbidding, hostile to those not familiar with its ways. Yet, she would rather they took their chances with the earth than stay one minute more with savages. Mary voiced none of these inner doubts to Melissa. For now they had to concentrate on getting as far away as possible.

They crossed a rock filled draw and paused on the other side to give the old horse a short rest. Mary looked back and figured they were at least five miles from camp, but she suppressed her joy for now. She was aware that as soon as the others returned, they would immediately start after them. And there was no way they could hide old Jake's big hoof prints in this sandy country. Mary concluded they were going to have to let Jake go as soon as they put another mile or two behind them.

"Mother, look!" Melissa said, pointing. Mary Stiles glanced back and saw the small dust cloud clinging low to the horizon like a yellow smudge against the blue sky.

"They're coming," Mary said grimly, giving Jake a good kick. "Only thing we can do now is look for a place to hide. Get up, Jake!" Mary shouted, using the end of the reins to urge the horse forward.

They had traveled less than a mile when Melissa pointed to a wall of gray rock that loomed off to their left.

"Maybe we could hide there," she told her mother.

Mary Stiles studied the jumble of earth for a moment before making a quick decision. Rather than riding straight for the rocks, she veered off to the right, continuing on until they came to a dry streambed, lined with rock and deep sand. She pulled back on the reins and slid off the horse at the edge of the rocks.

"Quick, Melissa, step down and be careful where you put your feet. Keep on these rocks." Melissa did as she was told and dismounted beside her mother.

"Hate to see old Jake turned loose," Melissa said sadly, patting the animals big neck. "I see him and I think of Jonathan racing across the waving grass, carefree and happy." Tears formed in her eyes.

"I know, honey. There's a hole in my heart that will never be filled again." Mary Stiles seemed suddenly tired and looked as if she had aged ten years in the last thirty-six hours. She hugged her only living child to her, both sobbing deeply over their loss.

Mary pulled back and wiped her eyes. She turned loose the reins of the horse and slapped him on the rump. Jake ran off a few paces, stopped and looked back at them.

"Get out of here!" Mary shouted and picked up a small stone and hurled it at the docile animal who didn't seem to understand what was being asked of him. The horse moved off a few more paces and stopped.

This time both women hurled stones at the horse who finally loped off when a stone stung him on his ample rump.

"Let's go," Mary said, moving out in front. "Keep to the rocks, child. One misstep and they'll trail us for sure." They worked their way carefully toward the gray rocks, fearing any moment the Indians would come charging up.

Melissa slipped on a loose rock and fell against a stubby cactus, her hand catching the brunt of thorns that jutted out from the plant. She screamed and Mary Stiles hurried back to help her daughter to her feet.

"You okay, child?" Mary said, seeing the dozen or so thorns protruding from her hand.

"I'll be okay, Mother. We can pull these out after we find a place to hide," Melissa said, trying to ignore the burning pain.

"It's not much farther, but we must hurry," Mary Stiles cautioned as she resumed the lead. They arrived at the slash of land where the rocks seemed to have been heaved upward from below ground as if by a great force. Among the wagon-sized rocks, cactus and small shrubs grew that made walking difficult between the crevices filled with small loose stones. One wrong step and either of them could easily twist an ankle.

Mary Stiles angled upward across a field, littered with stones, searching for some place they could hide. Her eyes scanned for a narrow opening or ledge, anything that would offer concealment. A buzzing noise pierced the still air and Melissa screamed as a prairie rattler, disturbed by their passing, slithered away among the rocks.

"Are you hurt," Mary called, her face showing concern.

Melissa clutched at her heaving chest and nodded her head. "I'm sorry for crying out like that. I just hate those things."

Mary continued her climb, with greater caution now that she knew snakes were about. It didn't make much sense to escape from the Indians only to be bitten and die here among these gray rocks. Then she found what she had been searching for, a crevice covered by an outcropping of rock. The surrounding terrain tended to conceal the dark crack from any angle other than a straight-on approach. It wasn't the ideal hiding place, but Mary figured it was the best they could do. They needed to get off the face of these naked rocks before they were spotted.

They found the crevice just big enough to squeeze under. In the shade of the overhanging rock, Mary felt temporary relief and her hopes inched upward a notch. They sat there for the better part of an hour, the first fifteen minutes devoted to pulling the painful thorns from Melissa's hand. Tiny pricks of blood followed each thorn to the surface as they were removed.

"Wish we could wash off the blood," Mary Stiles whispered, "but we'll need every precious drop of water before we find more."

For what seemed like an eternity, the two women sat unmoving, listening to the world around them. When a stone rattled down the side of the ravine, it startled them so bad, they clutched each other for support. They strained to catch any further sound, but all was quiet. Mary Stiles was just beginning to relax again when she looked across the narrow wash and straight into Tall Feather's angry eyes.

Chapter 12

Jack Dawson studied the lone set of tracks that veered away from the trail left by the Indians as he took a short sip from his canteen before handing it to Josiah Catt. They had shifted the pack load between the two animals in order for Catt to ride the mule. Without a saddle, the ride, at best, was uncomfortable, yet Catt never complained.

"Ain't more'n three hours old," Catt commented, tilting the canteen up for a quick drink before giving it back to Dawson.

"Don't appear to be heading in any particular direction," Dawson said, squinting against the bright sun.

"Know what you're thinking, so lead on," Catt said, biting off a piece from a slab of dark tobacco.

"Guess it won't hurt none to check it out."

Three miles farther, they had their answer. They found the old draft horse, standing in a rocky gully with reins trailing. Both Dawson and Catt spent a few minutes searching the immediate area for footprints, and concluded whoever was riding the animal had gotten off earlier.

"Probably belonged to that emigrant I came across," Dawson said, watching Catt mount the big animal. Trouble was, did the horse break away from the Indians or had someone been trying to escape, possibly the women? Dawson discounted the first thought, for the draft horse was too slow to outrun Indian ponies.

"I'm just thankful I got me a horse to ride again, saddle and all."

A few miles farther north, Dawson had the answer to his question. There was plenty of signs in the sandy wash where the draft animal had been turned loose, mixed with the tracks of unshod ponies. Near a rock was the unmistakable footprint of a woman in the sand.

"Looks like the women tried to escape," Catt said, studying the upthrust of gray rock in the distance.

"And headed to the most obvious place the Indians would check first," Dawson added, moving out again.

"Never said pilgrims and pikers had good sense," Catt said, falling behind Dawson. Once they reached the rock formation, Catt rode a wide circle around them to pick up their trail again. In a few minutes, Dawson joined him at the lip of the dry wash.

"It was the two women all right," Dawson said. "Two sets of tracks back there in the wash. Tall Feather found them easy enough."

"And they all headed north again," Catt pointed to the churned earth. "Them tracks ain't two hours old if that."

Dawson nodded, looking out across the wide expanse of rolling country that rose in the distance.

"How far to Potter's Settlement?"

Josiah Catt scratched his tobacco-stained chin. "Expect we cut over to the left, we ain't more'n ten miles, maybe less."

"Suppose we ride on to Potter's. Somebody there may have seen Tall Feather and his men. May be able to pick up a man or two to help us."

"Got a point," Catt said, taking the lead now that they were abandoning the trail.

Less than an hour later, they topped out on a slight rise. Below them, the ground fell away to where the South Fork of the Republican River cut across the parched earth. The gray smoke, rising against the blue sky, told them they could expect no help from Potter's Settlement.

"Looks like you were right. Tall Feather's been here and gone," Dawson said, putting his horse into a lope.

They rode slowly into the tiny settlement with their guns drawn against unexpected trouble, but all they found was a young boy sitting next to a freshly dug grave. Dried tears marked the boy's grimy face. He looked up at the two men with dazed eyes.

"You okay, boy?" Dawson said, dismounting. The boy never answered, just turned his pain-filled eyes back to the grave. A shiver ran through his thin body. Dawson and Catt exchanged looks and Dawson motioned for Catt to check the charred buildings.

"Anybody else alive?" Dawson asked, squatting down beside the boy. The boy looked at him with dull eyes and shook his head.

"I hid in the root cellar, 'neath Mr. Potter's. Weren't nothing I could do. They hit us so fast, just as day was breaking." His voice was thin and reedy, and broken now by grief.

"A relative?" Dawson asked, indicating the grave.

"Just somebody I cared for . . . a heap. She was more like an aunt to me." He turned to look at Dawson closely. "They took Iris Kelsey. She was Miss Kathleen's sister," he added softly.

Dawson's face turned grim. Things had gone from bad to worse. Now Tall Feather and his band had three women and most likely all the whiskey they could hold. There would be hell to pay for the women once they stopped for the night . . . if their luck held that long.

"Were any of the Indians killed in the attack?"

The boy's face brightened. "Yes sir, Miss Kathleen killed one who was trying to come through the door at her. I tried to find a gun, but by then they had taken over Potter's store and street and was shooting anything that moved. I . . . I hid after that," his voice dropped to a whisper and he looked down at his blistered hands from digging in the hard ground.

"You did the right thing, son," Dawson said quickly.

"All you would have done was get yourself killed as well. This way, you still got a chance to help free Iris Kelsey once we ride them down."

The boy looked up quickly, "I can shoot if you have an extra rifle. I'm not afraid."

"Know that," Dawson said, standing up again to look around at the destroyed settlement. Only walls of sod marked each building left standing, their roofs collapsing into their interiors.

"I walked down to the Stringers, they grow vegetables down yonder," he said, pointing at a farm house a quarter mile away. He swallowed hard before continuing. "The Indians killed all of them . . . they were still in their beds. Little Andy and Johnny Stringer was something awful to look at. Ain't had time to bury them yet."

"Josiah and me will give you a hand, son," Dawson said gently.

It turned out to be a grim task, burying the bodies of the Stringer family in their bloody sheets. Jack Dawson and Josiah Catt did most of the digging while they sent the boy into the house to look for extra ammunition and guns.

When they rode away from the smoldering ruins of Potter's Settlement at mid-afternoon, the boy, Linny Eaton, carried an old rifle that once belonged to Isaac Stringer. He rode Dawson's mule, rigged with a saddle found down at the corral. Josiah Catt had borrowed something from Isaac Stringer as well, a floppy hat which he plopped on his sunburned pate.

They backtracked the Indians to their camp and Dawson found a scrap of women's clothing. Catt checked the fire with his hand, moving the ashes around for a better feel.

"Still warm underneath," he informed Dawson.

"Evidently, they camped here last night and attacked the settlement this morning," Jack Dawson said, examining footprints and horse tracks carefully. "I suspect while the Indians were busy below, the two women decided it was now or never and lit out on that old plug horse. That must have thrown a kink in Tall Feather's plans once they returned from their killing and looting."

"Explains why the coals are still warm," Catt added.

"So what do you think?" Dawson asked the old prospector. "Only decent place to camp between here and Frenchmen Fork is the Arikaree River."

"Way I'd figger it, too," Catt said, wiping his sooty hand on his trousers.

Dawson cocked his head at the western sun. "Ought to put us there just before dark."

"We gonna need all the advantage we can get," Josiah Catt said, taking a chew.

"I'll be ready to fight, Mr. Dawson, just say the word," Linny said, holding the old rifle tightly to him. He was determined to free Iris Kelsey and he told them so.

"And we appreciate your help, son," Dawson said. "But you gotta do exactly as I tell you when the time comes."

"I will," Linny promised.

"Mount up and let's go then," Dawson said, getting on his horse. Between them and the Arikaree were twenty miles of gullied country, broken ridges, and loose rock that had to crossed. The going would be slow at best. Dawson hoped Tall Feather and his men would leave the women alone until they made camp that night. But when he found the empty whiskey bottle, Dawson knew all bets were off where the Indian renegade was concerned.

"Damn, but Black Hawk is taking his sweet time down there," Colin Jackson said to the others who waited with him in a clump of evergreens that jutted up from a field of huge boulders.

"Black Hawk just wants to be sure," Cove Stillman replied. "Wants to separate the braggin' from fact. You know how it is with most of these placer claims. They won't tell you the honest to God truth for fear of facing up to their own failures."

Colin Jackson turned to look at the outlaw beside him.

"Cove, I swear you sounding more and more like a professor than a horse thief."

Cove Stillman allowed a small smile to crease his unshaven features. "Never got much formal schoolin' back there in Tennessee, but I read everything I could get my hands on. Got myself in trouble with the law. Shot a man for trifling with my girl's affections."

The gunman lit a black cigar and laughed. "So you headed out here figuring to become a bad outlaw."

"Not exactly," Cove Stillman said, slightly embarrassed now that he had told the gunman the truth about himself. "What I mean, the man I shot didn't die. What sent me packing was his four brothers. They were a tough and mean lot, the Parkers. If I stayed, somebody would have died. So me and Whit Coleman jest drifted West."

"What about your sweetheart?" Colin asked, blowing a blue ring into the thin air.

"She didn't hold with guns and the like and wouldn't leave home, so I left her behind."

"Well, Cove, that's all very interesting," Colin said, studying the end of his cigar. "What was it you use to read?"

"English Literature mostly, and anything else I could get my hands on," Cove Stillman said softly.

"Get away," Colin said, surprised.

"It's the truth."

"Quote me something," Colin said, eyeing Stillman closely.

"You mean here . . . right now?" Cove asked, looking around at the other two riders who sat off by themselves, smoking.

"Now is as good a time as any," Colin said mildly. "We got to wait for Black Hawk to give us the sign, so we ain't going anywhere right now."

"You won't laugh, will you?"

"I won't laugh, now go ahead, quote me something educated."

Cove Stillman cleared his throat, "Well, guess it won't hurt." He quoted several sonnets and a few lines from

111

Shakespeare, quoting it as it was written in the Old English style. Colin Jackson listened, amazed by Stillman's ability.

"Dang, Cove, shoulda told me you was good at this sort of thing. You could be working the Apollo Theater or Cibola Hall."

Cove Stillman was slightly embarrassed by the gunman's attentions. He broke eye contact and looked through the trees down to the wild creek where Black Hawk sat smoking and talking with two miners.

"Just because I can quote stuff from old books, don't make me educated or an actor either."

"Hell, ain't none of them other fancy dressed fellows either one, yet it ain't stopped them," Colin said, puffing on his cigar once again.

Colin froze. "Black Hawk's giving us the sign," he said.

Colin Jackson threw the cigar to the ground, his face all business once again. He looked at Black Hawk through the trees. Sure enough, the outlaw had his hat off and was mopping his brow with a red bandanna.

"Get your horses, boys," Colin said. "Looks like we got ourselves a paying claim."

The clatter of hoofs over loose rock startled the two miners seated next to Black Hawk as four men rode single file from the dense woods and pulled up before the group.

The two miners looked a little uneasy by the sudden appearance of the riders and they stood up slowly.

"Relax, boys. I believe I know these gentlemen," Black Hawk said, giving them a reassuring smile. The men seemed relieved, but remained on their feet.

Colin Jackson and Black Hawk exchanged knowing looks as the gunman stepped down from his horse. A two-man rocker system sat idle near the bank of the rushing stream where the miners had been shoveling gravel all morning.

"Didn't know there was any color on this stream," Colin said casually. "Most other folks are working the drainage across this ridge," he said, indicating the steep slope rising up behind them and covered with thick stands of lodgepole and spruce.

"We making it pay," one of the miners said cryptically.

"Hell, boys, you don't have to be shy here with my friends," Black Hawk cut in. "Fact is, these boys have been raking it up by the shovelfuls," he said to Colin whose eyes widened in mock surprise.

"Ain't so?" Colin said.

"You fellas looking to work claims?" one of the miners asked, wanting to steer the conversation away from their good luck. It was obvious they were ill at ease and a little bit concerned by a camp full of armed strangers.

"Now, boys, do we look like miners?" Colin Jackson asked, pulling aside his frock coat and exposing the walnut butt of his Colt. He smiled at the two miners with eyes cold as the mountain stream flowing nearby. Before the smile faded from his lips, his hand dipped down and his Colt flashed fire, once and then twice.

Both miners died instantly, their eyes wide with surprise. Black Hawk rolled one away from the fire after one of his arms fell into the flames. Both had been heart shots.

"Dang, Colin, you didn't give me time to find out where they cached their dust," Black Hawk said.

"Well, Black Hawk, me and the boys been waiting so long in them trees up there, I figured you not only knew where they kept their gold, but got their pedigrees as well."

Black Hawk shook his head, "Only what they taken out of the rocker." The outlaw reached into one of the dead men's pockets and brought out a rawhide bag which he tossed to the gunman.

Colin Jackson shook the pea-sized gravel into the palm of his hand and studied the smooth gold.

"There must be several hundred dollars worth right here," he said, hefting the bag.

"Professor, you and the boys, go through their tent and belongings real careful. They got more here, you can count on it," Colin said to Cove Stillman. The gunman turned back to the fire and knelt down and helped himself to the dead miner's coffee.

"Them two going to work the claim?" Black Hawk asked Jackson.

"That's what I brought'm along to do," the gunman said, sipping the hot coffee. "Told you this could be a sweeter deal than stealing horses."

"It's working out that way, for a fact," Black Hawk said, keeping his eyes on the men who were rummaging through the tent.

"I found it!" Cove shouted in a few minutes. He emerged from the tent holding up a quart can. Black Hawk took the heavy can from Stillman and lifted off the rawhide covering. The can was filled with nugget gold like the bag Jackson was holding.

"Would you look at that," Black Hawk whispered when the others crowded around him. "Must be five, ten thousand here." He grinned at the cold-eyed gunman.

"Like I said, man has to look long and hard to find a sweeter deal," Colin said, lighting a fresh cigar. "You boys, drag these two unfortunates off there in the rocks and cover them up. We got to look respectful case others come by."

"What you want us to do, Colin?" Black Hawk asked, putting the leather covering back on the can of nuggets.

"Expect you boys best stay in camp and work hell outa this claim. I'll drift back into town and in four or five days, file on it so's it's legal-like."

"What if they already filed papers?" Cove Stillman asked.

"Don't you worry none, Professor. I'll just say we found it abandoned and started working it. Happens all the time. Claim office ain't about to spend time riding back in here to check things out. We free and clear and that's that." He emptied the coffee cup and turned to his horse. "Oh, and I'll take the gold down to the new mint and exchange some of it for them new gold coins, then deposit the rest for us."

"What about the others?" Black Hawk asked, handing Jackson the can of nuggets.

"I've been thinking on that as well," the gunman said,

tying the leather flap of his saddlebags down over the pocket holding the can. Colin and Black Hawk were alone. Cove Stillman had walked down to the rocker and was inspecting the contraption while the other two men were busy lugging one of the dead miners away from camp.

"Figure we cut Ford in on this deal and let the others ride."

"You think they'll stand by for such treatment?" Black Hawk asked.

"They won't know any different. I'll have Ford explain we're laying low for awhile after Bradley's death to let things cool off. They'll go for that. Meantime, we'll take what gold we can from this claim. Once it goes to looking more like work, we'll find ourselves another."

"Sounds good to me," the outlaw said as Colin Jackson swung his leg across his horse. "Just you take care of our money," Black Hawk grinned. "Wouldn't want to hear you been robbed by a pack of ruffians on your way back to Denver City."

"You just keep those boys working this claim. I'll see you in a few days." With that, Colin Jackson turned his big black around and headed downstream.

Black Hawk walked down to where Cove Stillman was tinkering with the rocker.

"We really going to placer mine?" he asked the outlaw.

"They are," Black Hawk said, jerking his thumb in the direction of the sweating men who were carrying the second miner from camp. "Like Colin said, we ain't miners. You and I will sit back and keep an eye on things and let them do the shoveling. Ain't about to get blisters on my shooting hand." Both outlaws laughed and went back to the fire to warm themselves. The air cooled off fast in high country.

Chapter 13

Tall Feather set a punishing pace northward as if driven by a desire to put Potter's Settlement as far behind him as possible. In doing so, the captive women suffered the most at the hands of his drunken warriors. One minute they were threatening them with the point of their lances, the next making lewd gestures. Tonight would be different from the past two, they seemed to be saying.

As hard as Mary Stiles tried to give comfort, Iris Kelsey was inconsolable over the loss of her sister. She didn't appear to comprehend what was happening to her. Under Tall Feather's orders, the three women were isolated again from one another as soon as they started north. Even though Mary was thankful they had not been physically abused, she knew the Indians would extract their payment tonight. Fueled by the whiskey, there would be no way to stop them. Mary shuttered inwardly, yet resolved to protect her young daughter even if it meant giving up her own life. Worse still, there would be no help forthcoming from the destroyed settlement. It was up to her to do something. What could she possibly do? She was as trussed up as the others, and with no hope of ever escaping again.

Tall Feather paused at a wide gash in the ground only long enough for the horses to be watered from the tiny trickle that was barely more than a wet streak in the red sand. The women were not allowed to dismount or to wet their throats. There was no doubt in Mary Stiles's mind that they were being punished for having escaped.

Iris Kelsey sat on a bony horse with her head bowed and her eyes closed. Her hands were bound tightly to the saddle horn. A dark-faced Indian, so drunk that he wobbled on his horse, held a rope that was tied to Kelsey's mount.

As they started across the shallow gully, the Indian leading Mary Stiles's horse passed Kelsey by and Mary whispered a word of encouragement to the woman. Iris Kelsey gave no indication she had even heard Mary, her eyes were tightly shut against the outside world.

Melissa appeared off to Mary's left and the young woman called to her.

"Are you okay, Mother?" Melissa shouted over the distance separating them.

"I'm fine, honey," Mary said, "but we must not talk."

"Why? They understand nothing we say. Has the other woman spoken yet?"

"Nothing," her mother called back as the Indian leading her horse spoke sharply to her, giving Mary a fierce look. Both women lapsed once more into stony silence as the horses picked their way through the field of loose rocks.

After everyone had crossed the gully, they resumed the ride north, single file. Mary Stiles looked down at her bound hands that were now a dark blue. For well over an hour now, she had felt nothing below the wrists. Besides physical agaony, she suffered great mental pain to knowing her only child was being subjected to such cruel punishment. But what worried her more was the fate she knew awaited them once the big Indian called a halt for the night.

Without warning, Iris Kelsey lifted her head, opened her eyes wide and began screaming loudly and kicking her poor horse wildly. The startled animal reared up and began crowhopping across the rough ground, dragging the tethered Indian and his horse along.

Yelling and racing their ponies after the melee, several drunken Indians swept by Mary Stiles at full speed. Through the dusty haze, Mary watched as Iris Kelsey flew into the air from the bucking animal. Mary heard the woman screaming, her hands still tied to the saddle, as she flopped along side and then under the plunging horse who was terrified of the thing bouncing beneath its belly.

"Oh God!" Mary Stiles whispered as she saw the woman being tossed about like a rag doll while two Indians tried quelling the wildly bucking horse. In agony, the Indian who had been leading Iris Kelsey's horse got up slowly from the ground, holding his arm, after being unseated by his own horse.

It seemed forever before the Indians got things under control once more and cut loose the dangling figure of Iris Kelsey. The woman collapsed in the dust and lay there, unmoving.

Mary Stiles turned to her captor and spoke to him trying to make him understand that she only wanted to go to the woman. The Indian looked at her with impassive eyes, but did not move.

"Damn you! I said let me go! Can't you see she's hurt?" Mary Stiles kicked her horse in the ribs and the startled animal crashed into the Indian's horse before he could react.

The Indian pulled hard on the reins to calm his mount, keeping the rope taut that held Mary's horse. They pranced around for a minute or two before both animals settled back down.

Tall Feather, calmly watching the proceedings, rode over to Mary Stiles and cut the rawhide bindings. He nodded for her to go to the fallen woman.

Mary Stiles doubled over in pain as the blood rushed into her numbed hands. It was a few minutes before the stinging subsided and she could even flex her fingers. Finally, she slipped from the back of her horse and ran over to the prone woman and knelt down, noticing the blood seeping from Iris Kelsey's mouth. Her face was covered with dirt and she was barely breathing. Her legs were bloody from being trampled by the horse and a foot was pointed at an odd angle. Mary knew, at the very least, it was broken.

Mary smoothed back the woman's hair from her face. Iris Kelsey looked up at her with pained eyes.

"Are you able to speak?"

"I hurt something awful," Iris Kelsey managed to whisper. Several Indians had crowded around and one reached down to straighten her foot causing her to scream out in pain.

"Leave her alone!" Mary said, slapping the Indian's hands away.

"Listen, you must get back on your horse," Mary warned.

Iris Kelsey shook her head, "There's no way I can ride now. My chest feels like it's filling with fluid . . . I can barely get my breath."

"They'll kill you if you can't ride . . . please try," Mary begged, tears forming in her eyes.

"I can't. There's no reason to live anymore. My sister was all the family I had."

"You have us now, Melissa and me," Mary said. "Together, we can make it through this if you would only try."

Iris Kelsey smiled, her face pale as death. "Thank you for caring." The injured woman reached up and touched Mary Stiles's face. Then, Iris Kelsey closed her eyes, her hand falling way from Mary's face. Her breathing stopped.

Mary Stiles shook the woman. "Please, no."

An Indian grabbed her roughly and dragged her away from the dead woman. Mary Stiles tried to gain her footing but the Indian would not stop long enough for her to do so.

"Stop it!" Melissa shouted. The Indian ignored her pleas and continued to drag her.

Melissa wanted to go to the aid of her mother, but her captor kept a tight rein on her horse. There would be no more demonstrations as was displayed by the dead woman.

The Indian finally dropped Mary in the dust by her horse. She lay there breathing the fine powder into her lungs and coughing loudly. Tall Feather spoke to the Indian who turned back and helped her to her feet and got her on the horse. He retied her hands as tightly as before and the group started up the trail again, leaving Iris Kelsey to the desert animals.

Jack Dawson watched as the slim youth's shoulders shook uncontrollably as he knelt by the shallow grave, containing the body of Iris Kelsey. As bad as death was, both Dawson and Catt knew the Indians had been cheated of the pleasures they had intended for the woman. . . . Acts so horrible most women would prefer death to such savage treatment.

Right now, Dawson was more worried about the other two women being held by Tall Feather's band. By all accounts, they were only two hours behind them, and luck was on their side for Tall Feather could not know he was being followed. Even if he did know, Dawson wasn't sure how worried the Indian would be, considering pursuit consisted of two men and a young boy. What Dawson had to worry about was being spotted by one of Tall Feather's braves. That happened, they would become the hunted instead of the hunters.

Linny Eaton wiped his red-rimmed eyes, replaced his hat, and got back on his horse. His face reflected a new determination and his eyes were cold and hard. Dawson figured Linny may have knelt by Iris Kelsey's grave as a boy, but he stood up a man.

"I'm ready," Linny said to Dawson. "Want to thank you for allowing time to bury Miss Kelsey."

"Could do nothing less," Dawson replied, moving the buckskin into a ground-eating lope. There would be no more stopping, Dawson concluded, if they intended to make up the two hour difference and prevent what he knew the women faced that night. The Indians had whiskey and that could turn out to be a two-edged sword for them. Good from the standpoint of preparing a surprise attack, but bad from the women's point of view. Dawson felt sure Tall Feather had not allowed them to be mistreated as of yet. But with the whiskey and the security of their old hunting grounds once again by the Arikaree, all bets were off. Dawson only hoped the women were prepared mentally in case they couldn't get there in time to help.

The smell of rain swept across the prairie in front of a cold wind as dusk settled over the broad swales and low hills, marking the Arikaree. Fed by four creeks to the west, the Arikaree was a major source of water for this region of the Plains during the spring months. Melting snow further supplemented these spring storms and allowed the Arikaree to flow even during the dry months of early summer and fall.

Dawson slipped into his coat against the evening chill as a few pats of water struck the brim of his hat. He looked back at the boy who was hunched over in his saddle against the cold.

"You got an oilskin or coat other'n that thin thing you're wearing?" Dawson asked.

"I'm all right," came the reply. Dawson drew up and untied the oilskin from behind his saddle and handed it to the boy.

"At least put this on. It'll break the wind and keep you dry somewhat. Looks like we're in for a storm."

Josiah Catt grinned at Dawson. "Good Lord's looking after us."

"Should make things a little easier, but we still got to be careful. One wrong move or we stumble on them too soon, and we'll be doing the running."

They rode on through the pelting rain and blowing wind as full darkness descended across the broken land. Dawson's long coat was completely soaked and he was chilled to the bone after a few minutes and Josiah Catt was facing the same condition. Worse still, the rain made following the Indians more difficult in the darkness. Dawson figured however since Tall Feather had barely deviated from his northern trek, there was no reason to believe the Indian would change direction this late in the day.

Catt pulled alongside Dawson and whispered, "We gettin' close to the Arikaree. There's a tree line up ahead."

121

"I know, been watching it for the last few minutes during flashes of lightning. You know Tall Feather, think he went up or down river?"

"Up most likely, toward the forks. Good place for camping among them trees there."

"Way I figure it, too. We angle that direction now, we could shave off another ten, fifteen minutes, but if we're wrong . . ."

"Tall Feather's camped at the forks, bet my life on it," Catt said.

"The way I see it, too, only it won't be our lives we betting on, just those two women."

"Don't remind me," Catt said with an audible sigh.

Dawson turned the buckskin toward the northwest and rode on through the slanting rain, keeping his rifle at the ready. His eyes constantly swept the lightning-charged sky for signs of danger. They were close enough now that Tall Feather may have a sentinel posted, no matter it was raining hard as hell.

The North and South Forks of the Arikaree are joined by Gordon Creek to the north and by Hell Creek to the south. Low growing juniper and cottonwood trees line the river at this juncture mixed with heavy underbrush. As the river flows east, the trees thin out, making campsites more open and exposed to prying eyes.

Just as Dawson and Catt figured, they located the camp by the smell of woodsmoke. Since it would be hidden well by the underbrush, they had to be careful not to ride in too close and announce their presence. While they were still two hundred yards from the forks of the river, Dawson called a halt and dismounted. Catt and the boy huddled close to Dawson for instructions.

"We can't take a chance in riding any closer, a horse or guard will spot us for sure. Pile a few rocks on your horse's reins and get your rifles. Looks like the rain is starting to slacken some, so we need to move fast."

Catt and Linny Eaton did as directed and the trio slipped quietly into the screen of trees and began working their way slowly up river. The smell of woodsmoke grew stronger and they heard a horse clear his nostrils in the distance. When they caught the flicker of firelight up ahead, Dawson stopped to study the layout. Voices drifted to them on the dying wind as the rain ceased altogether. There was deep guttural laughter followed by a woman's high-pitched scream.

Dawson turned to Catt and Linny Eaton. "This is it, boys, we got to move in fast. Want you two to cover me. Stay back in the shadows. If there's a chance of getting to Tall Feather, we might be able to free the women without a lot of shooting."

"You crazy, Dawson," Catt whispered. "We got to kill as many we can while we still hold the edge. There must be at least eight . . . maybe ten of them. You walk into their camp, we won't stand a chance of saving ourselves, much less them women."

Dawson grinned at the old prospector, "You got to learn to trust me, Josiah. I may not know much about prospecting, but Indians are kinda my specialty." Dawson led them through the trees with the leaves dripping cold water down the backs of their necks.

Moving forward with great caution, Dawson was surprised to find Tall Feather had posted no guard. They made a wide, half circle around the grazing horses so as not to disturb them and came up to the fire on the down wind side.

Dawson dropped behind a screen of brush and swept the camp with hard eyes. Catt and the boy settled in next to him. To keep off the rain, several hide lean-tos had been set up close to the fire where fresh meat of some kind was being roasted on green sticks. Several Indians sat cross-legged before the sputtering fire, passing a bottle back and forth between themselves while two more wrestled with a woman beneath one of the elk skin lean-tos. The woman was struggling with all her might, yet Dawson could see the drunken Indians were gaining the upper hand. Those by the fire shouted words of encouragement and laughed loudly, knowing their turn would come soon.

Dawson's angry eyes found the motionless figure of Tall Feather across the fire from the others. Beside him sat a young girl with golden hair, her head bowed, rocking back and forth with her hands over her ears as if trying to shut out the other woman's screams. It looked as though Tall Feather had saved this young one for himself. He, too, was drinking, yet Dawson knew the wary Indian would never allow himself to become drunk. Very soon the woman beside him would suffer the same fate as the other, if he, Catt, and Liny didn't put an end to it now.

Jack Dawson shifted his eyes to the struggling woman, hearing her clothes being ripped from her. He saw her nakedness, her exposed breasts, heavy and fish belly white in the glow of the campfire. Now was the time to move while the Indians were preoccupied.

Dawson motioned for Catt and the boy to stay put, and over Catt's protests, slipped quietly away through the underbrush without making the slightest sound.

"Moves like a varmint," Catt whispered to the boy whose eyes were glued on the woman now pinned beneath a big Indian who fumbled with his breechcloth. Two Indians held her arms flat against the ground. It made him think of Iris Kelsey whom he had seen one day bathing down at the river. Even though she was a whore, Linny had been ashamed, yet a little excited, at seeing her nakedness, her rose tipped breasts and the dark patch between her legs. The image was forever burned in his brain. And now, he saw that same nakedness once again, except this time he was enraged by the violent sight. Linny brought his rifle up to shoot the Indian but Josiah Catt touched his arm, indicating he should wait a few seconds longer.

Dawson circled the fire until he was directly behind the lean-to where Tall Feather sat with the rocking woman who appeared to be in shock. He had to act fast now or the other woman . . . .

Jack Dawson stepped quickly away from the surrounding brush and in two long strides was beside the surprised In-

124

dian, his Colt aimed at Tall Feather's head. The Indian did not flinch as Dawson spoke to him in Cheyenne.

"Tell the others to stop or you die with your next breath." Dawson's command had been spoken softly, yet there was steel in his voice.

Tall Feather cocked his head slightly to see who was holding the gun and a flicker of recognition crossed his black eyes. He knew the white man who stood there would not speak again before he fired and Tall Feather shouted quickly at the men across the fire. In the heat of passion, the Indian with his breechcloth pushed aside did not heed Tall Feather's command as he began his descent into the woman. A roar of yellow flame licked out of the night and the naked Indian was slammed against the side of the lean-to by a big bullet. Linny Eaton would wait no longer.

The other Indians froze. Still having the presence of mind to free herself, Mary Stiles jerked her hands free of the two Indians holding her while they stared at the bloody back of their dead companion. Grabbing up her torn clothes, she tried to cover herself as best she could.

Suddenly one of the Indians came to his senses and leaped at her with his knife drawn. A deep roar thundered from the brush again as Josiah Catt fired the big Sharps. The Indian was blown backward like a charging animal tethered on a short rope. Bright gouts of blood pumped out of the Indian from a gaping wound.

"Melissa!" Mary Stiles screamed after seeing Dawson standing there with his gun at the head of the big Indian. Melissa stopped her rocking, raised her eyes to her mother who was edging away from the fire, and jumped up quickly, looking around at Dawson standing there.

"Step over there with the other woman, miss," Jack Dawson said quietly. Melissa didn't bother to walk, she ran to her mother who hugged her close.

"Over here, ma'am," Josiah Catt whispered just loud enough for them to hear. The older woman looked over at Dawson who nodded his head, indicating they should leave.

125

Still holding tightly to her daughter, Mary Stiles guided them into the shadows.

"I thought the Blackfeet had taken your miserable life three winters ago," Tall Feather said calmly.

"Not a chance. They are too much like the Cheyenne, little boys with weapons they do not know how to use," Dawson said tauntingly to the big Indian.

"You will soon know that the Cheyenne are not little children, Jack Dawson, when I cut your heart out and show it to you while it still beats. Then I will cook and eat it."

"I've been threatened before, Tall Feather," Dawson said, keeping his eyes on those around the fire. "I should kill you now for what you've done back there at Potter's Settlement and to those poor women. You try following us, I will."

"Like you, many have tried to count coup against me and their bones lie bleaching in the sun . . . and so will yours, Jack Dawson. Many have tried to dishonor me by touching me with a war club and racing away. They have failed."

"Maybe, but it's going to take better men than a bunch of misplaced Digger Indians from Texas to bring it about," Dawson said, reaching down and taking the Henry rifle that lay beside Tall Feather's side. The big Indian tensed, stung by the reference to the Red River Diggers who lived closer to a coyote than a man.

"Go ahead, try me," Dawson said softly.

"There will be another time, this I promise," Tall Feather said. One of the Indians by the fire picked up his lance as if trying to decide whether to attack Dawson. Tall Feather held up his hand to stop the drunken Indian, knowing full well Dawson would not hesitate to kill him now.

"If you follow us, I promise it will be the last trail you take." Dawson reached out with the barrel of the Henry and touched Tall Feather on the shoulder, knowing how it would incense the renegade Indian to have a white man count coup. Just as suddenly as he appeared, Dawson was gone.

Tall Feather did not move from his place. He sat there,

furious, for having lost the many shots rifle and then having to endure a white man's insulting coup. Those by the fire howled their protest, jumping up and running back and forth, first to check their dead comrades and then over to Tall Feather who sat unmoving.

"Why did you not let us kill this white man?" Black Grasshopper said, seething with fury. "He has even taken the gun that shines like the sun from you."

Slowly, Tall Feather rose from the ground to his full height. He looked around at the others, counting only six.

"You do not know this white man," Tall Feather replied, his voice dark with rage. "He is a great warrior and knows the ways of many tribes. This white man, Jack Dawson, took Red Deer's life five summers ago. He is not afraid to travel alone." Red Deer was a great war chief who had gone out to raid an emigrant wagon train along the Platte that Dawson had been guiding. It was Jack Dawson who had followed them back to camp and knifed Red Deer while the others slept, leaving his knife on the dead Indian's chest as evidence that a white man had done this thing. The Cheyenne were impressed enough, they returned to their village that same day.

Some of the fire left Black Grasshopper at the mention of Red Deer. No white man he knew ever displayed enough courage to ride into an armed camp of fifty Cheyenne warriors and kill their leader.

"Still, this white man is responsible for Short Grass and Otter Back's death," Black Grasshopper said, pointing to the two dead Indians.

Tall Feather looked at the upset warrior with burning eyes, "It is better we only lost two, rather than us all. We will hunt this white man and kill him slowly, this I promise."

"We are ready then," Black Grasshopper shouted, holding aloft his lance.

"Would you track a grizzly at night?" Tall Feather asked. Black Grasshopper hesitated, lowering his lance. He did not understand Tall Feather's statement.

127

"Why do you suddenly speak of bears? We only track white men."

Tall Feather threw his blanket over one of his powerful shoulders. Taking the whiskey bottle he had been drinking from by the neck, he flung it into the rock where it smashed into a thousand pieces.

"You have heard nothing of what I have said," he told Black Grasshopper contemptuously. "It would be better to track a bear with no weapons than to go after this white man at night."

Black Grasshopper who had been a close friend of Otter Back lusted for immediate revenge, but what outraged him more was that none of them had gotten the opportunity to violate the two women.

"I am not afraid," he said coldly, looking Tall Feather squarely in the eyes.

Tall Feather pointed into the darkness, "Then go, but you will have to walk, for Dawson has taken our horses." Black Grasshopper and the others were startled. He saw the doubt on their faces.

"Go on, look for yourselves. This white man will take horses for the women and scatter the rest for that is what I would do." Black Grasshopper stepped into the darkness and was gone for a few minutes. He reappeared, holding the lance low at his side and he did not look at Tall Feather again.

"We will wait until light and track our horses. Once we have them again, we will hunt down this white man and end his life and those with him. The women you can take immediately." After he had finished speaking, Tall Feather turned to his blankets beneath the lean-to and fell asleep.

Black Grasshopper and the others huddled around the fire, eating the half-burned meat and drinking the last of the raw whiskey in silence. There would be no further celebrating until this white man was staked to the ground with flames licking at his crotch.

Chapter 14

Dawson didn't call a halt until they were four hours away from the forks of the Arikaree River where Tall Feather had his camp. After he had scattered the Cheyenne's horses, Dawson cut straight west across dry country, electing the shortest possible route to Denver City and to spare the two women further suffering.

While Josiah Catt built a small fire and made coffee and fried meat for the hungry women, Jack Dawson and Linny Eaton tended to the horses, giving them a good rubdown following the hard ride.

Catt came over to watch them work while the women ate their real first meal in days. He had his pipe going as he came up shaking his head.

"Them women's been through Hell," he said to Dawson. Jack glanced at them, huddled beneath a blanket before the fire, eating.

"Not half the suffering they would have, had we not come along when we did."

Linny Eaton put to words what he had been thinking since they rode away from the Arikaree. "Do you think they'll follow us?"

Josiah Catt chuckled, "Tall Feather's got no choice, son. Not after the way ol' Jack humiliated him in front of his braves."

Linny looked puzzled, "What do you mean, humiliated? You mean the way we snuck up on his camp thataway?"

"Aww, Hell, no. Didn't you see Jack touch that big Injun with the tip of his rifle? That's big medicine to an Indian. For Tall Feather, that means one or the other of them's got to die next time they meet."

Linny turned to Dawson who was wiping the big buckskin down with a piece of cloth. "That true, Mr. Dawson?"

"Don't have to be that way. But I expect Tall Feather's pride won't let him rest until he gets satisfaction."

"Then why did you do it? I mean touching him that way?"

"It's called counting coup," Dawson said, finishing up. "It's when an Indian touches the enemy during battle with a war club or just a plain stick and then races away. It shows the others in his band how brave he is. It also moves him up in rank a notch or two, depending on the number of times he does it."

"Still makes no sense," Linny said.

"I counted coup against that Indian with his own weapon. Now to Tall Feather, it can't get any worse than that. I shamed him, there's no doubt."

"Shouldn't you have just killed him instead?" Linny asked matter-of-factly.

"Boy's got a point, Jack," Catt spoke up.

"Yeah, well, I could use a cup of hot coffee." Catt and the boy watched as Dawson approached the fire and poured himself a cup and moved back inside the shadows after speaking to the two women.

"You could do worse, learning from him," Josiah Catt said to Linny as they walked slowly back to the fire. Catt squatted down and helped himself to coffee.

"I want to thank you Mr. Catt for . . . for shooting that Indian off—" Mary Stiles could not finish the sentence.

"You can thank Linny here, ma'am. He's the one done it. I kilt the other one with the knife."

Mary Stiles turned her pain-filled eyes on the boy whose face reddened clear up to his ears.

"Thank you both, and you, as well, Mr. Dawson," Mary Stiles said. As yet, Melissa Stiles had not spoken since leav-

130

ing the camp and Dawson was afraid there may be some lasting effects from being held by Indians.

"Heck, ma'am, we was glad to do it. Only wished we coulda come along sooner," Catt said.

"We were so afraid they had killed you," Mary said.

Josiah Catt grinned through his whiskers, "Came almighty close. Hadn't been fer my old Sharps, expect I wouldn't be here now . . . and for Jack Dawson who found me wandering across the prairie like a dried out lizard." Both women looked at Dawson in the shadows. Even in their pain, their eyes reminded him of gentle deer.

Dawson cleared his throat and told the women how he came upon the burned wagon and their dead relatives.

"I buried them decent," he added at the end.

"I'm so grateful for that, Mr. Dawson," Mary said. "I couldn't bear the thought of poor little Jonathan lying there exposed to God knows what." Melissa was openly weeping now and the men turned their heads, giving them as much privacy as was possible in their personal grief.

Later, Dawson told the women to try and sleep for a few hours, he wanted to be under way again by daylight.

"Where are you taking us?" Mary asked.

"Nearest place is Denver," Dawson said. "You can catch the stage back east from there."

"I see," was all Mary Stiles said, gathering the blanket around her. Dawson hesitated.

"Ma'am, if you wouldn't mind, I got an extra pair of pants and shirt in my pack you could use."

Mary Stiles gave him a waning smile, "I would be ever so grateful, Mr. Dawson."

"Call me Jack, ma'am," Dawson replied, getting up to retrieve the clothes. He came back and knelt down in front of the woman and handed her the clothes. As he started to get up, a slim hand shot out from beneath the blanket and gripped his arm. Dawson found himself looking into Melissa's face at close range for the first time and he was somewhat startled by her unblemished beauty. He could certainly see why Tall Feather had kept her for himself.

131

"I won't forget all the things you've done for us . . . for my family back there on the trail and for looking out after old Jake. I hope one day we can repay your kindness."

"There's no need . . ." Dawson searched for the right words, "as for the draft horse, he came in mighty handy, just ask Josiah. Mules are made for packing, not riding."

"I'm Melissa Stiles," she said, removing her hand from his arm.

"Jack Dawson. Proud to know you . . . and your mother," Dawson added.

"How come you didn't shoot that horrible Indian for what he did to those poor people?" Melissa asked, her eyes burning once more.

"Hard to explain to folks new to the West," Dawson said slowly. "I'm not denying Tall Feather don't need killing and, given the right circumstances, I wouldn't hesitate."

"But you had him at your mercy, why didn't you shoot him?" Melissa persisted, her voice suddenly hard.

"It was because he was at my mercy, I couldn't. Don't fully expect you to understand, you either ma'am," Dawson said to Mary, "not after what they were trying to do. Tall Feather and I are a lot alike. We both been free most of our lives, go where we want and do as we please. Except the roles are reversed now, Tall Feather's freedom is ending. The white man saw to that with the killing off of the buffalo."

"And are you free, Mr. Dawson?" Mary Stiles asked.

"I was getting to that," Dawson said ruefully. "Normally, I don't talk this much." He smiled at the women. "I grew up in town, constrained by laws and people. Out here in the mountains, I been free for nearly thirty-odd years and will continue to be, while Tall Feather's days are numbered, as all Indians are."

"I think I understand," Mary Stiles replied.

"I still believe you should have shot him while you had the chance," Melissa said, pulling the blanket tightly around her shoulders. "As it is now, we have to worry about him attacking us again."

Dawson tried to reassure the girl with a smile, "Perhaps, you are right, Miss Stiles. Now you both best rest awhile if you can. We got three hard days ahead of us before we reach Denver City." Dawson turned away, carrying with him the hauntingly beautiful face of Melissa Stiles.

By the middle of the next day, Dawson called a rest at the East Fork of Plum Creek where they built a fire and ate their first hot meal since early light. The butternut pants Dawson had given Mary Stiles fit her loosely yet the checked shirt strained to contain the woman's chest. Since last night, Mary Stiles appeared to have regained her confidence and was in complete control of her emotions once again.

Melissa Stiles came down to the small creek and washed her face and hands in the shallow water while Dawson stood back, watching her, trying to appear nonchalant about her presence.

Melissa stood up and looked out across the distance at the purple line rising above the horizon. She dried her face with the corner of her skirt and looked at Dawson with frank, open eyes.

"Are those clouds I see in the distance?"

Dawson shifted his gaze from her face to the ragged chain sweeping up from south to north in the distance.

"Those are the Rocky Mountains. Must be seventy, eighty miles away."

With renewed interest, Melissa Stiles shaded her eyes from the brilliant sun and scanned the long line of dark shapes once more.

"They don't seem to be very high," she finally commented.

Dawson chuckled, "That's because of the distance. Just wait until this time tomorrow. You'll notice a difference, believe me. They're high all right."

Melissa looked back at Dawson and a sadness filled her eyes. "My father used to tell Jonathan and me stories about the Rocky Mountains and how one day we would all be rich, that the mountains were full of gold, just for the taking. I sometimes would fall asleep thinking of the gleaming bands of gold flowing down their sides just waiting to be scooped up."

Dawson shifted his feet and looked down at the toes of his boots, trying to choose his next words carefully. He didn't want to shock her further by speaking the truth, yet he didn't want to be labeled a liar later on. In the end he just said what he had to say.

"Most folks have that same notion about the Rockies; you're not alone. That's why we got sixty thousand people working up and down the mountain range right now."

Melissa looked at Dawson keenly, a small smile playing across her unmarked features.

"In other words, I might be more than a little disappointed when I see them up close?"

"Not at all. The Rockies are impressive. I never tire looking at them. It's beautiful country full of game, secluded valleys and mountain streams like nothing you've ever seen before. Country that's once in the blood, you can't ever wash out again." Dawson grinned at her sheepishly.

"But no gold?" Melissa prompted.

"Oh, there's plenty of that, too. Least that's what I hear. I've trapped that country for twenty years and seen plenty of color in creeks and such, but it never interested me very much."

Melissa straightened to her full height and taking a deep breath said, "I guess then I'll just have to see for myself, won't I?"

"You folks aren't headed back East?"

"Possibly, but not right away. I have to see this dream through . . . for my father. I've got to know that he and little Jonathan didn't die in vain."

To Dawson this line of thinking reflected a maturity that went way beyond a person of her age.

"If I can be of help all you got to do is ask," Dawson found himself saying and for a moment he was flustered by his admitted statement.

"Thank you, Mr. Dawson, that's very kind and I'll keep that in mind."

134

"Please, call me Jack." He held her with his eyes for a long moment.

"Jack it is then," Melissa said softly. "I like that name. And do call me Melissa, ma'am sounds like you are addressing my mother." She gave a little laugh, bringing her hand to her face.

Dawson grinned, not knowing what else to add, and brought her horse over for her to mount.

"We best get going. Like to make Beaver Creek before dark. By now, Tall Feather and his bunch have rounded up their mounts and are pushing hard after us." He held Melissa's arm while she mounted the chestnut that once belonged to a Potter's Settlement resident. Melissa looked down at him with renewed fear in her eyes.

"Will they catch up to us?"

Dawson handed her the reins and patted the neck of the horse.

"Anything's possible. But Tall Feather knows who he's up against. We'll stay alert, no matter."

Dawson got them straightened out once more after they crossed Plum Creek. Linny brought up the rear behind Mary Stiles with Dawson leading the way. Josiah Catt rode flank from time to time.

Catt pulled in beside Jack Dawson and tossed him a whiskered grin. He bit off a chew of tobacco and held it out to Dawson who shook his head.

"What's eating you, old man?" Dawson asked.

"She's a real looker."

"Who?"

"Hah. Who do you think I mean? That young gal you fawning over."

"Wasn't fawning over her," Dawson said, slightly irritated it had been so obvious to the rest. "Just offering any help she or her mother might need once we reach Denver City."

"Mighty upstanding of you. Count me in as well."

Dawson looked at the grizzled-faced prospector. "What you got up your sleeve?"

"Nary a thing and then maybe I do," Catt replied cryptically.

"Mary Stiles?" Dawson asked, looking closely at Catt.

"I allow she's a fine mature woman, don't you think? How old you reckon she is? Forty-five, fifty?"

Dawson laughed. "More like fifty-five or sixty, I'd say."

Catt nodded, spitting a large glob of tobacco juice into the dust. "The way I figger it too, but she holds her shape mighty well and ain't a wrinkle on her purty face."

"Josiah Catt, I don't believe you. That poor woman's just lost her husband and son, she's not the slightest bit interested in your old carcass."

It was Catt's turn to laugh. "Ain't admittin' she is, but a man's got to make his move, take advantage of the situation so to speak. Hell, Jack, you know how it is out here. Women like her and that young gal, Melissa, ain't gonna last long in Denver City without every man making a fool of himself. Besides, didn't see no buffalo gnats sticking to you, way you was carrying on with her daughter."

"Wasn't carrying on, dang it. You best ride back aways and check our trail. Don't want Tall Feather and his men giving us any surprises," Dawson said, hoping to rid himself of the old prospector.

"I'll take a look, but you and me both know, Tall Feather ain't nowheres around . . . leastwise not yet." Josiah Catt laughed at Dawson's obvious discomfort and reined around.

"I swear, that old man . . ." Dawson muttered aloud to his horse who merely flicked his ears at Dawson. How old was Melissa anyway . . . eighteen, twenty? Here he was pushing forty and with nothing more to offer a woman than a cracked skull and a changing of clothes. She deserved better, a lot better. Jenny Logan was more to his style and liking. There was no pretending with her or a need to be somebody he wasn't. Jenny let things be, a man could grow naturally, unlike some women who went to work on changing a man once they thought he was hooked. But as Dawson continued across the broken country, it was Melissa Stiles that occupied his thoughts, not Jenny Logan.

In a dark thin-striped suit, A.C. Ford cut quite a figure of respectability around Denver City and what's more he knew it. With dark features and black hair that curled stylishly down the back of his neck and clean-shaven face, bachelor Ford had the picking of the girls in Denver. No matter they were prostitutes. He was more than satisfied to lavish his attentions on a select few down at Ada Lamont's place, like the one he was now bedding on Fifth Street. Fact is, he had been with the dark-eyed madam on several occasions, but Ada favored the gambler, Charlie Harrison, who had recently arrived in town. It didn't matter to Ford, there were plenty others more than willing to help spend his money.

"Will I see you tonight?" Sarah Jane Vailes asked from the rumpled bed.

A.C. Ford stood before a mirror adjusting the tie at his throat. He spoke without looking around.

"I'm playing poker tonight. Expect I'll sleep over at the office since it will be rather late. You know how those boys are at keeping a card game going."

"I don't care how late you come in, honey. You know how soundly I sleep. You won't disturb me. I just like to wake up in the mornings and find you here beside me," Sarah Jane's voice had grown husky and provocative.

Ford cast a sideways glance at the woman saying, "Sarah Jane, you sure it ain't something else you like waking up to?"

The woman yawned and stretched beneath the thin sheet, and Ford could see the clear outline of her full breasts rise and fall in the process.

Sarah Jane grinned and deliberately inched the sheet down over one full breast. "I like waking up to that, too, A.C., but I'm being serious. I just like you here in the mornings."

Ford knew he was being toyed with and he loved every

minute. "Like you're being serious now, looking like that."

"A woman plays the cards she's dealt," Sarah Jane said sweetly.

"Don't I know that," Ford said, coming over to the bed and giving her a peck on the lips. She caught his face in both her hands and kissed him deeply then released him.

"That's so you won't forget."

"Not likely to," Ford said thickly, turning to leave. He paused at he door and looked back at the woman who had snuggled beneath the sheets once more. "See you later tonight." He stepped through the door and closed it behind him. At once, his mind shifted from the woman to the business of the day as he started across the street for his usual breakfast.

Colin Jackson found him there eating. The gunman wasted no time in asking Ford what was on his mind.

"How did the others take it?"

Ford laid aside his morning paper and began eating after this food was set before him.

"Sure you wouldn't care for something?"

"Ate already. You late getting to it."

Ford gave him a knowing smile, "Had a good reason."

"What did they say?" the gunman asked, not interested in Ford's latest love affair which was known to everybody.

"You kinda testy this morning, Colin. We met again last night as you know," Ford said, leaning across the table and lowering his voice at the same time. Since the majority of Denver City's populace had already eaten, the restaurant was empty except for two miners who occupied a table near the door and out of earshot range.

"I must say, Bradley's death was a shock to some of them. It's the kind of thing we don't need. Forces some of us to, ah, take some sort of action."

"What kind of action?" the gunman asked, his voice growing cold.

"As you know, certain members of the secret committee are sworn to uphold the law. They have to investigate Bradley's death. The people of Denver City demand it. Once it's known that Bradley was killed by horse rustlers, there'll be more public outcries for the law to bring the killers to justice."

"Bradley's death was forced on Black Hawk. Hell, Whit Coleman died in the shoot-out." Ford gave the gunman a thin smile as he scooped up the last bit of runny eggs from his plate with his spoon.

"Decent citizens of Denver City are not going to cry over one dead horse thief and you know it."

"Well, it don't matter a damn anyway, we're through with that," Colin Jackson said, waving his hand about in the air. "You can get Jim Latt and his boys to keep it going if you want, but we're through." He took a leather pouch from his coat pocket and dropped it before Ford's plate.

"What's that?" Ford said, picking up the heavy rawhide bag.

The gunman smiled, "It's your share . . . so far."

"From the horses?" Ford whispered, leaning forward again.

"From our new enterprise," Jackson said with a hawkish smile.

"You've found a claim already?" Ford's eyes went wide.

"Didn't see the need to announce it in the papers," the gunman said casually. "Course, this ain't to be shared with the other committee members. With us out of the horse stealing business, they won't be expecting any more money for a while, unless like I said Latt is interested and I suspect he is."

"Latt is more than willing and you know it. Where's Black Hawk now?" Ford asked, plainly worried.

"Relax, counselor, Black Hawk's back at the claim, riding herd on production."

Ford's eyes grew furtive. "Is it a good claim?" he whispered, slipping the leather pouch into his suit pocket without opening it.

"You got three thousand in nuggets in that bag for your share. The rest me and Black Hawk split after paying Cove and them other two we hired to work the claim." Colin fished in his pocket for a piece of paper and shoved it across the table to Ford whose eyes were shiny with excitement.

"For your part, want you to file this claim with the land office in a few days. No one will suspect you. You can even say you took the claim from a couple miners who owed you for legal services."

Ford picked up the scrap of paper and read the land descriptions Colin had written out before shoving this in his coat pocket as well. "Never heard of this place."

"You might say we picked an isolated spot and struck pay dirt." Colin Jackson stood up. "Ain't another soul on this drainage system."

"There will be soon's I file on it. People can smell gold."

"Let'em. We ain't there to work every nook and cranny. Fact is, we could ride away now and be way ahead of the game. Once the color starts to fade, me and Black Hawk will have lined up another claim someplace else that's real private."

Attorney Ford stood up and picked up his derby hat. "I like it," he said, following the gunman out into the bright sunshine.

"Figured you would," Colin said. "Now if you will excuse me, I got business down at the Cibola."

"Always looking for a game, eh, Colin?"

"Keeps me from getting bored and you know how I get when things get boring for me."

Ford stood in the middle of the busy street, unmindful of the lumbering oar wagons rumbling by, dropping a fine layer of gray dust on his clean suit. Right now, Ford didn't care if he was splashed with mud, he was walking on air as he folded the newspaper, tucked it beneath one arm, and headed off down the street to his office.

Chapter 15

"Never woulda figgered it," Josiah Catt said as they eased their horses across Boxelder Creek, now flowing strong with the spring rains that shifted down from the seemingly impenetrable wall of high country, rising up in the distance less than a days ride west. Pikes Peak shouldered its massive snowy head above the chain of mountains, standing there like a beacon to trail-weary emigrants, fresh from the hot Plains.

"Figured what?" Dawson said, his eyes on the women as they forded the rippling waters. Bringing up the rear, Linny Eaton kept a careful eye on them as well. Dawson hadn't failed to notice how the boy was attentive around Mary and Melissa Stiles, fetching their horses in the morning and laying out their bedding at night. Dawson also noticed Mary Stiles had taken to Linny as well. Maybe she was trying to fill the void created by the death of her own son, Dawson didn't know. Whatever it was, their shared grief drew them close and he figured that was good for them both.

"Tall Feather. Figgered he woulda come up on us by now, sore as he is."

"To tell you the truth, I keep expecting him to thunder up in full war paint any minute myself."

Josiah Catt's eyes twinkled, "Don't suppose it was our prowess kept him off our backs?"

"Against two men and a half-grown boy? Tall Feather

will pick a time best for him and now we can almost see Denver City, expect it better be soon."

"You're right about that renegade. Tall Feather ain't likely to give up easy, not after what you did to him."

They climbed out of the bottoms, away from Boxelder Creek, and topped out on a gently rising plain that collided in the distance with the beginning foothills. The view of the Rocky Mountains as breathtaking and even Dawson found himself drinking in its beauty.

"Oh my, you weren't exaggerating, were you?" Melissa said, reining up beside Dawson, her eyes fixed on the line of jagged mountains that cut across the Plains as far as the eye could see.

"It's a pleasant sight for sure," Dawson said, "and I guess I've seen this view a thousand times and still it takes my breath away."

"If only my father could see this," she said wistfully. "That's all he talked about, how he couldn't wait to see these mountains."

"I'm sure he would be happy to know you are here to enjoy them in his place."

Melissa turned her beautiful eyes on Dawson, "Thank you for caring. My mother and I will never be able to repay your kindness."

"No need to try. It was the least I . . . me and Josiah could do, and Linny," Dawson added as an afterthought.

"You could have kept riding west. No one could have blamed you for not facing that many Indians."

Dawson grew flustered and he removed his hat to wipe away the thin line of sweat from his forehead.

"Anybody would have done the same," he said lightly, putting his hat back on his head and giving Melissa a self-conscious grin.

Melissa studied his face for a moment, "I don't believe you, Jack Dawson. We think you're real special."

Linny Eaton came riding up at that moment cutting off any response Dawson may have had.

"Mr. Dawson, better come quick! I saw some riders a

142

mile back on our trail!" The boy's face was flushed and his eyes fairly danced with excitement.

"Ride out and tell Josiah and then you stay here with the women," Dawson said, reaching for his rifle while reining his horse around. "You hear shooting, take the women down to those bushes along the creek and stay there."

"Be careful," Melissa called after Dawson as he sank his spurs into the flanks of the big buckskin. The horse crossed the waters of Boxelder Creek at full gallop, barely slowing down. A few powerful strides and the horse was out on dry land and running at top speed again.

Melissa and Linny watched Dawson fade from view over a gentle rise. Mary Stiles came up, her face an expression of concern.

"Where was Jack going in such a hurry? Are there Indians near?"

"No, ma'am," Linny said, "least they weren't dressed like Indians. I best go fetch Josiah." The boy kicked his horse in the ribs and raced away.

"Well, whoever they are, we'll be ready this time," Mary said, her voice hard and determined. She removed the shiny new Henry from the saddle scabbard and jacked a shell into the chamber. When Dawson realized the gun had belonged to her dead husband, and not Tall Feather, he presented her with the weapon their second night on the trail. Mary could only hug Dawson back, too moved to speak.

"Mother, can you shoot that gun? Father never took the time to teach us."

"Nothing like learning under pressure. Besides, I'll not let us be taken captive again . . . by Indian or white."

In a few minutes, Linny and Josiah came charging up in a cloud of dust. The boy drew rein but Josiah Catt streaked past them, bent low over the saddle with his big Sharps held out from him in one hand.

"Josiah rides like he was born to it," Linny said appreciatively.

"So does Jack," Melissa added. Mary gave her daughter a curious look, but said nothing.

Jack Dawson approached the crest of the low ridge with caution and finally dismounted and slipped the rest of the way on foot, leaving the buckskin ground hitched. He heard the riders coming and flattened himself out on the ground, inching forward until he could see over the crest.

Dawson studied the five men now less than a mile out and closing at a steady clip. Dawson allowed himself to relax a little now that he knew it wasn't Tall Feather and his bunch. He saw their rifles flashing in the sun and knew they were well armed. From what direction had they come? The Smoky Hill or Republican? Dawson heard a horse approaching from the rear and knew it had to be Catt. In a minute or two, Josiah Catt slipped up beside Dawson.

"What we facing?" Josiah asked squinting his eyes against the sun as he studied the dust cloud.

"Don't yet know. Could be anybody, hide hunters, prospectors or—"

"Or cutthroats," Catt added.

"Linny stay with the women like I asked?"

Catt nodded and cocked the big bore rifle, "How you want to handle it?"

"Straight on and standing up," Dawson replied, rising from the ground while the riders were still a quarter mile away. Catt got to his feet as well, his Sharps held at the ready. It was then they heard the crack of the Henry followed by the unmistakable, dull boom of Linny Eaton's big rifle. Both Dawson and Catt froze for an instant. There was no time for words. Catt jumped for his horse while Dawson sprinted the few yards back down the slope where he had left his horse. Catt flashed by spurring his horse and Dawson cursed savagely as he hit the saddle and jerked the reins, bringing the buckskin around. He quickly closed the gap between himself and Catt. As he drew abreast, he heard the Indians yelling in the distance.

Damn! Tall Feather had played his hand well, waiting until the group was divided to make his move. This thought

144

flashed through Dawson's mind as he plunged ahead of Catt. The creek was coming up quickly and without warning a painted face suddenly appeared on his left, riding up from the bottom. Letting go of the reins, Dawson raised his rifle and fired quickly, but missed as the Indian ducked low over his horse and disappeared into the thick growth along the creek.

The Henry kept up a steady crackle of fire now and Dawson saw painted bodies moving swiftly among the trees along the other side of the creek. A riderless horse, with reins trailing, bolted from the brush. Dawson recognized it as belonging to Mary Stiles.

When Dawson got to the edge of the creek, he dropped his single-shot rifle and pulled the big dragoon from its holster and plunged into the water. The air was filled with yelping Indians and gunshots. Behind him, Dawson heard Catt ride up to the creek and stop. A second later his Sharps spoke and an Indian toppled into the water in front of Dawson. Another Indian, Dawson recognized from the campfire the night the women were rescued, charged out of the brush at him with his lance raised over his head.

Dawson shot the Indian from his horse as he climbed out on the bank and dismounted. In the thick of things now, the underbrush seemed to be filled with screaming Indians. Somewhere up ahead a woman screamed and Dawson plunged into the thick growth, unmindful of Indians and the noise he was making.

A shadowy figure came at him through the dense green and Dawson barely had time to block the downward swipe of a knife blade before shooting the attacker at point-blank range in the chest. The Indian screamed and stumbled backward, blood splattering the leaves around him. Dawson forged ahead, wondering if others had joined Tall Feather's band, and how many.

The Henry exploded almost in his face and Dawson ducked, realizing he could easily be mistaken for an Indian moving through thick brush.

"Linny, Mary? Are you okay?" Dawson called. Dawson

145

felt the rush of air as an arrow embedded itself in a tree near his head. Dawson shot instinctively, without thinking and heard a low grunt as the big slug found its mark. Something thrashed around in the leaves for a minute and then stopped.

Linny's voice called to him through the dense woods and Dawson responded. Suddenly the air grew silent and still. Dawson took more care now and worked his way toward the boy's voice without making a sound.

He peered through an opening in the leaves and saw the two women and Linny huddled near the base of an ancient cottonwood, among its exposed thick roots. Protected by the tangle of roots, the Indians had but one way to attack the small group and that was head on. Two warriors lay sprawled several feet away, mute testimony to the folly of a frontal attack.

"It's me, hold your fire, I'm coming out," Dawson shouted at the besieged group. He stepped silently into the clearing.

"Be careful, Jack," Mary Stiles warned. "There's at least two more." Melissa screamed, bringing her hands to her throat as a dark object hit Dawson at full speed. Dawson barely had time to crouch down before being bowled over by a big Indian.

Filtered sunlight caught the descent of a knife blade, warning Dawson an instant before he felt the slashing burn on his cheek as he tried to roll free of the body, pinning him to the ground. The Indian raised his knife once more and Dawson brought his knee up swiftly and flipped the Indian over his head.

Dawson scrambled to his feet, turning to face the Indian and found himself staring into the dark eyes of Tall Feather who was crouching for another lunge. Having lost his Colt in the struggle, Dawson reached down and grabbed the big knife he carried strapped to his lower leg. Tall Feather hesitated a moment.

Dawson began circling to his left, his knife out from his body, his eyes glued to Tall Feather.

146

"Unlike the great warrior, Red Deer, I will not honor you by leaving my knife between your ribs," Dawson spoke softly in Cheyenne.

Tall Feather worked his knife back and forth between his big hands, his black eyes narrowed in their purpose.

"It is you who will die here today, Jack Dawson," Tall Feather said, low and threatening.

"I can shoot him, Jack!" Linny called, his rifle tracing the Indian's movement in the air.

"No! This is between us. Been a long time coming," Dawson said to the boy. Out of the corner of his eyes he saw Josiah Catt step into the small clearing with his Sharps ready. Dawson reached up and wiped the trickle of blood from his cheek.

Tall Feather lunged at Dawson and was nicked on the arm by Dawson's razor-sharp knife as he sidestepped the Indian and moved back in. The Indian turned to meet the attack and both men grappled, straining for an advantage, each knife arm locked in a steel fist.

Dawson faded backward, bringing Tall Feather with him. The Indian lost his balance and crashed heavily into Dawson, sending them both to the ground. They thrashed around, first with Dawson on top and then Tall Feather. The stink of the Indian filled Dawson's nostrils, their eyes just inches apart.

This time it was Tall Feather who flipped Dawson over his head and regained his feet, catlike. He rushed Dawson who was still on his knees, slashing downward with his knife as he did so. Somewhere behind him, Dawson heard Mary or Melissa scream as he blocked the Indian's knife arm with one hand while burying his own knife in Tall Feather's broad chest.

Tall Feather gasped, his eyes flaring wide in surprise. He had been so sure of the kill a second before. He stabbed feebly with his knife, last desperate attempts that were ineffective as his great body sagged against the kneeling Dawson.

Dawson withdrew his knife and pushed the dying Indian

aside. Tall Feather rolled over on the ground and lay staring up through the trees at the dappled sunlight now fading to black.

Both women rushed to Dawson's side while Catt stepped over to Tall Feather and relieved him of his knife.

"Are you okay, Jack?" Mary said, touching his face where Tall Feather's knife had left an angry trail of red.

"I'm fine . . . just need to get my breath."

"Tall Feather's dead," Catt said matter-of-factly.

"Good!" Melissa added.

"Are there anymore?" Dawson asked.

"Only one," Catt grinned, "but he ain't ever going to see his squaw again."

Dawson closed his eyes and sat back on the ground, totally exhausted by the ordeal. The powerful Indian would have been more than a match for anybody.

They heard a man shout from the opposite side of the creek and Catt slipped through the trees to have a look, taking the boy with him.

"Looks like the Henry came in handy," Dawson said.

"Linny killed the first one and I shot the other," Mary said simply. Dawson looked at the woman. She was learning.

They heard voices and the movement of horses through the woods. Dawson found his Colt and Melissa handed him his hat. Her eyes were bright and dancing and he wondered what she was thinking.

Catt came up leading his horse and five men who looked around at the dead Indians with open curiosity.

"Sent Linny across the creek for your rifle," Catt said to Dawson who nodded his head. He looked up at the white men, noting their homespun clothes and sorry equipment. He pegged them immediately as more hopeful miners, nothing else.

"Howdy. Name's Walter Dumont . . . appears you've had a little trouble, friend."

"Nothing we couldn't handle," Dawson said, remaining watchful.

"Yes, I can see that," Dumont replied.

"Jack Dawson. This old coot is Josiah Catt, case he hasn't said." Dawson reached up and took Dumont's outstretched hand. "These ladies are Mary Stiles and her daughter, Melissa."

"Ladies," Dumont said, tipping his hat.

"You boys headed fer Denver City?" Catt asked, running a careful eye over the group.

"That we are," Dumont said, his eyes clouded with concern.

"By way of Smoky Hill or Republican?" Dawson asked. Walter Dumont looked sharply at Dawson.

"Republican, why? Should we have taken the Smoky Hill Trail?"

"Both can be tough going early spring," Dawson said. "Then you came by Potter's Settlement?"

There was that sharp look from Dumont again, Dawson noted. Were they hiding something?

"We did," Dumont finally replied.

"Then you must know Potter's no longer a settlement," Dawson remarked.

"You seen it too?" Dumont asked, the air rushing from his lungs. Dawson nodded. "Mr. Dawson, don't mind telling you, me and the boys been kinda skittish since we rode through there. Ain't nothing alive back there but a few coyotes slipping around the empty buildings. Saw some fresh graves."

"We did the burying," Dawson said.

"You know what happened back there?" Dumont asked.

Dawson pointed to Tall Feather. "It was his bunch who did it." And then he went on to explain what had happened to Mary and Melissa Stiles after their capture. Walter Dumont shook his head over their tragedies.

"My, my, we sure sorry to hear about your menfolk, Mrs. Stiles," Dumont responded. Mary Stiles murmured her thanks. Dumont turned to Dawson.

"You taking the women on to Denver City?"

"No other place to take them case you ain't noticed," Catt spoke up.

"How come you boys aren't traveling with a wagon train?" Dawson asked, knowing green men and wild country didn't usually mix with trouble stirring them together.

"We were. You're the first people we seen since leaving the train."

"Why'd you leave?" Dawson asked.

"Cholera. Figured we'd take our chances on our own. Glad now we did. Mr. Dawson, we'd be pleased to ride on to Denver City with you if you don't object."

"You're welcome to, but it's going to be a short ride."

"How do you mean?" Dumont asked.

"We're less than a dozen miles from Denver. For all practical purposes, the trip is over."

Walter Dumont smiled and turned to his men, "Hear that boys, this time tomorrow we'll be panning gold."

Catt smiled ruefully at Dawson as he turned to his saddlebags and reloaded the chambers of his Colt, using paper cartridges of powder which he poured into each hole. Once the lead ball had been rammed home by the lever, Dawson placed a brass cap over the nipple of the chambers he had fired. The whole operation took less than thirty seconds.

"Looks. like you got yourself five more competitors," Dawson said dryly as he reholstered the big dragoon.

"Green pilgrims ain't never a worry," Catt said, as Linny came up leading several horses and carrying Dawson's rifle.

"We best get to riding," Dawson said to the group.

Two hours later they stopped at a small, two-storied log structure, framed by huge cottonwood trees. A corral and two out buildings served as a waystation for the Leavenworth stage. A cheery woman who said her name was Mary Cawker offered them food and a place for the two women to wash up. Linny Eaton gawked openly at Mary Cawker's daughter until he became embarrassed by Josiah Catt ribbing him at every opportunity.

"How far to Denver City, ma'am?" Walter Dumont asked when they sat down to a meal of fried elk steak, hot biscuits, honey, homemade cake and a gallon of hot coffee.

"Four miles. That's why it's called the four mile house," she said laughing. "You boys come West looking for gold, too?"

Walter Dumont gave the woman a sheepish grin and had to finish the mouthful of food before he could answer.

"Yes, ma'am."

Mary Cawker turned to Dawson and Catt, giving them the once over.

"What are the two of you doing running with the likes of these boys? You both ain't seen the East for a spell by the looks of you." Dawson only mentioned finding Mary Stiles's dead husband and their rescue from the Cheyenne.

"You poor things," Mary Cawker said to the Stiles women. "Why don't you rest up here? I know you both must be exhausted. We have plenty of room." Widow Cawker turned to the men, "You boys are invited back Saturday night for the dance we hold upstairs."

"Thank you, ma'am, but we best push on to the diggings," Dumont said wiping melted butter from his chin that dripped from a biscuit he was eating.

"Well, you're all welcome back after you strike it rich, got plenty of good whiskey to celebrate with, and ice cold well water for your horses. Don't forget," she said, moving back to the kitchen for more biscuits and a platter of steak.

"What about you, Linny?" Josiah Catt said, pushing back his plate. "You gonna hang around here fer the dance?"

Linny Eaton sputtered and turned red clear to the top of his head. "Don't have any plans yet, I mean, I ain't really give it much thought."

"Now is the time, boy," Catt grinned, "that's a mighty fine looking filly of Widow Cawker's."

"Dang it, Josiah, I done told you I ain't decided on my next move."

Widow Cawker came out with another heaping plate of food and Dumont and the others tore into the plate of steak like they hadn't eaten in months.

"What was that you were saying?" she asked Catt.

"Oh, nothing," Catt said dryly. "Just Linny here is kinda taken with this place and—"

"Josiah!" Linny blurted out, jumping up and running outside. Catt roared with laughter until Mary Cawker cut him off.

"I could use a boy like that around the place now that the stage has taken to stopping here and all."

Josiah Catt looked surprised, "Well, I'll be danged."

"You'll find Linny a hard worker and as good a man as any at this table the way he stood up to those Indians," Dawson cut in.

"I'll vouch fer that," Catt said.

"Then that's settled if he wants to stay awhile," Mary Cawker said, cutting them each a slice of frosted cake.

"Ma'am, you set the best table I ever stuck my feet under," Catt said, accepting a huge slice of cake from the woman, giving her a wink for emphasis.

"Glad you think so, Mr. Catt, but I'm not interested in another man. One was enough for me."

"Aw, Mizz Cawker, you hurt me to the quick," Catt said, cutting into the cake with his fork. "Jest trying to pay you a compliment is all."

When they rode out a little while later, Linny Eaton stayed behind, trading shy glances with Widow Cawker's daughter.

"Danged if I don't believe Linny's got the best of this deal, all the grub he can hold and the affections of a pretty young thing to boot," Catt said to Dawson.

Two hours later the group watered their horses at Cherry Creek while taking in the sights around them.

Dawson was stunned as was Josiah Catt. Where only empty prairie stood slightly more than a year before, the makings of a town were well underway. The streets of Denver City were a veritable display of madness. Crowds of eager miners, buckskinned individuals, and painted faced ladies rubbed elbows with businessmen in thin-striped dark suits. There seemed to be a fever about the place. The smell of fresh cut spruce and yellow pine lumber was all pervasive. In between mud huts of adobe, stood shiny new yellow buildings, some complete and others still under construction. The ring of hammers and the shouts of carpenters mixed with the lumbering oar wagons that rolled by, leaving a thin layer of gray dust over everything. Along Cherry Creek were rows of tents as far as the eye could see, all shapes and sizes and colors. Across the creek was another section or two that looked to be slightly older, yet nevertheless as impressive as the side they were standing on. Up ahead was a footbridge that spanned Cherry Creek, connecting what was until recently, two towns; Denver and Auraria.

"By grabs, if I hadn't seen it with my own eyes, I'da never believed it," Josiah Catt said with wonderment.

Dawson admitted there was a fever about the place, and he could feel himself being drawn in like every other piker that set a trail-dusty foot in town.

"What we got to do is find the women a decent place to stay," Dawson said to Catt. He asked a man who was sweeping fresh sawdust from a false-fronted building not yet occupied.

"Down Larimer. Third block. You'll find the Broadwell House at the corner of G Street. She's as fine a place as you'll want to stay this side of Chicago."

They parted company with Walter Dumont and the others who inquired of the storekeeper the direction to the diggings and the nearest saloon.

"Them boys ain't gonna find nothing but trouble, they hang in town very long," Josiah Catt said, shaking his head.

"They look old enough to handle whatever comes their way," Dawson said. "Let's get the ladies over to the Broadwell and settled in. Could use a drink myself . . . if you're buying."

"Probably ain't neither one of us can afford a drink in this town, I figger."

They found the imposing two-storied Broadwell House just like the storekeeper had said. The hotel was plush and contained a large dining room to the left of the lobby. Dawson checked them in and paid for a week's lodging over Mary Stiles's protests.

"Is there an attorney in town I might do business with?" Mary Stiles asked the hotel clerk.

"Yes, ma'am, we have several good lawyers. Your best bet is Mr. A.C. Ford. He lives over on Ferry Street and has an office two blocks down across from Hawkins Gun Shop. Just ask anybody, they can point you in the right direction."

"I'll see you to his office," Dawson said as he gave her the key to their room.

"Melissa and I can find it. We won't be a bother to you any longer. As soon as Mr. Ford arranges things, I can repay you for the room. I left some money with my sister back home."

"You don't have to do that."

"Oh, but I insist. We owe you much more than we could ever repay with money. You, too, Mr. Catt."

"Well, until then, I insist you take twenty dollars to live on," Dawson said, pressing the money into Mary Stiles's protesting hand. "Furthermore, Josiah and I ain't about to leave two pretty women alone on the streets of Denver. We'll see you and Melissa over to Mr. Ford's."

Melissa smiled at Dawson and squeezed her mother's arm. "If you insist then, Jack Dawson," Mary Stiles said with warm eyes.

"And it would be our pleasure if you would have dinner with us tonight here in this fine hotel," Josiah Catt said, giving Mary Stiles his best smile.

"That would be nice, and yes we accept," Mary said.

They had no trouble locating Hawkins Gun Shop near the corner of Third and Ferry Street and Ford's clapboard office painted white with green shutters. A sign lettered in black against a background of white hung from a metal hinge near the door. Josiah Catt elected to remain with the horses, and Dawson held open the office door for Mary and Melissa to enter.

A dark-haired man rose from behind a desk piled high

with assorted legal papers and came around to greet them. He was dressed in a black, thin-striped suit, accented by a string tie and a silk handkerchief neatly tucked in his lapel pocket. He exuded quiet confidence matched by a smile from a tanned face exposing dazzling teeth. A.C. Ford was a prominent Denver City attorney, and he carried himself thusly.

"Good day ladies, I am A.C. Ford, may I offer you seats?" Dawson hadn't failed to notice how he suddenly had turned on the charm and ignored Dawson's presence. He took an instant dislike to the lawyer. Mary and Melissa Stiles took seats across from the cluttered desk.

"Guess I'll take my leave now," Dawson said to the two women. "See you for supper at seven o'clock." Ford had taken his seat again and still hadn't acknowledged Dawson.

Mary Stiles looked back at Dawson and nodded her head, "7 P.M. then." Melissa never looked back, her eyes obviously locked on the suave attorney.

Back on the street once more, Dawson and Catt walked their horses down to the nearest saloon which turned out to be Wootton's Western Saloon and Hotel. It was nothing fancy, but it suited them just fine. They tied their horses to the railing. Dawson cast a quick glance back up the street at Ford's office.

"What did you think of Mr. Ford?" Catt said, spitting out the cud of tobacco he had been chewing.

"Not much. Too fancy and slippery-looking to suit me."

"Ain't they all?" Catt said, stepping first into the darkened interior of Wootton's.

Chapter 16

Late afternoon found A.C. Ford, Judge Slaughter, Colin Jackson and D.C. Oakes over a hand of high-stakes poker in the reserved room of Cibola Hall. For the last few hands, Judge William Slaughter had won a sizable pot each time. An Ohioan out of Nebraska, Slaughter had arrived on the banks of Cherry Creek in October of 1858 and brokered real estate until a town was built. Also a lawyer, Slaughter was a delegate to the First Constitutional Convention and presided over the People's Court by virtue of appointment from Governor Steele of Kansas Territory.

"If I didn't know you better, Judge, I'd say you were cheating," A.C. Ford said with an easy laugh.

"Ante up, boys," Judge Slaughter said happily as he raked in a pot worth several hundred dollars. "Looks like lady luck is in my corner and I don't intend to let any of you off lightly tonight."

Ford consulted his gold watch. "I can stay for a couple more hands and that's it."

"Sarah Jane can wait a little longer now that I'm winning," Slaughter said, dealing the cards.

"It's not that. I have an important meeting with a client at seven o'clock."

"If you're having a meeting tonight it's got to involve a woman," Colin Jackson spoke up, lighting a thick cigar.

Ford allowed his white teeth to frame his tanned mouth, "There's always that possibility." He picked up his cards, the smile growing as he looked at the three kings he had been dealt first round.

The paneled door opened quietly and a square-shouldered man entered, wearing a worried expression. A marshal's badge was pinned to his coat.

"Howdy, Tom," Judge Slaughter said, "pull up a chair and you can sit in on the next hand. Gotta warn you though, I'm hot tonight."

"Don't have time for poker," Tom Pollock remarked, coming over to stand next to Ford who looked up at the burly giant quizzically. The normally genial Pollock wore a frown on his heavily bearded face. Pollock, a fearless and enterprising man, started out in Denver City as a carpenter and cabinetmaker which coincided with his interest in undertaking. A jack of all trades, Pollock had tried his hand at horse trading, hotel keeping, farming, and ferry-boating on the Platte. But on this late afternoon day, the redheaded Pollock was a lawman on a mission.

"Need to see you in private, A.C."

"It's going to have to wait," Ford said, spreading his cards so Pollock could see his hand. Pollock's worried expression never changed.

"Play it out then, ain't got all night."

"Uh-oh, boys," Colin Jackson said, blowing a blue ring of smoke upward. "Ford's standing pat. Means only one thing." As if to emphasize his point, the gunman tossed his cards on the table. Ford gave Jackson a look that could kill.

"I'm staying," Judge Slaughter said, raising the pot by another twenty.

"Guess I'll ride for one more round," D.C. Oakes said, keeping his cards close to his chest. Oakes was the same man much maligned for his flagrantly optimistic view of the Pikes Peak gold rush. The notorious guidebook author was now a well-to-do sawmill operator.

The one thing that bound them all together, including Marshal Pollock, was that they were members of the Vigilance Committee, established to preserve law and order and take what measures necessary—namely hanging—when

157

guilty people were brought before the hooded group for swift trial. Made up of nearly a hundred members, some who had come from as far away as California where that state meted out secret and swift retribution to wrongdoers, they held the noose high over the heads of criminals as a warning.

But, as with any boom town, violence was a way of life and politicians who couldn't be bribed were simply murdered by the criminal element of Denver City. When the Vigilance Committee decided to play a more active role in ridding the city of rustlers, confidence men, petty thieves and the like, their nightly meetings at the Byeau Brothers Store leaked immediately to the outlaw faction. When it came time to arrest these outlaws, they had simply faded away.

Embarrassed over obvious leaks, the Vigilance Committee selected ten of their members, all presumably trustworthy and above suspicion, to oversee outlaw activities. Known as the Secret Ten, they commanded virtual authority over life and death decisions in the community and A.C. Ford was a member of the Secret Ten.

Slaughter raised the ante and Oaks covered the bet and called Ford. Smiling broadly, the attorney showed the two men his cards.

"Dang!" Slaughter said, throwing his cards down in disgust. "Guess that breaks my winning streak. It's time to go home to supper."

"May as well get along home, too," Oakes said, putting away the remaining greenbacks in front of him. Both men stood up.

"See you boys tomorrow night then," Ford said with a grin. "And Judge, don't forget to bring back your winnings."

As soon as they were gone, Tom Pollock took a seat, looking around him at the other tables and lowering his normally booming voice to a whisper.

"My tail's been chewed out twice today, once by Bradley's widow and by Editor Byers, wanting to know when I was going to do something about his death and the rustling going on."

Ford shuffled the cards and began playing a hand of solitaire. He looked over at the long-haired marshal with keen eyes.

"So?"

Pollock squirmed in his chair. "You know elections are coming up in a few weeks. With Bradley's killers still on the loose and with nobody's horse safe even in town, the citizens of Denver are going to take a mighty dim view of my performance."

"You worry too much, Tom." Ford continued to play while Colin Jackson sat back quietly smoking his cigar.

"Hell! That's fine for you to say. Ain't nobody eating your tail out every time you walk down the street."

"I'm telling you, don't worry about the elections. You know we got the political means to see you stay in office."

"Yeah, but dang it, people like Byers can make my life miserable if he wants to."

"Byers can be handled," Ford said softly.

"Think I got an idea that may help," Colin spoke up, leaning forward. Both men stopped and looked at the gun-man.

"I'm listening," Pollock said.

"What you need, Marshal, is a few dead rustlers to show the town you're doing your job, correct?"

"That would help," Pollock said dryly.

"You up to taking a ride tonight? You too, A.C.?"

"Whoa, leave me out of it. Got to meet a client in . . . twenty minutes," Ford said, consulting his watch. "Fact is, I should be going."

"Then we'll wait for you to finish," Colin Jackson replied. "You need to be along to pull this off."

"Why me? And what is it you got up your sleeve this time, Colin?"

The gunman gave the two men a cold smile, "Always an ace, A.C."

"That figures for a gambler," Pollock snapped. His patience was wearing thin with the first talk.

"I play because I enjoy it, Pollock," Jackson said evenly. "I'm a businessman, same as you or A.C. here."

Tom Pollock let go with a booming laugh, "I *know* what you are, Colin, so get on with it."

The smile left the gunman's face and his eyes bored into the marshal.

"You hire out your gun, Pollock, same as me," Colin said stiffly.

"Ain't the—"

"Hold it," Ford said, lifting a hand. "Why don't you tell us what you got in mind, Colin, that'll help the situation? You two can draw on each other after I'm gone."

"Byers is itching to see dead rustlers. I say we give him some to write about."

"How we gonna do that?" Pollock said peevishly.

"You got a spade?" Colin asked.

"I can get one," Pollock said, his voice starting to rise.

"Then, I happen to know where there is three fresh killed horse rustlers you can dig up." Colin sat back and relit his dead cigar.

A slow smile spread across Ford's face and he slapped Jackson on the shoulder.

"That's brilliant, Colin."

"Should do the trick," Colin said casually, studying the end of his cigar.

"But I don't see where I'm needed," Ford said.

"You're a prominent attorney. No one would doubt what happened if you and Pollock came riding into town with three rustlers draped across their saddles, ya'll were forced to kill in a shoot-out."

"That would sure ease the pressure some," Pollock agreed begrudgingly. Ford still didn't looked convinced it was necessary for him to be there.

"Then we can ride out soon's A.C.'s done with his meeting," Colin said.

"When'll that be?" Pollock asked Ford.

"8:00 P.M. or 8:30 P.M.," Ford said absently. He hated being rushed, especially tonight.

"Good, then we'll meet over at my office around 8:30 P.M.," Pollock said, standing up. He looked down at the cold-eyed gunman.

"Got to hand it to you, Colin, coming up with a trick like this."

Ford and Jackson watched as the big man lumbered away. Ford looked at Jackson with a renewed respect.

"That is a good idea, Colin."

"Pollock ain't got to know horse rustling around here is over for the moment. And with you two bringing in three dead outlaws, everybody will just naturally think the others skedaddled out of the territory."

"I like it," Ford pronounced, standing up. "Got to run. See you over at Pollock's."

"Tell the little lady hello," Colin said with a smile.

"Now how do you know a woman is involved?" Ford asked lightly.

"With you, there usually is." Ford laughed and settled his black hat on his head and took his leave. Colin Jackson watched the attorney step through the door before getting out of his chair and stretching. A freshly painted lady slipped through the opened door and up to the gunman.

"Could use a drink, Colin?"

Colin Jackson settled his eyes on the pretty woman.

"How long you been after me to buy you drinks, Cora?"

The woman smiled, exposing a good set of teeth along with an ample amount of bosom.

"Gal's gotta keep trying. That's how I make my living."

Colin Jackson laughed, "No, it ain't how you make your living." In her early twenties, Cora Blackburn was the prettiest girl working the Cibola and Jackson couldn't figure why she bothered with him. She could have anyone in the saloon. Fact is, Colin had seen her turn down offers plenty of times in the past.

"You like champagne?"

Cora's eyes widened, "You serious?"

"Fetch us a bottle, then, the expensive stuff. Got an hour and a half to kill and I can't think of a better way then up in your room." Cora Blackburn swished her Spanish style skirt for effect and headed out of the room, giving him a seductive smile.

Colin Jackson shifted the gun on his hip and headed for the stairs.

"Knew we were going to be late," Dawson said gloomily.

"Ain't my fault," Josiah Catt said, trying to match Dawson's stride.

Dawson opened the door to the Broadwell House and stepped inside. The dining room was packed with formally dressed ladies and businessmen. He saw the two Stiles women in a far corner sitting with A.C. Ford. Ignoring the obvious stares at two men in plain clothes, Dawson, with Catt close behind, threaded his way to the table. When Ford realized Dawson's presence, a faint trace of irritation crossed his handsome features.

"Ah, Jack, we were thinking you and Josiah weren't going to make it," Mary Stiles said, giving them both a smile.

"We almost didn't," Jack said, pulling up a chair between Melissa and A.C. Ford. Josiah sat down beside Mary Stiles. Melissa gave Dawson a half-warm smile when he asked how she was doing. Ford merely stared at him with hard eyes.

"You remember, Mr. Ford?" Mary Stiles said, "and this is Josiah Catt," she said, patting Catt's arm. "We owe our lives to these two fine gentlemen." Ford was barely civil to the old man before turning his attentions to Melissa once more, a difficult thing, now that Jack Dawson blocked his path.

"Apologies for not having gotten cleaned up, but we've been taking in the sights and time just slipped up on us," Dawson said mildly.

"No need," Mary Stiles soothed, "you and Josiah still look good to me. As a matter of fact, I've never seen anyone

162

look better that night you found the Indians' camp." Mary Stiles's voice was tinged with emotion, mixed now with a little embarrassment at having been found under such circumstances, half-naked with a wild Indian on top of her.

"Do you think I could entice you and your lovely mother to remain here in Denver City, rather than travel back East?" Ford interjected as smoothly as he could with Dawson blocking the way. "There are many opportunities out here just waiting to be taken advantage of," Ford hurried on. "This town will someday be the center of trade for the territory. Statehood won't be far off after that."

Melissa looked at her mother, then back to Ford. "I don't know about mother, but I love it here already. The excitement, the exhilaration one gets just walking around town and looking up at those beautiful mountains. I want to stay," Melissa said with conviction, picking up her water glass and taking a sip.

"Mrs. Stiles, didn't you say you taught school back East?" Ford said, his confidence returning.

"Why, yes I did, but this is all so fast. There's things back East I need to tend to now that Henry's gone."

"I'm an attorney, I can handle it all from here for you. There's really no need to make that awful trip back across the Plains unless you feel it's absolutely necessary."

Dawson sat there listening to the conversation, feeling as out of place as a mustang in a thoroughbred race. Suddenly, Mary Stiles was addressing him.

"What do you think, Jack? Should we stay in this rugged country?"

"Well, teaching school is a mighty fine occupation and anyone can see this place, growing like it is, will need school teachers." Ford smiled broadly at Dawson's words. "On the other hand, this ain't Philadelphia. There's every kind of criminal known to man out here, ready to take your money or your life if you hesitate one second."

"Come now, Mr. Dawson, things aren't that bad. We do have laws you know." Ford was scowling.

"And vigilantes, I found out."

"My word," Mary Stiles said in alarm.

"It's nothing you or Melissa should worry about. Decent folks are as safe here, probably safer, than on the streets of any city back East." Ford gave Dawson a look meant to shut him up.

"What will you do, Melissa, if you decide to stay?" Dawson asked, turning to the girl. There was none of the softness in her eyes that had been there on other occasions for him.

"I am not helpless, Mr. Dawson, let me assure you. I am perfectly capable of taking care of myself now that I've reached civilization." Her voice was a little too hard to suit him and so was her defense. He had only meant for her to think about what she was doing, although Dawson wanted her to stay. But with the high-priced lawyer underfoot, he knew he didn't stand a chance with her. Suddenly, he felt the need to get out of there. This was not where he belonged. Most likely, Mary Stiles had asked them to supper only because she was grateful for what he and Catt had done for them. He reached down and picked up his hat from the floor.

"What will you do, Jack?" Mary asked. It was obvious to everybody at the table she was trying to steer the conversation away from her daughter to a more neutral position.

"Oh, me and Josiah plan on doing a little prospecting. Been through this country fifteen years ago. Got an idea or two where to look if someone ain't staked a claim on it."

"The mountains are full of people like you, Dawson, hoping to strike it rich," Ford said with a smirk. Dawson turned cold eyes on the lawyer.

"That's where you're wrong! Not another person like me anywhere, Ford, and that goes for the Rockies," Dawson said evenly. He stood up and put his hat back on his head. "You coming, Josiah?"

Catt's mouth fell open and he started to rise from his chair before Mary Stiles laid a hand on his arm.

"Jack, please stay and eat with us," Mary Stiles said. Dawson noticed Melissa didn't try to prevent his leaving.

"Not really hungry anymore, ma'am. Thanks just the same." With that, Dawson walked away without looking back.

"We've hurt Jack's feelings in some way," Mary Stiles said worriedly.

"Mother, it was Jack who put a black cloud over everything," Melissa said.

Mary caught herself before she admonished her daughter like she would a child. Melissa was far from that anymore, not after what they had been through the last few days.

Josiah Catt stood up, bowing slightly to the women. "Expect I better catch up with Jack. Excuse me, sorry things. . . ." Catt left the rest hanging and headed for the door.

"Those two will never amount to much out here," Ford said, once Catt was out of earshot. "This country swallows men like them everyday."

Mary Stiles bit her lip to hold back the stinging reply that formed on her lips. She saw the way Melissa was looking at the lawyer; more importantly, the way he was looking at her. If there was one thing more important to her than anything in the world right now, it was Melissa. Even with her teaching school, things would be tight, but with Melissa married to a rich attorney, she would be free to look out after her own needs. She prayed to God her decision to stay in Denver City was a good one.

"What's eating you boy?" Josiah said, once he caught up with Dawson.

"I tell you what's sticking in my craw, that darn lawyer, Ford," Dawson said, gathering up the reins of his horse.

"Now I understand," Catt said, climbing into the saddle. "Mister Big Time's moving in on the little lady." He grinned at Dawson.

"Too slick for my liking. See the way he was fawning over Melissa?"

"Appears she's taken with him," Catt said as they rode away from the Broadwell.

165

"Just wish I could make her see what lies behind a man like Ford."

"Know what you mean. Money ain't everything," Catt said.

"I'm afraid it might be to someone like Melissa."

"Mary Stiles wasn't taken in by him," Catt said. "That woman has a level head on her shoulders." They crossed the foot bridge over Cherry Creek and proceeded to Wootton's where they had rented a room for two dollars.

Dawson was in no better mood when they stopped in front of the hotel-saloon a few minutes later. His stomach growled.

"Think we can get something to eat here?" Dawson said, taking his gear off his horse.

"Probably got some fat Mex cooking for him and that means freeholees and tortillas if we're lucky. Course, we coulda had a fine meal at the Broadwell had we stayed," Catt said casually.

"Ain't neither one of our systems could have taken that kind of eating and you know it."

"Expect you're right. In all them fancy surroundings, don't think I could have digested it anyway," Catt said. "What you reckon they eat in places like that?"

"Nothing we're ever going to find out, 'less we hit pay dirt."

"We still leaving tomorrow?"

"Got no reason to hang around here," Dawson said, "Not with the money I got left."

"Amen to that," Catt added, as they climbed the outside rickety stairs to their room.

It was well after midnight when A.C. Ford let himself in with his key. He was bone tired after the long ride. He wished a thousand times while they were stumbling around in the black night he had had the good sense of waiting until the next day to go looking for corpses.

Ford walked into the bedroom and sat down on the edge

of the bed and removed his shoes. What he needed was a bath, but that would have to wait till morning. The covered figure moved beside him and he reached over and stroked the woman's thigh.

"That you, honey?" Sarah Jane asked, thick with sleep.

"You expecting somebody else?" Ford replied, not expecting an answer. He stood up to remove his trousers. The woman rolled over in bed, looking at the shadowy figure through half-lidded eyes.

"What's that smell, A.C.?" Sarah Jane asked, sniffing the air.

"It's nothing," Ford said, removing his sweaty shirt. Moving rocks from a grave had been hard work and something he didn't intend to repeat in his lifetime.

"It smells like . . . old earth."

Ford slipped between the covers and took the woman in his arms. It felt so good just to lie down. Tomorrow he intended on going to the office as late as he wanted.

"A.C., you're sweaty and there's a funny odor about you. You haven't been playing cards."

Ford gave the woman a peck on the cheek. All he wanted right now was sleep.

"No, and I wasn't with another woman either. That's all you'll get out of me, Sarah Jane, now go back to sleep."

"Way you smell, I know you haven't been with anyone else," Sarah Jane said, rolling on her side away from him. Ford fell into a deep sleep with Melissa's pretty face in front of him.

Chapter 17

After buying supplies, ammunition, and two new pickaxes, Dawson and Catt pooled their money. They barely had enough left over for a bottle of Taos Lightning from Wooton's Saloon.

"Never thought I'd be in such a poor financial condition at my age," Dawson remarked as they packed the supplies aboard their one mule.

"You! What about me?" Catt said, his pipe stuck between his teeth. "Here I am nigh on to sixty-three with no more to show fer life than wrinkles and swollen joints."

Jack Dawson gave Josiah Catt an affectionate pat as he finished tying a rope down over the piece of white canvass used to cover the pack supplies.

"What do you want with a lot of money at your age?" Dawson said, grinning. "There's no way you could spend it before you go under if we were to strike it rich tomorrow."

"True," Catt said ruefully, "only thing is, I'd shore like to *feel* rich just once before I die."

"What you mean is you'd like to impress Mary Stiles, maybe get something started before all the juices dry up."

"I don't deny it, Jack. Trouble is I feel like that old Cousin Jack from Cornwall when asked by a newcomer where to dig for gold. He replied, 'Well, soor, where gold is, it is, and where it ain't, there be I,' " Catt said mocking the Cornishman.

Dawson laughed, "That's the worst John Bull rendition I've ever heard."

"You get the picture," Catt said crustily. "We gonna stand around here in the street all day or are we gonna go find some gold?"

"Soon as you put your butt aboard your horse we can leave," Dawson said mounting the buckskin. "As for the gold, I leave that up to you, you're the expert."

"Being an expert implies I've had some measure of success, and I admit to showing enough color ever so often to keep body and soul alive. But just because I've spent the last twenty-five years a-looking don't make me an expert, no siree."

"Maybe not, but you got a sight more experience than most pikers who's never stood on anything but level ground."

Catt had managed to trade the two Indian ponies for a plucky little mountain pinto that once belonged to an old Ute who finally fell off his horse near the Platte the winter past and froze to death. Catt mounted up and they started out of town by way of the Larimer Street bridge which took them by Ford's office on Ferry. It was nearly ten o'clock.

"Say ain't that the silver-tongued lawyer from last night?" Catt said, pointing at a dapper man who moved along the crowded street with a determined stride.

"Him all right," Dawson said, recalling the last night's dinner table, and seeing Melissa's adoring eyes on the attorney.

As if realizing he was the subject of scrutiny, Ford looked around and spied the pair on horseback. He slowed his step and angled over in their direction.

"Pulling out I see," Ford said mildly. Dawson never reined in, just kept walking his horse forward.

"That's right," Dawson replied as he passed the lawyer.

"You'll want to know then that the Stiles have definitely decided to remain here in Denver. Just this morning, Mary was hired by Professor Goldrick to teach school."

"I wish them luck," Dawson called back.

"Wait up a second," Ford called. Dawson reined in as the lawyer hurried up to him.

"Here, I'm suppose to give you this," and he shoved a wad of bills into Dawson's hand. "Mary asked me to give it to you. She has money coming from back East. Wasn't sure she would see you again, so she wanted to repay you."

"This your money?"

"Don't worry, Mary insisted. She signed a note for it."

Dawson shoved the money into his coat pocket. "Figured as much coming from a lawyer."

Ford turned red, but said nothing. He stood there until the two riders were out of sight before turning back to his office with a pleased look on his face.

They splashed their horses across Cherry Creek and continued west, out of town, joining a horde of other travelers.

Josiah Catt looked around him as they rode along. "Don't this beat all?" he said to Dawson who seemed to be lost in his own thoughts.

"What does?"

"All these people," Catt replied, waving a hand about at the sea of men, some walking with packs on their backs, others riding whatever four-legged creature they could afford. "Ain't enough creek space fer all these pikers."

"Guess most are like us; hoping to find an out-of-the-way spot that's been overlooked that will show color."

Catt surveyed the polyglot of people following the serpentine rushing waters of Clear Creek that spilled down out of the western foothills, guiding them deeper into the country like some wet beacon. There were young boys in floppy hats walking beside pack mules, eager hopefuls sporting new clothes and equipment, anxious to get to the diggings. And then, there was the other types moving up the trail to the source of riches as well. Men who were drawn to the diggings like a mosquito to its host; there to plow the miners' pockets rather than shovel gravel. Like a giant tide of human hope, Clear Creek was covered with men as far as the eye could see.

"Never would have believed it if I hadn't seen it with my

own eyes," Dawson said. "Three years ago, a man could water his horse anywhere along this creek, now he can't even get down to it without crossing a claim." Dawson heard someone calling his name and he turned in the saddle to see Walter Dumont and the others cantering toward him. He pulled up and waited.

"Looks like we meet again, after all," Dumont said, reining up, smiling. "We have a beautiful day for it, don't we?"

"That we do," Dawson said, looking up at the brilliant blue sky as if to confirm Dumont's statement.

"You fellows headed to the Gregory diggings?" Dawson asked.

"Not us," Dumont replied cryptically. "And we ain't stopping at Russell Gulch either."

"By the looks of all these men tramping west, a man best have another spot in mind," Dawson agreed. At this point, nearly a year after Gregory and Russell had made their discoveries, every tributary feeding into the Clear Creek Canyon system was overrun by eager miners numbering into the tens of thousands.

"We do," Dumont said with a twinkle in his eyes. "My brother sent me word. He had located a good claim last winter. Me and my kin here are going there now."

"Good luck to you then," Dawson said, turning back to the trail.

"Listen, we don't mind you fellows coming along. Ought to be plenty to go around."

"Thanks, but Josiah is steering this buggy and he's determined to find a place where there aren't any other souls."

"Never said no such thing," Catt shot back. "Truth is, this intrepid trapper came across color in these mountains years ago or so he says and he is bound and determined to find it again."

"Just the same, you find your luck cold, look us up," Dumont said, pulling away from Dawson and Catt, the others in his group following close behind at a lope.

"Reckon we should've taken them up on it?" Catt said, breaking out his pipe, his eyes twinkling.

"Sounded like a sure thing," Dawson replied, moving along again as he looked out across the backs of trudging hopefuls.

They heard the rumble long before it came into sight. As Dawson and Catt were squeezed by the horde of anxious miners pouring through narrow Gregory Gulch, they spied the source of the thunder. Three steam-powered stamp mills, consisting of four hundred pound iron hammers, was busy falling like pile drivers onto chunks of lode-bearing ore, pulverizing it so the gold could be removed later by chemical means. The thudding mills produced a ground shaking racket that made normal talking impossible along with the clouds of dust and steam billowing up into the crystal blue sky. The gulch was packed with miners scurrying to and fro from the stamp mills while others lined the creek, shoveling gravel into sluice rockers from placer claims that was already beginning to peter out. Above the creek, yellow-white mine tailings marked numerous hard-rock mines that would sustain the gold rush for years to come after placer mining was history.

It was here on May 10, 1859 that John H. Gregory had first struck pay dirt along a little creek bed that fed into Vasquez Fork of the South Platte, better known as Clear Creek. In spite of the ice and snow still clinging to everything, Gregory panned four dollars worth of gold from a single scoop of earth. Working his way up slope, Gregory found gold-bearing quartz which had been dislodged from the lode by erosion.

And now, five to eight thousand people looked to be crowded into the gulch, by Dawson's estimate. He could barely tell the original lay of the land having been through here years before. If he had only known then . . . Catt was saying something and Dawson strained to catch it above the crashing rumble.

"Place stinks with the filth of humanity not to mention them stamp mills." A yellowish-brown smoke poured into the air from the giant ore crushers. It cast a pallid feel across the rocky gulch that Dawson didn't like either. Clusters of ramshackle log huts and brush shanties clung to the steep sides of Gregory Gulch like ticks to a hound. A crudely lettered sign at the entrance to the gulch where the stamp mills and refineries were located proclaimed it to be Black Hawk. Some of the arriving miners were asking questions of anyone who would stop long enough to answer. When they tried approaching those men working their claims along the creek bed, they were waved back with a warning.

Dawson noted their long faces and dazed expressions now that they were actually in gold country. Some looked lost and simply sat down on their meager belongings with their head in their hands, too tired to go another step and too overcome by it all. Before nightfall, Dawson figured many would turn back down the trail for home, overwhelmed by the crowd, the lack of claim space along the creek, and the sheer physical abuse suffered just getting to this place.

"Mountain City's just up the gulch," Catt said, pointing. "Could use a plate of grub and a shot of whiskey to wash it down with."

"Sounds good if it's away from these thunder mills." They passed on up the gulch, guarded by watchful men who stared silently at them; their clothes filthy, torn, and wet from constant irritation by the gravel beds they worked. Most were thin, their faces deeply lined by the rigorous work and exposure to the elements. Dawson found no expression of warmth or welcome in their looks, yet he noted the relief on a few faces as they passed on without stopping.

Mountain City proved to be only a little quieter with the stamp mills rumbling loud in the distance. Like rungs in a ladder, Mountain City had three streets cut into the side of the canyon; two were filled with private residences while the third, Gregory Street, became the false-fronted business district. They rode up the steep street, muddied by heavy traffic and passed a hotel in the process of shrugging off its tent portion as bright yellow logs were being rolled into place. Ore wagons and miners on foot and horseback competed for space on the crowded street. Dawson looked around him at the frenzied movement and shook his head.

"Amazing what gold does to a man."

Josiah Catt smiled through his whiskers, "Just you wait, Jack Dawson. The fever will hit you just as hard once you pan a few flakes, I'll warrant."

"Seen gold before and it never did," Dawson replied pulling up in front of a new log structure serving food. The scent of fresh cut pine was a pleasant relief after the sulfurous smell below. Catt laughed and stepped down from the mustang.

"Maybe so, but you was trappin' back then. Gold was just another rock to get in your way. Ain't that right?"

"You do have a point," Dawson admitted, wishing now that he had paid more attention to the gold he stumbled over and less to beaver. Besides himself, he knew several old trappers who had passed over color while searching for good beaver water so he wasn't the only one to play the fool. Still, it didn't make him feel any better.

"It's different now, you'll see. Once a man goes to lookin' fer gold seriously, things change. I've seen it too many times fer it not to be true."

Dawson looked around him at the hurried crowds of people. "If this is what it does to a man, I'm not sure I want to find any."

"Ha! These fools you see here ain't likely to find nothing more'n a bad head from booze and swelled joints fer their troubles."

Dawson looked back at the crowd, "How do you know that?" They stepped into the freshly skinned log structure and found a crude table that gave them a view of the street and their animals. A fat man smoking the stub of a black cigar came over.

"What'll it be, gents?"

"Grub and two glasses of alkyhall," Catt ordered.

"Got plenty of venison, but nary a drop of whiskey." And then he rushed on to explain, "Too high for my customers by the time it's hauled up from Denver City. Enough

174

saloons in town that'll oblige you." Without waiting for a reply he disappeared behind a thin curtain where they could hear meat being fried.

"Don't matter. We got our own. Just as well wait fer supper now to enjoy it," Catt said.

"How do you know about these people?" Dawson asked again; not willing to give up on the subject now that he was going looking for gold . . . come root, hog, or die.

"Just do is all," Catt snapped back. "You got to git back into the country now to turn a profit. These placer claims are being worked by third or fourth generation miners green to the mountains. Probably ain't enough gold in them to pay fer a week of drinking, but they ain't about to let go unless they can pass it along to others coming up the trail fer a little money. There's always a sucker that'll come along and bail them out, like they did the one before them."

"Suppose so," Dawson said, cutting the thick venison steak with his knife after the fat man set the plates down and turned away. He found the meat tough and stringy. Catt frowned as he chewed on a piece.

"Bet my last chew of tobacco, this mule deer died of starvation, not a bullet."

"The time of year figures about right," Dawson said, "and with all these men about, I doubt a deer stands much chance anyway."

"That'll be two dollars," the fat man said, wiping his pudgy hands on a filthy apron the color of mine tailings.

"I could get the finest meal in Denver City fer fifty cents. Two dollars!" Catt exploded.

The fat man stared at Catt with angry eyes, "That's two dollars apiece. And this here is Mountain City, not Denver," the cook said flatly.

"Suppose I trim a little fat off your hide to make up the difference," Catt said half seriously.

"Wait a minute," Dawson said, laying the money down on the table. Even though the price was too high, he figured it would be awhile before either one of them paid for a meal again out of their dwindling supply of money. Right now,

175

all he wanted to do was get free of the noise and breathe clean air again. "Let's get on up the trail," Dawson said to the fuming Catt. The fat cook gave them a scornful look as he swept the money off the table, putting it in his pocket. Back out in the rutty street, Catt paused a moment to light his pipe.

"Dang thief. Shoulda left him a dollar apiece, that'd been plenty."

"Yeah, well it wasn't worth the trouble it would have brought us and frankly I'm ready to put all this mass of humanity behind us as quickly as we can."

"Amen to that," Josiah Catt said, mounting up.

They rode on for three or four miles to Russell Gulch which looked nothing like the Gregory diggings. Russell Gulch consisted of a large open meadow to the south of Quartz Hill with frame houses and log huts dotting the hillsides. Russell, a fellow Georgian like John Gregory, had taken part in the gold rush of 1827 in northwestern Georgia and knew what he was about. Rather than stake a claim at an established digging, Russell and several of his Cherokee relatives suspected that the placer gold he had found at Dry Creek had washed down from the hills. He was right and the rush was on. More than twenty-five hundred residents were busy washing free gold, both nuggets and dust from the creek that bisected the town.

Here the snow was still deep, and the late afternoon air was crisp and cold. Both Dawson and Catt slipped into their warm coats and continued across the broad gulch until they left the town behind. Still, miners dotted the meandering creek that fed out of a grove of spruce, tumbling over a course strewn with small boulders. As the sun dipped behind the mountains to the west, the temperature dropped dramatically.

"We gonna stop anytime soon?" Catt asked, his breath coming out as frost.

"Want to clear this valley first. Know a place on the other side where we can make camp. A small creek where I used to trap beaver."

176

Catt pulled his coat tightly about him. "That where you seen gold?"

"There and one other place," Dawson added, guiding his horse over slippery rocks still coated with snow and ice.

Catt looked around him. Prospecting had been a lifelong habit with him and it looked like they were leaving the most likely spots behind, but he kept his thoughts to himself.

An hour later, they topped an icy ridge where winds swept across the rocky surface like a locomotive, instantly numbing exposed flesh. It was here that Catt got his first look at the alpine studded valley that lay below them in the lengthening shadows. It was hard to make a judgement about a place when icy winds threatened to tear you from the saddle. Had they followed the stream flowing into Russell Gulch, it would have taken them in an entirely different direction. Catt wondered if others even knew of this small valley.

Dawson wasted no time lingering on the crest and dropped down immediately into a thick forest of spruce-fir and wagonsized gray boulders. Catt was grateful, and the winds were reduced to gentle sighs by the dark trees. No stamp mills shook the ground and the air smelled of fresh spruce and alpine fir.

"My butt's froze to this dang saddle," Catt complained.

"Just a little farther, I promise," Dawson called back as he led them deeper into the valley.

Before Dawson called a halt, it began snowing; tiny flakes at first, mostly ice crystals, later turning to big wet flakes. The spring snow didn't last long and was quickly pushed east by the strong winds.

As darkness approached, Dawson pulled up at a thin stream of water and stepped down. Catt just sat there in his saddle looking like a giant snowman. Finally he spoke.

"This is it? This the place you been raving about?"

Dawson was busy undoing the cinch on his saddle. He looked up at the snow-covered figure and nodded.

"The beginning of it. Down below, a few hundred yards, the stream widens out into a small meadow. Beaver had a

177

dam there musta held back three four acres of water. That's where I saw the gold." Catt still didn't look convinced but he got down slowly from his horse, his legs stiffened by the cold and hours of riding.

"I'll get a fire going," Dawson said and began gathering up dead spruce limbs. "Unpack the coffee pot and skillet will you, Josiah? Could use something hot right about now."

"Ha! What I need is about two or three days among buffalo robes with a warm squaw jest to thaw out," Catt said solemnly.

Dawson grinned as smoke curled upward into the night air from the fire he was building. "Can't help you there. Should have asked Mary Stiles to come along."

In spite of the penetrating cold, Catt laughed uproariously. "I kin jest see a woman like that traipsing around in these cold mountains. Woman like that usta good living and a warm house. Doubt if I went back to town with a load of gold she'd even look my way."

"Oh, I don't know about that," Dawson said, warming his hands over the tongue of yellow-orange flame that leaped away from the pitch-rich limbs. "Mary strikes me as a sensible person who would accept a man for what he was and not for what he carried in his pockets."

"Well, she may be thataway fer some men, but don't go lumping me with them," Catt said as he fumbled with the rope holding the pack on the mule. He finally freed the pot and filled it from the stream before setting it in the fire. Catt squatted down beside Dawson and held his reddened hands out to the fire.

"You ever been married, Josiah?"

"Nope. Oh, I had me a squaw or two over the years, same as you trappers, and I bucked the tiger with a few whores while the sap was still flowing, but I ain't never come close to a real woman . . . except'n maybe Mary."

"It's never too late," Dawson said, getting up to dump coffee into the boiling pot.

"That what you plannin' to do after you strike it rich, marry up with her daughter?"

It was Dawson's turn to laugh, his breath coming out as puffs of white smoke in the frozen cold.

"Hardly. Got a feeling Melissa Stiles is looking for someone who can offer her a lot more than creature comforts."

"Meaning that silver-tongued lawyer?"

"Appears he's available," Dawson said, slicing meat into the skillet. "You going to make us some biscuits to go along with this meat or you just going to hover over the fire and smother it out?"

"Ain't no gettin' warm this night," Catt said, standing up stiffly. "May as well do something to take my mind off the cold."

After supper, Dawson walked off to check the horses, leaving Catt smoking by the fire with a cup of coffee. The night was blue-black and the glittering stars provided enough light to see where he was walking. Once he was sure the horses and mule were properly hobbled, not that they needed to be since the patch of tender spring grass would keep them busy, Dawson decided to explore the creek farther down. He wanted to see if the beaver pond was still there after all these years, yet knowing it couldn't be. The ice-encrusted snow crackled beneath his boots as he trudged downstream, using the gurgling waters as a guide. It made such a peaceful sound and Dawson knew wherever he finally settled his bones, he wanted a rushing stream nearby to ease his spirit from time to time.

The farther down slope he dropped, the wider the creek became. The plunging waters foamed over rocks with a fury backed by more than a mile of rising terrain.

Dawson emerged from the thick stand of timber along with the rushing creek and scanned the meadow. What looked like gray bones, bleached from years of exposure to the sun and elements, turned out to be the old beaver dam, dried up and decaying. Most likely someone had come along behind him and trapped the little creek clean of beaver, Dawson thought as he climbed up on the shifting pile of rotten sticks. The creek continued on its way some fifteen feet away, the beaver dam a distant thing.

Dawson watched a mule deer emerge from the surrounding timber and come down to the creek for a drink. The animal appeared fat for the end of winter and he wished he had remembered to bring his rifle along. They could use a supply of fresh meat before they started in with gold hunting.

Just before stepping down from the four foot high pile of sticks, Dawson swept the area with practiced eyes born to detect subtle changes and hidden dangers. His eyes caught the winking light through the trees some distance away and he froze in place. His first thought was of Indians, yet he knew almost immediately that it was probably a prospector's camp. He studied the campfire for a long moment, deciding it was over a mile away. Dawson was glad they had made their camp among the trees. He looked back and could see nothing of his own campfire.

Dawson eased down from the woodpile, snapping a rotten stick in the process. The nearby deer bounded away from the stream on silent hoofs. Tomorrow before daylight, Dawson figured to slip downstream and see for himself who was camping there. He still hadn't ruled out the possibility the camp might belong to a band of Utes or Arapahoes. He hadn't lived as long as he had by taking anything for granted.

Chapter 18

"You look lovely this evening, Melissa," A.C. Ford said, sweeping his hat from his head and bowing to Melissa Stiles as she descended the carpeted stairs of the Broadwell House.

"Oh, Mister Ford, please, you are embarrassing me," Melissa said with a smile that clearly indicated she was enjoying the attention from the prosperous lawyer.

"Please, call me A.C., everybody does. Will your mother be joining us this evening?" Ford settled his expensive derby hat back on his head.

Melissa looked back up the stairs, "No, no, she won't. Mother isn't feeling well."

"I'm sorry to hear that. Please give her my best," Ford said, giving Melissa his arm.

"I will do that, Mist . . . A.C."

"Ah, now that's better. What shall we do first? Take in the play over at Cibola Hall? James Reid told me just today it shouldn't be missed. What do you say? Or, we can eat if you like."

"No, I would love to see a play, besides I'm not very hungry at the moment." Slipping her arm into his, they crossed the plush lobby.

"Then the play it is. We can eat afterward," Ford said, holding the door open for Melissa.

"Who is this James Reid?" Melissa asked as Ford guided her into the carriage.

Ford came around and got in the buggy and expertly guided the matched blacks away from the railing before answering.

"James is a dear friend and the co-owner of Cibola Hall. But please do not say that out loud to anyone."

"Why not?" Melissa asked, holding on to her new hat she had bought today while shopping with her mother.

"Don't get me wrong. James Reid is a fine man and very influential here in Denver City, but most politicians would just as soon not be linked with the man in the same sentence."

"I still don't understand," Melissa persisted.

Ford laughed lightly and patted the young woman's gloved hand.

"Because Reid owns a saloon or two, and some of the so-called decent folk around here believe he encourages the bad elements of this fair city, the lowlifes, gamblers and whor . . . ah, certain ladies who work for a living."

"And what do you say?" Melissa said, giving him a sideways smile.

"I say a man ought to be able to do as he pleases as long as it doesn't interfere with anyone else. You have to understand, Melissa. Things are vastly different here in the Rockies. Out here, there's room to grow and spread your wings whatever direction the wind blows. A man can make his mark . . . a woman, too. Something few of us could ever do back East."

Every head in the Cibola appeared to gravitate toward Melissa Stiles and A.C. Ford as they entered and took reserved seats near the front of the planked theater stage. Ford appeared more than comfortable with the stares and spoke quietly to several men as they walked past.

"Seems you've caused quite a stir," Ford said, looking around him and nodding to others in the audience. The air hung heavy with the smell of alcohol and cigar smoke. Roughly-dressed miners mingled with business-suited men at the far bar, drinking and talking in low tones as they waited for the curtain call.

182

A young boy came by and gave them each a handbill printed with tonight's performance. Melissa read the large type: The Haydee's Star Company proudly presents *The Maid of Corissey*, performed by the brilliant actress and ballerina, M'lle Haydee, her leading man, Samuel D. Hunter. Ford was saying something to her.

"What?"

"I said, Miss Haydee is quiet talented and clear of voice. I think you'll like tonight's performance. It's one of Denver's favorites."

A beefy man wearing a ridiculous checked suit of bright colors came out on stage and in a booming voice asked everyone to take their seats so the play could get underway. It was a few minutes before the word filtered back to the bar, but finally everyone had taken their seats on the hard planks and the curtains slid open. It was precisely at that moment A.C. Ford slipped his hand over Melissa's and squeezed softly.

At that moment, Black Hawk was sitting in his tent . . . the dead miner's tent . . . where he was putting away the day's working under the flickering light of a coal oil lantern. He hefted the poke of dust, judging its weight. From the shadows, Cove Stillman watched the outlaw through slitted eyes.

"You think them boys are holding out on us?" Black Hawk asked the slouching outlaw.

Stillman's eyes never opened further when he spoke. "Been watching them like a hawk every time they pan the riffles of that rocker. Ain't no way."

Black Hawk nodded his understanding and dropped the heavy sack of mostly gold dust into the pack at his feet and tied the flaps together.

"Guess that leaves only one explanation, . . ." Black Hawk said, taking a sip of whiskey directly from a bottle setting on the crude table. "Gold's petering out."

"Way I see it. And frankly, I don't care," Cove Stillman

said, reaching over for the bottle and taking a long pull. "Ain't cut out to be no miner in some lonely canyon. I could use a bath and a soft bed . . . and a bad woman."

Black Hawk yawned and scratched himself beneath his dirty shirt.

"Know what you mean. Weren't for hauling the gold down to Gruber's and Clark to have it minted, Colin wouldn't have bothered riding out this way."

"I don't see him bedding down here in the cold, eating out of tin cans," Stillman complained further.

Black Hawk gave him a sly grin. "What say we give it a couple more days and slip in to Denver City for a little fun?"

"Suits me just fine, Blackie, but I don't have to slip around. Don't nobody know me from a grizzly. I can walk down the streets of Denver free of mind."

Black Hawk frowned and his eyes seemed to smolder in his bearded head. "Told you not to call me that, Cove."

"Well, if you was to use your real name, for Godsakes, people wouldn't confuse you with the town so much."

"Ain't looking to change it any time," Black Hawk said, tight lipped.

Cove Stillman stood up and stretched. "Think I'll turn in."

"Check the horses before you do," Black Hawk called to him as he slipped from the tent.

Standing in the cold mountain air, Cove allowed his eyes to adjust to the darkness. The two miners were already fast asleep beside the dying fire. He found the horses standing quietly in a nest of boulders, out of the icy wind. Cove ran his hand over his horse and the animal nudged him in the chest.

"Looking for a treat, huh, boy?" he whispered, stroking the animal's head while he surveyed the other horses in the subdued light from the overhead stars. Things seemed normal. Cove fished in a coat pocket and brought out several thick slivers of dried apple and offered them to his horse. He liked the feel of velvety lips on the palm of his hand as his

184

horse picked the apple slices up in his sensitive lips, moving them to his back molars to chew.

"Like that?" The horse nudged him in the chest once more. "No, that's all, boy. Maybe tomorrow."

Cove Stillman started to turn away and stopped short, his head held high in the air, sniffing like some wild animal. What he smelled was woodsmoke and it couldn't be coming from their fire for the wind was blowing down slope and he was on the opposite side of camp.

He studied the darkened features of the gulch as far as the ridgeline, searching for a fire. Cove stood there for well over an hour, patiently searching with narrowed eyes and sniffing the icy breeze. In the end, he found nothing and turned to his own blankets, chilled to the bone. Before he dropped off to sleep, he made a mental note to ride up the narrow valley and have a look around in the morning even though they were pulling out soon. Wary as an injured wolf, Cove wasn't about to take any chances now that he was accumulating real money for the first time in his life.

Melissa turned back from the door with heart pounding and looked into A.C. Ford's beckoning eyes.

"I had such a wonderful time tonight," she said favoring him with a smile. "The play was marvelous and the dinner was incredible."

Ford moved a step closer and placed a hand on the door jamb above Melissa's head. His eyes seemed to change right before her, and she knew he was about to kiss her. Looking into his eyes now, she was powerless to prevent it.

His mouth was soft and yielding and without realizing it, Melissa found herself responding to him in an all out embrace. Seconds seemed like hours before she finally broke free. Both were breathing hard and Ford's eyes were dancing with emotion.

"You are so beautiful, Melissa," he whispered to her.

Melissa got a grip on her breathing and her emotions and gently pushed the attorney away from her.

"I must go in now," was all she could think to say.

"Can I see you tomorrow?"

"Perhaps," Melissa said, not wanting to appear overly eager, yet afraid that her true feelings were showing through the thin facade.

Ford bowed and kissed her hand, "Until tomorrow." And then he was gone. Melissa slipped into the darkened room and closed the door quietly behind her.

Her mother spoke to her out of the darkness, "All I ask is that you go slow, Melissa. We've been here only two days. Mister Ford seems like a nice man, but go slow. If he's the one, you'll know."

"Oh, Mother!" Melissa exclaimed and rushed to sit on the bed beside the woman. "He's the most charming man I've ever met; cultured, educated, and very rich, I'm sure of it." Mary Stiles sat up in bed and hugged her only child close to her.

"I'm happy for you, dear. But I thought you enjoyed Jack Dawson's company as well?"

"I do mother, but not in the same way I feel about A.C.'s. Jack is a friend, someone who can teach me about the wilderness, the mountains."

"Well, just don't let Mister Ford teach you anything you aren't ready for," Mary Stiles warned. "Remember, I brought you up to be a lady."

"Mother!" Melissa said, slipping away from her embrace to dance around the room.

"Come to bed, child, it's late."

"Mother, he wants to take me to a ball later this week. All the important people of Denver will be there. Can I go, please?"

"We shall see," Mary said, settling beneath the covers once more. "Now come to bed. Tomorrow we move into our very own cabin and I have to teach school."

Melissa lay awake in bed long after her mother had gone back to sleep, thinking of nothing else but Ford and how glorious the night had been. And then she thought of Jack Dawson and how much he paled in the same light as Ford.

* * *

"You want me along?" Catt said, rolling from beneath his blankets to work the stiffness out of his joints. Dawson was up and dressed and checking his guns. The overhead stars were beginning to pale and sunrise was less than an hour away.

"No need. Expect they're nothing more than green miners, but it don't hurt none to have a look. You go ahead and scout the creek. Find any likely prospects, go on and dig a hole or two before I get back."

"Expect the hole diggin' can wait till you're back. Wouldn't want to deprive you of your education when it comes to proper prospecting." Catt gave Dawson an evil grin as he turned to build a fire.

"Keep the coffee hot," Dawson joked and disappeared into the graying light.

Dawson had no trouble coming up to the camp without being seen. He settled behind a pile of rocks some thirty yards out and waited for light to come to the narrow valley. He brushed the snow away from the rock in front of him and laid his rifle down. He used the time to scan the camp thoroughly, noting the horses in the protected lee of boulders where spring grass was breaking through. There were six animals, all of them riding horses. The camp showed signs of having been there for sometime with beds of sieved gravel heaped up on the side of the creek. Behind the creek was a white canvas tent. Through the cold fog of early morning he could see the figures of three men rolled up in blankets beside a blackened fire.

Dawson's eyes left the obvious and scanned the wide area around the camp, wondering if this wasn't one of the spots he had found gold in so long ago. If not, it was close.

Suddenly, the flap on the tent was shoved aside and a heavily bearded man in rough clothes stepped out into the gray mists. He said something Dawson couldn't catch and a man stirred in his blankets, rolled over once, and then got up to build a fire while the man from the tent went down to

187

the creek and washed his face in the cold waters. It was then Dawson felt the first jab of caution about the man. He moved with a certain weariness, like a man accustomed to studying his back trail a lot. Dawson watched as the man's eyes played over the rugged landscape while he drank from the stream.

Dawson was used to men being careful in Indian country, but there was something else about the man he couldn't quite put his finger on. Also he was very heavily armed for a mere prospector.

Dawson watched as the other men climbed out of their blankets and got breakfast started. Only two of the four looked remotely like miners. In fact, the slim one, who hung by the side of the bearded fellow, had the look of a gunman about him. Were they guards, hired by the two miners? Wasn't unheard of, Dawson figured, especially if a claim was paying well.

He decided to chance it, and stood up from behind the rocks, starting for the camp. The two gunmen noticed him immediately and Dawson smiled to himself as he walked along, careful to keep the barrel of his rifle pointed downward, yet ready on an instant's notice. He still hadn't decided about the two men.

"Howdy," Dawson called as he drew close.

The four men stared at him silently for a moment, their faces registering mild shock by his presence. Cove Stillman was the first to speak.

"Come on in, we ought to have coffee here in a minute." Dawson waded across the cold creek that rose up to his knees.

"You alone, friend?" Black Hawk said, his eyes scanning the rocks and timber behind Dawson who stepped out of the creek and dropped his rifle, butt first to the ground and leaned on the barrel.

"Camped back aways. Saw your fire last night and decided to come down for a visit," Dawson explained.

"You still haven't answered my question. You alone?" Black Hawk repeated.

Dawson looked the outlaw dead in the eyes for a skipped beat to let him know he wasn't up to being toyed with.

"Aw, hell, Blackie, that ain't any way to treat a stranger," Cove Stillman said, stepping forward to extend his hand. The bearded one gave the other a pained look. "Name's Cove Stillman." Dawson gripped the man's hand, yet felt no better at having done so.

"Jack Dawson," he said quietly.

"You prospecting?" Stillman asked, making sure his hand stayed away from the Colt strapped over his thick coat. Dawson felt sure the man carried a hideaway as well and wondered why he thought so.

"Trying. You fellows having any luck?"

Cove Stillman looked around the tight group and back to Dawson before answering, "Some, but it looks like it may be playing out on us."

Up close now, Dawson knew by looking at their hands which were the real miners. He had not been wrong on that score.

"Tate," Cove said to one of the miners by the fire, "pour Jack a cup of coffee." He turned back to face Dawson. "Still cold as hell up here, don't look like spring's ever going to get here fast enough to suit me." He gave Dawson a false smile and a warning light went off in Dawson's head. When he took the proffered coffee, he made sure the one called Blackie never strayed from his vision. Dawson took the cup, swallowing the hot coffee as fast as he could. He didn't like this setup and wanted out of the camp as quick as he could manage it. He handed the empty cup to Cove Stillman.

"Guess I better get back to camp," Dawson said, "can't make any money standing here and I don't want to keep you fellows from working either."

"Get lonely, you drop back by," Cove said, his eyes as friendly as a rattler's. It was all Dawson could do to recross the creek without hunching his shoulders, half-expecting a bullet any minute. None came, and Dawson felt sure it was only because the one called Blackie didn't know for sure if he was alone or not.

* * *

The tiny group of men watched Dawson until he disappeared into the thick timber.

"Wary as a lobo wolf," Cove responded.

"And we still don't know if he's alone," Black Hawk added for emphasis.

"Think he bought what we are doing?"

Black Hawk turned his snake eyes on Stillman, "Does it really matter?"

Chapter 19

A week of pecking and probing, Josiah Catt called it "crevicing", of the ancient streambed began to show good color. While Catt searched for the lode with pickax and shovel, Dawson was given the job of hauling likely samples of sand and gravel down to the creek to wash and separate in the cold waters with a wooden sluice Catt had constructed. Twice a day, the riffles were panned by Catt for free gold. As yet, Catt didn't trust Dawson to do such fine work with a gold pan. Promising rocks, the size of a man's fist and larger, were thrown into a pile by Catt for a closer look later.

Jack Dawson slowly stood upright to relieve cramped back muscles as he shoveled gravel into the sluice. Leaning on the handle of the shovel, he looked around him at the natural beauty of the small valley. Suddenly it occurred to him where he had first seen the free gold. Dawson looked closely at the timbered slopes to the west for a few minutes until he separated the tiny thread of silver from the surrounding green. Twenty years had been a long time ago, yet the more he studied the area, the more he became convinced he was right.

Dawson leaned the shovel against the sluice rocker and waded the three or four steps to shore. Josiah Catt was doubled over some fifty feet away, tearing loose rock with the pickax. He caught sight of Dawson moving to his horse.

"Here now, this ain't no time to be leaving off work. We got more'n a ton a rock to go through."

Dawson ignored the prospector and threw his saddle on the buckskin and tightened the cinch. Dawson climbed aboard the animal and started off with Catt staring at him openmouthed. He rode past Catt and suddenly wheeled his horse and came trotting back to the sluice where he reached down for the gold pan.

Turning his horse once more, Dawson offered a single comment as he passed Catt a second time. "Gonna check something out, won't be long." He rode away.

Catt stared after Dawson with a perplexed look while he fished out his pipe and tobacco. He had heard of men going plumb loony over gold like a mad dog with the fits. But Dawson had struck him as being real sensible when it came to building air castles. He scratched his beard and lit his pipe, deciding now was as good as time as any to heat up the last drops of coffee.

Dawson entered the thick timber where the tiny sliver of creek water cascaded over the jumble of low rocks. He drew up and looked back at their campsite, some half mile to the east. Things looked right, but he couldn't be sure. Dawson moved up slope for a hundred yards and left his horse in a small aspen grove whose buds were beginning to swell in the spring sun. He followed the little creek upward and was confronted by a mass of downed timber and rocks the size of wagons. A massive snowslide in recent years had virtually wiped out the creek bed at this point, and water exited from the wall of timber and rock at various points before regrouping again.

Dawson spent the next thirty minutes working his way around the massive slide to rejoin the streambed. He didn't like what he saw. Behind the avalanche was devastation where the earth had been gouged by sliding boulders. Nothing looked remotely the same now. In places, he could see where the creek had changed beds several times due to the scraping away of timber and rock. The small pool of dark water he remembered was no longer there. Dawson sat glumly down on a fallen log next to the quiet little creek to catch his breath. He had worked his way up several hundred feet above the valley floor over rough terrain and was panting heavily. What he saw caused him to stop breathing for a full minute. Dawson knelt down by the water's edge and probed at the dull blinking light with his bowie knife. The creek bed was only three inches deep at this point and he worked feverishly to free the object which seemed to be standing in it. He worked the point of his knife deeper into the gravel, clearing away rock and sand as he labored to free the shining object. Suddenly the rock, which seemed to weigh a pound, came loose and Dawson rolled it from the creek with his knife. He sat back on his haunches, staring at the gleaming rock, shot through with thick threads of wire gold. Dawson reached down and gently picked it up, turning it slowly in his hands. He had never seen anything like it. Laced together like a mat, wire gold completely encrusted the rock while black-coated crystals were shot through the rest. He placed the gold ore beside his hat which he had taken off.

Dawson moved carefully into the water, keeping his eyes peeled for other promising rocks. Evidently the slide had scraped away the overlying rock and sand, exposing the wire gold. What he had seen twenty years before were a few pea-sized nuggets, nothing to match this. Seeing a dull gleam, Dawson drove the point of his knife down beside it and lifted free a solid gold nugget the size of his thumb. It weighed at least an ounce, maybe more. He slipped the nugget into his pocket and grabbed up the gold pan and filled it with sand and rock. When he had it panned down to coarse black sand, a half dozen fingernail-sized nuggets stared back at him along with a fair portion of gold dust. Dawson felt his heart thump heavily against his ribs. He didn't know for sure, but what he had here could very well turn out to be a major strike. With shaking hands, Dawson lifted out the nuggets, cursing himself for not having brought along a pouch to put the gold in. The nuggets he put in his pocket and poured the remaining dust on a flat rock to dry while he went back to panning.

In a little over an hour, Dawson had filled up one of his pockets with nuggets and had another three or four ounces of dust drying in the sun. Next to the dust lay a fist-sized rock that glittered in the light and was shot through with a bluish-gray mixture unknown to Dawson. He figured to show it to Catt. It may be worthless, but then again. . . .

It was late afternoon when Dawson emerged from the edge of timber and rode across the flat to their campsite. Catt was busy cleaning out the riffles from the rocker and pretended not to notice his arrival. Dawson smiled. Probably mad and Catt had every right to be for his shirking his work.

"Howdy old man," Dawson said, dismounting stiffly, his leg muscles cramping from squatting the better part of the afternoon. "Any coffee?"

"Nary a drop. Shoulda been here fer dinner," Catt said, filling his pan with the debris from the riffles and squatting down over the creek, gently rotating the pan like he had been born to it. Dawson smiled to himself.

"Well then, take a look at what I've been doing while you wasted the noon hour to eat." Dawson unbuckled the flap on his saddlebags and retrieved the rock encrusted with wire gold. In the blazing sun of a late afternoon, the burnished gold seemed on fire. Josiah Catt nearly dropped his gold pan, his eyes growing wide at the sight. He came out of the water, dripping rock and sand from his pan.

"Holy Mother of . . ." he squinted up at Dawson, "where did you find this?" Catt set his pan down and took the stone from Dawson as if it were alive.

"Back up that steep slope," Dawson jerked his thumb behind him. "Remember, I said somewhere around here I had found several gold nuggets, back when I was trapping this area?" Catt nodded his head, never taking his eyes from the encrusted stone. "Thought all along it was this creek, till today."

"One rock don't make fer a strike, boy," Catt said, squinting up at Dawson with fire in his eyes.

"What about these?" Dawson pulled out a handful of big nuggets from his pocket to show Catt.

"Boy, you done fell in it, fer shore," Catt cackled, as Dawson poured the heavy nuggets into the old prospector's outstretched hand.

"Brought back something else you might be interested in," Dawson said, going back to his saddlebags. Catt watched him like a hawk; his eyes fairly danced in his head with excitement as Dawson lifted out the strange-colored stone.

"What do you make of this?"

Catt replied instantly. "That's galena, boy, and shot through and through with gold and silver."

"So that's what the dark stuff is," Dawson mused.

"More than that, boy, that ain't placer rock. You done gone and struck the mother lode!"

Not until they had finished supper and were lounging around camp, did the full impact of what Josiah Catt had said sunk in. If it was true, and Dawson had no reason to doubt Catt, they would soon be rich men. All they had to do now was file on the claim and take away the surface gold to expose the lode-bearing rock underneath.

"Lucky fer us that slide blocked the way," Catt was saying. "Preserved it from pryin' eyes. And they ain't no tellin' how many pikers came face to face with that avalanche and turned away."

"Just lucky, I guess," Dawson said, grinning at the old prospector. Dawson was beginning to feel as excited as Catt and a restlessness grew deep within him.

"Think I'll take a ride downstream and see how those miners I told you about are making out." It was still an hour before full darkness would set in.

Josiah Catt put away his pipe and stood up. "Reckon I'll

tag along with you. See fer myself what kind of pikers we got fer neighbors."

"Can't be still either?" Dawson said.

"Gold'll do that to a man sometimes. Hell, as much as John Gregory was an old hand at finding gold, when he struck it rich, he was up fer three days and nights a-muttering gibberish to himself and guarding his gold. It took that editor fella William Byers to settle him down and get him back on track."

"Well, I've never talked to myself, gold or no," Dawson responded as they rode away from camp.

"That's cause you ain't never been the one woke up at night, like me. You carry on something awful at times."

"No such thing, Josiah, and you know it."

"Un-huh. Next time, I'll jest write down what you say and read it back to you one morning."

Dawson laughed, "Only one thing wrong with that, we both know you can't write."

They closed in on the camp with the proper amount of caution but all they found was a few rusted tin cans and a pile of unused chopped firewood.

"Looks like they pulled out," Catt said, stepping down from the saddle to look around at the discarded trash. He shook his head. "Ain't an Indian alive would leave behind a mess such as this."

"Guess they gave up on mining," Dawson said.

"Huh?"

"They left behind their sluice rocker."

"Don't mean no such thing," Catt shot back. "They get where they going, they'll jest build another. Same as this one."

"Maybe, but two of those men had never mined in their lives."

"Hell, boy, you got eyes. Ain't one in a thousand . . . no, more like one in *ten* thousand ever held a pickax or gold pan. Can't hold that against them."

"Just the same, something wasn't right about this setup. It was more what I felt than what I saw," Dawson said. Catt kicked aside a few tins and put a hand in the blackened fire pit, feeling the stones.

"Been cold fer a day or two," he said before swinging back aboard his horse. With the sun now setting behind the steep ridge to the west, the air temperature was dropping rapidly. Catt hunched his shoulders against the mounting cold.

"Let's get back to the fire and heat what's left of the coffee," Dawson said.

"Coffee. By grabs, tonight we'll break open a bottle of Taos Lightning and do a little celebrating, I figger," Catt shot back. "You the one got us ridin' around in the cold."

They started back to camp without brothering to recross the creek. It was Dawson who first noticed the inconsistency in the rocks and reined up.

"What is it now?" Catt asked, following suit.

"Notice anything different about those rocks over there?"

Catt studied the rocks with a frown on his whiskered face. "Close together like that, they look like—" Catt turned to look at Dawson.

"Graves?" Dawson asked. Catt nodded. Dawson walked his horse closer to the rocks. "They've been disturbed all right. See how some of them still have that shaded look, like they been turned over in the last week or two?"

"I see it," Catt said. "Looks like you might be right about them pilgrims." They dismounted and Dawson began removing rocks from one of the piles. Catt joined in. After a few minutes, the unmistakable smell of death filled the air.

"Been here long enough to get ripe," Catt commented as he strained to remove a big flat rock. When they had uncovered the first miner, Dawson wasn't surprised to find the man had been shot and at close range.

"We gonna uncover the other man or not?" Catt said holding his nose as he watched Dawson search the dead man's pockets. There was nothing to indicate who the man was. The odor was almost unbearable even for Dawson and he had experienced a lot of it over his lifetime.

He turned to Catt who stood a few feet away. "Why don't

197

you walk back to their camp and make us a torch with some of that wood. It'll be dark in a few minutes and since we've gone this far, we may as well finish it tonight." Catt turned away, glad for the opportunity to get a little fresh air.

Rather than repile stone on the dead man, Dawson began taking rocks from the second grave and using them to cover the first. In spite of the cooling night air, Dawson was sweating from the work when Catt returned, holding a length of lighted pitch.

"Dang, Jack, how do you stand it?" Catt said, bringing his arm up to cover his nose.

"Bring that torch over here," Dawson commanded, ignoring the question. He had uncovered the chest and head of the man and wanted to get a better look. Catt came over, holding the pitch pine down over the shallow grave.

"Believe this'n worse than the other one," Catt commented, but Dawson didn't seem to hear as he studied the dead man closely. He, too, was shot at close range, and in the heart. Whoever did them both was good, Dawson would give him that. He straightened up and turned to Catt.

"Take a look and tell me if you've seen this man before."

Josiah Catt edged closer, holding a lung full of tainted air, and looked quickly down at the dead man. What he saw made him forget about holding his breath and the air rushed from his lungs.

"Why, hell, he's the spittin' image of—"

Dawson nodded, "Walter Dumont. Looks like we've found his brother."

Chapter 20

"Well, it was good while it lasted," Colin Jackson said to Black Hawk as they sat in A.C. Ford's office that night. Ford was behind his desk and seemed to be preoccupied with other thoughts, even to the point of ignoring the bulging leather sack of nuggets that lay on his desk. His share from the claim-jumped placer mine.

"Beats hell outa rustling horses, don't it?" Black Hawk said expansively, looking from the gunman to the attorney as he sipped a large jigger of Ford's expensive whiskey. Ford could well afford it, having cleared over five thousand in gold for his part.

"I say we do it again. What do you think, counselor?" Jackson asked Ford. Ford stirred behind his desk and picked up the heavy sack from his desk and swiveled his chair to face his safe. He spun the dial expertly a few times, his back hiding where the tumbler stopped from Jackson and Black Hawk. Colin smiled at Ford's actions. The attorney didn't know he and Black Hawk had each kept ten thousand. So much for trust.

Ford turned back and looked at the two men for a moment. "We must be careful. Stealing horses is one thing, claim-jumping and murder is quite another."

"How so, dead is dead, whether he owns horses or a mine?" Black Hawk asked, downing the last of his drink. He refilled it immediately in spite of the slight frown that crossed Ford's face. Black Hawk didn't stop pouring until the glass was full.

"For one thing, there are over ten thousand men out here scrambling to find gold. They could care less about horses, but you start jumping their claims and killing a few of them, we'll have more trouble around here than we can handle."

"Got nothing to worry about," Black Hawk said confidently. "By the time anybody finds them two miners, if they ever do, won't be no way they can trace it back to us."

"Didn't you say there were two other miners in the area?" Ford asked, pushing his steel-rimmed glasses further up his nose. "What about the one visited your camp? What if he puts two and two together?"

"Got to admit, this Dawson ain't no green piker from back East. Looked more to be a trapper at one time, hard-edged, but down on his luck. Me and Cove kept a close watch on their camp from time to time. An old threadbare prospector's up there with him. The old man's doing most of the looking while Dawson's doing the shoveling," Black Hawk elaborated.

"Think Black Hawk and Cove ought to nose around in the mountains again, except farther out this time. Could be, with one more claim like the last we can settle back a while and pick up with the horses again later on. I agree with you A.C., we got to walk a fine line here," Colin Jackson said to Ford.

Ford nodded and was about to speak when the office door opened and John Shear stepped inside. A stout New Yorker and a free spender at the sporting houses, Shear was regarded as one of the better citizens of Denver and a close intimate of Ford.

"Howdy, boys, looks like I'm just in time for the meeting." Shear retrieved a chair from the back wall and joined the others.

"It's about over, John," Ford said, flipping open his pocket watch for the time.

"Aw, Ford's only wanting to get back to Sarah Jane," Black Hawk said, his speech slurring a little from the potent whiskey. "Me and Colin'll talk long's you want." Ford's eyes blazed, but said nothing.

Colin Jackson drew aside his coat and pulled out a leather pouch, tossing it to Shear whose eyes brightened. He hefted the heavy pouch, giving the gunman an approving look.

"Seems business has been good," Shear offered.

"It was until two days ago," Ford cut in, wanting to end this quickly. With Melissa waiting, time was growing short for idle chitchat. "Colin thinks we ought to try our luck again."

"So soon?" Shear questioned with eyebrows arched.

"With any luck we can pull one more job before anyone finds out about the first. After that, we can all relax or take a trip to San Francisco," Colin said.

"See nothing wrong with that, Colin. You and Black Hawk know more what you're doing than either me or A.C." It was plain to Colin that plain old greed fueled Shear's thoughts, nothing more. Even though John Shear had prospered in the Gregory diggings, he had spent considerable money trying to win votes to become a delegate to the first Constitutional Convention, not to mention what he squandered on expensive drinks and the ladies. Shear was looking to recoup losses and didn't care what Colin and Black Hawk had to do to keep the money flowing.

A.C. Ford stood up. "Gentlemen, I must excuse myself. John, lock up when you are through here for me, will you?"

"You bet," Shear responded, getting up for a glass so Black Hawk could fill it from the dwindling bottle of whiskey.

"Tom coming by?" Colin asked as Ford pulled on his dress coat.

"Told him to, but something may have come up. You know how it is with a city marshal," Ford said, setting his hat on his head.

"Yeah, well, we'll hang around a little longer, see if he shows up," Colin said. "You coming over to the Cibola later?"

A grin spread across Ford's tight features. "Not tonight, Colin."

"Must be that little blond lady I seen you with yesterday," John Shear said. "What did you say her name was?"

"Didn't," Ford quipped, opening the door. "Don't forget to lock up," and then he was gone in the night.

Shear shook his head, "Can't figure it. Ford's got the best looking woman around in Sarah Jane, but still it ain't enough."

Colin stood up, suddenly restless. "It never is for a man like Ford. Other men's weaknesses may be alcohol or money . . . or in my case cards," Colin said, stretching his lanky frame. "Think I'll go back to my room and rest awhile. Come by the Cibola later and I'll win back some of those nuggets you're carrying," the gunman said to Shear.

"Might just do that, but it's me that'll do the winning."

Colin opened the door and found Tom Pollock standing there. The marshal stepped in and closed the door.

" 'Bout to give up on you, Tom," Colin said quietly. Tom Pollock dropped his big frame into the nearest chair, looking tired.

"I tell you, sometimes I wonder why I ever pinned a badge on in the first place."

"Trouble?" Shear asked, emptying the last of the bottle in a glass for Pollock. Black Hawk looked sadly at the empty bottle.

"Oh, the usual. Couple bummers got in a row with a greenhorn from back East over at the Louisiana. Plugged him four or five times . . . can't tell yet with the blood and all. Shot him just because he refused to buy them a drink." The bummers were a bunch of idle, shiftless drifters from the goldfields of California and Nevada composed mostly of Southerners from Georgia, with no thought to law and order.

"You arrest them?" Shear asked.

Pollock shook his head, "Scattered. Most likely'll have to flush them out of their nest down on Indian Row. Expect we'll need a meeting later tonight to deal with them," Pollock added, referring to the vigilante committee.

"Ford won't like that," Black Hawk said, swaying in his chair, his bleary eyes bloodshot and unfocused. He was drunk now.

Pollock studied the outlaw for the first time, noting his condition. "Where is he?"

"Squiring a new lady around town," Shear responded.

"No matter, we need him and the others there at midnight, John. See you get the word to him."

"Do my best. What about the others?"

"I'll see to it myself," Pollock said, downing the drink and standing back up. "Gotta go." He stood there shifting from one foot to the other, looking from Shear to Jackson. He ignored Black Hawk.

"A.C. put your share in his safe if that's what's keeping you," Colin Jackson said, his cold eyes smiling. The two big men tolerated one another and that was about all. Jackson figured it was because he was a gambler and pure death when it came to drawing one of his five-shooter Colt revolvers. Colin figured Pollock didn't like the idea of having to associate with a known gunman and killer.

"That's fine, I wasn't worried about that," Pollock said smoothly. Colin spent his free time reading people and he knew the marshal had just lied. What's more Tom Pollock knew he knew. Pollock's face grew red and he tried to cover it by going to the door where he stood with it open.

Black Hawk staggered to his feet. "Anybody want to join me and Cove for a drink down at the Criterion?"

Pollock frowned, "Don't you think you've had enough?"

Black Hawk fixed his alcoholic eyes on the big marshal. "You ain't the one been stuck up there in a lonely canyon for the last three weeks. I'm just fixen to howl so you best stay clear of my way tonight, Pollock." With that, Black Hawk staggered from the office and disappeared into the night with Pollock shaking his head.

Colin came over and stood shoulder to shoulder with Marshal Pollock as he lit a fresh cigar.

"You know how Black Hawk is when he gets oiled, Tom," Colin said quietly, turning to look him in the eye. "Best give him all the space he needs. He may be well on his way to being drunk, but he can still jerk a gun if the need arises."

Marshal Pollock looked at the gambler-gunman with eyes that betrayed how he truly felt about his kind. In the end, he said nothing and simply walked away.

Colin Jackson turned to Shear, "Guess you can lock up now," and with that the tall gunman headed for his room.

A soft tap at the door brought Colin Jackson off the bed like a coiled rattler with his fangs bared. He cocked the Colt and stepped up next to the door, keeping his back against the wall.

"Yes?" His voice was low, yet penetrating.

"It's me," a feminine voice replied. Colin stuck the revolver in his waistband, unlocked the door and stepped back, holding the doorknob in his hand.

The stunning woman gave him a smile and stepped quickly inside. Colin relocked the door and lay back across the bed while the woman dropped her coat in a chair. She came to him with a smile on her face, crawling up the gunman's chest, shivering.

"I'm cold, Colin." Colin Jackson wrapped his arms around the perfumed woman and forced her head up to his where he kissed her hard. The woman struggled to free herself. Colin finally released her, but not until she quit struggling and lay against him. He laughed quietly.

"You kiss too hard, Colin," she complained.

"What's the matter, Sarah Jane, thought you was used to rough men like me and A.C.?"

Her eyes blazed with raw fury. "Don't mention that low-down dog's name while I'm here!" Sarah Jane bounced up and sat on the side of the bed, pouting. Colin raised up and snaked a strong arm around her waist and pulled her to

204

him. He kissed her hair and moved down to nuzzle her neck.

"You smell good, Sarah honey," Colin said thickly. Sarah Jane Vailes sighed and turned to meet the gunman's embrace.

Chapter 21

Even though the horde of miners who packed the streets during the day had, by now, either drank themselves into a stupor or gone back to their camps, there was still a lot of foot traffic for midnight. But those stumbling along darkened streets from one saloon to another did not notice a small knot of well-armed masked men escorting two sober-faced individuals down Blake Street. When the group reached the darkened glass front of Byeau Brothers, a guard, with rifle in hand, stepped from the shadows and quickly opened the door for the men. After they were inside, the guard closed the door, and melted back into the dim recesses of the building.

The knot of men proceeded through the store to a rear door which opened into a storeroom housing various boxes and crates. A small clearing had been made and a makeshift table and chairs brought in so the prisoners could sit. Six other men were already present. All ten men were wearing flour sacks over their heads except for Sheriff Middaugh and Marshal Tom Pollock. Pollock's face was etched with the weariness of the past few hours as he and Middaugh had conducted a search for the two men down on Indian Row. They finally found them drunk and in bed with two whores; neither man was capable of much defense.

Forced now to take seats before the imposing figure of the hooded judge, both prisoners were cold sober and sick.

"The People's Court of Jefferson Territory is now in session," the judge said. Both prisoners raised their heads and stared at the masked man.

"This ain't legal," Edward Noel said, his voice barely more than a whisper. The dark eyes behind the judge's hood found Noel's. Silence filled the storeroom for a minute until Ed Noel's eyes returned to the floor.

"This," the judge said, waving an arm around him, "is a legal court of law. We have both the sheriff and marshal present as well as an attorney present in case either of you wish to seek counsel." The prisoner next to Noel stirred and looked around him at the room full of determined men.

"I know what we done was wrong. God knows if I could change things, I would," Gordon Raymer said remorsefully.

"Damnit, Gordy, you shouldn'ta said that," Noel shouted.

"Ain't no use denying it, Eddie, we done it and now it's time to ante up."

"Edward Noel and Gordon Raymer, you both are hereby charged with the wanton death of one, John Osgood, late of Illinois," the judge intoned. "Do we have the coroner's report, Sheriff Middaugh?"

"Yes we do, your honor," Middaugh said, unfolding a piece of paper.

"Read it to the court, please."

Middaugh cleared his throat, "We, the undersigned persons, summoned by the marshal of Denver City to hold an inquest over the body of John Osgood, deceased, do hereby return the following verdict: The deceased came to his death from eight gunshot wounds inflicted upon his person at the hands of Edward Noel and Gordon Raymer . . . [Signed] George Towner, E.B. Bennett, M.A. Smeed, J. Smeed, H. K. McGrew and Curtis Brown." Middaugh looked up from the paper after he had finished reading the verdict. A strained silence filled the little room as the two doomed men dropped their heads.

"Do you have anything further either of you wish to bring to this court's attention before I pass judgement?"

Gordy Raymer merely shook his head, his eyes shut tightly against the scene around him.

Eddie Noel jumped to his feet, "I got something to say."

"Speak then," the judge said.

"Me and Gordy never intended to hurt nobody. We was drunk and just wanted to have a little fun with Osgood."

"Eight bullet wounds in a man is more than having a little fun," the judge cut in.

"If Osgood hadn't acted so high and mighty, refusing to drink with us, none of this woulda happened."

"Refusing a drink is a low call for deliberately killing a man, don't you think?"

Eddie Noel tried ducking the question, "He insulted us when we offered to buy him a drink. Then other people started laughing at us and well . . . " Eddie's voice trailed off.

"Ain't no use, Eddie, sit down," Gordy Raymer spoke up. "Can't you see that?"

Eddie's desperate eyes looked around the room at the well-armed men. Had his hands not been bound, he would have bolted for the door.

"You can't hang me for this," Noel said, his voice cracking.

"Will the other prisoner rise and face the court," the judge commanded. Middaugh stepped closer to the wild-eyed Noel while Pollock moved next to Raymer who rose unsteadily from his chair.

"It is the sentence of this court that you, Edward Noel and you, Gordon Raymer, be hanged publicly for your crimes, at 10:00 A.M. tomorrow! This court stands adjourned."

"God! Somebody shoot me! I can't be hanged," Eddie shouted, trying to wrestle free of Sheriff Middaugh's steely grip. Gordy Raymer merely stood by passively while Noel scuffled with two of the guards who finally subdued him.

After the doomed men were led from the room, Judge Slaughter removed the cotton sack and wiped the sweat from his eyes. He looked over at A.C. Ford who was smiling after taking his sack off as well. He was in a good mood and wanted Slaughter to know why.

"Hot work," Judge Slaughter commented. Ford came over to the desk and pulled a silver flask from an expensive suit coat pocket and offered it to the seated man.

Slaughter removed the top and tilted his head back and took a long swallow before handing it back to Ford who drank as well.

"Should be a good crowd for the hanging," Ford commented, slipping the flask into his pocket once more.

Slaughter looked sad, "There always is." He gained his feet and reached for his hat. "I'm tired. Going home to sleep. Too many late night poker games with you has me worn out."

The attorney laughed at the departing judge. "See you at 10:00 A.M., Judge." Slaughter merely waved his hat and left the storeroom.

Ford lingered behind, looking around him at the crates of supplies and lit a fresh cigar. He guessed his good news could wait until tomorrow. And there was the matter of Sarah Jane, who waited for him now. Ford smiled and blew out the lantern and left the darkened store. It was nice to have another woman to turn to in time of need, he figured, although he knew Melissa would throw a fit if she ever found out about Sarah. Ford stepped into the street and nearly lost his hat to a cold wind that had sprung up in the last hour. The guard wished the attorney a good night before relocking the store and moving off toward home in the opposite direction. Ford sauntered down Blake Street, appearing not to have heard the guard, the wind whipping his expensive suit coat about him.

That same wind gave forth moaning sounds around the snug cabin where Melissa Stiles lay awake, staring up in the darkness, too excited to sleep. Through the thin curtain that offered little privacy, she heard her mother roll over on the

209

straw ticking in the next bed. She listened for her breathing to become regular again.

"You still awake, Melissa?" Mary Stiles asked.

"I simply can't sleep, Mother," Melissa said, turning to face the curtain. A long silence filled the cabin as they lay there listening to the moaning wind in a place far away from familiar places and friends.

"I remember when your father asked me to marry him," Mary started out. "My family had gone to a barn raising for a Mr. Hillrose who lived in the next valley from us. I must confess, I couldn't keep my eyes off your father, so tall and proud, with skin the color of summer wheat. My, what a day that turned out to be," Mary said, recalling it with such vivid clarity some thirty-odd years later. Melissa couldn't be still, wiggling deeper into the straw ticking.

"Is that when father proposed to you, Mother?" Mary asked excitedly.

"It was. And I was bursting with happiness. Don't even remember the buggy ride back home, but I can still remember the honest smell of him near me; fresh sawdust and sweat." Melissa jumped out of the bed, no longer able to stay there. She came around the partition and got in bed with Mary.

"Oh, Mother, that's how it is with me." Melissa hugged her mother to her and it was a minute before she felt the wetness on her arm. "Are you crying, Mother?"

"I was just thinking how much I miss your father and little Jonathan. What I wouldn't give for them to be here now . . . for your wedding." Melissa jumped straight up in bed; bouncing up and down on the firm ticking, squealing.

"Mother, Mother, then I do have your permission!" She fell into her mother's arms, hugging her tightly.

"I guess so, child," Mary Stiles said a little sadly. "Under normal circumstances, I'd say wait a respectable amount of time. But times aren't normal and neither is this place next to the mountains. My only hope is that he will make you happy."

"I am happy, Mother, so happy." Melissa sank her head

to Mary's shoulder and silence once more invaded the tiny cabin.

Mary Stiles lay there, trying to sort through her runaway thoughts and mixed feelings. True, she should have seen it coming, and did to a certain degree. What she had expected was a longer courtship. It was just one more thing she had to deal with, and all too soon since coming to Denver. A lot of things had happened to them in the past month: the death of her husband and son; their abduction and subsequent rescue from the Indians by Jack Dawson and Josiah Catt who asked for nothing other than a chance to help those in need; and now her only living child was about to be married to a prominent lawyer. Mary Stiles felt a little twinge of sorrow that Jack Dawson hadn't been the one to catch Melissa's eye. He was strong and would stand firm in the face of adversity. She wasn't sure about A.C. Ford. He was too much like the others, fresh from the "states." But Jack Dawson knew this terribly beautiful land, how to live with it, and how to overcome its harsh ways. He was a man of the mountains and the Plains, a survivor. Ford belonged in the city like most folks. But would he take care of her daughter like Jack Dawson could if things suddenly went wrong for them? Beside her, Melissa mumbled in her sleep as Mary Stiles offered up a prayer for them both. Still, she couldn't help thinking, had it been Ford who stumbled across their tracks out there on the Plains, would he have attempted to rescue them? The moaning wind died to a whisper as Mary finally drifted back to sleep, clinging tightly to her only reason for living.

Chapter 22

Word spread through the infant city like a prairie fire through dry buffalo grass in late autumn. By nine o'clock, the streets were jammed with men, youths, and bonneted women awaiting the hanging. Dazzling sunshine greeted the stoic guards as they stepped into the street from the Cherokee House at the corner of Blake and F Streets. Leading the way were Sheriff Middaugh and his deputized sons, Asa and James. A few steps back Marshal Pollock, standing head and shoulders above the pressing crowd, walked along with a ten-gauge shotgun clutched in his big hands while the butts of two pistols protruded from his waistband. Behind him, the manacled Edward Noel and Gordon Raymer, ashen and silent, followed with faltering steps. Six more heavily armed guards brought up the rear. The tense group eased slowly through the curious onlookers, heading for the east bank of Cherry Creek, one long block away and to the gallows erected there last month for a hanging that never took place. The prisoner, James Gordon, had escaped custody and was rumored to be somewhere in the "states." Bill Middaugh was leaving that very afternoon on the stagecoach to track him down.

The crowd was thick along the grassy banks of Cherry Creek and Middaugh shouted for them to give way, barging ahead with his rifle cocked. Businessmen, miners, emigrants as well as the unruly crowd from the Criterion and other drinking establishments were gathered in the shadows of the gallows, smoking cigars and talking quietly. A hush fell over the assembled men, women, and children as the doomed men came up.

With desperate eyes, Edward Noel scanned the crowd and caught sight of the flamboyant Charlie Harrison, proprietor of the Criterion.

"For the love of God, Charlie, shoot me!" Edward cried hoarsely.

Charlie Harrison smiled at Noel, "Now if I was to do that, Edward, those gentlemen with you will shoot my new suit full of holes and I just paid a hundred dollars for it." A smattering of nervous laughter rippled through the tense crowd.

Marshal Pollock prodded Edward Noel up the first step, Gordon Raymer went quickly up the steps under his own power even though his face reflected the look of a man about to die. It took two deputies to get the blubbering Noel to the top of the platform where Middaugh had already placed a hemp noose around Raymer's neck. Raymer stood there, silent and drawn, but holding on to what was left of his courage, determined to go out like a man.

Noel had to be supported while the noose was dropped over his head and properly set; even then he squirmed like a worm in hot ashes.

"You don't be still," Middaugh whispered just loud enough for Noel to hear, "when you drop, the rope ain't going to break your neck properly and you'll be sometime strangling to death." Middaugh's words brought him up short and he straightened enough to allow the noose to be adjusted behind his left ear.

Marshal Tom Pollock held up his hand to quiet the crowd and waited for the din to die down enough for him to read the People's Court verdict in a thundering voice. Noel and Raymer stood by pale and drawn, their eyes darting over the sea of onlookers.

Pollock turned to the two men, "Either of you got any final words?" This time it was Edward Noel who shook his head silently.

213

"I want to say how sorry I am for my part in shooting John Osgood," Gordon Raymer said in a steady voice. "I only ask his family to forgive us for what we done. Know it won't do no good to ask the Lord's," he finished in a faltering voice. A few minutes of strained silence followed as the black hoods were slipped over the two men's heads. Hats came off in the crowd.

"You men just stand like you are," Middaugh instructed them as he stepped back and gave Pollock the nod. Pollock yanked the handle of the trapdoor and the popping sound of it falling away raced over the crowd like thunder on a clear day. Audible gasps rose up from the crowd of watching men and women.

The pair shot through the hole in the platform, jerked up hard as they came to the end of their ropes and did a slow half circle to the left. Quick and efficient and it was only five minutes past ten.

"Guess I'll round up a few of the fellows and start a game," Colin Jackson said, turning away from the death scene to Ford who sat in his shiny carriage tightly gripping the reins of his two horses. "You interested?"

"I never want to be hung," Ford whispered reverently, his eyes still glued to the dead killers, their faces already a purple gray. He had not heard Colin's question.

Colin laughed and brought out two cigars and handed one to Ford.

"Relax, Counselor Ford, you ought to be thinking of your upcoming wedding, not of dying." He put a match to his and held the flame out for Ford, who didn't seem to know he was holding the cigar. Colin flicked the match away from the buggy.

Ford turned to the gunman, "Just promise me one thing, Colin. If I ever get caught, I want you to shoot me, just don't let them hang me."

"Nobody's going to get caught, A.C. Christ, we got the law and a judge on our side, remember."

* * *

A week slipped by quietly after the double hangings with Colin playing cards with vigilante committee members, Ford, Shear, Judge Slaughter and D.C. Oakes at night and entertaining Sarah Jane whenever Ford was preoccupied with Melissa Stiles and the upcoming wedding. Ford was coming home less and less each day to Sarah Jane who reacted by showering her steady attentions on the gunman as if to get even with the attorney.

It was in the middle of the following week when Mademoiselle Carolista, the star of a traveling variety troupe, came to town that Sarah Jane found out about Ford's plans to marry Melissa Stiles.

Sarah Jane burst into Colin's room unannounced and nearly got shot in the bargain. She ignored the gun pointed at her by the tight-lipped gunman.

"That lying bastard! Do you know what he plans to do?" Sarah Jane literally screamed, her face flooded with anger.

Colin Jackson put the pistol on the night table and closed the door behind the woman.

"No, what?"

"He's going to marry that pasty-faced little wench, that's what!" Sarah Jane stormed around the room too worked up to sit down. To make matters worse, she had to find it out from that little tight-assed whore, Cora Blackburn.

Colin lay back on the bed, propping himself up with the pillows. A thin smile played across his hard features.

"You still got me, Sarah Jane," Colin said teasingly. She stopped her prancing and looked at the gambler for a moment.

"I'm being serious, Colin. What should I do?"

Colin beckoned her over and slowly Sarah Jane approached the bed with a certain amount of caution. She was not up to fooling around, not the way she was feeling. She sat down on the bed, but kept her distance.

"Not much you can do less you want to tell him about us. That case, I'd be forced to shoot him."

Sarah Jane's eyes grew wide. "Would you shoot a friend?"

The smile on Colin's face grew thin and finally disappeared altogether. He reached for her. Even though she wanted to resist, knew she should, Sarah Jane felt herself move closer to the gunman.

"I got no friends in this world, Sarah honey," he said, stroking her arm. "I learned long ago not to put my trust in any man . . . or woman for that matter. That way, life is a lot less complicated."

"What about me, Colin? You care anything for me?"

"As much as I can about anyone, Sarah Jane." He pulled her closer to him, kissing her hair. "Any man would be fool not to want you, take care of you," he said.

Sarah Jane pulled back and looked at Colin with tears brimming in her eyes.

"I only want him to hurt, like I do now."

"I know, but the best thing you can do for yourself is to pitch him out . . . before he's ready. That'll hurt his pride more than anything."

"I can't do that, Colin."

"Why not?"

"It's his place."

"That case, go back and pack your things and move out before he gets back. Knowing A.C., he's probably never had a woman leave him in his life."

"But I got no place to go."

"You can stay here . . . with me. Until I leave." Sarah Jane considered what Colin Jackson was saying while he stroked her arm. What did she have to lose? In a week or two, A.C. was bound to give her the boot. Then, what would she do? She turned and gave Colin a fiery kiss on the lips and jumped up.

"I'll be back shortly with my things." And then she stopped at the door and looked back. "What if A.C. finds out about us?"

"Does it matter?"

Sarah Jane considered this for a moment and finally nodded. What could he do? He wasn't about to go up against the likes of Colin Jackson. She never said A.C. Ford was

216

stupid, only lecherous when it came to women. All men suffered from the same weakness, some more than others. As she turned to leave, she wondered what Colin Jackson's weakness was. As she crossed the street and headed down the two blocks to Ford's place, she concluded the cold-eyed gunman didn't have any. Unless it was the fact he was only half-human.

From a curtained window, Colin Jackson watched the woman move off down the street, the smile back on his face once more. He hadn't the heart to tell the woman he was leaving tomorrow for a while. He would pay the rent on the room for a week or so. That would give her time to get things straightened out. Like a few women he knew, Sarah Jane was like a cat thrown off a building, she would land on her feet every time.

Colin dropped the curtain back into place, picked up his coat, and headed for the door. He needed to find Black Hawk and "Professor" Cove Stillman. And he knew his best bet was probably Ada Lamont's place.

"You still headed out in the morning?" Josiah Catt asked, stirring the slurry of sand and mud around in the big pan with an experienced flick of his wrist.

Jack Dawson stopped rocking the sluice back and forth for a moment and wiped the sweat building beneath the brim of his hat. In spite of the cool air, under the blazing sun, the rocker could make a man sweat on a cold day.

"Thought I would. Figure to swing back across the ridge and over through the Jackson and Gregory diggings. See if I can locate Walter Dumont. Then push on to Denver with what gold we've taken out."

Josiah Catt nodded, his eyes never leaving the swishing pan. "You'll find Clark and Gruber's Mint at the corner of McGaa and Blake Street. A two-storied red brick."

"I'll find it, don't worry so."

Catt stopped working the pan and squinted up at Dawson with one eye shut against the sun. "Just be careful, Jack.

You'll be carrying over twenty thousand in gold. Make any man think twice when it comes to knocking you in the head for it."

A determined look spread over Dawson's face. "Needn't worry about that either. I've had enough knocks on the head to make me wary of late." Catt went back to working the dregs of sand over the lip of the pan until all that was left was a dozen shining nuggets.

"Hand me a pouch, will you, Jack? You may as well take this little dab along with you when you go. Just about enough fer a twenty dollar gold piece."

Chapter 23

Jack Dawson asked every group of miners he passed by of the whereabouts of Walter Dumont. To a man, the name meant nothing to them. He had the same luck at Jackson's diggings and found only one old sourdough at the Gregory site ever having heard of Dumont. The grizzled miner stopped just long enough to tell Dawson what he knew.

"One of his group had a horse gone lame and they rested over to that cottonwood for a spell while this Dumont fella went looking for another horse." The miner squinted up at Dawson on horse back and spit a brown stream of tobacco into the rushing waters where he stood up to his knees.

"They say where they might be heading?" Dawson asked, feeling he was getting nowhere fast.

"Only that this Dumont fella was looking for his brother. Claimed he had made a good sized strike and had sent for him to come out. But lots of folks do that, most just feeling homesick and wanting to see a familiar face. Most times, they ain't found enough gold to keep a cat alive through the winter."

Dawson gathered up his reins. Chances of flushing Dumont out of these mountains was next to none.

"You happen to see Dumont again, tell him I got news about his brother."

"He make a strike?"

"He's dead," Dawson said. "My partner and I found him

and another fellow covered with rocks. Both been shot through the heart at close range."

The features on the old man flattened somewhat. "Claim jumpers! That's bad business. Any idea who done it?"

"Could be, just can't prove it."

"A man can't be too careful nowadays, not with all the pikers we got pouring in here everyday. I see this Dumont, where will I tell him to find you?"

Dawson thought for a moment. He didn't want to give away the location of their claim just yet.

"Tell him, I'll leave directions with the agent at the land office in Denver City."

The old miner smiled. "Found you a good claim I reckon. Don't blame you none for wanting to keep it a secret."

"It's more than that. Figure I owe Dumont first crack at a good site before others crowd in."

"Mighty commendable of you," the miner said, bending over his pan once more. "I'll give him the message, but don't count on my seeing him again. More people a-coming and a-going in this gulch in one day than they is in the whole city of Denver."

Dawson thanked him and continued on down the canyon feeling hopeless. He realized the chances of finding Walter Dumont were slim at best, yet he continued to ask any miner he met, coming up the trail. Most rushed on by him as if their tails were on fire, too anxious to get on to the diggings than stop and talk.

Dawson had no further luck and by the middle of the afternoon, splashed across the South Platte and entered Denver City through a few Indian lodges, thrown up on the banks of the river among huge cottonwood trees. The Arapaho had been camping in this spot for over a hundred years. Now they came to buy things from stores they could not get anyplace else, bringing pelts of beaver, soft buckskin and buffalo hides to trade.

Several women were down at the river getting water and when they saw Jack Dawson, they scampered into the thick underbrush. One of the women had obviously been bathing for Dawson caught sight of bare buttocks and shapely legs as they fled to the safety of the woods.

He steered his horse away from the site and skirted the dozen or so lodges, respecting their right to be there. Dawson continued east and picked up G Street and four blocks away came upon the imposing brick structure of Clark and Gruber's Mint. He tied his horse to the hitching post and lifted the heavy saddlebags to his shoulders. He stood there getting his balance for a moment, looking up at the building which stood all alone. The nearest building was Lawrence's Livery, four or five lots down McGaa Street. Across the street was a tinsmith shop declaring William Mark, proprietor, in red letters above the door.

Dawson stepped up to the stone platform edifice where four white marble columns held up the front of the mint. Above these columns in white, two-foot letters were the inscription, Clark, Gruber & Co. Bank and Mint were framed in black letters across the top of the two-storied building. It was then he noticed the heavily barred windows and iron shutters. He opened the door and stepped inside, surprised at the ornate interior of the bank. He went over to the marble teller cage and hoisted the heavy saddlebags to the counter. A youthful appearing man in a starched white shirt with black garters around his upper biceps got up from a desk and came over.

"Can I help you?"

"Got a little free gold I want to trade for gold pieces."

"Yes, sir. That will only take a minute," the teller said, dragging the heavy saddlebags over to his side of the cage. He unbuckled a flap and lifted out the heavy leather pouches and began weighing the contents on a scale set up next to the cage. A man dressed in a dark, expensive suit got up from a large gleaming desk and came over to where Dawson stood watching the teller weighing the gold.

"You've made good I see," the man said, looking over at the gold pan piled high with nuggets. "And pure quality by the looks of it."

"My partner and I have done okay," Dawson said, not

wanting to boast. Gold in this amount could loosen a lot of tongues, and he didn't want to be hounded by people looking to follow him back into the mountains when he got ready to leave.

The man laughed easily. "There's no need to be concerned about any business conducted in this establishment. Our policy to our customers assures you of complete privacy. I'm Austin M. Clark," he said, extending his hand to Dawson. "I own this bank along with my brother, Milton, and E.H. Gruber."

Dawson felt relived as he shook the banker's hand. "You been in business long?"

"Opened our doors a month ago today, isn't that right, Bates?"

"Yes sir," Bates replied without taking his eyes off the scales.

"Having gold coins ought to improve transactions around here," Dawson commented, recalling the brawls he had seen in several saloons over the bartender's ability to take more than a pinch of gold dust from a miner's poke for the price of a drink.

"It has indeed. Have you seen our coins?"

"No I haven't. Just got in a little while ago. Yours is the first place I stopped.

"Wise decision," Clark said, fishing out two gold coins he kept in his pocket for just such an occasion. He handed them both to Dawson. "That one is a ten dollar gold piece, the other is a twenty."

Dawson hefted the coins, liking the feel of them as he examined one closely. On one side were the words, Pikes Peak Gold and a crude outline of Pikes Peak, while the other side carried the name of the mint.

"At the present time we are only equipped to coin ten and twenty dollar pieces, but they are of pure gold and their value exceeds the government's issue," Clark explained.

Teller Bates interrupted them, "You have a total of twenty-two thousand, three hundred fifteen dollars and

222

sixty-six cents. Do you wish to open an account, or will you take it all with you?"

"Well, I'll leave you in good hands, Mister Dawson," Austin Clark said smoothly. "Don't hesitate to let me know if I can be of further help." With that, Austin Clark, attorney and co-owner, returned to his desk.

Dawson stared for a moment at Bates. In two weeks time, he and Catt had made more money than he had ever seen in his life. He thought of the hardships he and Tom Fitzpatrick had suffered trapping beaver and guiding emigrants across the Plains. The most he had accumulated at one sitting was the twelve hundred dollars he had stolen from him in St. Joe. And now he had over eleven thousand dollars for his part alone! Never in his wildest dreams had he ever thought he would have that kind of money.

"Mister Dawson?" Bates waited.

Dawson brought his runaway thinking under control, clearing his throat.

"Guess you better open me and Josiah Catt an account. I'll take five hundred in those new gold coins for supplies and such," Dawson mumbled, still in shock. A few minutes later he had signed for the account, deposited the coins in several of the leather pouches, and retrieved his horse from the hitching post. The next thing he had to do was record their claim over at the land office and leave a message for Walter Dumont, then he would report the murders to the sheriff.

Dawson noticed the flurry of activity as men hurried east toward Cherry Creek and he shouted at a young boy.

"Ain't you heard! Mademoiselle Carolista is doing a tightrope walk between two buildings down on Larimer Street. Town's taken up a hundred seventy dollars to pay her. You coming, ain't you, mister?"

Dawson smiled down at the freckled boy and guessed his age at twelve or thirteen. Scraggly looking, with pants worn thin in spots and no shoes for his dusty feet, Dawson suspected the boy was having a tough time of it.

"What's your name, son?"

"Andy. Andrew Philmore, sir."

"Well, Andrew, you looking for employment?"

The boy's face brightened, "Yes, sir! You got anything I can do?"

"Might have. It's backbreaking work, but honest. You interested?"

"I'm your man," Andy Philmore said quickly. "And you can just call me Andy."

"I'm Jack Dawson." Dawson took the slim youth's hand in his and felt his hard, muscular grip. Whatever the boy had been doing to earn his living, he was not soft.

"Consider yourself on the payroll then." Dawson tossed him a new twenty dollar Clark & Gruber, and Andy caught the shiny coin expertly.

"But I ain't done nothing yet," Andy protested.

"You will," Dawson promised. "Now get up behind me and we'll go have ourselves a look at this tightrope walker. You got any family?"

Andy Philmore swung up behind Dawson. "No, sir. I ran away from an orphanage back in Kentucky. Caught a river steamer to St. Louis and headed West first chance I got. I figure to strike it rich soon's I can earn enough for a grub-stake." He realized what he was saying and stammered. Dawson laughed.

"That's okay. Expect everybody in Denver ain't running a business is looking to head to the mountains and stake a claim."

"I'm not going to run off first chance I get just because you advanced me money, Mister Dawson, that's a promise."

"Know you won't, son. And call me Jack, okay?"

"Okay," Andy said, feeling all warm inside with the gold coin tugging at his pocket as they rode along. Things looked different from the back of a horse. God, what he wouldn't give to own one like this big buckskin he was riding now.

"You got a horse?" Dawson asked as if knowing what the boy was thinking.

"No, sir."

"After we get done watching Mademoiselle Caroletta—"

"Carolista," Andy corrected. He liked to roll her name over his tongue and he had practiced saying it out loud again and again until it came out as natural as his own name.

"Whatever. We'll see about finding you a horse and some work clothes and boots."

In spite of his effort to control his emotions, Andy felt hot tears stinging his eyes. He couldn't remember anyone treating him this nice in his whole life. He wanted to thank Dawson, but he didn't trust his voice not to reveal he was crying. Besides, there was a large lump in his throat that hurt when he swallowed.

They drew up well back in the crowd a block from Cherry Creek and Andy slid to the ground while Dawson remained where he was, studying the thin cable stretched tight across the street, twenty feet above the ground.

"Look!" Andy said, pointing.

Dawson and the crowd watched as a dainty woman in pink slippers and flowing white skirt eased out on the taut cable. A roar of approval rose up from the crowd. Dawson looked down at the beaming youth and wondered what had possessed him to hire the boy on the spot. There were plenty of other youths in the crowd that could probably use a little looking after. Catt would be surprised to say the least when he came riding up with the kid. True, they could use some help around the camp, keeping fire wood and the coffee pot going for Josiah, but Dawson finally admitted to himself the real reason he had befriended the boy. He saw the reflection of his own youth in the kid and the desperate eyes that asked only for acceptance, understanding, and a chance at life to prove his worth.

While the crowd kept their eyes glued to the suretooted slip of a girl dancing her way across the swaying wire, Dawson caught sight of a familiar face, peeking from beneath a sparkling clean buggy across the street. It was Melissa Stiles! Although he could only see part of an arm which held the reins, Dawson didn't need to see the rest to know it had to be attorney A.C. Ford squiring the girl around. Dawson sought her face again and realized how beautiful she was. He was tempted to go over and get reacquainted, but he checked the impulse. His clothes were grimy and trail worn, and he needed a bath and shave. It was best to wait until later.

Thunderous applause broke out, and it was a minute before Dawson realized Mademoiselle Carolista had completed her dance across the wire. The crowd started breaking up.

"Wasn't that just great?" Andy asked, his eyes shining.

"Never seen better, son. I see a clothing store over next to that confectionary shop. What do you say we both get us some new clothes?"

"Great," Andy said, wanting to shout instead.

They were moving through the crowd when a buggy came crashing through with a woman lashing out at the charging animal with a whip. Men and horses gave way in front of the driving woman. As she passed them, Dawson caught a glimpse of a redheaded woman in tight bodice and flowing skirts. He looked back in time to see her yank back on the reins as she came alongside the surrey carrying Melissa Stiles. Her voice was sharp and clear in the afternoon air.

"Damn you, A.C. How come I'm not good enough to go riding with you anymore?" the woman screamed, laying her whip across Ford's exposed arm.

"Sarah Jane!" Ford shouted surprised by the sudden onslaught. "This is completely uncalled for."

"Uncalled for!" Sarah Jane screamed at him, her face livid. "You don't think I deserve knowing about your little sweet cake here, that you two are planning to get married? My God, A.C. that's low-down even for you. At least Colin would never string me along like this."

"Colin? What about Colin?" Ford wanted to know.

"Never mind," Sarah Jane said, cutting him off. She turned to Melissa Stiles who sat there speechless, both hands to her mouth.

"Honey, you can have him. Just make sure he don't come

226

scratching around my door late at night like some stray dog looking for a bone." With that, Sarah Jane put the whip to her animal and thundered away.

"Wonder what that was all about?" Andy asked, standing next to Dawson who smiled knowingly.

"Women, Andy, women. You'll understand when you get older, but I can give you some advice now you can carry with you all your natural life."

"What's that, Jack?" Andy asked, climbing the two steps leading up from the street to the clothing store.

"Never court two women at one time, no matter how tempting . . . unless of course they live in separate towns." Dawson laughed and slapped the youngster on the shoulder. "Come on, let's get some new duds."

Ford stared after the departing buggy, seething with rage. Melissa placed a hand on his arm.

"You're bleeding."

Ford looked down where the whip had cut through his suit coat and shirt and saw the red streak. He fought to get his emotions under control for Melissa's sake.

"I'll be all right," he managed to say.

"Who was that woman?" Melissa asked.

"I'm sorry you were exposed to that outburst," Ford said, taking Melissa's hand. "That was a lady friend I used to see."

"Why was she so mad?"

"I honestly don't know. I've had nothing to do with her for quite a long time now," Ford lied. He slapped the reins across the backs of his horses. "Come, I'll get you home. I still have some business to attend to at the office. We'll have dinner later if you like."

Melissa squeezed his arm. "That would be nice," she said, snuggling close to him as Ford guided the carriage expertly through the thinning crowd, his mind replaying the scene with Sarah Jane. What bothered him most was the reference to Colin Jackson. It was a slip. He knew Sarah Jane well enough to know that when rattled things slipped out that normally she keep secret. He had never in his life beaten up a woman. But if he found her at his home when he got there, she stood a good chance of being his first.

Chapter 24

Dawson pulled the dress coat over his lean frame and stood there admiring himself in the mirror. The coat bulged outward where the big dragoon lay strapped against his waist. He turned to the clerk.

"I'll take it, and throw in a pair of pants."

The balding clerk nodded with a smile, taking the coat from Dawson. "Shall I get you a pair of boots as well?" he asked, recognizing a man with new money. Dawson hadn't even asked the price of the dark coat.

Dawson looked down at the scuffed boots. "Guess these'll do a little longer. You got the boy fixed up?"

"Yes, sir, the works. And I must say your son is happy with the selections I made for him." Andy Philmore had gone out on the sidewalk with his packages where he waited by Dawson's horse.

"Kid ain't mine. Works for me," Dawson said, digging in a glass jar on the counter for a handful of cigars. "I'll take these, too."

Dawson got them two rooms at the Broadwell House and learned Mary Stiles had checked out several weeks back. The clerk thought they had moved into a cabin owned by A.C. Ford over on St. Louis Street. Dawson figured as much as he ordered up two hot baths for him and the kid. There was still the matter of the two murdered miners he needed to report, but that could wait until he had cleaned up.

"Kid, you look like a new man," Dawson said later to the boy as they descended the stairs together.

"Feel like one, too," Andy Philmore said happily. "You clean up pretty good yourself."

Dawson laughed, tugging at the coat by the lapels. "Can't get this dern coat to lay just right."

"It's that big pistol you're carrying. I've never seen one that big before," Andy said, eyeing the weapon. "What kind is it?"

"A .44 Colt Dragoon, boy, and bucks like a mustang in a fight. Come on, let's go find the sheriff before it gets dark. You getting hungry?" Dawson asked, realizing the boy probably had not eaten this day.

"I'm okay. I can wait." Dawson asked the desk clerk where he might find the sheriff.

"Most likely over at one of his businesses on Ferry Street." Dawson recalled seeing a lawman standing in the doorway of a building across from Wootton's Hotel when he and Josiah Catt were staying there. They rode over to the sheriff's office on Dawson's horse since they had yet to get Andy his own.

A skinny man of sixty looked up from his evening paper and stared at the big man for a moment as if considering the question important enough to answer. In the end, the old man decided in favor of Dawson, impressed with his steel blue eyes and the Colt strapped to his waist.

"Sheriff Middaugh ain't here. He's gone to Leavenworth, Kansas, tracking a killer. No set time for him to be back."

"You the law?" Dawson asked.

"Heck no. I'm kinda the jailer, do the cleaning, keep the coffee hot, that sorta thing. You need a lawman, you got to go next door to Pollock's Saloon, just across third street. Tom Pollock's the city marshal," the man added as an afterthought.

Dawson instructed Andy to stay with his horse as he pushed through the door of the saloon. Pollock's place was no different than the countless others Dawson had been in over the span of his adult life. Constrained by the usual size

230

of the town lots, a typical drinking establishment tended to be longer than it was wide with the rear of the building being divided into rooms to accommodate the elite who could gamble, drink, and socialize in private from the front-hall crowd.

Dawson surveyed the crowded saloon, his eyes sweeping the men at the long bar with practiced eyes. He found himself trading glances with a bearded man who looked familiar to him and Dawson dug into his memory as he approached the bar. He intended to ask the bartender for Marshal Pollock's whereabouts when the bearded man called to him. Dawson angled over in his direction, giving the other two men who were obviously with him the once over. Both were tall and broad-shouldered; one wore his flame-colored hair and beard long while the other had the look and polish of a gambler or gunman. Dawson didn't know which.

"You Dawson, ain't you?" Black Hawk asked, as Dawson strode up.

"That's right. Met you over in the mountains, didn't I?"

"Yeah," the outlaw said, studying Dawson's new clothes. "Appears you run into some good luck. Hit the lode, did you?"

"It's showing some promise," Dawson replied. "I'm looking for the marshal, want to report a double murder."

"You don't say?" Black Hawk responded, rubbing his beard thoughtfully.

"That's right. Don't suppose you know anything about it?"

Black Hawk looked startled, "Now why would I know anything about such things?"

"My partner and I found them near your claim. Both had been shot in the chest at close range and their bodies covered over with rocks."

"I swear," Black Hawk replied, feigning surprise, "you hear that, Tom?" The outlaw asked turning to Tom Pollock.

"I heard," Tom Pollock said, stepping away from the bar.

"I'm Marshal Pollock. You say you and your partner found these men, when?"

"Maybe a week ago, or less."

"And you just now reporting it?"

Dawson felt the first sting of anger rising in him. "Look, we must be thirty miles back in there. It's rough country to get in and out of. Besides, they were already dead. Figured they could wait another week."

"You did, did you? Waiting gives the killers more time to make good their escape. You should have come straight to town and reported it," Pollock said, glaring down at Dawson. "What's your partner's name and where is he now?"

Dawson looked at the big man who stood several inches above him, feeling himself beginning to lose control. He noticed the gambler-gunman's face had not so much as twitched during the entire conversation.

"Josiah Catt. He's still working our claim."

"And where is that?"

"Four or five miles up the same drainage from this man's claim," Dawson said, indicating Black Hawk.

"We done give up on it, Tom. Weren't enough there to pay for cheap whiskey." Dawson caught the look and the lie traded by marshal and outlaw, and he knew he may have let his emotions overstep his sense of caution. But is was too late to change things now.

"I feel sure one of the murdered men is a brother to a man I met on the trail, a Walter Dumont. Left a message at the diggings and over at the land office in case he shows up."

"Uh-huh. Well, I'm just the city marshal, don't have any jurisdiction outside of town. You'll have to tell your story to the federal marshal since the sheriff is out of town."

"Where will I find him?"

Black Hawk gave a small snicker, and it was the first time Dawson had seen the gunman's face express any feeling by the slightly upward turn of his lip.

"Why Kansas, of course," Pollock replied. Dawson's features flattened out somewhat as his anger flared. Damned i he was going to stand there and be toyed with like some greenhorn pilgrim.

"You got the word," Dawson said coldly. "You tell him!" With that, Dawson wheeled on his heels and started for the door.

"Just a damn minute," Pollock bellowed, "ain't through questioning you yet!" Dawson stopped, turned back and as he turned he swept his new coat aside, exposing the big Colt.

"I'm done talking," Dawson said flatly, "less you planning on using force." The noisy saloon fell silent and men froze in place, their eyes on the scene.

A long moment of silence built between the two men as Black Hawk tried to ease away from the marshal without anybody thinking he was a coward. But he was blocked by Colin's big frame, so he just stood there looking at a man with no fear in his eyes.

"Aw, hell, go on," Pollock waved a big fist, "I know where to find you if I need you later." Dawson traded looks with the bearded outlaw and recorded the uneasiness he saw in the man's eyes. When he looked at the gambler-gunman, he saw absolutely nothing. The man showed no fear at all. Dawson turned back and left the quiet saloon. As soon as he was through the doors, the din from inside settled back to its normal level.

Dawson stood there for a moment in the gathering darkness, angry at himself. What had come over him? Bracing a marshal wasn't the way to win friends in this town.

"You okay, Jack?" Andy asked, noting the look on Dawson's face.

Dawson let out a long sigh, "I'm okay, kid. Whattaya say we grab ourselves something to eat. Know a good place?"

"Heard the Vasquez House has excellent meals." Andy dropped his head slightly, "But I ain't never eaten there."

"Well, by golly, you are about to. Lead the way."

* * *

Pollock and the other two turned back to the bar and the marshal ordered them fresh drinks. There was a frown on his face.

"I don't like it," he finally said, after they had their drinks.

"Nothing to be worried over, Tom," Black Hawk said reassuringly. Then he dropped his voice a notch, "Ain't nobody can pin this on us and certainly not that blowhard trapper, Dawson."

Pollock shook his head doubtfully, "Things have a way of snowballin', you ain't careful."

"We will be," Black Hawk replied, downing his drink. "Fact is, me and Colin before we came over here for a final drink, was talking about going back up there and silencing them two for good measure. Now that it looks like they hit good pay dirt, we might just take over their claim as well."

Pollock looked quickly around to make sure nobody had overheard what Black Hawk had just said. "You got to be real careful how you talk, Black Hawk," Pollock whispered uncharacteristically. "Just take care of the problem and lay low for a while. Claim-jumping and murder ain't like stealing horses."

"We'll handle it, Tom," Colin Jackson spoke up. "Just like we always have."

The tension stayed in Pollock's face. "Did you have to go and kill those two miners?"

Colin's gray eyes flashed fire, "What did you want us to do, run them off so they could squeal later? Your problem, Pollock, is you don't mind the gravy but you haven't the stomach for the blood."

"I've spilled my share of it!" Pollock snapped, his face showing his dislike for the gunman.

"Tom . . . Colin. Both of you get hold of yourselves," Black Hawk said, feeling the building heat between them. "We got us a good thing going here, no use spoiling the yeast before we done mixing the flour." Abruptly, Tom Pollock stomped off toward his office without another word.

"You going to push Tom too far one of these days," Black Hawk warned Colin.

"And what? Pollock's no coward, but he's no fool either."

"Seen him in a fight. Tom's pretty handy with that short gun when he needs to be," the outlaw said. "I know he ain't in your class, Colin, but as you know a lucky shot sometimes wins the battle."

"I think I'll go play a few hands," Colin said, dispensing with such unproductive talk. Tom Pollock could practice for the rest of his life and never come up to his standards. But this Dawson . . . there was something about him that made him feel uneasy. Colin had seen no give in the man when he faced down Pollock. He also noticed how Dawson kept him in his sight the whole time, case Colin wanted to offer trouble.

"We still pulling out tomorrow?"

"First light. Meet you and the professor down at the livery."

"Why you suddenly calling Cove Stillman that?" Black Hawk asked, emptying his glass. Colin laughed softly as he turned to the door.

"You wouldn't understand, Black Hawk." With that Colin stepped into the night, leaving the outlaw flustered and a little mad without really knowing why.

"You think this might be the cabin?" Dawson asked Andrew Philmore as they approached the structure under a full moon. A light shone in the cabin's only front window.

"I think so, that is, it could be," Andy responded, not wanting to chance disappointing his new friend. They had walked over from the Vasquez House after an early supper since the cabin wasn't far out of town.

Dawson stepped up to the door and knocked twice before taking a step back with his hat in his hand. Beside him, Andy took the cue and pulled his new hat Dawson had bought him from his head. From within, they heard a flurry of footsteps and suddenly the door was thrown open. They were greeted by a smiling Melissa Stiles wearing a pretty dress of blue and white with a tight bodice trimmed in lace. Dawson smiled back.

"Oh, I thought you were . . . someone else," Melissa said, her smile fading.

"Who is it, Melissa?" her mother called from behind her.

"It's . . . it's Jack Dawson, and a boy," Melissa said, looking down at the youngster standing next to Dawson.

"Ask them in, child, where are your manners?"

Melissa stepped quickly aside. "Please come in, won't you?"

Dawson found his voice, "Hello Melissa, how have you been? This is Andrew Philmore." They stepped inside and were greeted by the smells of fragrant cooking. Mary Stiles turned away from the stove and came over and offered Dawson her hand.

"It's so good to see you again, Jack." Mary looked down at the boy. "Is this your new partner?" Andy blushed from ear to ear under her close scrutiny. He had never said more than a dozen words in his life to a woman.

"Meet Andrew Philmore and I guess you could say he's a new partner. He answers to Andy when he's able to talk," Dawson said, enjoying the youngster's discomfort.

"Never you mind, Jack," Mary said. "Would you like a piece of hot pie, Andy?"

Andy could only nod his head. Mary directed them to the table while Melissa slunk behind with an unhappy expression on her face.

"Heard you were teaching now," Dawson said, pushing aside the empty pie plate and picking up his coffee cup. Mary had joined them with coffee of her own.

"Yes, and I'm enjoying it so much." Dawson let his eyes roam to Melissa who sat quietly with her hands folded in her lap.

"So you think you might stay around Denver City for a while, then?"

"I have to admit, the place grows on you. The mountains,

so majestic, looking like you can reach out and touch them." Mary's eyes grew dreamy. She straightened up and looked at Dawson. "And how is Josiah doing?"

"Happy as a newborn colt. He's still up there in the mountains working our claim."

"And you've found gold?" Mary asked wide-eyed.

"That we have and I don't mind telling you, it's paying a lot better than anything I've ever done in my life. Fact is . . . ." Dawson took out five twenty dollar gold pieces from Clark and Gruber's Mint and stacked them up before the woman. They caught the light from the lamp, casting off a burnished color and held those at the table spellbound. Even Melissa stared at the small stack of gold coins.

"Whatever is this for?" Mary asked.

"I was hoping to buy that new Henry once belonged to your husband," Dawson said softly. "The one I took from Tall Feather."

"I would be honored for you to have the rifle," Mary said getting up to fetch the Henry. "We have no need of it now," she said, placing the brass-plated rifle in Dawson's hands. "Nor can you buy it. It is my gift . . . for all you did for us."

They heard a horse and wagon approaching the cabin, and Melissa jumped up and rushed to the door. Dawson caught the concerned look of a parent on Mary Stiles's face as when a child is doing something unsettling. Dawson didn't have to guess who was at the door. He stood up and Andy did likewise.

"Put the money away," he whispered to the woman. "Me and Josiah have plenty more. You may need it later." Reluctantly, Mary Stiles picked up the money and put the coins in her apron pocket before the dressed-up lawyer stepped through the doorway. There was a faint trace of irritation on Ford's face when he saw Dawson standing there holding the rife.

"You remember my attorney, Mr. Ford," Mary Stiles said, still the gracious hostess. Dawson nodded, but did not speak.

"What are you doing back in town so soon?" Ford asked,

as Melissa slipped an arm into his. "Busted already?" he grinned.

"Just paying my respects," was all Dawson said.

"Well, if you're still around next week, you can come to our wedding," Ford smiled triumphantly.

"Oh? You finally settling down with that woman you been living with?" Dawson said with an evil grin.

Ford's face paled and then flooded with congested blood, his eyes pinpricks of fire. Melissa's hand flew to her mouth, her eyes full of hurt. Dawson was instantly sorry for having said what he did.

"It's Melissa I'm marrying," Ford said in a clipped voice, cold as ice.

"Pardon me," Dawson said, bowing slightly to Melissa who ignored his gesture.

"Shall we go?" Melissa whispered to the attorney.

"Yes, let's," he said, getting his temper under control once more. Mary saw them to the door while Dawson and Andy waited for the noise of the buggy to die away. Mary closed the door and leaned against it, her bosom heaving.

Dawson didn't pretend to know too much about women, especially this type, but what he saw in Mary Stiles's eyes made him think things were not all right where Melissa and the lawyer was concerned. Dawson laid the Henry across the table and helped himself to more coffee.

"See you're not too taken with your future son-in-law either," he said, coming over to the woman. Mary Stiles looked absently around her, running nervous fingers though her graying hair.

"What do you mean, Jack?" she asked without looking directly at him.

"Saw how you looked. That wasn't the look of a happy mother, unless I miss my guess."

Her chin dropped to her chest. For a moment, Dawson thought she was going to cry. In a few minutes she lifted her head and looked at him.

"I've tried to see the good in this . . . for Melissa's sake. What, after all, can I provide for her on eight dollars a week teaching school?" It was Dawson's turn to drop his head and he wished now he had said nothing, yet he was sorely rankled by the lawyer where Melissa was concerned.

"I apologize for my rude behavior," Dawson said. "I had no call."

Mary found a small smile somewhere down deep inside of herself and she gave it to Dawson.

"There's no need for an apology, Jack. I know you really came by tonight to see Melissa, but I'm afraid all is lost in that respect. If it's any consolation, my money was on you the whole time."

Dawson grinned ruefully and drained his cup, "Yeah, well, that's how it is with me." He turned to pick up the Henry from the table.

"Will you come to the wedding?"

"Don't expect that would be such a good idea," Dawson said, moving to the door.

"I wish you would come and bring Josiah along. You, too, Andy, you're invited as well." The boy blushed again.

On the way back to the Vasquez House to pick up Dawson's horse, Andy suddenly found his voice.

"She is real nice, Jack. Do you like her a lot?"

"I'm getting old, boy, but I ain't that old to take up with a woman could be my mother."

"No, not Miss Mary . . . Melissa. I saw how she looked at you when she thought you wasn't looking at her."

"You experienced with women now, are you?"

"Well, no . . . that is, not exactly," Andy stammered. "But I seen her look."

"Which was?" Dawson asked, hefting the Henry to his shoulder. Josiah would be pleased at his having bought the lever-action rifle. He would probably become tongue-tied when Dawson handed it to him as a gift.

"Can't explain it. It was kinda a faraway look, mushy like." Dawson laughed and laid a gentle hand on the boy's shoulder.

"Maybe so, boy, but you see who she's out with tonight.

239

Let's go get some sleep and tomorrow we'll find you a horse to ride and a few supplies. Expect old Josiah is about out of coffee now and getting meaner by the day we don't show up."

Chapter 25

"You sure this is the right place?" Colin asked Black Hawk as they sat looking at the huge avalanche of rock and twisted timber.

Black Hawk nodded, "It's got to be higher up. We need to work our way around this mess and pick up the creek again." The gunman still looked doubtful.

"It'd help if we didn't have this foot of new snow covering the ground," Cove Stillman said, pulling his coat closer to him in the howling wind.

"Cove, you bend around this pile of stuff to the right. Me and Colin'll work the other direction and meet you on the other side. And keep a sharp lookout for any signs, you know, broken branches or scuff marks where a horse maybe crossed exposed rock."

Cove Stillman turned his horse away from the cold wind saying, "I know how to read signs, Black Hawk." Cove was irritated by the statement and the wind. "Just hope there's something to see once we get to the other side."

"We ought to be free of this danged wind soon's we in thick timber," Black Hawk responded, raking his spurs into the flanks of his horse.

Thirty minutes later the three men joined back up beyond the slash of rocks and broken logs.

"You smell smoke?" Cove asked, wiping his dripping nose. Even though they were out of the wind, the air was brilliantly clear and cold.

"Uh-huh," the outlaw Black Hawk said. "Let's move out." They worked their way carefully up the rocky slope, staying close to the rushing creek for guidance. The new snow muffled their approach and they pulled up fifty yards out from the camp, keeping a few large boulders and big Ponderosa pines between them and the open ground.

As they sat their horses watching smoke rising from a brush hut, an old man emerged from the shanty wearing an old buffalo robe and carrying a skillet. His head was bald as an onion.

"Reckon that's Dawson's partner?" Cove whispered to the other two.

"Ain't but one way to find out," Black Hawk said, nudging his horse forward from the trees. Instantly, the old man by the creek froze. A second later he turned and disappeared into the brush hut only to emerge with a buffalo rifle.

"Wary old geezer, ain't he?" Black Hawk said.

"Wouldn't you be if three strangers came riding up to you in the middle of the mountains?" Colin said, chewing on the half-smoked cigar he held clamped between his teeth. Black Hawk only grunted his answer, his eyes probing the hut for further trouble. They rode slowly forward, keeping their hands in plain sight for the benefit of the old man by the creek.

"Good day to you," Colin spoke first, tipping his hat.

"Howdy," Josiah Catt replied, his eyes flashing a warning if they expected to cause him trouble.

"Would this be Gold Creek?" Colin continued.

"It is," Catt replied.

"Good, then you must be Josiah Catt?" The three men could see the flicker of surprise cross the old man's face.

"You've found me. What's this about?"

"You don't mind if we step down, do you?" Colin Jackson asked. "Long, cold ride from Denver City."

"Guess that'd be okay," Catt said, remaining alert while the three men dismounted carefully.

The gunman looked around at the rising land and timber

before letting his eyes come to rest on the old man once more.

"Beautiful place here and secluded, too," Colin said. "You would never guess until you rode around that wall of slash and rock that anything was on the other side. Good thing Dawson told us about it, huh, boys?"

"Woulda rode right on past," Black Hawk said, picking up on the thread Colin Jackson was working.

"You've talked with Jack?" Catt said, quite surprised. The Sharps dipped slightly lower.

"That we have. Said if we wanted to get in on a good deal, we best get up here in a hurry and stake a claim before the others stormed in," the gunman lied. It was also the wrong thing to say.

Josiah Catt's eyes flashed a warning to the gunman as he was bringing the big Sharps up. And in a flash, Colin Jackson had his Colt out, spurting flame. Catt staggered backward, the Sharps swinging wildly as he pulled the trigger. The belch of smoke and flame hung between the men for a second before being whipped away by the wind. Cove Stillman howled in pain and he twisted in his tracks as he fell to his knees, holding his arm.

Colin's revolver bucked twice more in his hand as Black Hawk cut loose with his own gun. Josiah Catt was knocked backward by the bullets and flattened out on the rocky ground beside the sluice rocker with five bullets in his chest. He gasped twice and stopped breathing.

"Tough old buzzard," Black Hawk commented, walking over to the prostrate form as he fed two fresh cartridges into his pistol. "Nice robe. Think I'll get it off him before he bleeds all over it."

"You okay, Professor?" Colin asked Cove Stillman who was still on his knees, his face clouded with pain.

"Think he's shot off my arm," Cove managed to say. "Can't feel a thing in my hand."

"Come on, let's go over to the hut and out of this weather. You can take off your coat and we'll see how bad you're hit," Colin said, watching Black Hawk peel the buffalo robe from the dead man. "Take that big knife and pistol off him as well," he said to the outlaw as he helped Cove Stillman into the brush hut and over to the small fire.

"Looks like he's left us a swig of coffee," Colin said, picking up the pot and shaking it. "Want some?"

Cove shook his head, breathing hard as he began taking off his coat. "Need a drink . . . bad."

"Well, maybe Black Hawk has some in his saddlebags. Here let's have a look at that arm." Colin used his knife to slit the wounded man's shirt open to expose the ragged wound that was bleeding profusely. The gunman probed the wound with his fingers.

Cove howled in pain. "Damn, Colin, that hurts, take it easy."

"You're lucky professor, another half inch and that big slug would have shattered the bone. I've seen what a Sharps rifle can do to a bull elk at six hundred yards. Cuts through bone and gristle like it was cotton."

"Spare me," Cove said. "Black Hawk! You got any whiskey?" he shouted through the brush shanty as Colin looked around the small structure. There was no furniture, just two makeshift beds of pine boughs in one corner and a few items of clothing and empty tins scattered about.

"Gimme that old man's shirt over there, Colin, and make me a bandage before I bleed to death," Cove Stillman said. "Black Hawk!" he shouted again.

"I'm coming," the outlaw said, pushing aside the ragged blanket that acted as a door to the hut.

"You get the whiskey?" Cove asked.

"I got it," Black Hawk said, fishing a bottle from the pocket of the buffalo robe he was wearing. "This thing's real warm. How's it fit?" Black Hawk asked, squaring his shoulders so they could get a good look at him. Cove took a long pull on the bottle, ignoring the outlaw.

"Hey, go easy on that bottle. It's all I got," Black Hawk said.

"Where do you think the old man's been storing the

gold?" Colin asked as he scattered the bedding material aside.

"Think he's been showing color?" Black Hawk said, his interest in the robe and bottle forgotten.

"You saw Dawson. That coat he had on cost a pretty penny and I saw him leave with a kid all dressed in new clothes and boots. There's gold here all right. We just got to find it."

Black Hawk joined in the search while Cove watched the two men with lessening pain as he took another long drink from the bottle.

Colin turned to Black Hawk, "You know how to pan. Suppose you check that sluice out. He's had the better part of six hours to work it. Could be he's not cleaned the riffles out yet. I'll keep looking here."

"That's a good idea, Colin," Black Hawk said, hurrying out to find a gold pan.

Colin searched every inch of the place to no avail. If the old man had any gold it was hidden well.

"Maybe he hid it in some rocks nearby," Cove Stillman said, half-drunk on Black Hawk's bottle of whiskey. Colin looked at the wounded man and came over and cleaned the wound with a little of the whiskey before tearing strips of cloth from a discarded shirt and bandaging Cove's arm.

"Thanks Colin," Cove Stillman said, "that danged Black Hawk woulda let me bleed to death before he offered to help."

"Just rest easy, now." The gunman stood up and looked around, not satisfied with his search of the place. If the old man had buried the gold in nearby rocks they would never find it. And then he realized there was one other place he hadn't looked.

"Watch yourself, Professor," Colin warned as he came over to the fire and began kicking aside the hot coals.

"Dang, Colin, whatcha putting the fire out for?" Cove asked, swinging his legs away from the fire. The gunman never answered.

Using the blade of his knife, Colin scraped away the

245

remaining hot ashes and probed the ground underneath. The knife slipped easily into the dirt and he smiled. Cove watched the gunman, wondering if he was losing it all of a sudden. And then he saw the first leather bag being exposed. The gunman turned and gave the wounded man a smile.

"Wily old geezer, wasn't he?" he said to Cove.

"I'd a never thought to look there," Cove said, his voice full of wonder. In a few minutes, Colin Jackson had lifted out five leather pouches filled with big nuggets and dust.

"Don't that beat all," Cove said, staring at the sacks. "How much you reckon's there?"

"More than enough to make the trip up here and to pay for you being shot," the gunman grinned at Stillman. They heard Black Hawk give a shout as he came running up to the hut, throwing aside the thin blanket door.

"Boys, take a look at . . . " His eyes found the five sacks and the hole where the fire use to be. He whistled low. "Found it I see."

"Got anything in that pan?" Stillman asked.

The outlaw snapped out of it and held the pan out for them both to see. The bottom was covered with six to eight ounces of big nuggets.

"Looks like we got ourselves another paying claim," Black Hawk said, grinning at the two men. "What's more, it's real private. Ain't going to be nobody snooping up this way with that wall of rock facing them."

"We got one that will," Colin reminded him, "Dawson."

"Aw, hell, Colin. He ain't but one man. We can take care of him like we did his partner."

"Got a better idea," Colin said, smiling at the two men. "Last thing we want to do is kill him."

Black Hawk stared at the gunman, "You gone plumb out of your head, Colin?" But Colin only laughed softly as he knelt to gather up the sacks of gold, leaving them to wonder what he was thinking.

* * *

246

The sun stood four hours high over the eastern prairie as Dawson and the boy entered the foothills to the west of Denver City along with hundreds of other men. Andy looked down from the back of the small pinto Dawson had purchased for him at the sea of struggling men, small carts, and loaded wagons that stirred up a constant cloud of choking dust.

"Is there gold enough for all these men, Jack?" Andy wanted to know.

Dawson gave him a short laugh, "There never is, son, there never is."

"What will Mr. Catt say about you bringing me along?"

"Old Catt will be more than happy to have another hand to help out around camp." He winked at the boy. "I don't make the best partner when it comes to doing my share of the chores."

"I'll do whatever chores you want done, Jack."

"Know you will, boy."

Rather than continue up Clear Creek canyon to the Gregory diggings, Dawson crossed a low fold of open ground surrounded by red rocks and continued to the south until he picked up Bear Creek which angled deeper into the hills.

"I've never seen such country," Andy blurted out, looking around him at the high ridges of rock and timber.

"We get to Squaw Pass is when you can see some country," Dawson called back. "How is the pony doing?"

"I love him, Jack. It will take me years just to pay you back."

Dawson merely waved his hand and kept riding deeper into the canyon thickly covered with pine and spruce.

They stopped to rest the horses at Squaw Pass and Andy was astounded by the open vistas that lay before his young eyes.

"I never knew the world could be so high," he said breathlessly.

"Out here, it gets even higher," Dawson promised, passing the boy a strip of jerky. They let the animals graze near the tumbling creek bank now covered in spring grass and spotty with old snow. Dawson didn't bother to strip the pack from the mule since they would be leaving shortly.

"Named him yet?" Dawson asked, indicating the rugged pinto with his muzzle deep into the tender mountain grass.

Andy shook his head, "Not yet. Can't seem to think of a good one yet."

"Don't worry, it'll come."

"What do you call yours?" Andy asked, chewing the tough meat.

"Buck," Dawson said simply.

"Not very original for a buckskin," Andy said.

"Horse don't know it," Dawson returned, "and he comes when I call. That and carrying me around is about all I ask of him."

"How about the mule? He got a name?"

"Never thought to give him one. Suppose you come up with one for me," Dawson said.

Andy looked doubtful, "Gonna be hard."

"Well, nobody's going to rush you. You got plenty time to think on it." Dawson walked upstream a little ways and drank deeply from the ice cold creek.

They crossed the last high ridge leading into the sheltered valley where Catt had their camp at mid-afternoon. The wind on the ridge was fierce and clawed at their clothes with trembling, icy fingers.

"Looks like there's been a new crop of snow since I've been gone," Dawson shouted across the howling winds to the boy as he dropped down off the bare slope and entered the thick timber. The winds moaned through the upper branches of the tall trees while the limbs near ground barely rustled.

Thirty minutes later Andy sat his horse staring up at the monumental wall of rock and timber.

"How we gonna get past here?" he asked Dawson who seemed to be more concerned with the three sets of horse tracks clearly visible in the snow. He dismounted and looked closer where bits of snow had sifted back down into the tacks. From what he could guess, they were four to six

248

hours old. Dawson didn't like the way they split up, moving to either side of the rock wall. Were they miners simply scouting the area much like he and Catt had done, or the other kind like the ones who murdered Walter Dumont's brother and partner?

Andy saw the look of intense concentration on Dawson's face. "What is it, Jack? Something wrong?"

"Don't know. Could be nothing, but when we approach the camp, I want you to hold back in the timber with the pack mule. And wait for my signal before you decide to ride in on your own, understood?"

"Yes, sir." Dawson saw the frightened look in the boy's eyes.

"Don't mean to scare you, but things out here in the mountains is different than back in town. You got to be prepared for whatever comes at you, from any direction."

"I'll do as you say, Jack, I promise."

Dawson gave the boy a tight smile, "Know you will, Andy. Let's ease on around this deadfall and see what we're dealing with."

Dawson called a halt and studied the ground in the safety of the trees at the same spot where the three riders had come together. It was obvious they had spent more than a few minutes here by the way the horses had chewed up the ground with their hoofs. Dawson spotted a half-smoked cigarette on the ground. From this angle they had a clear view of the camp, and a feeling of dread came over Dawson as he looked at the brush hut he and Catt had hastily constructed to break the cold wind. The camp seemed peaceful enough as smoke rose from the brush shanty into the clear blue sky. Another hour and it would be dark. Josiah had probably stopped for the day and was preparing supper.

Try as he might, he could discern no other human activity, nor were there any other horses in sight. Yet Dawson knew Catt kept his own horse back among the trees, out of sight.

Dawson turned to Andy Philmore. "Whatever you do,

don't show yourself until I lift my hat and wave you in."
Andy nodded without speaking.

"If things go wrong and you see me in trouble, don't come running out to offer help. You'll only make things worse. That happens you head back to Denver and get some help. You have trouble, find Mrs. Stiles. Got that?"

"I got it," Andy answered.

"Here," Dawson said, holding out his hand and dropping several twenty dollar gold coins in the boy's hand. "You may need some money for whatever."

"Nothing's going to happen. Is it, Jack?"

"I'm sure everything will be fine. Remember, wait for my signal." Dawson gave his horse the reins and eased from the shelter of the big boulders with the Henry across his saddle, never looking back.

Chapter 26

"He's coming, just like you said, Colin," Cove Stillman remarked, peeking through the brush hut at the distant figure on horseback.

Colin Jackson turned to Black Hawk. "You know what to do."

The outlaw scrambled into the big buffalo robe and pulled Catt's hat low over his face. Taking the coffee pot, Black Hawk stepped from the brush hut and went down to the creek where he pretended to wash the pot. He kept his back to the approaching horseman while Jackson and Stillman covered the rider with their rifles.

"We'll wait until he's near the creek before we make our move," Colin whispered to the wounded Stillman. Cove remained silent, nodding his head that he understood.

"Remember one thing, this Dawson knows how to use a gun so if he starts to come unglued, you best shoot quick."

"I'm following your lead," Cove said, giving the gunman a grim smile, "my being winged and all."

"Just don't get in my way," was all Colin Jackson said as he watched Dawson close the gap. He could almost feel Dawson's eyes searching the terrain in front of him like a wolf scenting a trap.

"He ain't fully buying the bait we got dangling down by the creek," Colin whispered.

Cove Stillman took his eyes off the rider for a moment to look at the gunman.

"How's that?"

"Just by the way he's sitting his horse and holding that rifle. Notice how his hand's staying near that big pistol he's wearing?" Cove Stillman looked back at their quarry, not fully understanding why they just didn't go on and shoot him. They could still haul him to town and claim he murdered his partner and the other two miners. But he never voiced what he was thinking to Colin. Cove had learned long ago to keep his mouth shut around the dangerous gunman.

"Another thing," Colin continued, "when Black Hawk walked out into the open, Dawson never relaxed for one second."

"I truly don't feel up to getting shot again today," Cove said, not wanting Colin to think he was any less of a man.

"You won't." Colin eased over to the curtained door and squatted down. "Just back me up with that rifle if there's call to."

"Got it," Cove replied.

Colin watched Black Hawk twist his head around to get a handle on how close Dawson was.

"Damnit, don't look back!" Colin whispered to himself. The crouching outlaw finally turned back and continued to wash the pot.

With his hat pulled low over his eyes to shield the slanting rays of the setting sun, Dawson saw the familiar figure of Josiah Catt emerge from the brush hut and go down to the creek with the coffee pot. Although he remained outwardly alert, Dawson allowed himself to relax just a tiny bit inside. At least Catt was okay and Dawson began to think the riders who passed through had been miners, nothing more. Knowing Catt, he probably sent them packing as quick as civility allowed.

Dawson was less than thirty yards out when it finally occurred to him, Catt could be acting under duress and he called out to him. All Dawson got in return was a wave of the coffee pot. The crouching figure in the buffalo robe remained as he was. Instantly, all the alarms went off in

252

Dawson's head, and he lifted the Henry, ejecting a shell into the chamber.

"Wouldn't do that if I was you," Colin Jackson called out from the brush hut. Suddenly, "Josiah Catt" stood up and whirled around with a gun aimed at him. Except he was looking into a pair of cold eyes belonging to Black Hawk.

"Easy does it!" Black Hawk warned as Colin stepped clear of the hut with a rifle trained on Dawson.

"Drop that purty rifle," Black Hawk commanded.

For an instant Dawson debated his next move when a third voice called from the hut.

"Better do as he says."

Dawson's eyes found those of the gunman's and they looked at each other for a long moment. Finally, Dawson let the Henry slide from his hands to the ground.

"Ease that hog-leg out as well," Black Hawk said, coming closer. Dawson did as he was told, his shoulders slumping.

"Where is Josiah Catt?" Dawson asked.

"That his name?" Black Hawk asked as he retrieved the rifle and gun.

"Where is he?" Dawson demanded again.

"Step down off that horse, Dawson," Colin Jackson ordered. He wanted Dawson on foot and unarmed. Slowly Dawson swung down from the saddle and Black Hawk jerked the reins from his hands and led the horse a few steps away.

"Josiah's dead, isn't he?" Dawson asked, already knowing the answer to his question.

"Unlike you, your friend decided to do battle," Colin Jackson replied. "Even got off a lucky shot, winging Cove with that big Sharps of his." Cove Stillman came out of the shanty with his arm in a makeshift sling. Dawson's features grew bleak.

"You best kill me now, gambler."

Colin laughed softly, "Why, and miss a good hanging?"

In spite of Dawson's cold composure, he was surprised by the gunman's statement.

253

* * *

From the safety of the huge rocks, Andy Philmore was horrified as he watched Jack Dawson being disarmed and led away to the brush hut. A big man in a buffalo robe took Dawson's horse and disappeared behind the brush structure.

For a full minute Andy sat on his pinto, completely numb, as reality sank in. Tears filled his eyes. Where was Josiah Catt? How could a partner allow these men to treat Jack this way? Suddenly, Andy knew why Catt could offer no assistance; he was dead. Andy got himself under control and wiped away the wetness on the sleeve of his coat while taking stock of the situation. With darkness fast approaching, there was no way he was going to get down out of these mountains tonight. He would have to find shelter, care for the animals, and light out for Denver first thing tomorrow. He wished now he had paid more attention to the country coming in.

Andy felt the responsibility of Jack Dawson's trust settle down over him like a huge weight as he turned his little pinto deeper into the thick timber. He had to get off the trail so those men who held Jack would not discover his presence in the morning.

In the lengthening shadows, Andy passed beyond the stone wall and rode across the narrow open valley until he struck the main creek coursing through the area. He splashed across the stream and continued into the dark swath of green timber before stopping to make camp.

It was all he could do to get the bulky pack off the mule, the contents spilling into the snow at his feet. One thing he knew, there was no way he could ever reload the mule. He would have to leave the stuff here. As soon as Jack was free, they could come back for it. He managed to hobble the animals and started a small fire against the dropping temperature now that the sun had disappeared. Somewhere in the distance, Andy heard the crying of coyotes or wolves. He got up and rummaged through the spilled items until he found the extra Colt that Dawson had put there for emergencies. It was all Andy could do to hold the big gun in both of his hands, but he practiced cocking and uncocking the weapon until he was satisfied with his performance. Next, he sliced bacon into a skillet and made himself coffee.

Later, as he sat by the little fire wrapped in his blanket, Andy realized he never wanted to be this alone again, now that he had found someone like Jack Dawson to care for. His thoughts grew dark as he recalled the repeated beatings he had suffered in the orphanage. He unconsciously tightened his grip on the big Colt. Never again would he allow anyone to treat him like that and live.

As night settled in, Andrew Philmore dozed by the dying fire while the little pinto stood quietly by, nibbling at the swelling buds of an aspen.

Chapter 27

Dawson rode along with his hands bound to the horn of his saddle. The gambler, whose name Dawson learned was Colin Jackson, rode by his side. It had been that way since leaving the brush hut at first light, four hours ago. Dawson occupied his mind with thoughts of Andy Philmore and hoped the boy had not gotten lost in the mountains. Sensible and ready to please Dawson at every turn, Andy was still just a boy, and Dawson hated the thought of leaving him on his own so far from town. Dawson cursed himself for not having made better plans in case something like this happened.

In the lead, Black Hawk called back to Colin concerning the pouch of gold coins they had taken from Dawson.

"Ain't there some way we can get this jasper to sign over what he and that old coot we killed has in Gruber's bank?"

Colin looked over at Dawson. "What if we cut a deal with you, Dawson? Suppose we all swing by the mint and let you make a withdrawal for us in return for your life?"

Dawson looked at the gunman with burning eyes. "I'd as soon charge the entire Sioux Nation with an empty rifle."

Colin laughed softly. "You heard the man, Black Hawk," Colin shouted, "we're going to have to get the law to release the money." All three outlaws laughed, and Dawson had the sinking feeling there was more to this game than three outlaws out to line their pockets. He recalled how Jackson and Black Hawk had been socializing with Marshal Pollock a couple days back.

Colin lowered his voice so only Dawson could hear what he was saying.

"You pretty good with that Colt Dragoon?"

"Killed my share of snakes, Indians, and lowlifes," Dawson said tightly.

"So you got us pegged as lowlifes, huh?"

"About the size of it."

"Now that ain't quite true." Colin twisted in the saddle to indicate Cove Stillman bringing up the rear. "Cove, back there, is a man of books. Hell, he can quote all the great writers of our time . . . Shakespeare even."

Dawson gave the gunman a benign look, "What's the point of all this?"

"The point is, looks can be deceiving, except maybe where Black Hawk's concerned. He's always been bad, even when he was a young sprout. You know he killed his first man when he was only ten. Shot him in the back with his daddy's greener. Never did ask why. Not that it matters."

"What about you?" Dawson asked. "You bad to the core as well?"

"Dawson, you know my kind. We both been over the hump a time or two. This great land out here molds a man to fit according to his particular skills. Take yourself, for instance; once the beaver trade played out, you took up guiding emigrants West to make a living. I'm not any different, I simply turned to the only trade I'm truly good at, handling a gun. Made my living with these pistols in towns around the Missouri River for years. When it looked like the gold rush to Colorado was for real, I came out here to offer my services and to take advantage of any opportunities that presented itself."

"Why you telling me all this?" Dawson asked.

"It's important that you know I'm not just some gun for hire at any price. I consider myself a businessman."

"Never thought of murder as a business. Let's get something straight now, Jackson. If I get free of this, you and

257

both your friends can expect me to come with my gun at full cock."

"Fair enough, although there's little chance of that happening."

"I've not gone under yet, and that's the only warning you'll get from me."

Two hours later they crossed the South Platte by way of Tom Warren's ferry. Tom Warren, a thirty-year-old Kentuckian who immediately saw the need for a ferry as hundreds of Conestoga wagons lined up to cross the churning waters, had been in business less than a month. Already, he was taking in two hundred a day and rising. Warren had rigged up a system of pulleys and two ropes of different lengths which he tied off to two large cottonwood trees on opposite sides of the river. By lengthening one rope and shortening the other, Warren was able to let the river's own current propel the flatboat from bank to bank.

"What's he tied up for?" Warren asked Colin Jackson.

"Murdered his partner over their claim."

Warren shook his head and turned his back to Dawson.

"You'll find no sympathy in town either," Colin said to Dawson.

"Wasn't looking for it . . . only the truth."

Colin laughed, "You'll get none, only a quick miner's court trial and a sudden hanging."

Dawson kept silent as the ferry bumped the riverbank at the end of Ferry Street, and the group remounted their horses. In a few minutes they turned down the alleyway beside Pollock's saloon.

"Keep an eye on him and I'll go around and let you in the back," Colin told Black Hawk.

"Get down from your horse," Black Hawk ordered Dawson. "Expect this'll be the last time you'll ever ride again."

Dawson stood there beside his horse; his hands hurting from being twisted around while still tied to the saddle horn.

"Cut me loose of this saddle," he told Black Hawk.

The outlaw stepped over and withdrew his big knife, "What's the matter, Dawson? Afraid your horse'll spook

258

and drag you bloody?" He cut the rope and stepped back keeping his revolver on Dawson as the back door to the saloon swung inward.

"Let's go," Black Hawk prodded Dawson who stepped through the door into an office. Marshal Pollock, looking somewhat strained, sat behind an old, scarred wooden desk. Colin Jackson stood across the room with his Colt drawn.

"Sit down, Dawson," the gunman said, indicating the empty chair next to the desk. "The marshal wants to ask you a few questions." To Dawson, Pollock looked more like he wished he was someplace else than here.

"Well, Dawson, looks like your scheme failed," Pollock said, biting the end of a black cigar which he lit.

"What scheme?"

"Why, you come in here a day or so ago wanting to report a double murder and now you're back, accused of murdering your own partner according to Colin here." Dawson stared at the big man with open contempt.

"I can see you're open-minded to the truth," Dawson said bitterly.

"I *am* open-minded, Dawson. But in your case, I'm willing to make an exception."

"What I figured."

Pollock stood up, bringing his pistol with him. "Enough talk for now, let's get you down to the cellar where I keep all bad men like you." He turned to Black Hawk, "Grab that lantern, will you?"

Dawson found himself being lead down a set of rickety steps that descended into a dank black hole below the saloon floor. He could hear the muffled footsteps and the occasional scrape of a chair above him. He took a quick look around at the small room, noting the single bunk and one chair. Nor was there a window for light. Only after Pollock had him handcuffed to a thick iron ring by the bed and had bolted the thick door behind him, was Dawson overcome by the feeling of doom that assailed his senses in the pitch darkness.

For the first time in his life he felt utterly alone and

helpless as he sat there on the edge of the hard bed. He couldn't think of a single instance in his life, even the terrifying times fighting Indians and blinding blizzards alongside Broken Hand Fitzpatrick, that compared to being locked away in a hole with no light, facing a sure hanging. And then he thought of Andy and knew the kid would do everything in his power to help him. All Dawson had to worry about was whether the boy would find his way down out of the mountains in time to do him any good.

Chapter 28

"You did what!" A.C. Ford shouted, half-rising from his chair. Colin Jackson gave the lawyer a cold smile.

"Relax, counselor. There's no way Dawson can tie you to us if that's what's worrying you." Ford eased down in his chair again, his mind busy with implications if Dawson somehow managed to spread the truth to a few honest businessmen. He stood to wreck everything Ford had so carefully built over the past eight months.

"Where is he now?" Ford asked, lighting a cigar with nervous hands.

"Pollock's got him over at his place, in the hole. Figure he'll keep 'til the People's Court can try him tonight."

"Why didn't you just kill him and say it was self-defense? You could still pin his partner's murder on him, even the two other miners you killed as well."

The gunman nodded, sipping the drink Ford had poured for him. Colin had caught the attorney just as he was leaving his office for the evening.

"Could have," the gunman acknowledged, "except for this." And he tossed a heavy leather pouch onto Ford's desk. "Dawson and his partner are two lucky hombres. They got a claim looks like the mother lode."

Ford untied the bag and spilled some of the large nuggets across his desk. He sat there staring at the gold.

Colin Jackson continued, "We hang him legal-like, we got first crack at his claim and nobody can say different.

And this is one claim's gonna make us very rich, A.C. It's going to take us some time to work it, therefore we'll be needing legal papers to it." The gunman could see the greed in Ford's eyes.

"You leave anybody on guard?" Ford asked.

"Don't need to. Pikers drifting into the mountains around there could pass it by a thousand times and never find it."

"That may be, but you best get a couple men up there just in case," Ford said. Suddenly he remembered something. "Where's the young pup that was with Dawson?"

"Pup? You mean boy?"

"That's right," Ford said, his voice rising. "He was with Dawson the night they stopped by the Stiles's."

Colin's eyes narrowed. "Appears Dawson is a little smarter than I gave him credit."

"What do you mean?"

"Probably left the boy back there in the rocks when he rode in last evening." Ford picked up on the thread.

"That means the kid saw everything," Ford added, worriedly.

"Relax, conselor. Where's the boy going first for help . . . the law?"

Distracted, Ford nodded, thinking, *or maybe to Mary Stiles.* "What will you do with the boy?"

"Relax, A.C. Let me worry about that. You just call the court together so we can rid ourselves of Dawson . . . maybe tonight if we help spread the word how Dawson murdered his own partner and the other two miners. After that, we can let things run its course."

Ford got to his feet. "I'll round up the members of the vigilante committee and get things started while you spread a little free whiskey around to the miners and a word about Dawson." Ford resacked the scattered nuggets. "This mine?"

"The first of many," Colin said, reaching for the door knob.

* * *

It was completely dark when Andy Philmore slipped quietly into town. He had planned it that way. And now he headed straight for Mary Stiles's cabin avoiding busy Ferry Street. There was a light in the cabin's window as he dismounted and tied the pinto to the limb of a tree by the corner of the structure. Trying to remain calm, Andy took a deep breath and knocked softly at the door.

The cabin door swung inward and Mary Stiles stood there with a surprised look on her face. The yellow light from the interior spilled out the doorway and across the young boy standing there with his hat in his hand.

"Why, hello . . . Andy, isn't it?"

"Yes, ma'am," Andy said, feeling the tightness beginning to swell in his skinny chest.

"Come in, Andy," Mary said, standing aside. She closed the door behind him.

"Would you like something to drink? It's still rather cool outside."

Andy turned to face the woman, shaking his head. It was then Mary noted the stricken look on the boy's face.

"What's wrong, Andy? Where's Jack?"

The words came tumbling out of the boy like cascading water over the lip of a high canyon. Mary listened closely, her face revealing her own shock at the events.

"What about Josiah Catt, Andy? Did you see him?"

"No, ma'am. When they rode away, there was nobody but Jack with them."

"That can only mean poor Josiah is dead," Mary whispered as Melissa came out from behind the thin curtain, dressed for an evening out.

"I trailed them here to Denver this afternoon, but I laid up in some rocks across the river till it was dark, so they wouldn't see me ride in. Jack told me to come here if anything was to happen to him."

"I'm glad you did, Andy," Mary Stiles said, reaching for her shawl by the door. "We'll go fetch the marshal and straighten things out." Relief flooded Andy's face as Melissa stood there taking it all in.

"Mother, A.C. will be here any minute. Maybe he can help, after all, he is a lawyer." Mary Stiles stopped with her hand on the door.

"Why yes, Mr. Ford may be just who we need to help clear up this matter." She turned to Andy, "Suppose I make you some hot chocolate. There's a slice of cake left from supper I'll bet you could eat." The strain crept back into the boy's face. Mary put an arm around his slim shoulders.

"I know you want to help Jack as quickly as you can, but Attorney Ford should be here shortly. I promise you, we'll do everything we can to find Jack. Now sit down at the table and I'll fetch you something from the stove." Andy did as he was told and Melissa sat down next to him.

"Maybe, Jack rode willingly with those men," she offered. Andy looked at the girl with burning eyes.

"No way," Andy stated emphatically. "Jack's hands were tied to the horn of his saddle. Besides, if things would have been okay, he would have given me the signal to ride in.' Melissa seemed stumped over this logic but then perked up at the sound of an approaching buggy. She jumped up and ran to the door while Mary put the cake and hot chocolate down in front of Andy.

"Hello, sweetheart," Ford said, gathering the wisp of a girl in his arms. Ford never bothered to look farther into the cabin.

"I'm glad you're here," Melissa said, hugging him back

"Listen, Melissa, I'm afraid I can't stay. The town's in an ugly mood and I'm due to defend a murderer in cour tonight. There's talk of a lynch mob forming because o what he did."

Melissa pulled back and looked at the attorney. "Wil you be safe?"

Ford laughed, "I'll be fine. Don't believe a mob eve lynched a lawyer for defending a client before."

"What's this?" Mary said, coming up behind them. "Thi murderer you spoke of, wouldn't be Jack Dawson?"

264

"I was coming to that," Ford said, sighing deeply. "Seems he murdered his own partner over their gold claim. There's even the possibility now he may have murdered two other miners."

Andy exploded from the table with fire in his eyes. "That's a lie!" he shouted.

Ford was shocked to see Andy standing there. "Where'd you come from, boy?" Ford asked, recalling now the pinto tied to the side of the cabin.

Mary Stiles quickly explained, seeing Andy was so upset. Ford did a good job of covering his underlying feelings as he kept his eyes on the boy who stood his ground with lips pressed together.

"Won't you talk with the marshal and see if this can be straightened out?" Mary asked Ford.

"It's doubtful," Ford responded. "How do you know he hadn't already murdered Catt before hooking up with the boy? That's possible, ain't it?" Ford hurried on, "It's also possible that Dawson took the boy under his wing so he would have an alibi as well as a witness when they discovered Catt dead."

Andy's face remained resolute, "Jack Dawson ain't no killer, Mr. Ford."

"Andy's right," Mary Stiles joined in. "Jack refused to shoot Tall Feather in cold blood, even though Melissa and I both hoped he would."

"There's a difference, Mary," Ford said.

"How's it different?"

"Tall Feather didn't have any gold. And gold can do strange things to a man."

"I don't believe that for an instant," Mary said. "Jack is a decent man. Josiah Catt was his friend."

"I'm only looking at things from the law's perspective . . . and the miners. They won't take kindly to one of their own being murdered. Dawson's going to have a tough time proving he didn't kill Josiah Catt without witnesses."

"Will you talk to the marshal . . . let Andy tell his side of the story?"

265

"Most certainly," Ford said smoothly. "Didn't I say I would help if I could?"

"That's all we ask," Mary said, turning to give Andy a worried smile.

"Come on, boy, let's get over to Marshal Pollock's before this town blows sky-high." Andy picked up his hat from the table, ignoring the untouched cake.

"Please be careful," Melissa whispered to Ford as they hurried out.

"I'll be back. Wait up for me?"

Melissa gave him a warm smile. "All night if I have to."

"That's my girl," Ford said, giving her a squeeze.

Mary followed them outside, "I'm coming too."

"You can't . . . . What I mean is this trial is conducted in secret by the People's Court. General public is not permitted."

"That hardly sounds like a legitimate court of law," Mary said.

"I understand your sentiments, Mary, but this is Colorado. Life is raw and untested out here. If it weren't for the People's Court, there would be no law to deal with the thieves, murderers and cutthroats inhabiting Denver."

"But why must court be held in secret?"

"To protect those on the bench and others who stand firm against the criminal elements of Denver, otherwise, they would be prime targets." Ford turned to Andy. "Tie your horse to the buggy, son, and we can talk further as we ride over to the marshal's office." Andy did as he was instructed, yet he felt a little unsettled where Ford was concerned. What kept nagging at his young mind was whether he was really doing anything to help Jack by associating with the attorney.

"Climb on in here, Andy," Ford said, patting the seat next to him. Andy got in and took his seat. Ford cracked the buggy whip across the backs of the matched horses and disappeared into the night, leaving Mary and Melissa Stiles standing in the shadows of the cabin with worried faces.

266

Chapter 29

The long-haired Pollock reared back in his chair and studied the boy's worried face. He glanced over at Ford who seemed to be in complete control of himself in spite of this latest wrinkle.

"You get a good look at these men?" Pollock asked Andy.

"Yes, sir, I'd know them anywhere," Andy said with conviction. "They rode by real close where I was hiding. There were three of them. One had his arm in a sling, like he had been hurt . . . maybe wounded."

"I see." Pollock pursed his lips and looked again at Ford.

"Can I see Jack now?"

"Can't allow that, boy. Too dangerous for a man about to stand trial."

"Why not?" Andy persisted. Ford got up from his chair and came over to stand by the boy.

"Andy, you saw how it is out there. Men are getting likkered up, fighting mean. If they knew where the marshal was holding your friend, why they would just break in and hang him immediately. You understand?"

"I . . . I guess so," Andy said slowly. Ford patted the boy's shoulder reassuringly.

"The marshal and I will do everything in our power to see Jack gets a fair trial, ain't that so, Tom?"

"You bet, kid. That's part of my job."

"Andy, why don't you wait outside while I talk with the

marshal for a moment about the best way to handle the trial?"

"Yeah, kid. Tell the bartender out there I said give you a cold sarsaparilla," Pollock added as Andy moved to the door.

"I'll only be a few minutes," Ford said.

Andy looked at the marshal, "Will you tell Jack I'll be waiting for him?"

"Sure, kid, I'll tell him," Pollock said. Andy nodded and left the room.

Pollock immediately turned to Ford, "What the damn Hell we gonna do now, A.C.? That kid can identify Colin and the others."

"You worry too much, Tom," Ford said, pouring himself a drink from the bottle on Pollock's desk.

"Somebody's got to."

"This doesn't change a thing. You see how the town's stirred up. Dawson ain't going to last the night, and we both know it. After that, the kid can say whatever he wants. Won't change a thing. Dawson'll be dead, and that will be that." Ford downed the drink in one long swallow.

"What about Colin and Black Hawk? They ain't going to be happy to know the kid can identify them."

"True, but that's how the cards are dealt sometimes," Ford said, his anger rising suddenly at the thought of Sarah Jane and Colin in bed together.

"They going to have to stay outta town for a while," Pollock warned, "and fish-eyed gunman ain't going to like that one bit."

"I know," Ford said, smiling. "Knowing Colin and Black Hawk like I do, they might just decide to get rid of the kid and put an end to the whole affair."

"Count me out of that game," Pollock said quickly. "Ain't having nothing to do with killing kids."

"Nor I, but we both know Black Hawk has no morals when it comes to murder, woman or child."

"I know. Sometimes I'm sorry for having gotten mixed up in all this in the first place," Pollock said morosely.

"Don't worry, Tom, things will be fine. I'll handle Colin and Black Hawk myself, meet you at Graham's Drugs in an hour with Dawson. You need any help guarding him?"

"Middaugh's boys are lending me a hand."

"Good. That's a smart move, Tom."

"Why we meeting over Graham's? What's wrong with the old place?"

"Judge Slaughter's idea. Wanted to give maximum protection to the prisoner, I suppose." Tom stared for a moment and then a slow smile spread across his face.

"We'll have a hard time getting Dawson through that crowd of bummers down at the Criterion once the trial's over."

Ford stepped over to the door and looked back, "It certainly won't hurt our cause any." The Criterion Saloon was the headquarters of bummers and cutthroats. Ford had already seen to it the men bellying up to the bar were treated to free drinks and advice as to what should be done with a man like Dawson. Ford had paid Ed Jump, the proprietor, well. The two-storied frame structure rivaled the Broadwell House in its plushness. Besides the saloon, Jump had established a restaurant adjoining the bar that served meals equal to Delmonico's in New York. The ornate structure had delicate flower designs etched into its frosted glass windows while a liquor cellar was well-stocked with the finest champagnes and wines this side of Chicago.

Pollock sat there for a full minute letting his thoughts ramble a bit. He could hear the boisterous miners through the thin wall as they took on a load of free whiskey, he had ordered his bartender to dispense. He figured the night's drinking would set him back about two hundred at most, but his share from the other drinking establishments Ford was handling would triple that amount. He got out of his chair and, taking the keys, descended the stairwell to the cellar. At the bottom, a faint glow of light outlined the guard sitting there with a shotgun across his lap.

"Why don't you go get your brother and bring the wagon around to the back door? Time's growing short."

James Middaugh stood up and handed the shotgun to Pollock.

"Yes, sir, Marshal," the young Middaugh said, climbing the stairs.

"Knock one time when you get back with the wagon," Pollock called, "and I'll let you in." James nodded and kept climbing.

Pollock turned and unlocked the door; picking up the lantern, he stepped into the dank hole. The light caught Dawson's eyes and they seemed to glitter in the dim glow.

"You about ready, Dawson?"

"For what?"

"To stand trial."

"In the middle of the night?" Dawson laughed softly. "Suppose that was the only time open on the docket, right?"

"Ain't it at all," Pollock said, turning up the light.

"Then it must be to hide these criminal proceedings from the decent people of Denver."

"Listen, Dawson. It's important you know something. I'm only the law. When a group of men ride in bringing a man they claim has murdered someone, I'm bound to hold them for trial, until things gets straightened out."

"Yeah, and you got no interest either way," Dawson said bitterly.

"Exactly. That's why we're having the court hearing to-night. See, what you don't know is word's spread across town like fire. Miners are getting liquored up, threatening to break in and lynch you before the night's out. That's why we moving you to another location soon as court is over, case a mob comes looking for you."

"Guess I can thank my captors for that." Dawson looked Pollock straight in the eyes. "What I wonder is . . . who's paying the bar bill for all these self-righteous people?" It was Pollock's eyes that found the floor first.

"Don't blame you for not believing me, Dawson, but that ain't my problem. I'm here to protect you and that's what I aim to do."

270

"Oh, that makes me feel better. How many deputies you got out there? Five, ten . . . a dozen, maybe?"

"Got enough," Pollock retorted. "Ain't your worry."

"It is when it's my life hanging in the balance."

Pollock turned toward the stairs, "Be back in a minute soon's they bring the wagon around. I'll leave the light." Dawson watched as the big man ascended the narrow stairs, wondering where Pollock fit into all this. In a town flowing with fresh wealth from the goldfields, a town marshal would probably come pretty cheap. So far, he had no real reason to suspect Pollock of anything except doing his job.

Dawson looked down at his clenched fists in the flickering light and thought of Josiah Catt. He didn't yet know how, but there were three men going to pay the ultimate price for what they had done.

Andy stood in the deep shadows, shivering in the cold wind that funneled down Ferry Street as he watched Pollock's saloon. Ford had said for him to ride back to the Stiles's cabin and wait there for him, but Andy had seen and heard a lot while he waited in the saloon for the marshal and Ford to get done with their business. Nobody pays much attention to a young boy at the end of a bar drinking root beer and Andy had been all ears. What he heard disturbed him deeply. He wanted to scream at them, make them understand Jack Dawson would never do such a thing as they were saying. But what kept him quiet was the drunken miners, bragging how they were going to lynch Dawson before the night was out.

Now Andy waited in the cold shadows, hugging the big pistol Dawson had kept hidden away on the pack mule, his eyes glued to the frame building across the street. Waiting, knowing that the marshal would eventually have to move Dawson to wherever they were holding court. He had picked that up from a well-dressed man standing at the bar, talking with a fat-bellied man who looked to Andy like some kind of important public official.

He watched as an empty wagon came lumbering up Ferry Street and swung down Third before stopping near the rear of Pollock's Saloon. Andy's heart thumped heavily against his skinny ribs for he had caught the gleam of badges on the two men who climbed down from the wagon seat. While one stood guard with his back to the door, Andy watched as the other lawman knocked. The door opened immediately, and Andy caught a glimpse of Marshal Pollock framed by the light. The lawman stepped quickly in and the door was closed. The other man stayed where he was with his back plastered to the wall of the building.

In a few minutes, the door reopened and Andy wanted to cry out as he saw Jack Dawson step outside and was helped into the back of the wagon. A canvass tarp was thrown quickly over his head. Andy watched as Marshal Pollock jumped into the bed of the wagon while the two lawmen scrambled to their seats. A whip cracked in the night air and the horses lunged forward, disappearing down Third Street.

Andy leaped atop the pinto and crossed the street at a lope. He was determined to follow them wherever they were taking Jack Dawson, hoping somehow he might get the chance to help his friend get away. From a safe distance, Andy kept the wagon in sight as it turned down St. Louis and continued for three blocks to Fifth, where the driver turned left and headed north across Cherry Creek bridge. The wagon pulled to a stop at the end of the next block, and Dawson was hustled quickly inside a two-storied building by Pollock and one of the lawmen while the other man drove briskly away.

Andy waited for a few minutes until he thought it was safe to move forward. He rode slowly by a boisterous saloon packed with drinking miners. He could spell the letters above the saloon, but couldn't pronounce the word, Criterion. When he drew near the building where Dawson had been taken, Andy kept a sharp eye out for a guard. As he passed the darkened windows of Graham's Drugs and turned east down F Street, the area appeared to be empty.

Andy pulled up near the Western Stage and Pony Express

building and ducked down the side of the frame structure where he tied his pony. Hurrying back to the corner of the street, he squatted in the shadows once more and took up his vigil.

Andy was surprised to see the tall businessman and the fat man from Pollock's saloon approach the drugstore on foot. They were immediately let in by an armed guard who came out of the shadows. Andy had failed to see him when he rode by. Before another minute could pass, he watched as Ford drove up in his buggy and got down and went inside. This did not concern him much, for he knew the man was a lawyer. If they were holding court, he would need to be there. Behind Ford came another man Andy recognized immediately. He was one of the men who had brought Jack Dawson down out of the mountains. Andy's anxiety level shot up. He fidgeted nervously in the dark, wondering what he should do now. What would this man be doing here if it didn't mean trouble for Jack? Andy couldn't answer his own question.

Chapter 30

"Sit down, Dawson," Pollock said, pushing him into a chair. Dawson felt the heat rising in him from the rough treatment, but he knew he needed to stay calm if he planned on surviving the next few hours. He looked around the tiny upstairs room that served as the vigilantes headquarters. A door opened and closed behind him and Dawson turned to see two men enter, both wearing flour sacks over their heads. One had on a dark flowing robe while the other was dressed in a thin-striped brown suit.

"See now I'm going to get a fair trial," Dawson said bitterly. "Don't I even get a lawyer?" Pollock prodded him with his gun.

"Stand up, Dawson, while the judge takes the bench." Dawson did as he was told while the judge settled in his chair behind the table.

"You may take your seat, Mr. Dawson," the judge said in a deep resonant voice. Dawson lowered himself down.

The man in the brown business suit stepped up to the table.

"The People's Court of Jefferson Territory is now in session." And then he turned to the hooded judge. "Looks like the defendant's attorney is not here yet."

"How can you tell? Everybody here has hoods on other than those three lawmen," Dawson snapped. Four other hooded men who sat in nearby chairs shuffled their feet as the courtroom fell silent.

"I will not tolerate any outbursts from the defendant," the judge said coldly. The door opened again and a man hurried into the room and took his place next to the man in the brown suit.

"I apologize to the court, your Honor, for being late." Dawson stared hard at the hooded man whose voice sounded vaguely familiar even through the flour sack. The man turned to look at Dawson, "I'll be representing you at these proceedings."

"That's what this is, proceedings?"

"Mr. Dawson," the judge admonished, "may I remind you that this is a legitimate court of law and you are on trial for a serious charge. *Murder!* And not to be taken lightly, I might add." The judge looked at the man in the brown suit. "Call your first witness, Mr. Prosecutor."

"The People calls Mr. Colin Jackson to the stand." Dawson sat up straight as the door behind him opened and the gunman strolled in smoking a cigar. He was sworn in by the prosecutor.

"Tell the court, if you would please, the events leading up to the death of one, Josiah Catt, Mr. Jackson," the prosecutor said.

Colin Jackson gave Dawson a faint smile, their eyes locking in mental combat.

"Black Hawk, Cove Stillman and me were out riding, looking the diggings over when we heard several shots coming from a timbered slope above us. Upon investigating, we caught the defendant, dragging the body of his partner away from camp, and we managed to disarm him. Guess we surprised him before he could put up a fight."

"I see," the prosecutor said. "And how did you find Josiah Catt?"

"Why dead as Hell, of course," Colin responded. There were a few guffaws from those seated.

"How many times was he shot?"

"Didn't count exactly. Three, maybe four times, I guess. I figure once a man's dead, it doesn't matter how much extra lead he's toting."

275

Dawson looked over at his appointed attorney. "Aren't you goin' to object to something?"

"Nothing said so far that I can. Sounds like *in flagrante delicto* to me."

"Speak English," Dawson ordered.

"Simply means you were caught red-handed, in the act of committing murder."

"Least I know whose side you're really on now," Dawson said with some satisfaction, for now he knew who was hiding behind the hood: A.C. Ford.

"Order in the court," the judge said, banging his gavel on the wooden table.

"I have no further questions for this witness, your Honor," the prosecutor said.

"You got any?" the judge asked Dawson's attorney.

"None, your Honor."

Dawson wanted to shake his head at the travesty taking place, but he wasn't about to give the gunman the satisfaction of seeing him display emotion. Without another word, Colin Jackson strolled out of the room.

"Next witness," the judge said.

The prosecutor turned to the bench, "Your Honor, is there a need to call further witnesses to the stand just to prolong this trial? The court has heard explicit testimony from Mr. Jackson which Mr. Dawson has not denied in the death of Josiah Catt."

"So moved," the judge thundered. Dawson shot up out of the chair.

"Don't I get to tell my side?" he demanded.

"Damn it, Dawson, sit down!" Pollock roared, grabbing Dawson by both shoulders and forcing him back into his chair.

"Of course, you do, but only when the proper time comes," the judge said. "You have any witnesses to present the court, Mr. Attorney?" he asked the hooded Ford.

"No, your Honor," Ford replied, "other than the defendant himself."

"Well, in that case, the court will hear from you now, Mr. Dawson."

"Got nothing to say," Dawson said, catching everybody off guard.

"What do you mean?" the judge shouted. "Just a minute ago, you were itching to talk!"

Dawson looked slowly around at each hooded face, lingering on Ford who finally had to turn away, before stopping on the judge.

"This whole trial is a sham and a mockery to the judicial system, and I won't be a party to a system by defending myself against the very men who killed my partner."

"Then you offer me no choice in passing sentence," the judge said.

"Pass and be damned!" Dawson shouted, his jaw locked firmly in place.

"Have the prisoner rise, Marshal," the judge said. Pollock prodded Dawson with his gun once more. Dawson stood, looking straight ahead.

"Mr. Jack Dawson, it's the finding of this court that you are guilty of murder in the first degree of one, Mr. Josiah Catt. Further, this court sentences you to be hung by the neck until you are dead before the hour of 10:00 A.M. tomorrow. Court's adjourned!"

Rough hands grabbed Dawson and propelled him toward the door. Dawson stopped for a moment with James and Asa Middaugh trying to force him through the opened doorway.

"Ford!" Dawson called back. "I know that's you beneath that flour sack . . . sleep well." The young Middaugh brothers finally got Dawson out the door and down the stairs with Pollock charging ahead with the shotgun. Judge Slaughter was the next to leave.

Silence fell across the room as A.C. Ford reached up and took off his hood. The others did likewise.

Ford looked around at the faces of the Secret Ten, all prominent men of Denver.

"Means only one thing, boys. Jack Dawson has to die

and he's got to die tonight." The others nodded their heads in silent approval.

"Sounds like the boys down at the Criterion are working themselves up into a good one," Asa Middaugh commented as they emerged from Graham's Drugs with Dawson.

"May turn out to be a short night for you Dawson," Pollock said, "if we don't keep you under wraps." He helped the shackled Dawson into the back of the wagon.

"That's the way you and Ford planned it, isn't it?" Dawson shot back as the marshal covered him with the tarp.

"Like I told you earlier, Dawson, it's my responsibility to protect you, not offer you up to a drunken mob."

Two drunken miners came charging around the street on fast horses, yelling loudly as they reined up in front of the Criterion. The three lawmen stood there tense, with guns ready in case trouble erupted at that point, but the two miners left their horses at the crowded hitching rack and staggered into the saloon.

"They're in a hanging mood for sure," James Middaugh said, climbing up to the wagon seat beside his brother.

"That's why we ain't going back to my place," Pollock added. "Be the first place they'll come looking."

"Where then?" Asa asked, holding the reins.

"Drive two blocks west down F Street. We'll hold him in the cellar at the Cherokee House. Should be safe enough there til the miners cool off or head back to camp to sleep it off." Pollock had held other prisoners there in the past. It was much larger than Pollock's cellar with a table, two chairs, and a small barred window for lighting. Across the back wall, rows of dusty bottles of wine and champagne rested in wooden racks.

Once they had Dawson locked away in the cellar, Pollock left the two brothers on guard with the understanding he would be back to relieve them in three hours.

From the safety of the large porch of the Denver House, located directly across Blake Street from the Cherokee

House, Andy Philmore watched as Pollock emerged from the building and trudge back up F Street, alone.

What bothered Andy more than seeing the marshal was his feeling of helplessness. He had to come up with some kind of plan to save Jack, and he didn't have all night to figure one out either. A drunken lynch mob would eventually find Jack, no matter the marshal had moved him.

Reluctantly, Andy realized he needed help and he needed help fast. The only one he knew he could turn to was Mary Stiles. Taking one last look around, Andy turned back to his pony. Seconds later, the little pinto exploded down the street with Andy laying over the animal's muscular neck.

"Got him tucked away safe?" Ford asked, flashing Pollock a smile as he came walking up. Ford was standing in front of the drugstore with Joe Shear and several others of the Secret Ten.

Pollock nodded. "Left the Middaugh brothers on guard."

"Excellent," Ford said, turning to the others. "Thought I'd step down to the Criterion for a late nightcap. Anyone care to join me, I'm buying." Everyone declined except for John Shear.

John Shear gave Ford a nod.

"I'm always open to a free drink, A.C." They stood there for a few minutes while the other members of the Secret Ten disappeared into the night, leaving Pollock alone with Ford and Shear.

"That was a good idea, Tom, leaving James and Asa on guard," Ford said.

"Just don't want to be around when the mob comes for Dawson," Pollock responded.

"We were about to check the mob's pulse at the Criterion, want to come along?"

"Think it would be best if I hung around my own place, kinda act as a decoy like we planned."

"You're right, Tom," Ford admitted.

"Yeah, well, just hope things go as smoothly as you think they will. Dawson don't strike me as a man that'll go meekly to the gallows."

"With a hundred angry miners boiling up around him, he won't have a choice," Ford promised. "Let's go, John."

Pollock watched them fade into the darkness as a chilling thought settled over him. What if Dawson managed to escape? How would that affect him? Pollock mulled that over in his mind and concluded Dawson, for all his dislike of him, really could not tie him to Colin Jackson or the others for that matter. All he had been doing was his job.

With that thought in mind, Pollock hitched up his gunbelt and started back across town to his own establishment. The one thing he intended to do was keep the free whiskey flowing until Dawson was dancing on air.

Chapter 31

Rather than take time and cut over to the bridge, Andy splashed across Cherry Creek, barely slowing the pinto. When he rode up to the cabin a few minutes later, he was out of the saddle and at the door in a flash. Before he could knock, the door opened and Melissa stood there, surprised to see him alone.

"Didn't A.C. come back with you?"

Andy stepped in and closed the door, his eyes flashing. Mary Stiles was nowhere to be seen.

Andy shook his head, "Mr. Ford's been over to Graham's Drugs attending Jack Dawson's trial. Town's in an uproar. The miners are going to hang Jack for sure if we don't help him."

"Why, what can we do? They say he's guilty."

Andy's eyes turned to bright points of anger. "Told you, Jack ain't killed nobody. I seen the three men who did. Only chance Jack has of proving his innocence is to get him out of jail. And we got to help him now. Time's running out."

Melissa was shocked by the boy's words. "You mean break him out of jail . . . now?"

"That's just what I mean and we got to hurry. Those miners will start searching for Jack just any minute."

"What do you mean by searching? Isn't he in jail?"

Andy shook his head, looking around again, hoping Mary Stiles would show herself. He didn't like dealing with

Melissa, whose concern seemed to be mainly centered on Ford.

"The marshal moved him, maybe to throw the miners off, I don't know. Don't you see, this is our only chance to help Jack," Andy pleaded. "They'll hang him for sure if we don't."

Melissa was torn by the desire to wake her mother for advice, yet wanting to prove she was an adult and fully capable of handling tough situations.

"You ain't forgetting what Jack done for you and Miss Mary, are you?" Andy continued, pressing home his last ray of hope.

"I'm not forgetting . . . just, it's all so sudden. Don't know what's best to do," Melissa said, stalking around the room with her hand fluttering to her hair.

"Those Indians were sudden, too," Andy said. "Didn't take Jack long to figure out the right thing to do."

Melissa stopped, staring hard at the boy. "You seem to know an awful lot, considering your age."

"Had to know. Life on the streets is tough when you got nobody to care about you . . . that is till Jack came along." Tears welled up in Andy's eyes and he wiped them away, angry at himself for showing emotion at a time when they should be thinking about a way to help Jack.

Melissa heaved a deep sigh. "I'll do whatever I can. I know Jack never killed poor Mr. Catt," she whispered softly.

Andy looked relieved. "Think you ought to wake Miss Mary?"

"No, let her sleep. We can handle this ourselves," Melissa said, putting her thoughts in order.

"If you say so," Andy said. "There's two guards, both look to be about your age."

"Should we wait for A.C.? He promised to stop by later."

"He's a lawyer. Ain't no way he's going to help free Jack. No, ma'am, it's strictly up to us," Andy said with conviction. Then he remembered, "You got a gun?"

Melissa looked like she was ready to call it all off at the

mention of a weapon, but she finally nodded her head. Going to a side cabinet, she withdrew a small derringer.

"A. C. gave me this for protection while walking around town. He said there were a lot of people who could not be trusted to act as gentlemen."

Andy looked defeated by the size of the weapon Melissa was holding, but realized it would have to do. After all, he still had Jack's big pistol. If they surprised the guards, maybe it wouldn't make much difference.

"Let's go then." Andy turned back to the door.

"Wait, let me get my wrap," Melissa said, hurrying around the thin curtain. Just as quickly, she emerged with a thick shawl wrapped around her blond hair.

"Can you ride?" Andy asked, vaulting into the saddle. Melissa nodded and put her foot into the proffered stirrup. Using the boy's skinny arm, Melissa managed to pull herself up behind Andy while keeping her long skirt down over most of her legs.

"Hold tight," Andy whispered as he turned the pinto back toward Cherry Creek. In deference to the girl, Andy took the bridge across the creek even though it cost them time. Melissa hugged his thin body close and he could smell her sweet perfume. It made his head dizzy. He couldn't remember ever having been this close to a woman before in his life, much less having one hug him like she was doing.

They crossed the wooden bridge and were shocked to see the streets swarming with miners carrying pitch torches. Most glared hard as they passed by. One even lunged out of the darkness for his bridle, but Andy managed to steer the little pinto away from the drunken man.

"I think we're too late," Melissa whispered in his ear. "They are searching for Jack now."

"Don't you think I know that," Andy snapped, his own hopes flagging the farther they rode among the still unorganized melee. It would only take a few minutes more for them to solidify their drunken anger and get it pointed in the proper direction: the Cherokee House.

Andy deliberately rode past the Cherokee House and

stopped in an alley down the block next to a mercantile store. Melissa slid from the back of the pony. In the darkness, Andy stepped down and looped the reins loosely over the branch of a low bush. He had a feeling once they had freed Jack, there wasn't going to be time to untie reins.

"What now?" Melissa whispered almost in his ear.

"They're holding Jack in that two-storied building down there," Andy said, pointing.

"Where?"

"There, on the corner. The Cherokee House," Andy said, realizing Melissa could not see where he was pointing in the darkness. "They're probably holding Jack in the cellar."

"What! Don't you know?" Melissa exclaimed.

"I couldn't very well march in there and ask them that, now could I?" Andy said, irritated by Melissa's questions. Sometimes, he just didn't know about females.

"So what are we going to do?"

Andy felt the responsibility of freeing Jack shift totally to his shoulders, yet he felt a little proud the girl was looking to him to provide the answers.

"We're simply going to walk in, take a look around until we locate the cellar stairs, and go down."

"I'm ready then," Melissa said, taking his arm in hers. Andy felt awkward as he walked across the less crowded street and up to the glass-fronted door of the Cherokee House. When he glanced up at Melissa Stiles, she gave him a reassuring smile as he held the front door for her.

The buggy rattled to a stop in front of the cabin and Ford stepped down, his spirits bolstered even higher by the few drinks he and John Shear had shared at the Criterion. He left behind streets filled with angry miners under a 40-rod influence. Judging by what he saw, Ford calculated Dawson had less than thirty minutes to live.

He rapped softly on the cabin's door at first, then harder when he got no immediate response from inside. In a few minutes, Mary Stiles came to the door obviously roused from a deep sleep.

"Good evening, Mary," Ford tipped his expensive hat to the woman. "Melissa still up? I'm afraid I got carried away with business and forgot the hour, but I did promise to drop back by."

"She must be asleep," Mary said, running a hand through her hair, "come in while I see if she is awake."

Ford closed the door behind him, "Don't wake her up, I can come back tomorrow."

Mary was back in seconds, alarmed. There was a worried look on her face.

"Melissa isn't in her bed!"

"What do you mean?" Ford asked not fully understanding what the woman was saying.

"I mean, she's not there. Her covers haven't been turned down." Mary was frightened, and it showed. "I can't imagine where she could be," she said, wringing her hands.

"She must be with the kid then," Ford said.

"Andy? He never came back, least not before I went to bed."

"He should have been back hours ago," Ford said frowning, turning this bit of information over in his mind.

"But where could they have gone?" Mary asked.

Ford looked at the woman, "Only one place I know. The kid must have somehow talked Melissa into helping Dawson."

Mary Stiles stared at the attorney for a full minute as she gathered her runaway thoughts.

"What do you mean?"

"The town's in an ugly mood right now over the murder of Dawson's partner. The kid has eyes and ears. He must have realized the dangerous situation Dawson is in and convinced Melissa to help free him."

"What! Melissa would never do that . . . unless." She looked at Ford. "Was Jack found guilty of Josiah Catt's murder?"

"He was, even though I defended him myself."

"Any way Andy could know that?"

"Doubt it. I think the kid's simply operating out of a feeling of loyalty to Dawson, and it looks like so is Melissa."

"I don't believe Jack murdered Josiah any more than Andy," Mary said, reaching for her wrap.

Ford spread his hands, "I did my best, but there were three eyewitnesses that claim they saw him shoot his partner."

"Jack Dawson stood up for us when most men would have kept on riding," Mary said tightly, "and I'm not about to forget that."

"We can't very well go breaking Dawson out of jail, can we?"

Mary Stiles flung the door open, "You coming, counselor, or do we Stiles take the law into our own hands without you?"

Ford followed the woman out into the yard. "Mary, you can't be serious."

"I am," Mary said resolutely, climbing into the buggy. "You said yourself, the town was ready to explode. Given half a chance, a mob would hang Jack from the nearest cottonwood limb."

"Yes, but—"

"What do you think Melissa and Andy are trying to do at this very moment?"

Ford could see there was no use arguing with the woman so he climbed in beside her and slapped the reins across the backs of his horses.

"There's one good thing that'll keep Melissa out of trouble," he said as he turned the buggy around.

"What's that?"

"No one knows where Dawson's being held. The marshal saw to that after the way the town is spitting fire for Dawson's carcass."

"Wouldn't be too sure about that," Mary said, pulling the wrap closer to her against the night chill.

"What do you mean?"

"Andy is a resourceful boy . . . and he listens well. Furthermore, he's loyal, just like you said."

A scowl crossed Ford's face as he got to wondering why the kid hadn't come straight back to the cabin like he was told to do. Had he trailed him and the others? The marshal as well? If so, then it stood to reason, the kid knew where Pollock had stashed Dawson. Ford jerked the buggy whip from its stand and lashed out viciously at the horses. There was no more time to waste. If Dawson managed to escape before the lynch mob arrived, then all his plans would be shot to Hell. And then he thought of Colin Jackson and relaxed. What was the worst could happen? Dawson escapes, braces Jackson for lying in court about Catt's murder, and pulls his gun. Ford had seen Colin Jackson in action. Nobody he knew could match the gunman's skill and blinding speed with a short gun. Dawson was sure to be killed. *End of story!*

Ford breathed easier and reached into his coat pocket for a cigar which he clamped between his teeth. With daylight less than four hours away, things should be settled one way or the other where Dawson was concerned before another day passed.

Chapter 32

As Andy turned to close the door, he heard the growing thunder. Like fireflies dancing in the night air, a swelling crowd of angry miners, carrying pitch torches, rounded the corner of McGaa Street. Melissa saw the look on his face as he quickly closed the door.

"What is it?" she whispered.

"Nothing," he said, deciding not to tell the girl the latest problem. Obviously, someone had tipped them off to where Jack was being held. They had no time to lose now. Andy steered the girl as fast as he could across the broad lobby to a far door near the dining area he hoped led down to the cellar. Fortunately, the few people seated in the lobby, smoking and talking, paid them no mind. The hotel clerk was absent as well. So far so good.

Melissa gave him a sideways glance as he pushed her toward the paneled door, but said nothing as he opened the door carefully. His hand slipped beneath his coat and brought out the big pistol. Melissa's eyes grew wide.

Andy forced her to take several tentative steps through the door. Andy pulled it shut behind them. They stood there in the narrow hallway a few feet from a set of stairs that led downward. A lamp from below cast warm shadows across the narrow confines as they edged closer to the stairs.

"Remember, we got to catch them off guard. Tell them anything you can think of. That don't work, pull the derringer. I'll be right behind you, case there's trouble."

"And what makes you think there won't be?" she whispered.

Andy smiled up at the girl and without batting an eye said, "Because you're a woman . . . and pretty. They won't be expecting trouble from you."

Melissa smiled at Andy, "So you noticed?"

"Let's go," Andy said gruffly, "time's wasting." Melissa started down the stairs with Andy crouching behind her. He only hoped they couldn't see him, but he dared not try to look around the girl for fear of being seen. He was sweating by the time they neared the cellar's stone floor.

"Here now, girl, you lost?" Andy heard a young voice ask.

"I . . . I just couldn't sleep with all the noise in the streets, so I just decided to explore the hotel. You don't mind, do you?"

"Why, I, uh, guess not," Asa Middaugh said slowly, taken in by the girl's beauty.

"Is this where they keep the wine?" Melissa asked, as she stepped lightly from the stairs.

"Yes, but you can't go in there just now. We got—"

Andy stepped quickly away from the woman and lifted the heavy pistol with both hands, cocking the weapon as he did so.

"Don't move, mister," Andy said, aiming the gun at the man's chest.

Asa Middaugh stared at the youngster with his mouth open for a few seconds.

"Boy, what the hell you up to?" He looked back at the girl and was surprised to see her standing there holding a small gun in her hand as well.

"What's going on here?" he demanded, getting up from his chair.

"Said not to move, mister," Andy warned.

"Why you little squirt, I oughta—"

Andy brought the pistol to full cock as it wavered before Asa Middaugh.

"Ain't got time to argue, Andy said, "there's a mob coming for Jack Dawson at this very minute. Either unlock the door or I'll be forced to shoot you."

Asa Middaugh saw the determined look on the boy's face and knew he meant what he said.

"Okay, okay, I'll open it, just keep that big gun under control," he told Andy.

"Take his gun," Andy told Melissa who stepped up and relieved Asa of his rifle and Colt. Asa grew red-faced at having a slip of a girl disarm him. He turned to unlock the door.

"You both are going to be in a lot of trouble for this," he said over his shoulder. He removed the padlock and swung the door inward.

Inside, Dawson quickly sat up in bed and saw what was happening.

"Andy! Get his keys and unlock these leg irons." Dawson looked at Melissa. "Thanks for coming," he said softly. Andy tossed Dawson the pistol while he took the keys from Asa Middaugh and came over to the bed.

"Where's the other guard?" Dawson asked.

"He was the only one out there," Melissa said. Dawson looked at the young lawman.

"Sent James to fetch me something to eat," Asa confessed.

"Okay, get over here and take off your boots," Dawson said, once he was free of the irons.

"We got to hurry, Jack," Andy warned. "There's a mob will be here any minute."

"Okay," Dawson said, "we'll skip the formalities. Just sit down on the bed until we gone, you hear?"

Asa nodded, taking his seat while they scrambled from the room and relocked the door.

"Let's get out of here," Dawson said as they went up the stairs two at a time.

Just as they reached the top, the outer door opened and James Middaugh stood there holding a plate of food with a surprised look on his face.

"You want to live, you'll do as I say," Dawson commanded. All James could do was nod his head.

"Take his revolver, Andy." The boy stepped quickly forward and lifted the gun from its holster.

"Now get down the stairs and stay put until we're gone, got that?"

"Got it," James said, scurrying down the stairs. The thundering crowd was nearing the front door of the Cherokee House, and several people had gotten out of their chairs to see what the fuss was all about.

"Put the gun away," Dawson commanded the boy as he took Asa's rifle and pistol from Melissa after sticking his own weapon in his waistband. Andy was busy looking out of the cellar door. He turned back to Dawson, his face completely white.

"They're at the front door!"

"Okay, you two go ahead, out the front. I'll go out the back way. Meet you in fifteen minutes behind the Elephant Corral down by Cherry Creek. Know where that is?"

"We'll find it," Andy said quickly, grabbing Melissa by the hand. They were halfway across the lobby when the front door burst inward; spilling drunken, cursing miners into the lobby.

"Outta our way, kids, we got work to do," a loudmouthed miner said, pushing around Andy and Melissa who darted out the door and down the steps.

"Melissa!" a voice called to them. They both halted in the middle of the street as Ford brought his horses to a skidding stop.

"You go on, Andy," Melissa whispered, squeezing his hand. Without a word, Andy darted around the blowing horses and disappeared into the night.

"Melissa, what in God's name are you doing down here this time of night?" Ford said, jumping out of the buggy. "Can't you see what an ugly mood these drunken miners are in? You could have been hurt or worse." Ford lifted Melissa off the ground in a big hug. Melissa sagged in his arms, glad that it was over.

"Are you okay, child?" Mary Stiles asked emotionally. In the background, the roar from the miners quickly built to a crescendo when they learned Dawson had been freed just minutes before. They spilled back out into the street with blood in their eyes. Leading the pack was Asa and James Middaugh. The mob flowed around Ford and the women and stopped.

"What's happened?" Ford asked the two lawmen.

"Dawson's escaped, Mr. Ford," James said, his eyes on the girl.

"What! How did that happen?" Ford shouted as the crowd pressed closer around the tiny group.

"Two people freed him at the point of a gun," James said, not wanting to tell more with the drunken miners hanging on every word.

"We're heading over to Marshal Pollock's, see what he wants to do about starting a manhunt," Asa added.

"Maybe you and the ladies would like to come along as well," James said.

"Yes, I think that would be a good idea," Ford said, noting the looks the Middaugh brothers threw at Melissa.

James, the bigger of the two lawmen, turned to address the crowd.

"Boys, you might as well go on back to camp. Ain't going to be a hanging tonight." This news brought on a howl of protest from the miners, still furious from being cheated out of their quarry.

Ford held up his hand and waited for the crowd to quiet down so he could be heard.

"Men, listen to me. I know most of you, and you know me. Fact is, wasn't more than an hour ago we stood drinking together at the bar down at the Criterion." The more sober of the miners nodded their heads.

"This man, Jack Dawson, was tried tonight and found guilty of murdering his partner, Josiah Catt." A rumbling of disgruntled voices rippled through the crowd of miners.

"Now I know how you feel, believe me, but let the law

take its course here. Marshal Pollock can handle this if you will only let him do his duty."

"He damn well better!" came a voice from the rear. Others joined in and it was several minutes before the crowd got quiet again.

"For those of you wanting a nightcap, I'm buying," Ford said. "Just tell Ed Jump to put it on my bill. Now we gotta go. It's late and these ladies need to be in bed." For a minute the crowd held and finally gave way, some drifting back to the Criterion to drown their sorrows with more free whiskey, while the more sober simply eased away into the darkness.

"Thanks, Mr. Ford," James Middaugh said, "they were spoiling for trouble and it wouldn't have taken much to set them off."

"That's okay. Suppose I drop the ladies off at their cabin and meet you over at Pollock's?"

"I'm afraid that won't do," James said almost apologetically.

"Why not?"

"Because this girl and a young boy were the very ones set Dawson free tonight."

The Elephant Corral was located only one block down and one over from the Cherokee House. The corral itself was an eight foot high stone and concrete wall that served as a place where emigrants could park their wagons and stable their horses and mules without outlaws making off with them. It also served as a marketplace for those looking to buy and sell animals, and many of the local merchants transacted business there regularly.

Sticking to the shadows, Dawson made his way to the Elephant Corral and flattened himself against the high wall bordering Cherry Creek. He pulled off a boot and emptied the gold coins into the palm of his hand. It was all he had left of the five hundred he had kept out of the deposit. He guessed Colin Jackson and the others had split the rest.

Dawson put the money in his pocket. It was more than enough to buy a horse since he had no idea where his buckskin was. He hunkered down by the wall and waited for Andy to find him.

Chapter 33

Dawson watched as a figure on horseback rode slowly up the creek from the west. As the rider came closer, Dawson recognized Andy and he called softly to him.

Andy rode over to the wall, jumped off the little pinto, and threw himself into Dawson's strong arms.

Somewhat surprised, Dawson held the boy close for a moment, neither of them speaking.

"Where's Melissa?" Dawson asked after Andy had stepped back, a little embarrassed by his spontaneous act of affection.

"She's with Miss Mary and the lawyer," Andy said. "They drove up just as we were leaving the hotel. Melissa insisted that I run for it. Should I have stayed?"

"You did right, boy," Dawson said. "They won't do anything to the girl, not with Ford throwing his weight around. But you would have been another story."

"Still, I hated leaving her there," Andy admitted.

"Appreciate you coming along when you did. Another five minutes and I'd have been swinging from a cottonwood limb. That took a lot of courage . . . Melissa, too. How did you know where to look after Pollock switched locations?"

Andy told Dawson of following the wagon to Graham's Drugs, of seeing the gunman and Ford together before they entered the building, and afterwards trailing the wagon to the Cherokee House.

"Might explain why those drunken miners managed to

find me so quick. Which means Pollock must have said something to Ford about where he was moving me."

Andy's eyes grew wide, "You think he had anything to do with it?"

"Can't say for sure, but he did a mighty poor job of defending me in court."

"Then we've got to stop Melissa from marrying him," Andy almost shouted.

"Keep your voice down, boy. First things, first. Case you ain't noticed, I got troubles of my own . . . you, too, since you helped me escape."

"What are we going to do, Jack?"

"First, take this money and go around to the front and buy me the best horse you can find. Don't worry about spending it all, got plenty more down at Gruber's mint . . . least I did have, if that silver-tongued lawyer and the gunman haven't managed to make a withdrawal." Andy gripped the money in his small fist.

"I'll be back quick as I can," Andy promised and he slipped away along the darkened wall. Dawson held the reins of the pinto and stroked the animal's neck. If push came to shove and he was discovered before the boy returned, he'd be forced to ride the little horse even though it couldn't carry his weight for long.

Thirty minutes later Andy reappeared, leading a rangy-looking mustang the color of sandstone under a quarter moon rising in the eastern sky.

"Best I could do, Jack," Andy said. Dawson checked the animal's feet and legs and felt along his back. "That man who sold him to me acted mighty suspicious."

"You did good, boy," Dawson said, checking the cinch on the old saddle.

"Charged me twenty dollars for the saddle," Andy complained.

"Beggars can't be choosers. Come on, boy, let's get out o town," Dawson said, mounting the horse who acted like he was going to buck until he felt the steady hand of Dawson on the reins.

"Where we going?" Andy asked as he climbed aboard his pinto.

"Don't rightly know for now, just need some time to think, to sort things out without worrying about a mob breathing down my neck." Dawson turned the mustang west and entered the safety of the tree line bordering the Platte. He drew up and looked out across the dark waters running swift and cold in the pale light.

"Think you can swim that little paint across?" Dawson asked.

"Done it before. Once with you, and again after I trailed you and those men back to Denver."

"I know you did, but crossing at night can be tricky, dangerous even. You got to stick close."

"Me and Misstep will stick to you like glue," Andy promised.

Dawson smiled in the darkness, "That his name now?"

"I guess so," Andy said, surprised at himself. "I just now gave it to him."

Dawson moved his horse slowly into the swift current, "Told you when the time came, you'd come up with the right name for him. Move around to my right, boy. That way if there's trouble, I'll be downstream to help you." Andy did as he was instructed and they made the crossing without mishap even though they were both shivering from the cold waters once they emerged on the far bank.

"We'll move out a little ways and build us a fire. Dry out some," Dawson said. "After that, we got to hit the mountains. It'll be daylight in a couple hours and we both could use some sleep. We stay out here, someone'll spot us for sure."

It was close to an hour before they were sufficiently dry enough to ride on.

"You remember where those pack supplies are?" Dawson asked.

"I can lead us right to them," Andy said proudly.

"Good. That'll ease the pressure some for us. Give me time to find Catt. Got to give him a decent burial."

Andy didn't speak as they rode farther away from the South Platte and entered the deep foothills of the Rockies just as the sky to the east flared red.

Pollock sat at his desk with a disgusted look written all over his face. With defiant looks, Melissa and Mary Stiles sat up straight in their chairs across from him. A. C. Ford and the Middaugh brothers stood nearby.

Pollock was boxed in, and he didn't like the feeling one damn bit. Had it not been for the Middaugh brothers, the affair could be easily forgotten, swept aside. But James and Asa Middaugh were as honest and straightforward as their old man when it came to right and wrong.

"For the last time," Ford said, "Melissa never stopped to consider the consequences of her actions. She felt an obligation, a duty if you will, to help Dawson." He turned to face James and Asa. "Hell, you boys know the story well as I do. Hadn't been for Dawson coming along when he did, those Indians would have had their way with these ladies. After that, who's to know." Both James and Asa shifted from foot to foot, their eyes darting from the women, to Ford, and finally to the scarred wooden floor.

Pollock lifted his big frame from his chair, sweeping back his long red hair. "It don't matter what James and Asa think," he said coldly. Pollock had made up his mind and came to the only logical conclusion open to him.

"You boys were acting as *my* deputies, not as deputy sheriffs. As town marshal, I have jurisdiction over this case, not the sheriff. Therefore, I am releasing Melissa Stiles into Mr. Ford's custody." Pollock sat back down and picked up his coffee cup and took a sip of the cold, half-brandy, half-coffee mixture. "You boys are hereby relieved of duty as deputy marshals. Go home and get some sleep."

Both Asa and James Middaugh looked relieved rather than upset by Pollock's decision. Without another word they dipped their heads in the direction of the women and hurried out the door.

"Come, ladies, I'll drive you home," Ford said, giving Pollock a knowing smile.

Mary Stiles stood up and looked Pollock square in the eye, "I want you to know I would have been right beside Melissa helping Jack Dawson for what he did for us."

"Yes, ma'am," Pollock said, standing up as well. "Know you would have."

"Thank you for understanding," Mary said, turning to her daughter. "Come, child, let's go home." Ford ushered the two women from the room.

"If you ladies would wait in the buggy, I need to have a private word with the marshal," Ford said. The two women nodded and left the room.

"That was real smart of you, Tom," Ford said, "you're getting better at this political game." Pollock didn't look impressed. It had been a long night, and he was facing another long day with Dawson's escape.

"What we gonna do about Dawson?" Pollock wanted to know.

"Go find Colin for me, will you? Tell him to meet me in my office in an hour while I take these ladies home."

"Dawson wags his tongue, we're all dead meat," Pollock said unhappily.

"You got nothing to worry about, Tom. All you been doing is your duty. Dawson can't pin a thing on you. It's Jackson and myself that's got to worry."

"Still, I don't like these shady affairs much."

"Don't turn tail now, Tom," Ford warned.

"Ain't turning tail!" Pollock thundered, irritated by a plan gone sour now Dawson was running loose.

"Okay, okay," Ford said, lowering his voice. "I'll take care of Dawson like I said I would. Just you find Colin like I asked." Ford slapped his hat on his head and disappeared through the door, leaving the marshal sitting there with a hangdog expression on his face.

"Listen, it's important if Dawson comes around to get in contact with me," Ford told Mary and Melissa Stiles as they stepped down from the buggy in front of the cabin. "I'm the only one who can help him now."

"I have no idea where Jack has gone," Melissa said.

"What about the kid?" Ford asked. "Surely he said something?"

Melissa shook her head tiredly. There were dark circles beneath her eyes from the loss of sleep. Mary Stiles looked at Ford with searching eyes.

"Can you really help now? If Jack is caught, won't he simply be hanged now the court has passed sentence?"

"Not necessarily," Ford said smoothly. "There's the matter of *habeas corpus*. Which simply means, Dawson was convicted without the prosecution showing evidence of a body. In other words, it's Dawson's word against Colin Jackson's."

"That gunman," Melissa shuddered.

"If Dawson would agree to surrender to me, I'll see he gets an appeal and a new trial."

"I don't know if Jack would ever agree to such terms," Mary Stiles said doubtfully.

"It's at least worth a try, isn't it? Otherwise, the law will put a bounty on his head and every man with a gun will try collecting it."

"If that happens," Mary responded, "there's going to be a lot of blood spilled. I've seen Jack use his guns."

"All the more reason to stop this madness if we can," Ford said, pressing home his point.

"Guess you're right," Mary admitted.

Ford took a deep breath and let it out slowly. "Good, now here's what you tell Dawson if he comes around. There's an old cabin, down by the Platte, where an old mountain man used to live with his squaw among the woods. Indians use it as a camping area whenever they come to town. Have him wait for me there. I'll do all I can to see he gets a fair shake, that's a promise."

Ford drove directly to his office and pulled off his coat and tie, washed his face, and built a fire in the stove. He was

300

busy pouring himself a brandy when Colin Jackson showed up.

By his looks, Ford figured the gunman had gotten very little sleep either. He almost blurted out how Sarah Jane must be keeping him up at nights. Instead, Ford poured Colin a jigger of brandy as well. Ford tilted back his head and downed his drink. Sarah Jane was no longer important to him, he concluded, and certainly not worth the pain Colin could dish had he a mind to press the issue.

"Starting a little early, aren't you?" Colin asked, sipping his.

"Not when you've been up all night like I have," Ford said, taking his seat behind his desk. He was bone weary, yet he knew too much needed to be done before he slept again.

The gunman smiled thinly, "Heard Dawson had escaped. Some kid and that girl of yours pulled it off."

"Damn it, Colin, ain't in no mood to be toyed with," Ford warned. "It's that little brat's fault. He talked Melissa into it, played on her conscience. Told her how Dawson had helped her mother and her in their time of need."

"Boy ought to make a fine lawyer someday."

Ford bit back a sharp reply, getting up to pour himself another drink. Returning to his desk, Ford looked at the gunman over the rim of his glass.

"We got to end this soon."

"What is it you want me to do?"

"What I want is Dawson dead. Provoke him into a gunfight in front of the whole town when you find him. Gunfighting is your specialty, isn't it? Ought to be a certain thing for you."

"In a gunfight ain't nothing ever certain until the other man's lying face down in the dirt."

"Well, seeing's how you and Black Hawk were the accusers, Dawson may be a bit more determined, so be careful."

The gunman gave the lawyer a cold smile, "Dawson don't worry me none. He may be a seasoned trapper and such, but he ain't no gun hand."

"That may be, but I hear tell Dawson's a damn fine shot with a long gun."

Colin Stood up, "You worry too much, counselor. There is one thing though. I sent Black Hawk and Cove Stillman back out to cover that Dawson's claim. Wouldn't do to have ornery, fired-up miners moving in on us, would it?"

"You want to hire a couple men to track down Dawson?"

"Dawson's one man. Ain't seen the day I couldn't handle him and five others just like him at one time."

"Just be careful. Where will you be?" Ford asked. Silently, he intoned, *with Sarah Jane?* Even though the woman had humiliated him in front of Melissa Stiles and the whole town, the thought of her with the gunman still ate at him.

"Over at the Criterion when you're ready," Colin said, standing up, "or . . . in my room."

Ford didn't need to ask what Colin would be doing there as a sour expression settled across Ford's face.

Chapter 34

Dawson and the boy walked carefully among the scattered supplies, picking up tins of food and discarded clothing.

"Looks like the critters went through our supplies pretty good," Dawson said, holding up a ragged piece of gnawed bacon.

"I'm sorry, Jack," Andy said, standing there with his arms loaded with canned goods.

"No need to be, boy. Loading that mule was about more than I could handle. Besides, we don't need much now. Soon as we give Josiah a proper burial, we're going back to town."

Andy's face paled under the brilliant blue sky. "We go back there, they'll kill you for sure," he said, his voice edged with fear.

"You right about one thing," Dawson said grimly as he strapped on the extra holster he kept in his bedding gear and slipped the big dragoon Andy had found earlier into the leather.

Andy watched with eyes as large as silver conchas. "How come you have two pistols just alike?"

Dawson looked over at the boy, shucking the big revolver from its resting place with lightning speed. The movement was fluid with no wasted motion. Andy's eyes grew even larger. Dawson gave the boy a grin and reholstered the gun.

"Keep an extra for occasions such as this."

"You're fast, Jack," the boy said, filling a flour sack with food.

"Maybe so, boy, but I'm not crazy to believe I'm in the same class as Colin Jackson."

"You ever see him draw?"

"Don't need to. Man makes his living with a gun. And at his age, that means he's fast." Dawson gathered what he had and dumped them in the sack Andy was holding.

"Enough for now. Let's go see if we can find Josiah, okay?"

"Whatever you say, Jack," Andy said, looking up at the tall trapper with open admiration.

They approached the claim with caution from up slope and through a timbered draw choked with boulders of every size and description. The going was tough, but Dawson wasn't about to be surprised for the second time in a row.

Dawson motioned for Andy to dismount with his finger to his mouth once he caught scent of woodsmoke. Somebody was on their claim and most likely unfriendly.

"Hold the horses here," Dawson whispered, slipping the rifle they had taken off Asa Middaugh from its saddle scabbard.

"Be careful, Jack," Andy said softly.

"Stay here even if you hear shooting, understand?"

Andy nodded. "When it's safe, I'll call for you to come down."

Dawson jacked a shell into the chamber of the rifle and slipped quietly through the thick stand of lodgepole. A few minutes later he emerged from the dark stand and found himself less than fifty yards from camp. What he saw next sent a wave of anger shooting through him.

Dawson stepped into the clearing, leveling the rifle at the two men who were busy working the sluice.

"You men just hold it right there!" Dawson commanded.

They looked at Dawson as if they were seeing a ghost. It was Cove Stillman who got over the shock first, and he jerked his gun, diving for the ground.

Dawson's rifle cracked and Stillman was spun around by

Dawson's bullet as he hit the ground, firing his own gun wildly.

Up to his knees in the creek, gripping a shovel, Black Hawk was in no condition to offer much fight. He just stood there as Cove Stillman writhed about with blood pumping out of his neck.

"Ease that shovel to the ground," Dawson commanded of the outlaw. Black Hawk stood there unmoving with a perplexed expression on his face, as if to say none of this was making sense. Dawson was supposed to be dead!

"Do it!" Dawson's voice rang out.

Black Hawk dropped the shovel like the handle had gotten too hot to hold any longer.

"Now step out of the water and keep your hands where I can see them."

"Ain't got no gun on me," the outlaw said gruffly, finally finding his voice.

"Lucky for you," Dawson said, watching the outlaw with cold eyes. "Take a seat over on that flat rock." Black Hawk did as he was told, regretting his decision to take the gunbelt off while he shoveled gravel into the sluice. But then he changed his mind when he looked over at Cove Stillman who lay very still with both arms flung outward from his body.

Dawson glanced around camp. "You two the only ones here?"

"Got nothing to say to you," the outlaw said defiantly.

Dawson threw him a bleak smile. "Expect you might change your mind about a few things before I'm done with you."

Black Hawk's expression lost some of his bluster at Dawson's promise. Dawson whistled shrilly. In a few minutes, Andy emerged from the timber leading their horses.

"It's that dang boy," Black Hawk said incredulously.

"That's right, Black Hawk, the boy knows everything. Left him behind when I rode in the other day. He saw you, this fellow here, and Colin Jackson take my guns." The

305

outlaw looked as though he had been punched in the stomach.

"That still don't pin the tail on this donkey," Black Hawk said, trying to regain some of his confidence.

"Expect you'll confess."

"You got the wrong gobbler."

"Don't think so," Dawson said as Andy came up with the horses, staring at the captured outlaw. Dawson handed the rifle to Andy. "Keep him covered." Dawson lifted the rope from Andy's saddle, built a loop.

"You got a choice, Black Hawk, tell the truth or hang here and now," Dawson said flatly, his face hard as granite.

"You wouldn't," the outlaw said, half-rising from the rock.

"You had a hand in murdering my partner or maybe you done the killing yourself. I don't know, but there's one thing I do know," Dawson said coming over to the outlaw, "you don't agree to talk, you hang." He dropped the noose over Black Hawk's head. The outlaw shrank as the rope touched his exposed flesh.

"Wait a minute, wait one minute," Black Hawk said, losing his grip on his nerve.

"Got no more time to give you, less you willing to point fingers."

"I'm willin'," Black Hawk said, finding it difficult to swallow, his mouth gone suddenly dry as sand.

"Expect you best wait until we find ourselves a reliable witness. They ain't about to believe me," Dawson said, "or the boy, not after helping me escape jail."

"I want to make a deal," the outlaw said, gathering his thoughts to him. "I'll give you a list of names of the Secret Ten and sign it, if I can leave the territory."

"Secret Ten?" Dawson repeated as he bound Black Hawk's hands behind him with a leather string. "What are you talking about?"

Black Hawk seemed genuinely surprised by the question.

"Why, don't you know? They're the inner circle of the

Vigilance Committee who's been hanging people right and left. You get on their list, you're good as dead."

"This People's Court run by them as well?" Black Hawk nodded.

"Figures," Dawson said, scratching the stubble on his face.

"I can name some of them, Jack," Andy spoke up. "I saw several of them slip into Graham's Drugs last night. Including Mr. Ford and that gunman, Colin Jackson."

"Colin ain't no member," Black Hawk scoffed. "He just does Ford's bidding when they need somebody killed."

"Like Josiah Catt," Dawson said coldly. "So, a select few of these members are into horse rustling and claim-jumping. Pretty slick. Nobody would ever suspect them of such skullduggery. Who are these rotten apples?"

Black Hawk clamped his lips together, "Done talking till I get my deal."

"First we got to find someone in Denver we can trust," Dawson said. "Like a judge, maybe." He looked around at the dead outlaw sprawled in his own blood.

"Guess we better bury him." Dawson looked back at Black Hawk. "What did you do with Catt's body?"

"Back up in them rocks aways."

"Show me. While you're at it, we'll bring along the shovel and you can dig a hole for your friend here."

"Hell, I ain't digging no hole for him, just roll a few rocks over him. Be good enough."

"That what you do with Catt?" Dawson said, picking up the shovel. The outlaw dipped his head and stared at the ground. "Figured as much. Now move!"

After Black Hawk had shown Dawson where they had disposed of Josiah Catt, the outlaw was cut free and told to start digging. Andy stood by with the rifle watching every move the man made while Dawson began to uncover his dead friend.

"Got to be getting ripe by now," Black Hawk warned, sweating over the hard ground with the shovel.

Dawson gave him a cold stare and continued removing rocks from the shallow grave.

"Just make sure you dig it deep," Dawson ordered.

After Dawson had properly laid Josiah Catt to rest, he helped the outlaw bury Cove Stillman. By then, Black Hawk was exhausted from digging and flopped down on the ground to rest.

"On your feet, man, we're taking you into Denver," Dawson said, picking up the shovel.

"I'm tired," the outlaw complained, wiping his sweating face on the back of a sleeve.

"You can rest in the saddle. Now get up!"

The outlaw's face turned blood red. With the rifle trained on him, he managed slowly to get to his feet and started back to camp.

Dawson bound the man's wrists once again and saddled his horse. He set Stillman's horse free, knowing the animal would remain in the general vicinity since there was plenty of spring grass near the creek for forage. Dawson felt sure the horse was stolen but he didn't have time to worry about that right now.

Next, Dawson cleaned out the riffles in the sluice Black Hawk had been using and quickly panned out four ounces of gold which he poured into a leather pouch. That done, Dawson tossed it to Andy who looked surprised.

"Your share, partner," Dawson said simply and mounted his horse after helping the outlaw on his own. Andy was still too flabbergasted to say anything, holding tightly to the small pouch of nuggets, as they rode away from the claim.

With the dark gray massif of the Chicago Peaks at their backs, the trio crossed Squaw Pass and descended into the narrow cleft of Clear Creek Canyon in mid-afternoon with Andy dozing in the saddle. Dawson smiled back at the spunky boy whose head bobbed up and down. He had been without sleep now for over thirty hours. With the sudden turn of events, Dawson doubted he could expect to get any for the next twenty-four.

They passed hordes of miners, some working claims,

while others, with heavy packs strapped to their backs, trudged deeper into the mountains. Dawson urged the outlaw on, never stopping to give answers to questions forming on miner's lips.

By late afternoon, they broke free of the canyon where Clear Creek cut its way across the plains to enter the South Platte River just a mile north of Denver City. Rather than follow the circuitous route of the creek, Dawson directed Black Hawk to continue directly east. They crossed the Platte by way of Tom Warren's ferry. The ferryman stared hard at Dawson the entire time as if trying to figure where he had seen him before. Once free of the ferry, they entered that part of town known until recently as Auraria. It was also where the presiding judge of the county, William Slaughter resided.

"Hold up," Dawson told Black Hawk a block from the river. "You know which house belongs to Judge Slaughter?"

"Across from the Tremont, on Cherry Street," the outlaw said gruffly.

"Lead on, then," Dawson said. "Just remember, you try running and I won't hesitate to shoot you in the back. I'm already wanted for murder, one more won't make any difference to me."

Black Hawk looked closely at Dawson to see if he was bluffing, but he saw no give in the man's eyes. It was then he decided to take his chances with the judge rather than buck Dawson.

William Slaughter had just sat down to supper following a particularly long day in court, and he was in no mood for interruptions. When he was confronted at the door by Black Hawk with his hands still tied behind him, Slaughter opened his mouth to offer a protest. The words stuck in his throat when he peered around the outlaw and saw Jack Dawson standing there with a huge revolver in his hand. Involuntarily, Slaughter took a step backward and Dawson propelled Black Hawk into the parlor.

Judge Slaughter quickly recovered his voice. "What's the

meaning of this?" he demanded, looking at the two men and the small boy who trailed in behind Dawson.

"We got some business needs attending to," Dawson said quickly. "This can't wait."

Slaughter realized Dawson couldn't know he was the one who had presided at his trial last evening and he relaxed somewhat.

"Why is this man bound?" Slaughter asked. It was then he noticed the odd look Dawson gave him. Slaughter turned away, showing them to chairs.

"Calls himself Black Hawk," Dawson said, motioning for the outlaw to sit down. Dawson remained standing with the dragoon in his hand. "He's here to offer up the murderers of both Josiah Catt and the two other miners Josiah Catt and me uncovered back there in the mountains a few days ago."

"And who are you?" Slaughter asked, playing dumb where Dawson was concerned.

Dawson stared hard at the judge for a long moment and finally shook his head. "I might've played directly into the hands of the Vigilance Committee by coming here."

"Whatever do you mean?" Slaughter asked warily. Black Hawk looked from the judge and back again to Dawson, not understanding what was happening here.

"Think you know what I mean, Judge," Dawson said quietly.

"Yes, I see," Slaughter said, realizing Dawson had guessed his role in last night's trial.

"And you also know I barely escaped from a lynch mob last night. Fact is, hadn't been for Andy here, I'd be dead now."

"Marshal Pollock has his men combing the town for you, Dawson. Why don't you give yourself up to me and I'll do all I can?"

Dawson gave the judge a bleak smile, "Yeah, like you helped me out last night?"

"No, this is different. Fact is, several prominent members of this community and I have picked up on some rather disturbing news since your escape." He glanced down at Black Hawk who was all ears now.

"What sort of news?" Dawson asked, his interest quickening.

"Just this. We believe there may be members of our, ah, unique group who may be responsible for the latest rash of horse rustling. They may even be responsible for claim-jumping and murder, but we can't yet prove any of this," Slaughter said.

"So Black Hawk told the truth."

"What's that?" Slaughter asked Dawson.

"That group you just mentioned is the Secret Ten. Black Hawk spoke of it earlier; several of the members are carrying on crimes under the guise of being law-abiding citizens." Dawson nudged the outlaw with his big dragoon, "Go on Black Hawk, tell the judge what you told us."

"Ain't saying nothing till I get a deal," Black Hawk said.

"Depends on what you have to say," Slaughter responded.

"Got plenty to say. Enough to blow this town wide open . . . give you the names of the Secret Ten been sharing in the profits from horse stealing and claim-jumping—"

"And murder," Dawson prompted, thinking of Josiah Catt.

"Yeah, that too," Black Hawk said, licking his dry lips. "Well . . . what do you say, Judge?"

"In return for this important information, what do you expect from the court?"

"A fast horse, nothing more. I'll clear outta this part of the country for good." Black Hawk looked from Slaughter to Dawson and back again. "What do you say, Judge, we got a deal?"

"I want your share of the gold you stole from my partner and me," Dawson interjected before Slaughter could speak.

"What ain't in my bedding, Colin Jackson deposited for me in the Clark and Gruber's Mint. I can sign a letter turning it all over to you now," Black Hawk said, sensing things were about to go his way. Besides, he could always

311

get more gold. There was talk of gold strikes up in Montana, and the climate would be a lot healthier for him.

"Okay, your request is duly noted and accepted. Now tell me, who's the ringleader?" Slaughter asked.

"A. C. Ford runs the show, both the horse rustling and claim-jumping. Colin Jackson and me been doing his dirty work, but it was Colin done the killing," the outlaw added quickly after seeing Dawson's hard eyes.

Slaughter shook his head. "I never would have suspected A.C. Hell, we play cards together, three . . . four times a week," he said sadly.

"Who else?" Dawson prodded Black Hawk.

"I'll write out a list of names when you're ready to turn me loose, Judge. Not until then."

"I want your written confession as well, understand?" Slaughter said, getting out of his chair to fetch paper and pen. Dawson slipped his knife between the outlaw's bound wrists and sliced through the rawhide bindings.

"For now, I want you to write out a disclaimer for the gold you and Colin Jackson have down at Clark and Gruber's that belongs to Dawson," Slaughter instructed.

The outlaw slowly scribbled out the necessary words, as directed by Judge Slaughter, releasing the stolen gold. When it was done, he signed his name and gave it to Slaughter who countersigned as a witness and handed it to Dawson.

"That ought to do it."

Dawson read the poorly handwritten note. Satisfied, he folded it once and put it in his coat pocket. He looked at Slaughter.

"This mean what I think? You believe me when I say I didn't murder my partner?"

"Let's just say, with Black Hawk's written testimony, there's a good chance you will be quickly cleared of all charges. But later, it will have to be formally presented before the court for it to stick."

"Well, that's good enough for me," Dawson replied.

"I wouldn't go showing myself just yet, least not until I get with other members and set the record straight. And

God help you, if you come across Colin Jackson before then."

Dawson's face turned grim, "It's him will be needing help. And that slick lawyer Ford."

Slaughter gave Black Hawk a skeptical look, "It's hard to believe A.C. is mixed up in something like this."

"Greed can do funny things to a man, even someone like Ford who has everything anyone could want in life," Dawson said, binding the outlaw's hands behind his back again.

"You must try to stay out of trouble until we get to the bottom of this," Slaughter cautioned. "There are those in this town who will take charge of these new findings presented here tonight. Don't complicate things any more than they already are."

"You got till tomorrow morning to take care of things. After that, I'll do it my way," Dawson promised. "What I can't promise is whether or not Colin Jackson will force things."

"Understood," Slaughter said.

"What about him?"

"Two of my associates are due here any minute. We will see he's taken good care of." Black Hawk gave Dawson an evil grin.

"Just make sure you give that list of names to the judge here," Dawson said to the outlaw, turning to the door with the quiet boy trailing behind.

"Take care of yourself, Dawson," Slaughter called.

"Always," Dawson replied, stepping through the opened doorway.

"What now?" Andy asked. They were standing outside the judge's residence.

"Well, like the judge says, we need to keep a low profile. And with all these miners still hopping mad about my having shook free of their noose last night, expect if I'm spotted now, they'll come shooting. Won't be time for questions."

"So what are we going to do?" Andy persisted.

"Think we ought to pay a call on a couple of pretty ladies, don't you?"

Chapter 35

"I don't believe you!" Melissa Stiles shouted, backing away from Dawson who was standing in the opened doorway. He hadn't meant to broach the subject so quickly, but the girl questioned what he was still doing in town. Mary Stiles came over and closed the door. Andy Philmore stood there with big eyes watching the girl.

"That is a rather strong accusation, Jack," Mary said, hoping to calm her daughter.

"You're against A.C. and me getting married," Melissa said. "You're mad I didn't pay more attention to you, I know how men think!"

Dawson's eyes blazed, "Oh, you do, do you? Well, all I've been thinking of lately is Josiah's murder. And now I've found someone who can prove who was behind it all."

"A. C. would never murder anyone," Melissa shot back. "He's kind, gentle . . . and he's rich. He doesn't need to kill anyone for money."

Dawson smiled thinly. "Didn't say he killed anybody, just passed along the orders to his gunman, Colin Jackson."

"Whoever told you that lied!"

"It's no lie, Melissa," Andy spoke up. "Last night, I saw Mr. Ford and Colin Jackson talking in front of Graham's Drugs before they tried Jack for murder."

"They are friends, nothing more. They even play cards together, but that don't mean he does A.C.'s bidding."

"I heard Black Hawk say he did," Andy replied softly.

"And it was Jackson who testified against me. That I was the one murdered Josiah," Dawson said.

"Jack was with me the whole time, he couldn't have killed Josiah," Andy said. "Just like I told you last night. That's why you helped me."

"That was different," Melissa said coldly. "But now you are accusing A.C. of something I know he could never do. I'm not about to stand still for this kind of talk for one minute."

Dawson looked helplessly at Mary Stiles who was twisting her apron in her hands and looking worried.

"Listen, child, if A.C. is innocent, surely the law will get to the bottom of who's really behind the murdering and horse rustling. A.C. is an excellent attorney. He will see to it that right prevails."

Melissa stiffened and she turned her cold eyes on her mother.

"Mother, stop calling me that! I'm *not* a child anymore! And nothing you or anybody else can say will change my mind about A.C.."

Melissa ran to the door, threw it open, and was gone into the night.

Dawson was stunned by her outburst as tears welled up in Mary's eyes.

"I'm sorry," Dawson said lamely. "I'll go after her, make her understand."

"No," Mary said, dabbing at her eyes with the corner of her apron. "It will do no good. Melissa is like her father, headstrong and unwilling to listen to truth at times."

"I never meant to . . . ." Dawson's voice trailed off.

"Believe me, I understand," Mary said. "And in time so will Melissa. Right now she needs time to think over what you said. She'll be okay." Dawson looked doubtful.

"I'll talk to her," Andy said, darting from the cabin before Mary Stiles could call him back.

"Could work. Andy can do more than anybody," Dawson said, slightly encouraged by the boy's sudden action.

Mary clasped her hands together and brought them to her lips. She seemed in shock herself.

"Mary, I . . . I never meant to cause trouble for you or Melissa. God knows you both have been through more than your share. I will admit that I was a little disappointed she turned so quickly to Ford, but I could see why. I could offer her nothing while Ford promised her everything. I didn't do this out of spite or jealousy. Ford was specifically named by the outlaw now being held by Judge Slaughter."

Mary came over and laid a hand on his arm, looking up at the rugged trapper.

"I understand, Jack," she whispered. "Want you to know, I picked you, but Melissa took one look at Ford and fell head over heels. It's not your fault." Dawson nodded, feeling somewhat better.

Andy burst through the doorway, his face pale and etched with worry.

"What is it, boy?" Dawson said quickly.

"It's Melissa. She's gone . . . and she's taken my pony.

After Judge Slaughter and his three associates had Black Hawk safely locked away in the same room at the Cherokee House Dawson had been held in only hours before, they retired to one of the hotel's private rooms next to the bar to discuss the grave situation Denver was facing. Slaughter was the first to speak after they had taken their seats.

"We all knew it would come to this," Slaughter said. The others nodded quietly, waiting for him to continue. "Just a matter of time. What we must do is act swiftly, get it over with as quickly as possible, for Denver's sake . . . and ours."

"I agree, it's been going on much too long," Captain Edwin Scudder spoke up. "We now have the proof, or I should say, we will have as soon as Black Hawk provides us with a list of names." Scudder had come to Denver and established one of the first grocery stores in the area, first working from a tent and gradually progressing to a clapboard building as his business prospered. Scudder came up with the novel approach of delivering groceries free of charge. Until he could earn enough to hire another man, he could be seen trundling a wheelbarrow loaded with food, cheery-faced and singing. As his business grew, so did his standing in the circle of prominent merchants and politicians. Scudder was now a major voice in the Vigilance Committee, the Secret Ten, and now the Stranglers, formed just days ago to deal with those members of the Secret Ten who were themselves breaking the law.

"When do we act?" one of the other men asked.

"Tonight, before word leaks out. It must be done tonight," Slaughter said. The other men nodded and swallowed their drinks, standing up.

"We all know what to do," Slaughter said. "Ed, you alert the others, Bill I want you and Morgan to stand guard. Don't let anyone in to see Black Hawk. The rest of us will meet in the cellar in one hour. That's all."

The powerful men of Denver's upper crust filed out of the back room with Morgan Strasburg and Bill Brady going directly to the cellar where they took up positions in front of the locked door.

A.C. Ford was surprised to see Melissa Stiles standing at his door, but he showed her quickly in after he caught sight of her red-rimmed eyes.

"What's the matter?" Ford said, closing the door behind the woman and leading her over to a chair. He was so thankful he had resisted the temptations of the dancer at the Criterion to come home with him for the remainder of the night.

"It's just awful," Melissa said, burying her head in her hands.

"Melissa, tell me what's wrong?" Ford said, kneeling before the distraught woman, taking her hands in his. She looked at Ford through a flood of tears.

"Jack Dawson said you were responsible for Josiah Catt's death and the others," Melissa burst forth crying.

"What! When did you see Dawson? He came by the cabin?" Melissa nodded.

"When was that?"

"Just a little while ago," Melissa managed to reply, blowing her nose in her lace handkerchief.

"Tell me exactly what he said, leave nothing out," Ford commanded, his mind racing ahead of the conversation.

"He said some outlaw . . . named Black something or other . . ."

"Black Hawk!" Ford paled somewhat at the mention of the outlaw's name.

"Yes, Black Hawk." Melissa stopped and stared at the attorney. "Do you know this man?"

Ford waved a hand in the air. "Everybody knows about Black Hawk. He's a famous outlaw been stealing horses and committing other crimes against the populace of Denver for many months. Go on."

"Jack says this man named you as the ringleader, and you had this gunman, Colin Jackson, do your bidding whenever you wished somebody killed."

Ford laughed, as much to cover his own uneasiness and shock at the news, as well as to alleviate Melissa Stiles's fears.

"That's preposterous! Me, associating with known criminals? This Black Hawk is obviously trying to save his own neck from a noose."

Melissa had stopped crying and was looking at the attorney, pacing back and forth in front of her.

"Still, these charges are serious and I must do everything I can to see such vicious rumors are headed off before they spread around town. It could do harm to my practice even though there's not a grain of truth to what Black Hawk said."

"I knew Jack was mistaken," Melissa said, feeling better now she had talked with Ford. Ford came over and lifted her from the chair, taking her in his arms. They kissed.

"Don't worry about Dawson. He's probably jealous, and looking to blame me for his partner's murder."

Melissa pulled back and looked at the lawyer. "Jack didn't murder Josiah Catt, this I know."

"Well maybe it was this Black Hawk fellow," Ford said, pulling her close once more. He didn't want to upset her more than was necessary. He needed to send her back to her mother as quickly as possible without arousing her suspicions. There was much he had to do and he had very little time left to do it.

"I want you to run along home now, Melissa," Ford said. "It wouldn't do for people to see you alone here with me."

"I don't care anymore," Melissa said breathlessly as she pressed even closer into him. Ford felt the swell of her body against him and it was all he could do to keep his senses.

"There's nothing I would like better, darling," Ford whispered, kissing her lightly, "but we are going to set Denver on its ear after we get married. I won't have your reputation in doubt ever!"

"I tell you, I don't care anymore," Melissa said huskily as she kissed him deeply. "Even mother believes Jack, I could tell," she said when Ford forced them apart.

Ford felt the heat rising fast in him, and he knew he had to get rid of the girl now. In a few minutes he wouldn't have the strength left to resist, even in the face of his own self-preservation if Black Hawk should spill his guts.

It took all of his courtroom persuasion to get Melissa started for home on Andy's horse. Ford waited a few minutes to be sure the hot-blooded girl didn't change her mind and double back. Then he grabbed his hat and coat, and hurried off down the street to the Vasquez House.

Colin Jackson answered the frantic knocking, shirtless and in his stocking feet. He held the Colt breast high and aimed at the door as he jerked it open.

"A.C., what are you doing here?" Jackson said, surprised by the visit. Ford had never been in the gunman's room before. Ford rushed in before Colin could stop him.

"Whoa, wait, A.C." Colin closed the door. Ford saw the woman in the bed and gave her a wicked grin. Sarah Jane pulled the covers even higher around her shoulders.

"Hello, Sarah Jane."

"Now damn it, A.C. You got no call to barge in here this way," Colin said, his temper rising fast.

"Oh, don't worry, I'm not here to start a lover's spat. Fact is, I've been knowing about you and Sarah Jane for some time now," Ford said contemptuously. "Got more important things to discuss."

"Like what?"

"First, get the woman out of here so we can talk."

Colin Jackson was on the verge of giving the lawyer a good cussing until he looked into his troubled eyes. He turned to the woman.

"Sarah Jane, get dressed. I'll meet you in the dining room in a little bit."

"I'm not moving from this bed until A.C. turns around," Sarah Jane said flatly.

Ford laughed in spite of his predicament. "Hell, Sarah Jane, you ain't hiding something I ain't already seen, now are you?"

"You bastard!" Sarah Jane spat out, her green eyes blazing.

"Damn it, A.C., I'm warning you," Colin said.

Ford held up his hand, "Okay, okay, got more important things than watching a whore get dressed." Ford turned his back while the woman slipped into her clothes and out the door, but not without a backward glance at the attorney with a look that could singe hair on a cold day.

"This better be good," Colin said tightly, laying the Colt on the bed while he slipped into his shirt and pulled on his boots.

"It is. Black Hawk's locked up and about to spill his guts to the authorities," Ford said without preamble.

"What? When was this?"

"Seems like Jack Dawson surprised Black Hawk and Cove out at the claim. Expect Cove is dead, but I can't prove it just yet."

"Dawson brought Black Hawk in?" Colin said, buckling

320

his holster around his lean frame. "Who would he turn him over to, not Pollock?"

"Most likely Slaughter," Ford replied.

"That's good."

"I don't know about that anymore," Ford said, helping himself to some of Jackson's whiskey.

"What do you mean?" Colin asked, checking the loads in the Colt before slipping it into the well-oiled holster.

"Just a gut feeling is all that something's been going on of late that didn't involve the Secret Ten."

The gunman smiled thinly at Ford. "A circle in a circle."

"What?"

"Could be there's yet another group in the Vigilance Committee keeping tabs on the Secret Ten."

Ford had clearly never considered such a thing, and he collapsed into a chair. "They ever get Black Hawk to talking, he'll take us all down with him."

Colin Jackson reached for his black hat and settled it comfortably on his head. He looked down at Ford who seemed to be suddenly at a loss for words. The gunman had no such problem.

"Let's go," he said to Ford.

Ford seemed to snap out of his self-imposed trance. "We've got to break Black Hawk out of jail. Get him as far away as possible from Denver." Colin offered the lawyer a thin smile.

"My exact thoughts. Maybe as far away as Hell."

"You'll need to gather up a few men you can trust."

"Know exactly who I can get. Don't worry I'll take care of things," the gunman said smoothly, thinking of Black Hawk's share of the gold in Clark and Gruber's Mint.

"He's probably being held at the Cherokee House. They wouldn't trust Pollock or Middaugh's men if what you say is true," Ford offered.

"Why don't you go on back to your lady friend. No use you getting too involved in this, case they haven't tied you to anything yet."

Ford nodded, getting up from the chair. He wasn't thinking too straight still. Jackson was right, the further away from this, the better. He knew exactly where he was going first . . . to see his old friend Judge Slaughter and then out to the Stiles's cabin. He would use the women as an alibi once Colin freed Black Hawk.

Chapter 36

Black Hawk sat at the old wooden table with a scrap of paper and pencil gripped in his hand. He labored over each name he scrawled across the paper. Each name left him drained and feeling guilty, knowing he was signing each man's death warrants. Slowly, he added another name to the growing list. Better them than me, he figured as a thumping noise sounded at the door, followed by a strangled cry.

Black Hawk paused over the list, half-rising from his seat. Through the thick door he could hear the muffled sounds of voices and keys being turned in the padlock.

Were they back already for the list? Hell, he was barely getting started. Then a bolt of numbing fear raced down his spine, and the outlaw reached over and dimmed the wick on the lantern until darkness flooded the room.

The door burst inward and four brawny, hooded men rushed in and seized Black Hawk by the shoulders.

"What the Hell—" Black Hawk managed through clenched teeth as he fought back with all his strength. Rough hands pinned his arms behind him as the table overturned in the darkness. Black Hawk's confession and list of names fluttered to the floor where it lay unnoticed.

A tall man approached the bound outlaw. "You make a sound, I'll cut your heart out." Black Hawk caught the dull gleam of a steel blade. There was something vaguely familiar about the man as they led him from the cell.

Once outside, they marched Black Hawk quickly toward the creek. The night air was clear and cool; laughter could be heard drifting out of several nearby saloons. Denver was once more drunk on the gold flowing out of the mountains to the west. No one took notice of the tight group of men as they marched the long block southward to Cherry Creek.

As they neared the creek, Black Hawk realized what the silent group was up to and he balked hard. They ended up dragging him the last few yards.

"You boys can't do this. We had a deal, damn it." They positioned him beneath an ancient cottonwood and a rope snaked through the air and over the sturdy limb that had hung a few other outlaws in Denver's short life.

The tall man stepped forward and settled the noose around Black Hawk's bare head. It was then he recognized Colin Jackson.

"Colin, damn it, what are you *doing?*" the outlaw screamed.

Colin Jackson stood there a moment and slowly reached up and pulled the hood from his head.

"I knew it was you," Black Hawk whispered. "This is a joke, ain't it? Christ, you gave me a scare."

"It's no joke, Black Hawk," the gunman said solemnly. "You should have kept your mouth shut."

"But, Colin, I never—" the rope grew taut as several of the men hoisted the outlaw off the ground. For a long moment, Black Hawk remained motionless. But when he tried to breathe and couldn't, he kicked frantically, his legs pumping the air like he was running.

Colin Jackson watched until the outlaw's kicks grew feeble and finally stopped altogether. "Tie him off and let him hang," he said, turning away.

It was Morgan Strasburg who brought the word to Judge Slaughter, holding his bloody head with one hand where he had been struck with the butt of a gun. A gun he had recognized and now he told this to Slaughter.

"You sure it was his gun?"

"Positive. Ain't another man in this territory carries a Shawk." The .36 caliber Shawk & McLanahan was a rare pistol west of the Mississippi with fewer than a hundred ever being produced.

"How is Bill?"

"They conked him pretty hard. A couple fellows got him over to the Doc. He'll be okay though."

"And Black Hawk? You sure he's dead?"

Morgan Strasburg shook his head. "I'm sure. He's swinging a few feet off the ground down by the creek. Can't figger it. Why'd they hang him?"

"To shut him up," Judge Slaughter said, pulling on his big overcoat. "Best get over to the doc's and have that head wound looked after, Morgan. If Bill is able, meet me at Graham's in one hour. We got a bloody job facing us."

Chapter 37

John Shear rolled over in bed, awakened by the pounding at his door.

"Just a damn minute," he mumbled, staggering to his feet. Still groggy from having been awakened from a sound sleep, Shear threw open the door and found the proprietor of the Parks House standing there.

"Sorry to bother you, John, but there's a fellow waiting to speak to you downstairs. Said it was pretty urgent."

"What time is it?"

"Quarter past twelve."

Who the hell could be asking for him this time of night, Shear wondered. The pudgy proprietor shifted from foot to foot.

"You coming down?"

Shear yawned and rubbed his bleary eyes. "Tell'em I'll be down directly." The owner nodded and scurried back down the stairs. Shear closed the door and got dressed.

A few minutes later, Shear came downstairs and found Ed Scudder waiting for him.

"Ed, what's the meaning of this?"

"Trouble," Captain Edwin Scudder whispered, taking Shear by the arm and steering him over to a far corner and away from the proprietor's keen hearing.

"What kind of trouble?" Shear asked, his head instantly cleared of all sleep.

"Black Hawk's been hung."

"You don't say," Shear whispered softly. "When?"

"About three hours ago, but that ain't the bad part."

"What is?"

Ed Scudder shook his head, looking over at the fat man who pretended to be reading a newspaper behind the desk.

"I'm suppose to fetch you. Ford will tell you the rest."

"Let's go then," Shear said, wondering what all the mystery was about.

When they departed the Parks House, they were met by four other riders who moved out of the shadows and surrounded Shear.

"What's going on here?" Shear said, his voice betraying his sudden fear. In the darkness, he couldn't tell who the riders were in their long coats and their hats pulled low.

"Take it easy, Joe," Ed Scudder said, "they with us." Shear relaxed somewhat, but not completely. He had seen the gleam of rifles and short guns at their belts. These men were heavily armed as if expecting serious trouble. This concerned John Shear deeply for he had left his room unarmed.

They rode south along the Platte for two miles before stopping near a grove of big cottonwoods.

"What's A.C. doing way out here?" Shear asked Scudder. He got his answer when a match flared and Shear caught sight, not of A.C., but Judge Slaughter standing there with two other men. Slaughter touched the match to the trimmed wick and a weak light flickered across the faces of men with Slaughter.

Shear felt his heart hammering against his ribs. He knew most of those present. Four served with him as members of the Secret Ten. Before Shear knew what was happening, two riders came alongside his horse and forced his arms behind his back while a third tied his wrists with rawhide.

"There's one thing I neglected to tell you, John," Scudder said, his voice suddenly hard. "Black Hawk left behind a list of those guilty of horse rustling before he was hung. Your name was on it."

327

"That's impossible!" Shear squawked. "Slaughter, tell these fools to cut me loose."

Judge Slaughter walked slowly over to the frightened man, bringing the lantern with him. He looked up at Shear with sad eyes.

"Sorry, John," Slaughter said softly, turning away as a rope sang through the air and slapped Shear on the neck, knocking his hat off. A rider adjusted the noose and backed off.

Shear looked around the group with fearful eyes. "Boys, you can't do this. You all know me. Hell, we all rode together one time or—" The slap of reins across the rump of Shear's horse sent the animal plunging forward. The noose bit quickly into Shear's neck, cutting him off in mid-sentence.

A rider rode over to the stump where the rope had been tied off. He flipped a playing card from his coat pocket and watched as it settled next to the stump with the scribbled message, "This man was hung, being proved that he was a horse thief."

Slaughter looked over at Morgan Strasburg. "You boys know what to do next."

Morgan nodded to the judge and the group of men thundered away into the night, while Slaughter blew out the light and turned to his own horse. It was going to be one helluva long and bloody night, he concluded.

Dawson got up from the table where he had been drinking coffee with Mary Stiles and Andy Philmore.

"She should have been back by now," he said, slipping into his coat. Andy jumped up and reached for his.

"You stay here, boy, case she comes back. Way things are so unsettled in Denver right now, I'd feel better if you stayed and looked after the ladies."

"But I can look for Melissa better than you can," Andy protested. "Nobody will even notice me. Remember what the judge said, you get caught, they'll hang you for sure.

Dawson smiled and rested a hand on the boy's shoulder. "I remember, boy, and I'll be extra careful. Just make sure you let only Melissa or me in after I'm gone."

Mary Stiles pushed a strand of loose hair the color of gray sandstone away from her face and stood up. "Please be careful, Jack. Andy is right. The majority in town don't yet know it was someone else who murdered Josiah, and not you. By now they'll be as drunk, or drunker, than they were last night, and spoiling mad."

Dawson gave the woman a knowing smile and turned to the door. He picked up the Henry and checked the loads.

"I don't plan on dying just yet," he said grimly. "Make sure you keep Melissa here when she comes back." Without another word he was gone.

Dawson kept to the shadows as he slipped unobtrusively along Ferry Street. He planned on going to Ford's office first; if Melissa wasn't there, he would be forced to find out where Ford lived and go there as well.

He couldn't help but notice how tense the town felt. Worse than last night even when everybody had been fueled with free booze and itching to hang him. But there was a distinct difference tonight, he noticed. Men who passed him by were, for the most part, stone-faced and cold-eyed sober, and all were heavily armed. An ugly mood hung over Denver like dust from a stamp mill.

Dawson pulled the collar of his long coat up around his face as he pulled his hat lower across his eyes. Tonight, these miners would be a hard lot to confront in a gunfight. He only hoped he could find Melissa and get her back home without encountering any problems. After that, he could concentrate on finding the gunman, Colin Jackson and then Ford.

A miner stepped from one of the many saloons lining Ferry Street and almost bumped into Dawson. Dawson froze in his tracks, his finger on the trigger of the Henry. He watched as the man stopped and poured a bottle of whiskey over a pine limb wrapped with cloth. After the rags were soaked, the miner killed the rest of the bottle in one long swallow. Next, he fumbled in his pocket for a match and swore mightily when he failed to find one. He turned to Dawson.

"You got a light, friend?" The man slurred his words, an indication he had been drinking heavily.

"Sure thing," Dawson said, digging in a pocket. "What's all the fuss about, anyway?"

"You ain't heared?" the miner asked. "We done had ourselves a slew of hangings tonight. They's dead men stretched all up and down the river."

"Who?"

"Black Hawk fer one. The other's John Shear. Big business man I hear tell around these parts. Be hell to pay over that one."

"That all?"

"Nope. Some emigrant coming into town said he ran into a parcel of dead men hanging along the river like crows in a tree. One of them sounds like Jim Latt, has a red beard near touches his knees. There were five more bodies hanging next to him according to this emigrant."

"Who's doing the hangings?" Dawson asked, shocked by Black Hawk's death. Without his confession, Dawson figured he would be marked for death, if he wasn't already. Dawson found a match and lit the torch. The rags gave off a smokey blue flame.

"Hear tell it's a part of the Vigilance Committee, call themselves the Stranglers. Say, you want to ride out with me and see for sure if it's old Jim a-hanging there on tha cottonwood? Emigrant said it was about ten miles er so ou of town."

"Best get on home to the missus," Dawson said, keepin his face shielded from the torch.

"Suit yourself," the miner said, grabbing for the reins o his horse.

Dawson stood in the darkness of an alleyway while th miner managed to pull himself aboard his horse and rid away. He stood there, torn by the need to find Melissa an the desire to find Judge Slaughter. Dawson needed to kno

330

if Black Hawk had signed a confession, clearing him of the murder charges. In the end, it was Melissa's safety that won out.

Dawson paused by Ford's darkened office and peered through the glass front. The place was empty and silent.

Damn! Now what?

For one thing, he argued with himself, he had to find out where Ford lived and then it occurred to him. He could ask Judge Slaughter that question and find out about Black Hawk at the same time.

Dawson hurried across the street, hoping he didn't run into that blockhead Marshal Pollock or his two young deputies on the way.

Slaughter's wife answered the door and Dawson apologized for the late hour, explaining it was urgent he speak with the judge. It was then the woman told him the judge had left right after Dawson and hadn't returned. She didn't know where A.C. Ford lived either when questioned. Dawson thanked her and turned away, feeling stumped. He checked his watch by the pale light of a quarter moon and found it was nearly 2:00 A.M. in the morning. He rubbed his burning eyes. He had been without sleep for nearly forty-eight hours. More importantly, what was he going to do now?

A.C. Ford had gone from being fighting mad to deadly serious, all in a matter of an hour. Colin Jackson stood aside, looking grim and lethal. The attorney had just gotten the word concerning John Shear. It had left Ford feeling numb and with a rattled case of the nerves.

The normally cool attorney downed another drink and shot a worried look at Colin who sat playing solitaire.

"How the Hell can you sit there and play cards when the whole town's gone hanging mad crazy!"

The gunman appeared unruffled by Ford's outburst and carefully considered his next card before looking up at the distraught lawyer.

331

"Don't forget it was us kicked things off by hanging 'ol Black Hawk. You want me to go out and shoot somebody now?"

"Find out who's doing all this hanging. It damn sure ain't the Secret Ten!"

"You forget what I told you," Colin said, laying aside the stack of cards he held in his hand. "Circle in a circle?"

"But damn it, how could they know John Shear was part of the rustling?"

"Black Hawk musta talked before we got to him. Just the threat of a rope has a way of loosening a man's tongue . . . even Black Hawk's." Ford grew pale as he considered this.

"That the case, I probably head their list," Ford whispered. A soft knock at the door sent Ford scrambling for his own gun, his eyes wide with fright.

Colin Jackson grimaced, got up from the table, and cracked the door. Rafe Tidwell, the Criterion's bartender, was standing there.

"Who is it?" Ford croaked, gripping his pistol so hard his knuckles had gone white as the barrel of the weapon wavered back and forth in the air.

Colin closed the door and turned back to Ford. "You may be right, A.C. Rafe says some emigrant a little while ago found Jim Latt and his boys strung up to a cottonwood about ten miles out of town. And put that pistol away before you shoot one of us."

"God! I knew it," Ford said, slipping the short-barreled weapon into his coat pocket. Angry blood flooded his face.

"That damn Black Hawk spilled his guts just like I figured." Ford looked at the gunman, his angry eyes narrow and dark.

"And it's that damn Jack Dawson's fault. Bringing Black Hawk in to stand trial. Very clever." Ford's face was covered with a thin sneer. Colin had taken his seat and poured them both another drink from the bottle of expensive whiskey.

"And that means only one thing," Colin said, lighting a

fresh cigar as he leaned back in his chair. He picked up the full glass of whiskey and took a sip. It was smooth, just the way he liked it.

"What the hell you talking about now?" Ford snapped, clearly irritated and in no mood anymore for the gunman's rambling.

"You weren't so agitated, A.C., you could see it right off."

"See what?" Ford almost screamed.

"Judge Slaughter. It's got to be Slaughter leading the pack, hanging everybody. Don't forget, Dawson turned Black Hawk over to him."

Ford's eyes flared bright with hate. Never would he have suspected the affable old man of such a double cross.

"Just take care of Dawson," Ford said tightly, "leave Slaughter to me."

"Whatever you say," Colin replied, draining his glass and standing up. "If he's still in town, it's good as done."

"Follow him to Hell if you have to," Ford shot back as the gunman cleared the doorway and was lost immediately in the crowded saloon.

Chapter 38

Dawson finally located Ford's frame house in the pre-dawn darkness after the night clerk at the Vasquez House gave him the information in exchange for one of the gold twenty dollar coins he still had on him.

The single-story dwelling stood dark and silent. Dawson checked the front door, the side windows and the back door, finding everything bolted securely. Returning to the dark window he thought was the kitchen, Dawson used the butt of his Colt Dragoon to smash the window. The breaking glass sounded like an all out saloon fight. Dawson held his breath, expecting a light to flare, any second, inside the house. There was no sound from within, and Dawson let out a long sigh of relief, hooked a boot over the windowsill and hauled his lean frame inside. It was a minute or two until he found a lantern with the help of a burning match. Dawson touched the match head to the wick, adjusted the flame and lowered the globe.

With the big Colt in his hand, Dawson eased from the kitchen and headed, for what he hoped, was the bedroom. This time of night, there wasn't much use in checking the other rooms, less Ford had gotten too drunk to find his bed. But Ford didn't strike Dawson as the heavy drinker type.

Dawson was two steps into the bedroom before he realized there was someone beneath the covers. The faint glow of yellow light from the lantern illuminated the outline of body. Dawson's lips flattened, wondering how Ford could sleep so soundly with all that had happened tonight?

He stepped closer with the light and was startled to find not Ford's body, but Melissa's. Anger shot through him, hot and deep. How could she?

Dawson stepped close to the bed and gave the girl's shoulder a good shaking, not really caring now if he frightened her or not. Melissa came awake with a start, a scream forming on her lips. The dim glow of the lantern outlined her terrified face.

"It's me," Dawson said quickly, his voice sounding cold and distant.

"You nearly scared me to death," Melissa said, looking as though she might faint.

"What are you doing in Ford's bed?" Dawson asked gruffly.

Melissa looked around wildly, brushing the golden hair out of her face.

"I . . . that is, it's not what you think," she managed, her face turning a deep crimson.

"I hope not for your mother's sake."

Her eyes grew wide, "What are *you* doing here?"

"Searching for you," he smiled coldly. "You never came home."

"Hadn't planned to, but A.C. insisted I go," Melissa said, getting out of the bed fully clothed. "I came back and when I found A.C. gone, I lay down for a minute."

"Wise man," Dawson said, putting away the Colt. "What did you do with Andy's pinto?"

"Left him across the street. There's an empty corral behind one of the buildings."

"Where's Ford?"

"I don't know."

"Let's go."

Dawson let them out the front door and headed across the street to the corral. The pinto watched their approach with large silent eyes. Dawson threw the saddle on him and

335

slipped the bit between his teeth. He turned to Melissa and offered his hand.

"I can mount by myself, thank you," she said, snatching the reins from his hands.

"You best go home, like I tell you, till this business is over. One way or the other."

"Don't you dare hurt A.C.," Melissa snapped. "You do and I'll hate you forever!" She kicked the pinto in the ribs and the little horse bolted down the street.

Dawson stood there for a few minutes and finally shook his head. There was just no understanding women . . . least of all Melissa Stiles's kind. Now Jenny Logan was a different matter, and Dawson realized how much they both had in common. Both having had to scrape by best they could, fighting for everything that came their way and then some. It was then Dawson realized how he truly felt about Jenny and knew, once this was over, he was going back to St. Joe and let her know. But for now all that had to wait. He couldn't yet walk the streets of Denver a free man. And there was the matter of the personal score he intended to settle with Colin Jackson, concerning Josiah's death. Once Jackson was taken care of, he would take care of his silver-tongued boss, A.C. Ford, notwithstanding the warning from Melissa.

As Dawson moved along the early morning streets, holding the Henry in the crook of his arm, the sun erupted in a shower of red and cool yellows as it inched above the empty Plains behind him. Dawn found Denver a place ready to explode at the slightest provocation.

Dawson crossed the street and turned down Larimer. The Criterion was but a few doors down from Graham's Drugs where he had been put on trial. It was where Andy said Ford and Colin Jackson retired after leaving the drugstore. Maybe he would get lucky and catch them both there together. End it all quick.

"Hey, ain't that him?" Dawson heard a man shout from a group of miners standing beneath the canopy of a hardware store. Dawson kept walking, hoping they would no push the issue. He cursed his luck for not having come up to the saloon from the back alley.

"Who?" a miner asked.

"Dawson. The one killed his partner. I seen him over at Pollock's when they brought him in."

"That's him!" a brawny miner confirmed, "let's get him!" As a group, the knot of miners stepped away from the boardwalk, fanning out with their hands on their pistols.

Dawson stopped and turned to face them. He doubted he could talk his way out of this one, not without bloodshed, but he was going to damn well try. He wished Slaughter was here to set the record straight.

"You Dawson, ain't you?" a burly miner asked, who looked like he could move boulders by himself the way his muscles bulged beneath the coat he was wearing.

"Boys, you're making a grave mistake," Dawson warned. "There's been enough hanging for one day."

"You damn right there has," the husky man shouted. "We plan on shooting you outright so's you can't slip a rope again."

Dawson jacked a shell into the Henry. The metallic sound was like that of a blacksmith's hammer striking iron. Every man in the street froze in their tracks.

Andy barely looked at Melissa so intent was he on checking his pony. The girl's eyes blazed at him. He had been wandering outside the cabin while Mary Stiles was busy preparing breakfast when Melissa came riding up on his pinto.

"I didn't hurt him none!" she spat out.

Andy gave her a withering look, "You shouldn't took my horse without asking me first."

Melissa flounced away from the boy, tossing her golden hair in exasperation. "Would you have loaned him to me had I asked?" she said over her shoulder when she reached the door of the cabin. Before Andy could formulate a reply, she continued, "Jack Dawson would have stopped me as well."

"Where you been all this time?" Andy asked, stroking the pinto's neck. "With that lawyer?"

Melissa spun around, her eyes flashing. "And what if I have? It's none of your business!"

"Is when you take a man's horse," Andy mumbled, instantly regretting his words.

Melissa laughed at him, "A man? You?"

Andy Philmore wanted to bury his head in his horse's neck so the girl couldn't see the sudden flush on his face, but he held his ground. It was okay, let her laugh. He knew what he had to do, moving to retighten the cinch.

When Andy finished, he turned to look at the girl with determined eyes. "Jack's having to fight for his life right this minute and I aim to be by his side when the shooting starts," he said. He turned back to the pony and vaulted into the saddle easily.

"Jack took me on when times were good for him and bad for me," the boy continued. "He didn't have to do that, like he done for you and your ma. Jack could have kept on riding and no one would have been the wiser. Now the saddle's on a different horse, and I got to be there for him when he faces down that gunman, Colin Jackson." Andy could feel the tears welling up inside of him and he reined away from the cabin.

"Wait!" Melissa called. Andy pulled back on the reins and turned his head.

"I'm coming with you," she said.

Andy's mouth dropped open, "You're what?"

"You heard me," Melissa said, coming up beside the pinto. "Kick your foot from the stirrup and boost me up."

"I can't be bothered with no girl," Andy protested, "there's liable to be shooting . . . and all."

"Just do what I say!" Melissa commanded. Without thinking, Andy did as he was told and helped pull the girl up behind him.

"You can go, but I want you to do as I say when the

trouble starts, understand?" he stated, as if expecting the girl to follow his orders at this late date.

"Let's just go, Andy," Melissa whispered in his ear. "It's getting toward broad daylight."

"All right, just hold on tight 'cause I ain't stopping if you fall off," Andy warned.

Pollock and his deputies had been up all night as well, and it showed. Sour-faced and in no mood for more swinging bodies in trees, he looked up from his desk where he was sitting with his head propped in his hands at the sounds of footsteps. Damn! Couldn't he be left alone for one minute's peace! But it wasn't the night of sleep he had lost that had put him on edge and given him a bad case of the jitters, losing sleep like a marshal who just came to the territory. What had his system in such an agitated state was seeing the body of John Shear dangling from a cottonwood limb. It sent cold chills racing down his backbone for it told Pollock one important thing: Black Hawk had done some talking before being hanged. What he didn't know was—did Black Hawk indict him as well?

His office door opened suddenly, and Sheriff Middaugh stood there, looking hollow-eyed and disheveled. Pollock tried to covered his surprise at seeing Middaugh back in town.

"What are you doing here, Bill? You bring Gordon back with you?" Pollock asked, standing up to shake the sheriff's hand. Middaugh had gone to Leavenworth, Kansas, to extradite killer James Gordon back to Denver to stand trial for capital murder of Jacob Gantz, an elderly German immigrant. Gordon in a drunken rage had held the German down while he fired a bullet into his brain, killing him instantly.

Middaugh flopped down in a chair, exhausted from the long stagecoach ride. "No, came back alone." Then he corrected himself, "That's not entirely true. Shared the stage with a classy young woman from St. Joe. Made the whole trip worthwhile."

"Thought the Kansas authorities were holding Gordon for you?"

"They are. Unfortunately, the federal court claims I didn't have the proper authority to have him released to my custody. Got to find Judge Slaughter and get this matter cleared up. Right now, I want to know what the Hell's been going on in town? My boys tells me there's been several hangings overnight. When I arrived on the stage this morning, Denver looked like an armed camp."

Pollock went over to the stove and filled two cups. "Better have some coffee," he said glumly, "this'll take a while."

Chapter 39

Colin Jackson was just exiting the Criterion when he looked up the street at the group of tense men. Twenty yards out front, he spotted Dawson, standing square and gripping a rifle. Jackson grinned wolfishly and eased away from the saloon. This was going to be easier than he thought. He pulled aside his coat and slipped the leather thong from the hammer of his revolver as he walked slowly down the middle of the street.

One of the miners saw him coming and said something to the man next to him who turned to face Colin. Several other miners turned their attentions to the approaching gunman.

Dawson caught the sudden interest behind him, but he dared not turn around or take his eyes from the miners. The prickling sensation along his spine told him whoever was behind him posed a new threat. And then he heard a familiar voice and Dawson's anger erupted deep within his brain. Deliberately, he turned his back to the miners and faced the one man most responsible for Josiah Catt's death.

"You boys, stand aside," Colin Jackson said with authority, "this bird belongs to me."

"Like Hell!" the burly miner exploded, feeling things were slipping away from him in his brief moment of glory.

"Twobow, you best keep quiet," a miner whispered nearby. "That's Colin Jackson, you tradin' beefs with."

Twobow never flinched, yet his eyes acknowledged the gunman's reputation. "We was going to fry this hombre's meat for what he done to them miners," Twobow said, his voice sliding down a notch or two.

"Won't be necessary," Colin said. "Now you boys best step out of the way unless you want to catch a stray round of hot lead." The miners needed no further urging and they scrambled for the nearest boardwalk.

"Been looking for you," Dawson said, staring the gunman squarely in his pale eyes.

"Funny, been doing the same," the gunman said, planting his feet firmly, forty steps from Dawson.

"Yeah, bet you have now Black Hawk is swinging from a limb. You were next, but killing you this way will pleasure me more."

Colin's pale eyes blazed in the morning sun. "Put the rifle down and we'll see how good you are with that big pistol you been toting around. I'll even let you have first crack," he said, his face forming a hawkish grin."

Very carefully, Dawson eased the Henry to the ground and pushed aside his long coat while his heart hammered against his chest. He wasn't a gunman. Why in the Hell did he let Colin get him to lay the rifle down? In spite of his outward calm, Dawson felt a trickle of sweat forming between his shoulder blades. No matter what the gunman did, Dawson reminded himself, he had to concentrate on getting the big Colt Dragoon out and making his first shot count. With a man like Colin, Dawson doubted he would get a second. Then Dawson realized there was no way he was going to walk away from this one alive. Even if he got lucky and managed to kill the gunman, the miners would cut him down within seconds.

For some strange reason, Dawson had a momentary glimpse of Prince Albert Smith, flashing him a smile just before turning to embrace Big Yaak and the yelling Blackfeet. He could still smell the dust and blood. Old P.A. They didn't come any better . . . just like Josiah Catt.

Dawson mentally shook the image free and concentrated on lifting the big Colt out of its holster as quickly and as smoothly as he could. Even as he thumbed back the hammer, Colin's own weapon was spurting flame and something hot smacked him hard in his side. It was then Dawson saw the blur of black and white flash into view, nearly on top of the gunman.

Dawson regained his balance and brought the dragoon to bear on Colin Jackson, who had turned slightly to avoid the onrushing animal.

The big Colt bucked twice in Dawson's hand as Colin Jackson spun away from the charging horse. One of Dawson's bullets found its mark and Colin flinched, bringing his own weapon around to return fire. Dawson's second slug kicked up dirt two foot in front of the gunman. Dawson cursed and thumbed back the hammer on his Colt for the third time, but froze with his finger on the trigger. Andy and the girl joined the melee, yelling at Colin Jackson while the pinto kicked up such a dust cloud, Dawson's vision was obscured for a moment.

"Get out of the line of fire," Dawson screamed at Andy. The girl was yelling at the top of her voice as the pinto pranced around the dodging gunman who was trying for another shot at Dawson.

Suddenly, without warning, Colin Jackson shot the pony in the head and raked the girl from behind the boy in one long sweep as the horse fell headlong in the dusty street, spouting blood everywhere. Andy managed to kick free of the saddle, but not soon enough. As he fell, a flying hoof caught him alongside his head and he sprawled unconscious in the dust next to the dead pinto.

Melissa was screaming at Colin Jackson who held her tightly, pointing his gun at her head. Blood was spurting from the gunman's right chest and he was having to take in air through his mouth.

"Drop the gun, Dawson," Colin said hoarsely. Dawson hesitated.

"I said now! I'll kill her, you don't. Makes no difference to me that she's a woman," the gunman warned.

Melissa had suddenly gone limp in the gunman's arm. She looked at Dawson with pleading eyes.

343

Slowly, Dawson lowered his rifle. Colin Jackson just as quickly shot him in the chest. The slug spun Dawson around and he collapsed in the street, the dragoon flying from his hands. He could hear the girl screaming again and then he thought it funny how much it sounded like Jenny. But Jenny Logan was back in St. Joe. It was a struggle for him to keep his eyes open as darkness closed in behind his skull. Dawson rolled over in the dust just as Melissa broke free of the gunman. But it didn't matter to Colin Jackson now as he started up the street with his revolver cocked, ready to finish Dawson.

Desperate, Dawson looked around for his Colt and spied the Henry. With the last of his remaining strength, Dawson scooped up the rifle as Colin lifted his Colt for one last shot. Even as Dawson brought the Henry around, he knew he was too late, and he gritted his teeth against the coming pain that would end his life. Gunfire crackled nearby.

Suddenly, Colin Jackson stopped in his tracks. A look of disbelief spread across his face. His gun arm inched downward. Then he lost the willpower to hold the pistol any longer and it fell at his feet. The gunman took a faltering step, his eyes locked on Dawson and then he fell face down in the dirt. Blood stained the back of the gunman's coat where two bullets had entered.

Raising up on his elbows, Dawson looked beyond the burning pain and building fog. There was Melissa helping Andy to his feet. Good, the boy was a little shaken, but otherwise looked to be okay. But who had fired those shots? Then he saw her, running toward him, holding a revolver in one hand.

"Jenny!" Dawson croaked as the woman collapsed by his side, hugging him close. She rocked him back and forth.

"Don't you go and die on me now, Jack Dawson!" Tears streamed down her face. "Please, don't die," she whispered softly, stroking his hair. Through the dimming light and consuming pain, Dawson heard other voices. Angry voices.

"Get that woman out of the way," a miner bellowed,

344

"so's I can finish him off." It was Twobow, the big miner, talking.

Two miners rushed up and grabbed Jenny Logan. Jenny screamed and Andy Philmore jumped into the fracas.

"Damn it, get that brat outta the way," Twobow roared, trying to get a clear shot at Dawson who was barely hanging on to consciousness. The thunder of hoofbeats filled the street as a dozen riders came pounding up as Dawson gave in to the darkness and pain.

"Drop that pistol, mister," Slaughter demanded, dismounting from his horse. Ed Scudder, Morgan Strasburg and others followed suit, holding their guns on the advancing miners.

"Who the hell are you?" Twobow bellowed, still gripping his weapon.

"Judge Slaughter, and the next man fires a shot will be taken down to the creek and strung up alongside those other criminals." His strong voice echoed across the silent crowd that had suddenly appeared.

"Jack Dawson killed no one. I have a confession here," Slaughter said, waving a piece of paper in the air, "from an outlaw by the name of Black Hawk, clearing Dawson of the killings." The miners lowered their weapons just as Marshal Pollock and Sheriff Middaugh came charging up with guns drawn.

"What the hell's going on here, Judge?" Middaugh asked.

Judge Slaughter smiled at the lumbering sheriff and put away the piece of paper and his revolver.

"Hello Bill, when did you get back?"

From the front window of the Criterion, A.C. Ford watched the unfolding gunfight, the sudden appearance of the boy and Melissa on the horse, and finally Colin's death at the hands of some strange woman. Ford backed away from the window, licking his dry lips after Judge Slaughter came up waving the piece of paper. His loud voice had carried to where the lawyer stood. Without a doubt, Ford knew he was next.

He looked around the suddenly empty saloon. With that paper in Slaughter's hands, he was a marked man. There was only one thing to do to keep from being hanged. Ford left the Criterion by the back way, on a dead run.

Seven miles out of town along the Platte, the states-bound stage was help up by four well-mannered and well-armed men wearing masks.

"We got no gold this trip," the driver said with his hands in the air.

"Not after gold," the leader said, riding over to unlatch the door to the stagecoach. "A. C. you best come on out."

The three other startled passengers watched as the attorney adjusted his derby hat and stepped calmly from the coach. The masked rider closed the door.

"Get out of here now!" he told the stage driver and the man brought his hands down and cracked the long whip across the team of horses. The coach lurched away in a cloud of dust.

"That you Judge?" Ford inquired as another rider brought up a riderless horse.

"Mount up," the leader commanded without answering the lawyer's question. Ford did as he was told, and the group of men disappeared over a low rise as the stagecoach rattled along in the distance.

"This is far enough," the leader said, reining in. "Step down, A.C.," the man said as he removed his mask. The three other men did likewise.

With naked fear in his eyes, Ford looked at his friends. Damn Black Hawk anyway!

Judge Slaughter looked at his old friend with sad eyes. "Why, A.C.? You couldn't be wanting for anything. You had a pretty girl. Understand you two were going to be married?"

"We are, judge, soon's I . . ." Ford's reply trailed off,

realizing the folly of such talk now. Ed Scudder, Morgan Strasburg and Bill Brady held shotguns on Ford in case he suddenly got the notion to run for it.

"I'm sorry, A.C., but Black Hawk listed you as the ring leader of the horse thieves and, as it turns out, for claim-jumping and murder as well," Judge Slaughter said tonelessly.

"Claim-jumping was Colin's idea," Ford said weakly. "I never meant for him to kill anybody."

"No matter, it ends here. Get the rope Morgan," Slaughter said.

"No, wait, boys! You can't do this. I can't stand the thought of being hanged," Ford pleaded. "Judge, you know how I am about a rope. Please, just shoot me instead."

Slaughter looked at the other three men for guidance.

"I say we oblige, A.C.," Morgan said quietly. "It's the least we can do for a friend." The other two men nodded.

"Okay, A.C., looks like you get your wish," Slaughter said. The other three men dismounted and lined up next to the judge.

A shaken Ford looked down the row of his executioners, his eyes coming to rest on Ed Scudder.

"Ed, will you see to the arrangements of my property? I got some in Council Bluffs as well as Denver." He reached into his pocket and brought out his heavy gold watch. "And would you see Sarah Jane gets my watch? I got money for Melissa Stiles . . ."

Judge Slaughter answered for Scudder. "We can't do that, A.C. We can't risk implicating ourselves in your death."

Ford seemed to sag inside.

"I'm sorry, A.C."

The sudden thunder created by four shotguns simultaneously going off spooked an osprey from a cottonwood. The bird screamed its displeasure at the sudden noise and winged its way across the Platte.

Chapter 40

"I can't believe I let you talk me into this," Jenny Logan said, studying Jack Dawson's drawn face. They were lounging by Gold Creek while eager miners scrambled to and fro staking claims and shouting good-naturedly at one another.

"What?"

"Coming up here so soon. You've hardly given your wounds time to mend properly."

"It's been three weeks," Dawson protested.

"Uh-huh. I can see you're all better just by the pain on your face. Jack Dawson, don't try lying to me this early into our marriage."

Dawson grinned at her, his eyes dancing. "Aw, I'm fine, Jenny darling, really."

"What your are is pitiful," she replied, giving him a smile reserved only for him.

"That's what I've always liked about you, Jenny, ain't no fooling you. You can cut right through the fat clear down to the bone quicker than anybody I know. That's why we go good together."

"Too bad you didn't wake up sooner," she quipped. "We could have had children before you got too old."

"I'm not *that* old! Besides, we got Andy over there to raise."

She gave him another warm smile. "That was wonderful of you, sharing your claim with him."

"What Josiah would have wanted."

She reached over and gave him a peck on the cheek. "You aren't as tough as you make yourself out to be, Jack Dawson. And I know about the money you gave Mary and Melissa Stiles for their trip back home."

"Well, it wasn't doing much down at Clark and Gruber's, and they needed it more. There's plenty more right here, all we got to do is dig for it."

Jenny's face clouded. "You have to be careful around that marshal, I don't like him."

"Only thing left hanging's far as I'm concerned, but I can't prove Pollock was mixed up with Ford. Black Hawk never completed his list, so I guess we'll never know."

"Just the same, you be careful around him."

They heard a pair of boots crunching over gravel, and they turned to see Walter Dumont coming their way.

"Excuse me, Jack," Dumont said. "I never properly thanked you for what you done for my brother," he waved his hat behind him, "and all this. Everywhere you stick a shovel, you find gold. The boys really appreciate it, and so do I."

"I'm just sorry Josiah and I wasn't able to save your brother from the likes of Colin Jackson."

"That's another thing," Dumont said, rolling his hat in his hand, looking from Jenny and back again to Dawson.

"What is it?"

"Well, me and the boys been talking . . . how you're willing to share this strike with us and all. Guess what I'm trying to say is if you ain't got any objections then we'd all kinda like to change the name of this creek to Catt."

A broad grin spread across Dawson's face. "I think Josiah would like that very much."

WALK ALONG THE BRINK OF FURY:

THE EDGE SERIES

Westerns By GEORGE G. GILMAN

PINNACLE BOOKS HAS
SOMETHING FOR EVERYONE —

MAGICIANS, EXPLORERS, WITCHES AND CATS

THE HANDYMAN   (377-3, $3.95/$4.95)
He is a magician who likes hands. He likes their comfortable
shape and weight and size. He likes the portability of the hands
once they are severed from the rest of the ponderous body. Detec-
tive Lanark must discover who The Handyman is before more
handless bodies appear.

PASSAGE TO EDEN   (538-5, $4.95/$5.95)
Set in a world of prehistoric beauty, here is the epic story of a
courageous seafarer whose wanderings lead him to the ends of
the old world — and to the discovery of a new world in the rugged,
untamed wilderness of northwestern America.

BLACK BODY   (505-9, $5.95/$6.95)
An extraordinary chronicle, this is the diary of a witch, a journal
of the secrets of her race kept in return for not being burned for
her "sin." It is the story of Alba, that rarest of creatures, a white
witch: beautiful and able to walk in the human world undetected.

THE WHITE PUMA   (532-6, $4.95/NCR)
The white puma has recognized the men who deprived him of his
family. Now, like other predators before him, he has become a
man-hater. This story is a fitting tribute to this magnificent animal that stands for all living creatures that have become, through
man's carelessness, close to disappearing forever from the face of
the earth.